Also available from Lauren Dane and Harlequin

Goddess with a Blade

Goddess with a Blade
Blade to the Keep
Blade on the Hunt
At Blade's Edge
Wrath of the Goddess
Blood and Blade
Bad Blood
Blood and Magic

Diablo Lake

Moon Struck
Protected
Awakened

Cascadia Wolves

Reluctant Mate
(prequel)
Pack Enforcer
Wolves' Triad
Wolf Unbound
Alpha's Challenge
Bonded Pair
Twice Bitten

de La Vega Cat

Trinity
Revelation
Beneath the Skin

Chase Brothers

Giving Chase
Taking Chase
Chased
Making Chase

Petal, Georgia

Once and Again
Lost in You
Count on Me

Cherchez Wolves

Wolf's Ascension
Sworn to the Wolf

The Hurley Boys

The Best Kind of Trouble
Broken Open
Back to You

Whiskey Sharp

Unraveled
Jagged
Torn

Blood and Magic contains descriptions of violence, a great deal of foul language, and mentions of abuse and trafficking.

BLOOD AND MAGIC

LAUREN DANE

Recycling programs for this product may not exist in your area.

ISBN-13: 978-1-335-49084-1

Blood and Magic

For questions and comments about the quality of this book, please contact us at CustomerService@Harlequin.com.

® is a trademark of Harlequin Enterprises ULC.

Carina Press
22 Adelaide St. West, 41st Floor
Toronto, Ontario M5H 4E3, Canada
www.CarinaPress.com

Printed in U.S.A.

This one is for the readers
who’ve loved Rowan from the start

Chapter One

"Well, look at you, then," Clive said as he entered the room and caught sight of Rowan sitting with his assistant, Alice. He'd known she was in the building. Had been drawn to that energy she carried, magic that was uniquely hers. Spoken in a language somehow uniquely Clive's. Discovering the way his wife seemed to exist on a frequency tailor-made for him—dissonance and all—had been a delight.

They shared a physical and emotional bond that had settled between them like a deeply comforting weight. Nearness registered, but even when he'd been in a totally different state, he'd felt her…essence. He'd known she was alive and well, and a few terrifying times he'd known she was injured or in pain.

Clive Stewart, Scion of North America, an ancient, powerful Vampire who'd see five centuries before too much longer, was used to being in charge. Accustomed to the mantle of leadership. Comfortable with the responsibility, though certainly intelligent enough to have moments when he understood he faced a challenge.

In his life, he'd trained to be a Scion, stumbled, rose up and ascended to rule an entire continent of Vampires used to the half-hearted leadership of the robber baron who'd ruled before Clive. He did not clear his movements or direction with anyone other than the First and his Five. Though he certainly never forgot that every choice he made would echo outward and potentially impact those Vampires and humans he was responsible to lead and protect.

The being he gazed at, long and lithe, her deep red hair pulled back in a braid that reached her waist, her gaze constantly roving as she assessed threats without conscious thought, changed the Vampire he'd been before.

She made him painfully aware he couldn't control everything that mattered most. It was lowering and yet, in some integral way, it had lifted him up because though he couldn't protect her from everything, he did his very best to be as worthy as possible. For her.

Rowan was a queen. A goddess in a very real sense. A treasure beyond compare.

His.

Currently, her rather disarming mouth was arranged in a smirk that had a hint of a smile in it. "Evening, Scion. I'm here to question some witches. Maybe even a shifter."

"Why don't you settle in your office?" Alice suggested to Clive. "I'll bring in tea shortly and you two can update one another in private."

Rowan rose, leaning slightly on a cane of some sort. When he'd gone to daytime rest, she'd been using crutches.

Once inside his office, he asked quietly, "What did Dr. Jenkins say exactly?"

Just a few days before, during a very public ambush, Rowan had been at a traffic light when she'd been crashed into by three cars full of wolf shifters who'd then unloaded multiple weapons' worth of ammunition resulting in fourteen gunshot wounds and multiple broken bones. Witches, specifically the Procella family, had been behind the attack and Rowan was in the process of closing that case with all responsible parties arrested.

Which was a great deal to heal from in and of itself. But to top it off, one of the witches responsible for the ambush had attempted to kill Rowan via magic less than twenty-four hours prior. Also in public. In the presence of a chaos demigod and one of the most powerful witches on the planet. And thanks to the goddess inside his wife and the aforementioned witch and demigod, Clive's wife had lived.

It took a complicated situation and amplified it, involving one rather large and sticky mess of Vampiric and magical goings-on, and Rowan bore the weight of it all.

Most would have broken under the pressure long ago. But Rowan wasn't most, and she'd taken her pain and rage and spite and forged it into the sort of will and perseverance her enemies couldn't begin to fathom.

She'd been on their trail, pulling together all the pieces of this complicated mess. The closer she got to figuring it all out, the sharper her energy would get as she focused hot enough to start a fire. Watching her work endlessly fascinated and excited him.

And, poking at her to take care of herself was a delight for them both.

"Dr. Jenkins declared my broken leg healed as fuck. Okay, not that last part verbatim, but the story ends the same. Sort of the same," she amended when he gave her a bland look. "It's not back to one hundred percent. I'm free of the cast as you can see. There's like a brace thing I'm to wear, especially while I'm sleeping for the next week or two. The worst part was a three-month moratorium on kicking with that leg. *That's my dominant kicking leg.*"

She looked so aggrieved he wanted to laugh.

"I'll have to content myself with using this cane as an extension of my body. I was getting good with the crutch as a weapon so I figure I can use those basic principles. Bonus, there's a blade tucked into the handle. Star just pranced right into Dr. Jenkins's office and dropped it at my feet like she worked there."

He gave the hand-carved walking aid a look and nodded his approval. "I wouldn't have expected anything less of your dog."

Rowan's magic-dog-slash-familiar had a way of just showing up whenever she was needed. Given the utter violent chaos that was Rowan's life and her job, Clive supported any strong proponent in Rowan's corner, and Star was certainly entertaining to have in the household.

"Then I'm doubly impressed. And pleased you're free of the more constricting cast." After the most recent attack on her the night before, he'd been concerned there'd be a setback.

She sniffed, pretending to be indignant, and then ruined it by snorting. "Dr. Jenkins got a little *miffed* she couldn't write a paper about my super healing in some journal on account of me not being human and all. I'm not sure if I should be offended or not, but she cheered up after reminding me I'm prone to injury and need a local doctor, so she'd see me soon enough."

"Well, let's keep all your bones unbroken from today forward. It can be a life goal." He added a wink to rile her a little.

She groaned. "You act as if I love getting nearly killed on a regular basis. I do not. It hurts. Usually, I have a bunch of Vampire blood poured down my throat, which as you know isn't my favorite."

"On the plus side of the column though, all that ancient Vampire blood now coursing through your veins has made you so strong you're here in my office flirting with me after being shot not even a week ago. Broken bones nearly healed up. Four days ago, you could barely stay conscious. Today you've got that murderous gleam back in your eye." He did so enjoy it when she was murderous toward others.

She harrumphed.

"It's rather fetching, darling, and it gives you another weapon no one will see coming." Clive took her free hand and kissed her knuckles. Her smile in response was indulgent and affectionate.

Which lasted a few breaths until her scowl returned. "Okay that was a good point. I've had a dozen meetings today. *So many people* talked to me, and I had to be nice to nearly all of them."

"I know how much you hate that," he said with a bland expression.

She flipped him off and continued. "I approved a lot of money to be spent and nearly all of it was about witches and Vampires. As usual, wasting resources better put to use elsewhere. Since your self-titled Vampire lords decided to threaten—on Vampire Nation letterhead—to execute Hunters, we've had to raise our security protocols. That's very expensive. I'm billing the Nation for it."

"Naturally," he said. Normally, he'd argue. The Nation wasn't responsible for Hunter Corp.'s expenditures. *Normally.* In this case, the First had allowed six Vampires to be included in a process they had no business being involved with. From the start they'd set about to agitate, threaten, and degrade Hunter Corp. and Rowan specifically. At the start, Rowan had accepted it as Vampiric posturing. But because these fools were not fit for diplomatic communication, emboldened by their access, these lords went too far and that had blown up in everyone's face. The Nation owed more than money to repair this egregious mess. But money was a start.

They paused as Alice brought the tea in. Once she'd gone, they returned to the conversation.

"And because no one can act right, I had to also handle a bunch of witch stuff in the wake of that business with Hugo last night. The Conclave is having meetings about it so I'm expecting to hear more soon. Genevieve's office sent over footage of the interview with Bess Procella."

The mother of their as-of-last-night captive, Hugo Procella, had been on the other side of the planet.

"What is your impression?" Clive knew she chafed at not being able to do the interview in person, but she couldn't do everything. That and she'd been recovering from multiple attempts on her life.

"Why are you frowning so hard?" Rowan demanded.

"I find it agitating when the second attempt on your life in less than a week is referred to as *that* business."

Rowan consistently found herself touched and absolutely silly when he got this way in defense of her. No one else was this to her. Accepting of who she was and all the blood and magic that came with it.

"I'm good. I have a super-cool pain stick." She held her cane up. "It's got good energy. A little wild though. So there's that."

She was probably going to hell for how amused it left her when he eyed it warily.

"One does love a pain stick. My apologies. I was ruminating for a moment on the madcap series of events over the last three years. But you're here and I'm here. Tell me what you think of Bess."

"Granted, I don't have a lot of experience with mothers, but she comes off frosty and aloof. She's hiding something. Look, they straight up told her the Conclave and Hunter Corp. had her entire family in custody for all sorts of fuckwittery. Except for her husband, who's decided to run from the Conclave. Anyway, so she barely had any questions about the rest of the Procellas. She was irritated we'd pulled her off her swanky vacation. I'd like to think I'd demand some answers when confronted with such information. Even if she had to fake it a little. But none of that family make any sense. So maybe it's just who they are. As one bitch to another, her reactions didn't ring genuine to me. I get Antonia's bitchery. She's out here watching hours of those movies that make you cry. Practicing her big eyes and wobbly lip. Her brother is a homicidal stalker. They might get it from mom and none of them experience feelings."

Rowan was already pissed the Procellas had been given a demand for the location of their family members in the wake of a host of crimes they'd all been committing. There'd been a delay of multiple days until they'd finally discovered Hugo and Antonia's mother had been on a luxury cruise. Once Rowan had her location, they'd arranged to grab Bess at the next port. All the Procellas had managed to do was make her angry. Which wouldn't work out well for them.

"So that was my daylight. I'm sure it's not obvious

as I'm a model of grace and dignity, but I'm extra salty and in the mood to ruin the day of some asshole witches. Because of said grace and dignity, I waited until after sunset as they're here and I simply didn't want any more Vampire tears that I'd spoken to my own prisoners while you were all at rest."

Clive's attempt at being bland broke and he laughed. Ugh, he was so damned sexy.

"As always, the Vampire Nation is indebted to you for your professionalism. As I am continually learning things from your…methods, I'll accompany you."

Rowan shook her head. He'd been murderous for hours after she'd been attacked in the early hours of that day. He still had that gleam in his eye even if he pretended he was oh so suave.

"You'll scare him too much and then Konrad—he's on the way here now to conduct the interview with me—will have to intervene. That shit will be like candy for a narcissist like Hugo. No, let's deny him everything we possibly can. That's how we chip away at his reserve. That's how we get answers. He's got to be devastated first. We'll get that started. Genevieve's about ten minutes behind her father, so have her brought directly in so she can watch in your control room with you. She'll be in on the chat with Sergio, but there's no reason to give Hugo what he wants." Or expose Genevieve to him. Hugo had stalked and terrorized Genevieve. It was a traumatizing thing to have someone that obsessed with you. Rowan could protect her friend a little in this situation and that's what she planned to do.

They finished their tea right as Konrad arrived.

Chapter Two

"I'll have Konrad brought directly to the interview room. We'll go together and meet him," Clive said, inviting himself along.

The elevator opened and they headed through the various levels of security together.

Before they arrived at their destination, he pulled her to the side, backing her into a doorway for privacy.

"Stop flirting with me," she said, totally not meaning it.

A whisper of a smile skittered over his mouth. "I don't trust these witches. Be careful. Kill them before they can kill you. Are we clear?" Stepping back, he gave her a severe British reproof and all her sex parts went warm and a little soft. Except for her nipples.

Still. Bossy. "Easy there, Scion. I can't handle another thing on my plate at the moment. We both know if I go killing any Procella there'll be so much political bullshit I'll drown. At this stage anyway. There's always tomorrow." Rowan gave him a bright smile. "I don't trust Hugo either. But I do trust myself and my cane and all the strength in my general vicinity to handle this without execution. Unfortunately. If anyone needs to be wiped off the face of the planet, it's a predator like Hugo."

He straightened his cuffs and then shook his head at her. "It's impossible to stay angry with you."

She laughed hard at that one. "I don't think anyone else who knows me would agree with that point. But I'm smitten enough with you I'll let you get away with such blatant flattery."

They moved through the next set of doors, and she caught sight of their guest.

Konrad tipped his chin slightly as he approached. The tall, broad-shouldered witch looked like a sexy, silver-haired architect or lawyer in his early sixties. He wore a smoke-gray three-piece suit with a black shirt open at the neck and walked like he was hot shit. Fair enough, as the warlock was a thousand years old and the magical equivalent of the king of witches worldwide.

He was also Genevieve's father, so it was more than the murder attempts in full view of cameras, tourists, a sage, and a magical dog. More than using coercive magics against others in violation of Conclave law and the Treaty Rowan and the rest of Hunter Corp. were charged to enforce. It mattered that the object of Hugo's obsession was Genevieve. All the crimes he'd committed were in some way motivated by that. Konrad Aubert was very motivated to be sure Hugo faced justice for what he'd done to her.

"The Procellas have formally asked for permission to have Felix present as we question Hugo," Konrad told her.

Rowan thought that over. "Why not? I don't know what he thinks he can do. He has very limited authority in this situation. I'm absolutely certain about the parameters of this entire arrest, which means I've already gone over every possible way he might try to get out of culpability."

Konrad bowed slightly. "I'm certain you have. Whatever you decide, the Conclave will support it."

Good to know. "I've got no real opposition to letting Felix sit in on our interview. But we're starting in like," she glanced up at the wall clock and then back to Konrad, "two minutes, so he'd better be here already or move his ass because I'm not waiting."

It was going to take her a bit of time with the witches she had in custody to find all their fault lines and weak points. Then she'd know how to unravel them and get answers. While violence certainly had its uses, torture was ineffective. Mentally and emotionally breaking them? Well, that was very effective.

Spells could compel cooperation, but they needed to know what to ask before they compel someone to speak. There'd been multiple crimes and only some of them seemed connected. Rowan knew she and the others were only seeing a small part of the whole. There was more. The clues were all there, she just had to find them.

They looked toward the interview rooms where Hugo would be. "His type always gets high on entitlement. Gives them what they feel is permission to brag when an attorney is present. It's an added bonus when the lawyer knows shit is going left and they try to get their client to shut up. Everyone starts to panic. The entitled ass can't shut up, the lawyer is stretched thin attempting to manage a slow-motion car crash."

Suddenly, Rowan's day got a little brighter at the prospect of fucking so many people's shit up. "Chaos is a dam breaker," she said with a shrug. And super amusing to watch.

Konrad nodded. "It seems to be forever so. Do you have an order you prefer after Hugo? I imagine you'll want to speak with Sergio as well?"

Sergio was the patriarch of the Procella family and Rowan knew he'd been part of the first hit put out on her life. There was more skullduggery for certain and she couldn't wait to hang it around his neck.

"We do Sergio after. We'll most certainly learn new things from Hugo we can then use on grandpa. Genevieve should be arriving soon, so I think she should be part of his questioning." Rowan wanted to be sure to send the message that not having Genevieve in the room with her stalker was strategy, not punishment. None of this was her fault.

During those four minutes they'd given Felix—which he barely made as he jogged in, sweaty and out of breath—Hugo had been brought from his cell and placed in a room to await their arrival.

"You need to assure me you understand your role here," Rowan said to Felix before they opened the door.

"I'm here as a legal representative of Hugo and Sergio Procella."

Rowan told him as coldly as possible, "Neither have a right to legal representation at this point. This is not human law enforcement. His crimes are not human crimes. You are allowed into the process at the sufferance of Hunter Corp."

"Now see here." Felix got that expression men often did right before they leaned into some long lecture about their importance.

She held up a hand, palm out. Not in peace, but in warning. "No." Rowan's one-word sentence seemed to echo outward with the underline she gave it. "Hugo Procella violated the Treaty. Multiple times. I'm within my rights to execute him at this very moment for his crimes. As you're aware. Many of his crimes were committed in full view of witnesses. *His guilt has been decided* by both Hunter Corp. and the Conclave of Witches. What remains is judgment and sentencing. The severity of which, as I'm certain you understand, will be measured by cooperation of Hugo Procella during interviews. Do not mistake your place in the timeline as well as the process. This isn't a parking ticket. He didn't shoplift from Chanel or rough up a server at a casino. We are not in the county courthouse where you can sway humans with cash and good shoes. I've got plenty of my own. You are *allowed* in the room at my sufferance. That's it. Were our positions reversed, I'd attempt to help Hugo understand where he is in the process as well. Things will go much smoother if we all know our place."

Felix's eyes widened and Rowan waited for him to accept reality or push back. Either way, her path was clear.

Konrad cleared his throat before adding, "Precisely so. In or out?"

Felix sighed before straightening his spine and nodding to Rowan. "I will do my best to help Mr. Procella navigate the situation as it exists."

Konrad added, "And dissuade him from cleaving to any fantasies where he walks free and gets to go back to living his life as if nothing happened. Imprisonment will be Hugo's reality for some time to come."

Rowan really liked Konrad Aubert.

Along with David, Rowan's valet, and the person responsible for managing the US operations for Hunter

Corp., and Genevieve—who'd arrived only scant minutes before—Clive sat on the other side of the wall facing monitors with the camera feed from the interrogation room Rowan had just entered.

He settled in, stationed in front of several monitors feeding cameras recording the interview. Some of them were of a modern, technical variety, measuring things like body heat and pulse rate. Rowan was a far more accurate detector than any machine he'd ever seen. To her cells, she was made for the job she did.

Die Mitte, the casino and hotel they were in, served as the base of Vampire Nation operations in North America. His court. His ground. Clive had offered up use of its secure facilities to hold some of Rowan's prisoners, certainly to be helpful because they had the space and ability, but also because like all Vampires, he was nosy and loved to watch his wife at work.

"Felix looks defeated already," David murmured. "Rowan has spoken with him."

Clive withheld a laugh, but the boy was right. If she hadn't been using a walking aid and wasn't still recovering from multiple attempts on her life, he might feel more amused. At that point though, he rather looked forward to watching his wife eviscerate the witches on the other side of the table.

Rowan didn't address him at first as she got settled and looked through some of her notes. Clive knew she'd memorized exactly what it was she wanted to confront him with long before she'd even walked into the building.

His rather delightfully devious wife was toying with Hugo. Letting him know in no uncertain terms he was not in charge.

After two or three minutes, Hugo leaned forward a

bit and began to speak. Rowan put a finger up. "Quiet." Said without even looking up.

At Clive's side, Genevieve laughed quietly.

Finally, Rowan turned to Konrad. "Are you ready to proceed?"

Aubert kept a bland expression as he nodded.

"Go on, then," she said to Hugo.

"I demand you release me this instant. I was influenced by magic and can't be held responsible for my actions." Hugo put a hand over his heart. "I would never harm Genevieve outside duress. Everything that happened was beyond my control." He paused. As if that settled anything. A few breaths later, he asked, "Is Genevieve well? I'm sure once I can speak to her to explain myself, she'll understand and forgive me."

Konrad flicked his wrist and three slices appeared along Hugo's cheek, crimson drops of blood beading against pale, pale flesh. *Well.* Clive approved of him more by the second.

Rowan breathed in deep and a bolt of desire hit. She was taking in all that pain and fear, like a Vampire would. He added it to his encyclopedia of reasons he adored his wife.

Felix opened his mouth to speak, Rowan sent him a look and a cocked head—a snake watching a bird—and then he closed his lips without a word.

Konrad said, "If you must reference her, she is *Senator Aubert*. However, I'd suggest it's best not to bring her into your mouth at all." The words were full of sharp teeth and pain and even on camera, the way they seemed to slice through Hugo was impressive.

"Focus, Hugo," Rowan said, and rapped the table three times.

* * *

Genevieve sucked in a breath at that. Rowan simply *knew* things like very old magic. A combination of the goddess who lived within her and that spark that was inherently Rowan and her magic. Genevieve had seen a lot of magical practices over her three-quarters of a millennia, but none quite like Rowan's.

"What?" Clive asked.

"There is magic in ritualistic gestures. Old magic. Knocking wood. Rapping three times. It's a connection to the time when everyone accepted magic as real. Humans instinctually fall back to it because it's as much a part of them as fight or flight. Sadly, they'd rather be angry or scared than believe in the magic of small things these days."

Rowan spoke again. "Let's talk about the way you've attacked me using magic. Now's your chance to explain yourself."

"*As I said*, I was under the influence of coercion spells." Hugo's condescension was only going to make it worse in the end and Genevieve really couldn't wait to see what Rowan had in mind to punish him with. Her friend was so delightfully spiteful and Hugo was so absolutely dreadful it was therapeutic just watching.

Rowan caressed the head of her walking stick—that was new—for a moment before she said, "You have quite the history with this type of behavior. Before your weak-ass spells blew up in your face. This time, I mean, because it looks like you fail a lot. Amateur." Her sneer was magnificent theater. "Explain yourself. Or don't. But the only possible way for you to get out of this mess is to give us context. Because all we *do* have makes you look like a cock who thought he had better magic and more charisma than he did. Boo-hoo."

Rowan fisted her hands and made a parody like she was crying and wiping her tears. Hugo's face darkened at the—accurate—insult and there was more than one person in that room snickering.

"I was under the influence of magic! You know this. He," Hugo pointed at Konrad, "was the one who removed the spells."

"Tedious that you'd imagine us not seeing you clumsily dodging the issue. So. Let's talk about werewolves, shall we?" Rowan lobbed into the room.

Hugo flinched. "I don't know what you mean."

"Oh, I'm sure that's not true at all. I'd probably have gotten caught just like you if I'd used a bunch of dudes with the combined brainpower of spray cheese to do my dirty work. Honestly, who kills someone with a crew that big for half a million bucks? The overhead alone would have eaten up a huge percentage. But then you went and double-crossed the dumb, vicious hired killers with paper spelled to look like money. *And*, in what is the absolute karmic cherry on this shit sundae, you went and fucked over some Dust Devils by attempting to breach their village with the intent to do harm to their priestess. You could have lived your rich-asshole life, but instead, you made so many new and excitingly powerful enemies because your ego is bigger than your brain or magical talent." Rowan shrugged. "Great news for me and all. But for you? Your schedule will be busy, busy, busy. And for what? Why did you hire the Shanks to kill me?"

Even via video it was obvious that question had caught Hugo and he began to panic.

"I have nothing to say to you. I want to speak with my attorney," Hugo sputtered.

Rowan remained as she'd been, outwardly relaxed. She tipped her chin. "He's right here with you, sport. And he hasn't said boo. He's got nothing to save you with. Goddess. I did a basic background check on you. Good schools from the cradle. But you're fucking useless, even though they graded people whose parents gave the school big fat checks—more than you paid to have a Hunter killed in broad daylight in the middle of Las Vegas—far more leniently than the rest who had to work for it."

"I want to speak to my attorney. *In private.*"

Rowan waved a hand. "No."

"No?" Hugo's tone dripped with incredulity.

"Well, that was a mistake," Clive murmured, clearly amused.

Rowan sat forward; all her easygoing energy gone now as her attention lasered onto Hugo. "As you should certainly know since I've told you several times, I've researched your whole life. You've heard no enough from women over the years. I'm advising you to get yourself used to hearing it outside that context too. *No.* You're not in charge. You're not even in the same universe as being in charge. *I'm in charge.* The Treaty is in charge. You? You're fucked."

Hugo twisted to face Felix. The other witch looked pained, but he echoed Rowan. "You're in violation of the Treaty's most inviolable laws. You're in violation of the Conclave's laws for the same. You have been found guilty already by both."

Hugo was petulant when he asked Felix, "What good are you, then? Why am I still here?"

"Because your sentence hasn't been agreed upon yet. Hunter Corp. and the Conclave are still negotiating." Konrad spoke that time. "You are part of a conspiracy to hire shifters to murder a Hunter. In the presence of human witnesses. In the full view of cameras. You are similarly responsible for the attack on a Hunter last night. In a public parking lot full of cameras. You made multiple physical and magical attacks on a Senator and fellow Conclave witch. You have attempted to breach a Dust Devil village." Her father visibly shuddered at that.

Genevieve filled with pride and love because these beings who evoked such—rightful—fear had given her a real home. Safety. Acceptance. And more power than she'd ever imagined.

"I was under compulsion. They were keeping her away from me." Hugo's voice had gone thready.

Rowan snorted and then shook her head. "The Devils have made a formal request to recommend a sentencing suggestion for you."

Hugo spun to face her, his eyes wide, but not with nearly enough fear. "It has nothing to do with them!" he yelled.

"I know you'll lower your voice right now, you stalker piece of shit," Rowan said, leaning closer to Hugo. "It has *everything* to do with them. She is their priestess! One of them in a deeply integral way. You attempted to harm her. Repeatedly. Maybe you're as ignorant as you're acting. Doubtful. But maybe. So, let me explain. You sent *a human* armed with what was essentially a magical chemical weapon to breach their village. After you attempted to attack Ms. Aubert at her place of employment, which is also protected Devil ground."

"It has nothing to do with them," Hugo repeated faintly.

With the entire surveillance room watching the screens, Rowan continued, "And then last night, you attacked me and Ms. Aubert in a public parking lot. In the presence of a Dust Devil and on Dust Devil ground."

"Which has now involved the Vampire Nation, as Rowan is the wife of the Scion of North America and the daughter of the First," Konrad said. "So much trouble from so many powerful players."

Rowan sipped her water and got back to Hugo. "So. Step one is you learn your motherfucking role. You're in a listening place. An obedience place. No one cares to hear your demands. Your feelings are irrelevant."

"You're twisting what happened," Hugo said.

Rowan sighed and Genevieve bet the Hunter was thinking of how many ways she could strike Hugo with her cane. "Go on, then, tell me how it was."

"I am not responsible! You will let me go. I can't be held accountable for something outside my control. You know it was compulsion magic that bled onto me."

Her eye roll dripped with disdain. "The compulsion magic that bled onto you? That was *yours. You* created it to use on someone else. You're responsible for where you ended up because *you* put all this in motion. Before your magic rebounded on you. The fact is, you expected to control another person against their will. Magic you've used multiple times in the past. So, you're not going anywhere, Hugo."

Rowan counted off on her fingers. "You used coercive spells on her multiple times before you were infected." Another finger. "You and your grandfather hired shifter assassins to kill me before you were infected. You moved up the timeline and told them to go ahead and make it public. Also, before you were infected." Then she flipped him off. "By the time you attempted to send forbidden magics into a Dust Devil village to harm their priestess, you'd already gotten yourself exactly here. That bit in the parking lot last night? Icing. You're a danger to everyone around you and you're not going anyfuckingwhere."

Rowan got to her feet and Konrad followed suit.

"You'll remain in custody here," Konrad told Hugo, who attempted to stand until the chain holding him to the cuff in the floor prevented it.

"Surely he'd be better off in Conclave custody," Felix said.

Rowan's tone was icy when she replied, "What's *better* for Hugo Procella is pretty near the bottom of my priority list. He'll do well to be grateful. Be of use. Otherwise..."

"I can't be held—"

In a dizzyingly fast move, Rowan swung her cane up and twisted it, hooking the handle around Hugo's throat and shoving him back against the wall. In a snarl loaded with venom, she said, "I swear on all I hold dear in this world that if you try to say you can't be held responsible for what you did before your own shitty magic blew back into your *stupid*, *weak*, *inept* face, I will make you bleed."

No one said anything, because not a being on Earth would doubt that promise after witnessing it.

Hugo blinked quickly and closed his mouth, tearing his gaze from Rowan's to stare at the floor.

"That's my bride," Clive murmured softly, making Genevieve smile. The Vampire was—like all Vampires—

snotty and in everyone else's business. But his greatest virtue was how much he obviously admired and adored Rowan.

"Thank goodness he won't be roaming free to do this to anyone else," David said quietly as he stood.

The relief that he wouldn't see the outside of a cell for decades, and most likely would never be given his magic back, left Genevieve a little lightheaded.

Then with a slight *pop* of energy, the air changed slightly and suddenly Darius was in the room at Genevieve's side, bending to check in with her.

Chapter Three

When they got back to the control room, Rowan hid her surprise at finding Darius sitting—close enough to touch Genevieve—in a very expensive chair. A flow of protectiveness came from him and surrounded Genevieve. So brilliant and strong it was visible to the naked eye.

Good. It was about time someone protected Genevieve. Yes, Rowan's friend was a badass bitch. Utterly capable of slaying her own dragons. But Rowan knew from experience just how nice it was when someone shouldered that load with you.

Rowan tipped her chin in their direction. "What did you all think of that?"

"He's not sorry at all," David said.

"No. I don't think he is. Just that he got caught. He'll do it again if he can and though so far, we only know about witches he's done this to, a human wouldn't stand a chance. He's a risk to public safety." Rowan shrugged. Regardless of whatever else Hugo and the Procellas were involved with—and she knew without a single doubt this was about far more than Hugo's tiny pecker. There was something bigger, just out of focus—he needed to be incarcerated in some manner.

Darius told them, "He's a Genetic witch. Old enough

to know better. As magically imbued beings, we carry responsibility along with our gifts. To misuse them as he has is a violation of the oldest laws binding everyone in this room and more. We do not, as a general rule, interfere. We do not take sides in petty squabbles between supernatural beings. But we can—and we will—when the situation calls for it. This one does, and not only because Hugo attacked one of our own multiple times. The public nature of that ambush is a threat to our world and the fragile anonymity we currently have with humanity."

"The time is coming when we will no longer have that protection. One of our number will finally be incontrovertibly exposed to humans." Rowan took the mug David handed her way, the fragrant steam lifting from the tea within. "Thank you." She sipped. "It's getting to be such a regular occurrence Hunter Corp. is working on the creation of a unit whose only job is cleaning up these potential disasters. There are three people on erasing all the footage of the ambush as it is. Planting the right kind of story—that it was organized crime, and I was attacked because I'd been investigating them. Still exciting, but not as dangerous as the public discovering it was witches who hired werewolves to murder a Hunter. Toss in any tidbits about Vampires working with sorcerers to kidnap and drain humans and witches of their life force and magic and it's a recipe for pitchforks and torches."

"The Nation is similarly discussing such needs," Clive admitted.

"It has always been a matter of time. And that time—the time before humans know about a shadow world that exists right alongside theirs—is coming to a close." It wasn't that Rowan had a prophecy dream. But a feeling so strong it was something she knew was coming within her lifetime.

Darius stilled for a moment and then he nodded slightly, which only cemented that feeling.

"The Conclave takes your recommendations very seriously," Konrad said.

Rowan nodded. "Good. Here's what we're going to do to help Hugo move along. We need to shatter his illusions in the most uncomfortable way possible. He's not afraid of pain because he has no context for that. But the loss of luxury and all the perks the growing power of his family has given him? He's a big, soft, spoiled, evil baby. He's been so sheltered he doesn't understand the true depth of trouble he's in because he's never had to be responsible."

David took notes on his phone, so Rowan was sure everything she said would be heard and put into action in some way.

"Feed him. Make sure he's got access to water, and his basic needs met. There's a sink in his cell. He can use that. Use those tiny little cups they give kids at nursery schools for teeth brushing."

Genevieve snickered.

"Three square a day, as they say. But not the good stuff the chef makes for the employees. I want Hugo to get meals like sandwiches on the cheapest white bread you can find. Day-old bread for bonus points. He doesn't get anything pillowy soft. No mayonnaise or mustard. Bologna. Deviled ham. The cheap stuff that smells like dog food. Egg salad. But like vending machine egg salad. Those disgusting sausages in a can I give Star as a treat." Why the dog loved the smelly things Rowan couldn't say. But the little cans showed up and Rowan took the hint when Star dropped one on her toes. "Powdered scrambled eggs and cold, dry toast. Watery coffee in a plastic cup."

"Sweet goddess that cell will stink to high heaven," Konrad said, admiration in his tone.

"Even his hair will smell. Take his street clothes. Give him a prisoner jumpsuit and those shitty flip-flops. Those full-body wipes, no showers. David, have our friend at the county get their hands on a jail blanket and mattress." The more uncomfortable Hugo was, the quicker he'd get the picture and they could move forward.

"That will surely break him," Konrad said, approving. "He most certainly knows things. Some of the things he doesn't even realize he knows. Others? Well, he thinks he can hold back. What's a little pain if he can run back to his grandfather and claim he held out against it?"

"Yes. He craves Sergio's approval and protection. But. Not more than he values his own skin. We just need to knock him down a thousand pegs so he's cold, hungry, alone, and brutally aware of just how much trouble he is in. Then, he'll throw them all under the proverbial bus to save his skin."

Genevieve's skin still crawled every time she thought too long about Hugo Procella and the way he'd obsessed on her. Stalked her. Tried to use magic to turn her into a shell of herself, one under his control.

It helped to remind herself she was stronger than anything Hugo could have tossed at her. It helped that the Devils she'd been a relative stranger to just months earlier had opened their magic to her use. Had given her a family. A place to belong.

That sort of defensive magic rendered her fairly invulnerable to the malicious intentions of those like Hugo. She was safe. Protected. But it got under her skin. And brought up memories of a time several centuries before when something similar had been done to her. She survived. She rose and overcame and would again. It'd take some time to cast away entirely the fear and embarrassment. But she had no doubt she would.

Without a word, Darius reached out to brush his fingertips against her neck, just below her ear and the voices of centuries' worth of magical teaching that had risen within her head quieted.

He'd created a spell for her. A way to soothe and calm those voices on her own by activating it herself whenever she needed to. But she didn't have to, because he'd shown up out of thin air—literally—to do it for her. To take care of her.

She didn't *need* it. But she wanted it. From him. Which created a difference she was defenseless against. Choosing to trust him with the softest parts of herself was terrifying and thrilling. Despite the depth of emotion around it, she was certain her vulnerability, the sides of herself so few ever glimpsed, would always be safe in Darius's hands.

That certainty helped center her once more. "What of the other Procellas?"

Sergio, the patriarch of the family and Hugo's co-conspirator in the attempt on Rowan's life, was in Conclave custody for refusing to give up the location of his grandson or son. By that point they'd uncovered more crimes he'd taken part in.

"Sergio stays in custody. He's a flight risk and the crimes he's accused of are far too serious to let him free. Grandpappy is at the head of this…whatever the fuck conspiracy is going on. Sister and mom haven't done anything wrong now that we know where Hugo is, but we know they're up to something. The father is on the run still. Why run if you're not hiding something?" Rowan blew out a breath.

"I agree," Konrad said. "Sergio is already here to be interviewed and he'll stay after. Since we've already nullified the cells here and neutered both witches, it's safe. As for Antonia, she's not as innocent as she attempts to make us believe. However, mercenary as this may be, if we let her go, she's a shiny target for our unknown others. We watch her, we wait for them to attack or attempt a meet of some type, and we take them all."

Genevieve rather enjoyed her father when he was tracking his quarry. He'd been absent from her life for most of her youth. And then she'd been sent off to be trained. Many things had happened, most of them had made her more powerful. Some in ways she'd prefer to never repeat.

Still, watching him while he did his job as leader of the Conclave had always been a master class of sorts. He was clever, patient, and viciously single-minded in pursuit of his goal.

"Let's circle back to the sister in a moment. What's the status with the mother and father?" Rowan asked Konrad.

"Alfonso is still missing, though we've had a few sightings. Bess is on a plane, on her way back to the United States. She's to be transported to the Conclave building and held securely there until we've done more investigating. I assume you've reviewed the interview?"

"Maybe she was on medication or used a calming spell, but she didn't seem even slightly anxious about the fate of her spouse or children. Didn't much try to hide her dislike of Sergio. But I've met Sergio, so I understand." Rowan shuddered. "I'd prefer to have seen her reactions in person, but the video underlines to me that the whole family is involved in something far more than just trying to kill a Hunter because Hugo thought I stood between him and Genevieve. You don't go to the extremes they did for that. The rest aren't going down for Hugo's deviant bullshit. Not once they feel it's him or them. They're protecting someone far more dangerous than that fucking creep."

"The Conclave agrees with all that."

Relieved she wasn't going to have to fight the Conclave, Rowan finished her tea, only to have a fresh cup poured for her immediately. She nodded her thanks to David and said, "Now let's return to Antonia. I too think using her as bait could be useful. But before she's released, I want to perform another search of the Procella mansion. I know your people already went through and it was a very thorough search," she hastened to add. She didn't lie. Precisely. What had been searched had been searched as well as she would have. It just wasn't as comprehensive a search as Rowan felt was necessary, and that was the issue.

"I have no objection to Hunter Corp. performing a follow-up search. But I can assure you, my team was quite conscientious." Konrad spread his hands as if to underline it like a game show host. "Do you have something specific you're looking for?" Clearly he was feeling territorial.

"Staff have been allowed to return, and while I know you've spelled the place so no one can take anything out—so nifty, by the way—I do wonder what might have been brought back. Or what might have been missed because the servants' quarters were not examined."

"They're in a separate wing from the Procellas. We did perform a cursory search."

"I'm not criticizing your methods." Well, she was, actually. Just not as rudely as she might have in another situation. But he, like many other very powerful people, missed things that were right in front of them. Privilege sometimes made you blind.

"What would you have done, then?" Konrad asked. Not a demand. A genuine question.

"Some of my best intelligence comes from household staff because their employers act like they don't exist. They say and do so much in the presence of the people who work for them, it's a blind spot I'm always happy to exploit. Every room in that wing needs to be searched as carefully as the areas the family lives in. Secrets don't confine themselves to the family wing."

Konrad paused and thought that over before he nodded. "I take your point. My own intelligence network is routinely fed by servants of all types."

That was as close as she was going to get to Konrad admitting she was right, and it was more than enough. Rowan just wanted to see the place herself.

"Antonia is the type to imagine she's the one holding everything together. Her brother is an idiot led by his dick and an inflated sense of importance. Grandpa is an entitled asshole. She's on cleanup duty all the time."

Rowan bet Antonia had her own spy network to keep an eye on her relatives.

Her leg twinged a little and it made her feel even meaner.

"We can bespell all her visitors to be sure they can't speak of certain topics. Not quite a geas, but something similar. I think it's wise to keep her visitor list very short," Konrad said.

"To one. Just Felix. With Alfonso still in the wind, who would she speak to anyway? And speaking of Alfonso." Hugo and Antonia's father claimed to be estranged from Hugo. He was supposedly in Long Beach at the headquarters of their entertainment business, but no one was answering the phone, and the offices had been dark and locked when Hunters and witches alike had shown up looking for him.

"It will have gotten to Alfonso by this point that we've taken Hugo into our custody." Konrad looked at the monitor in the room with Sergio and Felix.

"We'll find him eventually and ask." Rowan turned her attention to Genevieve. "Shall we finish up with Sergio? Let him know he's staying here for the foreseeable future?"

"Won't it be fun to watch him react to that?" Genevieve stood.

Chapter Four

Sergio Procella had been brought in, looking far less confident than he had the night before. Felix had finished up with Hugo and arrived right after Rowan and Genevieve had gone in.

"Here's how this will go. You," she pointed at Felix, "know the score. Don't make me have to repeat myself about your place in this process. Because I won't. Instead, I'll have you removed. Are we clear?"

Felix clearly didn't like what she was saying, but he nodded his agreement.

"And you," she pointed at Sergio, knowing how rude he'd find it, "will answer my questions truthfully. If you plan to keep wasting time by not answering questions, this will end, and you'll still be in jail. Nothing you do outside telling me what I ask you to will free you from this predicament. We can have a conversation, or you can fuck off back to your cell."

The patriarch of the Procella family wasn't as smart as his attorney. "You can't keep me here."

Rowan leaned over and slapped his face three times in quick succession, leaving a red mark and a crack in his composure. A crack she'd wedge open until he split and spilled all his secrets.

"If that were true, you'd be at your club complaining about the temperature of your lunch or whatever rich people get up to all day. If that were true, you'd have scurried out the door after I slapped your face just now. Or attempted in any way to defend yourself. So. Let's focus on what's true, shall we? A week ago, Sergio, you got in contact with the Weres who do your dirty work. You very cheekily put a hit on my life," Rowan said.

Sergio's mouth dropped open and Rowan wished she'd have slapped him two more times for being such a dick. How could he be surprised she'd have figured it out?

"There's more," she said.

"Lies!" Sergio yelled. "You're making this up to frame me and my family."

Genevieve took up next. "And *then*, Hugo called them back and pushed up the deadline. Moreover, he told them to make it hurt, even if it had to be public. Which of course it was, as you along with a few million others watched numerous video clips filmed as the attack happened in real time."

Rowan indicated the room they were in. "So here we all sit. The problem is, Sergio, you have more money and influence than sense. Never a winning proposition in the long run. Money isn't that hard to come by, especially if you don't care about legality. Power though? You earn it and if you fuck it up, getting it back is a whole different story." She would spend a few hours every fucking day until the sun burnt out to keep him from ever achieving real power again.

"You have no proof of any of this," Sergio said less confidently. "You don't look that bad off to me."

While she didn't break eye contact with Sergio,

Rowan recounted, "Well, here's the thing. I do have proof. Because you have more entitlement than sense, you paid your werewolf hitmen with fake money. I've seen your fucking mansion. Half a million dollars wouldn't have broken your backs. And for what? You didn't think they'd notice after the spell wore off and they had a bunch of paper instead of US legal tender? Greedy and shortsighted. Especially when you were already being looked at by the Conclave and Hunter Corp."

She shrugged and then shared a look with Genevieve like, *can you believe the nerve of this guy?*

"So now you've gone and pissed off the shifters who do your dirty work and have *so much* evidence against you. If you'd paid them fairly, their masters back in Seattle wouldn't come after you. They'd go about their business because there's inherent risk being a hit man. Like being caught up and taken into custody. And then questioned. We found the ones who'd escaped and took those Weres too. None of them wanted to roll on you until they realized you'd double-crossed them. Now? *Multiple* parties have identified you and Hugo as the people they received orders from. I have the paper that was spelled to look like money and the duffel bags it was delivered in. Hugo's magical signature is all over the paper, but the duffel bags, well, I'm told they have *your* magic on them. Your life is so complicated right now." Rowan sent him a sunny smile.

"That certainly does seem like a lot of proof," Genevieve agreed. "I'm the one who was able to verify your magic on the duffel bags. I found several of that same brand and type in your home office along with some very illegal spells."

"This interview is over," Sergio said, voice shaky as he shot to his feet.

Rowan stood, slamming Sergio back into the chair. "I didn't give you permission to move, old man. David, please bring me the restraints," she said, knowing her valet was listening in the other room, awaiting any orders.

"Don't touch me!" Sergio shouted.

Felix bent to speak to him in soothing tone, so Rowan leaned over, flicked the tip of Sergio's nose, and said, "*Boop.* You're not done, Sergio."

"You can't do this. This is medieval," Sergio gasped out.

Rowan and Genevieve both laughed at that.

Rowan said, "That medieval stuff is unwieldy. Have you ever seen an iron maiden? They're huge and heavy. Where would I even keep one?"

Genevieve nodded. "Fortunately, we have lightweight materials now that are stronger or just as strong as iron. Implements that are mobile. Techniques that target the softest inner bits like memories and emotions. They take up less cleanup after use, and are far more brutal." She discussed it like she was talking about what sort of rosebush she was considering planting. So breezy and mundane it was rendered terrifying.

"Ah, David. Thank you," Rowan told him as he came in.

Sergio stood and put an arm out to shove Rowan from the way. Instead, she sidestepped—he'd pay for the twinge in her leg as she did—and then gave him two hard shots to his kidneys that sent him back down.

"Here I am yet again, dealing with a man who thinks with his ego instead of his brain." Rowan put a hand at her hip. "I've mcfucking had it with you. Try me again and see." She pointed again and then shackled his leg to the rung in the floor designed for that very thing.

"Do something!" Sergio barked to Felix, who leaned in and attempted to quietly rein his client in, reminding him of what was going on.

Naturally, Sergio wasn't used to being reined in, so he reared back, disgust on his face, and turned to Rowan yet again.

"This is an outrage. I'm a citizen of the United States. I demand to be freed." Sergio's breathing sped and his pupils were way larger than they'd been earlier.

Finally, the elder Procella seemed to sense the depth of trouble he was in.

Genevieve said in her snootiest tones, "What nation or state you reside in is meaningless. You are a Genetic witch. As such you are governed by the Conclave. To attempt to claim protection from humans would involve them in our business. Which is a crime punishable by death. As this is something you've already been found guilty of, you might want to avoid trying that again."

Sergio's mouth closed with a snap.

Rowan withheld a snort of appreciation for the way that was all delivered. Sergio was sweating again. Felix looked tired. She almost felt bad for him. Then again, his client tried to have her murdered. So there was that.

Genevieve had occupied every inch of her position. A Senator. One of their most powerful elders. An Aubert. Rowan would sit quietly and let that disturb Sergio while a witch handled witch business.

"Hiring wolf shifters is not against the rules. Many witches do this for a variety of reasons. We don't even care about the mildly illegal ones. But this isn't *mildly* illegal at all. You, a Genetic witch, have contracted with the Shank family—who in our files are designated a crime syndicate—to murder the Hunter Rowan Summerwaite. With explicit instructions to make it public. Violating several of our most sacrosanct laws. You're in a great deal of difficulty," Genevieve said and while her expression was mock sadness, her tone held zero.

"I will not be interviewed with her in the room," Sergio said.

Ignoring him entirely, Genevieve turned her attention to Felix. "A guard will escort you to your vehicle. Sergio will remain here until further notice. Along with Hugo. Their magic will be nullified, and they will be kept in cells that have been altered to make certain no magic other than that of a few recognized witches will be cast. You have been found guilty of the crimes previously mentioned, but a full investigation into the scope of your actions is in process. Should that investigation find more *deviations* from our law, charges will be added."

Sergio attempted to stand, but he was still shackled to the floor, so he didn't get far. Red faced, he yelled about being outraged, yadda yadda.

"Understand you won't leave this building, even if you work yourself into a stroke." Rowan shrugged. "Throw your fit, but you'll still be in custody. The more cooperative you are, the less harsh that sentence will be. If you want to talk about things pertinent to this situation, you can let a guard know. At some point we'll be back. You're on *my* schedule now, Sergio. And it's your fault I'm so busy."

"Let me talk to him," Felix requested.

Rowan gathered her things one-armed, and headed to the door. "No. I have the wolves in custody too. I've got the fake money and the duffel. I've got your ass, Sergio. And I'm serving it—and your family—up to the Conclave on a pretty platter. Whether or not you explain to help us understand why you did these things, you're fucked, and it couldn't happen to a more deserving person."

She walked out to the hall, staring at Felix until he assured Sergio he'd be doing all he could before he scurried around the Conclave guard, one of Konrad's personal team. The strawberry blond Vampire who materialized to move Sergio—still yelling—to a cell was someone who'd been in Clive's service for two centuries. She kept her expression utterly blank—Vampires were so good at that—as she hauled the witch out of the interview room and toward the specially prepared cell, Konrad's guard leading the way.

Genevieve said to Felix, "Get in contact with Alfonso. Tell him to get himself back here to Vegas."

"I don't know where he is. But," he added quickly, "I will get word as far as I can to those who might. Are there still charges against him?"

"That remains to be seen. How can we know if he keeps running away?" Genevieve asked in a silky purr full of violence Rowan approved of greatly. She wasn't going to tell Felix much because they couldn't trust him.

He looked like he was going to argue a moment but remembered himself in time. Point to him. "What of Antonia? Hugo has been found. You were holding her for a reason that no longer exists."

"Antonia, much like her father, has obstructed our investigation. But you do correctly point out Hugo has been arrested." Rowan didn't say anything else. She didn't want Felix telling anyone they had plans to search the Procella mansion. And until that happened, Antonia was staying her ass right where she was.

"Can she at least have her magic back until her fate is decided?" Felix tried again.

Rowan couldn't fault the guy. He was doing his job the best he could, even in the face of absolute loss.

Genevieve's nose wrinkled a moment as she processed the question. "No. Yours will return once you leave here. The spell in place prevents you from revealing the location of anyone in custody. If you even *think* about telling anyone, I'll know. You won't like the result."

"I'm attempting to represent my clients—my family—the best I can."

Genevieve straightened her spine and looked down her nose at the other witch. Power seemed to flow from her in wave after wave. "Don't make the mistake of thinking anything you or the Procellas have or are connected to can get in the way of my duty." When she paused, threads of Dust Devil magic began to flicker all around her, threading through her own. It locked together like chain mail, adamantine.

So. Fucking. Cool.

Genevieve's kill shot was, "There will be no further appeals to human legal structures. I will execute him myself if he exposes us to humans. If you're involved, I'll execute you as well."

Oooh. Genevieve was being scary. Rowan loved it.

Felix remained quiet. He must have sensed Genevieve was at the very end of her patience.

"We are *not* humans. We are the Conclave." Genevieve's magic swirled around her, mimicking dust devils in the wild. "I am beyond your petty powers and potions. Go and tell them, Felix. They can know and their choice after that will be on their shoulders."

Rowan had been watching the interchange, knowing Genevieve was the best person to deliver the scary witch stuff.

When it was appropriate and Felix had clearly understood the message, Rowan said, "Bess Procella has been interviewed in Auckland, and taken into custody. You could have told us, any of you really, that she was on some swanky ten-month-long world cruise and saved us time. Funny how you all just said she was on a work trip, but you didn't *know* exactly where. But we found out anyway. If you take nothing else away here, know to your core, I will always find out, Felix."

"I assure you, it was not a plan to hide her. She wasn't here during any of this. It didn't involve her in any way. And no one asked me directly."

Rowan sneered. "That's the *definition* of a plan, fucko. You know a thing is coming up and you decide how you'll react. To control the flow of information to what you want. And you *were* asked where she was. All of you were."

"She was in the middle of the ocean. I didn't know exactly where. That much is true," he insisted.

Rowan shook her head, disgusted. "This verbal loaf of absolute nonsense might fly with humans, or other dumbassed witches like you, but I'm not human or a dumbass."

"She didn't know of the arrests. No one has been in contact with her."

Which she doubted, though Bess had denied any knowledge during her interview. Rowan was very cruise averse, but even she knew they had internet and ways to communicate with the mainland. There was no way a bunch of rich people who could afford some swanky, nearly yearlong cruise would tolerate being inconvenienced by not being able to contact their brokers or whoever back home.

Hunter Corp. and the Conclave would find out anyway, because all her electronics had been confiscated, and there was currently a major search through the ship's systems for all incoming and outgoing communications.

Not that she was going to tell Felix. He must have known they'd look. Maybe he, like his family, thought everyone else was too stupid to find all the clues they'd dropped.

"Is this a tour run by the Procella family business?" she asked. Might as well use his fear and guilt to see what he'd say. And compare it with what Bess herself had claimed.

"Not directly. But the family is working on some collaborations with the company that she's cruising with currently," Felix answered carefully. "We like to have an understanding of each new venue before we decide to take on any business dealings with them."

"Tell me something, Felix," Rowan urged. "Next in line for the business. Who do you think Sergio will choose? Not who wants to be chosen most. Don't waste my time with that. You're their lawyer and some third cousin so you see inside with a unique perspective. You're not giving away state secrets or anything. It's a way to cooperate."

"It's not Hugo at all, is it?" Genevieve said quietly.

"One might argue Bess is ideally situated to take over. The company began with her family back in England in the sixteenth century," Felix said instead of directly answering that last question.

"Armbruster?" Genevieve used the name of the family line Bess had come from.

"Back then they were the Clares. Then Armbrusters married in."

Genevieve made no major outward indication of how she felt about that revelation, but Rowan noted the slightest narrowing of her friend's gaze.

"Get me the information about those contacts as soon as possible," Genevieve said with so much finality Felix shut his mouth and nodded his agreement before scurrying off.

Rowan gave her a sideways look. Something had been revealed and she wasn't entirely sure but it seemed to have come from that tidbit about Bess and her family.

"I think we leave off seeing Antonia tonight altogether," Rowan said quietly. "She'll still try you with all that big-eyed *I didn't know* bullshit. These families are as bad as Vampire families. Just know that."

"As it pertains to the Procellas, I totally agree." Genevieve laughed prettily and slung her arm around Rowan's shoulder a moment. "Hold," she murmured and then a shimmering wall popped into place. "Now, your husband will be annoyed he cannot spy. We should talk about this connection Bess has. It could be nothing, but the Clares have come up in another matter. They're one of the families my team has been quietly investigating. I'm not sure how we missed that link. I'm rather annoyed by that so once I leave here, I need to speak to my team and to Konrad. He'll have heard that bit with Felix in the hall and made the same connection I did."

"All right. I'll wager David has done the same thing.

Hopefully he's working with Konrad, but I get that your dad will take more time to come to fully trust me and Hunter Corp. the longer we work more closely together."

"He's coming around. He recognizes your nobility. Your honor and power. I will share what I find, regardless. You might see something I don't."

Chapter Five

"I'll see you in about half an hour," she told Clive as they walked back toward his office. They had plans to meet for dinner in a private dining room at Fleur shortly. David had gone into the office Clive had given Rowan at *Die Mitte* to check in at the motherhouse. Genevieve and Konrad had left. There would be a rotating Conclave guard personally appointed by Konrad should the Procellas manage to try anything.

"Will you come into my office for a moment? I'd like to speak to you in private."

The rest of the way to his office she considered how hard she'd pretend to be outraged by the idea of having sex in there, and then how much time she had to make it a reality.

Instead, once the door was closed, he leaned close to her ear and said, "Will you take my blood? You might meet with trouble and all progress made toward you recovering your strength, the better."

There were times when her spouse could be a supreme pain in her ass. He was a condescending know-it-all with a superiority complex. Mainly because he was pretty hot shit. Still, his attitude could work her nerves.

And then he'd do something like offer her his blood

so quietly no one could overhear because he knew she had...complicated feelings about giving and taking blood from Vampires.

For a very long time the emotional damage from the way blood had been used to manipulate her as she'd grown up in the Keep had created a wound so great, she was sure she'd never get over it. Vampires tied humans to them using blood. Sometimes to help them. To protect them and keep them strong. Other times—and sometimes at the same time—it was to create a bond so the Vampire could direct the human's behavior in whatever way they pleased any time they had a notion to.

Her foster father, the First and oldest of all Vampires, had done all those things. As a result of the blood he'd given her, she'd been stronger and faster. Healthier. No doubt, her lifespan had been extended. He'd taken her blood because as one of the protected humans who'd lived in his household, her blood was a tithe. Her blood, like her service, belonged to him. It marked her so that others within the world the Vampires ruled wouldn't poach her or take blood from her without permission. Theo's permission, not Rowan's.

Despite the positives, she'd been a possession. Always at the bottom of everything, the fact was, she was not in charge of her own fate. Theo's blood bond to her meant he could—and did—barge into her mind at any time he chose. She had no real privacy. No real time off. No moment when she wasn't always painfully aware of her status.

It had gone on until the Goddess had begun to manifest herself within Rowan. Theo hadn't liked that at all. But it had shifted the balance of power until the bond between Brigid and Rowan—Goddess and Vessel—

was strong enough Rowan was able to keep Theo out more often.

All of that was to say Rowan had some heavy-duty triggers and hot buttons when it came to blood exchange. And Vampires.

It wasn't until she'd been with Clive quite some time when she'd shared blood outside a life-and-death situation. It hadn't been terrible at all. In fact, it deepened their bond. There were so many ways this Vampire had changed the way she viewed things.

Rowan smiled up at him for just a brief moment. "Thank you."

He took her hand, turning it so he cradled it wrist up. He bent his head and brushed his lips over her veins there. Once. Twice. Then he struck. A slice of pain, gone in a breath as he sipped from her. Just a tiny taste before offering his own, two crimson beads of blood already welling against his skin.

She only needed a swallow or two. Warmth spread all through her, tingling at her scalp and the tips of her toes. There was a little sting as all that healing power seeped into the still-wounded parts of her body, knitting things back together.

"That will make walking a lot easier tonight," she told him before kissing the spot on his wrist she'd just fed from.

He wanted to preen but settled for a smirk designed to annoy—and therefore delight—her. "Try not to break anything else between now and when I join you shortly. Normally I'd say it was only half an hour, but I've loved you long enough to know you can find trouble anywhere at any time."

"I do what I want, Scion," she told him after delivering a smacking kiss.

"Allow me to accompany you downstairs to the garage. I've got something for you."

"Did you give me a tank? With rockets?" she asked, teasing as the elevator doors opened on the private garage level.

The replacement for her old heavily armored vehicle was a new, even more protected high-tech fortress on wheels. "Don't joke. If I could get away with it, I'd do just that."

She took in the beefy and yet elegant BMW SUV. Matte black. Not as giant as her previous vehicle, but the smaller size meant she had more maneuverability and speed when she needed it.

"I had this in production for you anyway." He'd learned early on that his wife destroyed cars on a regular basis so it was best to always have the next one in production. That allowed for upgrades to allow for advances in technology and weaponry.

He had trouble getting her to accept diamonds, but expensive weapons were one of her weaknesses so he indulged it however often he could.

"I like how sneaky and sort of mean it looks. But it's still classy. That's your touch, obviously."

He opened the liftgate. "There are *three* separate ways to get into the weapons lockers. So even if you don't have the keys and the fingerprint locks are shot out you still have another way." He tapped a panel that slid open. "Retinal scan. You know my feelings about having a point of access without a lock." Clive gave her a look as they both remembered the ambush and the way she'd been unable to get her weapons because the fingerprint lock had been destroyed and the keys had been lost in the crash.

He did not much care what anyone else thought about it. A lock slowed her down. Limited her options and he wished very much she'd abandon that altogether and said as much out loud.

"I have too much interaction with human law enforcement. If I got pulled over it'd be a whole thing. It's easier to do it right and avoid drama." She allowed a quick hug. "But I do love that you pulled this off in such a short period of time. It's very sexy."

He gave her a wary look, which only seemed to amuse her.

"I really do appreciate you. And the way you want me protected," she said quietly.

"There's a voice-activated control system as well. So you can make a call for backup or what have you, whenever you need that. And the windows are your magic windows. Darius made it work on a much expedited schedule."

The Dust Devils had created a proprietary and partly magical process that created spy-proof windows. She'd discovered this fact and had been obsessed with getting it for her own vehicles ever since.

She brightened considerably. "Ooh! You really get me."

It was easy to think Rowan's blunt nature meant she was simple. *Nothing* about her was simple. Complicated. Layered. Beautifully flawed. No one in all the centuries of his existence had held such fascination for him. Each new aspect of her only brought a deeper craving.

"I aim to get some more of you at day's end," he said, lips pressed to her ear.

"Looking forward to it."

David called out, and they both turned to watch his approach.

"Update?" she asked.

"I have information regarding Elmer Marsc."

Marsc's name had come up in the interview process when one of the Hunter Corp. candidates had revealed Marsc had been his Maker and had abused him and several other Vampires in his line.

From everything they'd uncovered, Rowan's new hire had been telling the truth and once Rowan had her day with Marsc, Clive would most assuredly handle him from a Vampire Nation perspective.

He hated it that this was yet another thing on her plate to be saddled with. But, given the gleam in her eyes, perhaps a little bit of therapeutic energy she would expend on this predator Vampire would be of use to her general mood.

Whatever the case, it wasn't as if Clive would tell her to stand down or that she'd taken on too much. This was her job. Her path.

So he'd do what he could to provide assistance, especially as this Vampire Rowan was hunting was a problem he would be pleased to solve.

Rowan nodded at David. "Appreciate it."

David gave his report efficiently. "Unsurprisingly, he's got a massive house at Red Rock."

"Lots of gates out there to protect those million-dollar estates. I get that. I like privacy too. However, why's *he* there? Instead of on the Strip in some luxury condo like the rest of the predators he knows? He can't play day golf, and he doesn't seem to like men over twenty-two or so and that place is awash with middle-aged human men. Elmer's like that one actor guy. The one who was a kid star but now he's well into his forties. He gets older but his girlfriends stay young. I bet he's one of those men who likes to believe he's *teaching* his younger lovers. Taking them under his wing to educate them on the finer things in life." She rolled her eyes.

David snickered. "Certainly, as they call it, he's a walking red flag but he's got a lot of money, so he gets away with it like other rich walking red flags." After a cheeky grin, David got back to his report. "We've managed to get into place to keep an eye on his home—I do know how much you love a good home invasion—but he's out a lot more. He likes a certain type of bar. The dual named dudebro type with games, vastly overpriced cocktails, and mid chicken wings."

Rowan shuddered. "I know the type."

"There are four different ones he frequents in a circle around Las Vegas. Henderson, Summerlin, North Vegas, and Spring Valley."

That was a hunting pattern. His attention homed in, and Rowan gave him a sideways glance. "That's a feed loop. There's no fucking way he's there for any other reason." She curled her lip. "Why would a Vampire who can't get drunk from anything served at Bob and Chad's or whatever the name be hanging out there? Does he crave skee ball at all hours? That racing simulator? An addiction to deep-fried onions to go with his diet of the blood of barely legal humans?"

Clive blew out a frustrated breath. They were nearly immortal with myriad gifts and Vampires took risks like this. It threatened them all.

David said, "At least at a bar you know they're all legal adults of drinking age. A change of pace for him."

Rowan made a sound of derision. "They're almost all spaces that include minors too, though. You need an ID to buy liquor, but the rest of the place is full of nineteen-year-olds playing at being legal and being ripe for weirdos like Elmer. You know he chooses those for a reason. He'll avoid the places near UNLV. Too many authority figures sniffing around along with the human predators. They'll have marked that territory for themselves."

Rowan gagged and David curled his lip.

Vampires like Elmer had gotten away with centuries of entitled behavior. Rule breaking that may have started off as minor began to worsen because they grew accustomed to the idea the law did not apply to them.

But in the end, they ended up like Clive's predecessor. Dead. Because eventually, someone who had enough power and will—like Rowan—would pay attention. His wife cared very little about rules, but what was *right* was paramount to her existence.

Rowan looked his way. "I just have a feeling about this."

Because Rowan was an entirely unique power, she had come into new gifts over the years. One of those gifts she'd been attempting to hone and understand better had been prophecy. Via dreams and what she termed knowings. Once he'd gotten to know her, Clive had always trusted her feelings. She was intuitive as a base setting, but these prophecies had come from Brigid, and had bound with whatever made Rowan an excellent Hunter. The end result was magnificent.

Rowan gave him a sideways glance and a wash of her amusement came through their shared bond. His wife knew him very well.

"As ever, your feelings are my command," Clive said, bowing low and kissing her knuckles.

She snorted. "I want to go to Marsc's house. I need to…there's something or someone I'm supposed to see or say or whatever." Rowan shrugged. "It's not quite nine, so I want to go and mess with Marsc's life before I eat obscene amounts of linguine."

Two of his favorite things about her was watching her wreck lives and enjoy food. The latter allowed him to spoil her without interference. The former just made him hotter for her. "Only if I am allowed to accompany you on this mission. This is my Vampire. His crimes are happening in my city." And whether she wanted to admit it or not, she was still healing from multiple attempts on her life. Having a Scion at her side would annoy her, but she'd know it was a good thing.

"I need to go to the motherhouse to change into more suitable clothing and to do a little bit of planning with my notes first."

"I will meet you there in fifteen minutes. I have some things to handle here first as well." Clive tossed the keys to David. "See you both shortly."

Chapter Six

When they arrived, David shoved an insulated mug of hot coffee and a little plate of cookies her way as they stood in front of the map of the area hung up in their operations room. "We've only been here like five minutes. How the hell do you produce this stuff so instantly?"

"It's my job," he said. "I have a feeling you'll need the sustenance before this is over and as you've shifted your dinner later in your schedule, this will give you fuel in the meantime."

She snorted. "My life is full of people who shove food at me every ten minutes. It nearly makes up for the reason I'm burning through all those calories constantly healing from assholes trying to kill me. Not complaining about cookies. Thank you." To underline that, she took a bite. "Oh, lemon? Yum." She ate another because it would be rude not to. "No need to delay this. I've wanted to rile up this Vampire since Aron told me about him."

Rowan's—Hunter Corp.'s—new Vampire employee had told her the story of how and why he'd left his Maker. And of the way he'd been still a teenager when Elmer had first brought him over. Elmer was a fucking creep who liked young humans because they were easy to manipulate.

"He's hunting. In my city. I don't like it and I want to be assured he's not violating any laws. Which we know I won't be. This guy is wrong in a dozen ways."

Her gut told her he was up to something far worse than cruising for young white men with popped collars, cargo shorts, and boat shoes.

Vanessa came in. "We've been able to tap into multiple traffic cameras and the security cams for the subdivision, as well as the outside of his house. Do you want to knock on the front door or break and enter? Vihan has managed to secure the code for the door leading into the house from the garage. Take the bay furthest to the west. It's empty and I've got control of that entrance to the house. I'm working on the interior cameras. I'll have it for you by the time you roll up to his place either way."

Rowan realized just how quickly and ably the other woman had become part of their team. "I'll let you know if I want to kick a door down or just show up in their sitting room when I get a look at the place when we approach."

"Roger that." Vanessa indicated a black case she'd opened on a nearby table. "I'll be on overwatch here through David's earpiece. I brought these body cams. They clip onto your button here." She indicated Rowan's chest just below the hollow of her throat. "Vihan will be with me at the controls."

Good. David's new assistant was smart and a very fast learner, but the more experience he got, the better he'd be prepared. Rowan liked that her new employees were creating relationships with the rest of the team. That sense of unity would keep them all safer.

Rowan snapped the nifty little camera into place and David did the same before seating his earpiece.

"I'll have a Scion with me, FYI. You might see Patience or Seth because they're not going to let him travel without a guard either. Any other Vamps and I want to know. He can't be doing this alone and I don't want to be ambushed again." Clive would never let her leave the house if that happened.

Malin called up to say Clive had arrived. Rowan polished off the last three cookies before she told David, "I'm going to kit up. You do the same. Bring weapons."

After David left, Rowan slid the custom back sheath for her blade on first and then loaded knives into their slots on each boot. Should be enough, though she had handguns in a weapons locker in the back of her new car.

As they reached the first floor, she said quietly to David, "I'm sandbagging the news that Aron was hired until the perfect opportunity. I want to pop him in the nuts with it. He might already know given the way the information was disseminated within the Nation. But if he doesn't, it'll be fun. And people make mistakes when they're caught off guard."

There was a leak—most likely more than one—within the Nation that was feeding her enemies sensitive information that left her vulnerable. She'd figure *that* out too.

"Do you think the Nation will ever accept Vampires on our mixed teams?" David asked. All this drama and extra work for Rowan was because Hunter Corp. had wanted other paranormals on their teams when the case they were investigating needed the eyes of someone from that group. The Vampire Nation actually benefited from these special teams but they were so dramatic and petty more than one group of them had caused trouble over the choice.

"They already have. They'll act aghast and play the victim because that's what they do. No matter what we do they're going to complain so we may as well do what we want and let them die mad. It's done and they can't change it."

Clive approached looking suave and dangerous. He gave an approving glance toward the tactical gear she wore, the style mirroring his. *Sexypants.*

"Let's go to his house first. Then we try the other places if he's not around. That way, we can perform a search before he gets a tip-off that we're looking for him and starts trying to dump evidence. If he's not there, he won't be under my feet. If he is there, I can fuck with him. Win/win."

"And for those who get to watch you in action," Clive said.

David took the wheel and Rowan frowned, annoyed her leg was still keeping her from the driver's seat, but satisfied herself, screen on her lap as she worked with Vanessa remotely and they were able to get through two layers of guards and gates.

"Drive past and turn around," she told David.

Elmer's house was gigantic with a big, circular driveway. Angled to shield the front door from the street. It was bright enough from the rising moon and she could see there were no guards stationed anywhere at the front of the place.

Though she did love some breaking and entering, Rowan decided subtlety wasn't the angle she wanted right then. "Yeah, I say we ring that doorbell. Park right in front of the steps to the door," she told David.

"One moment," David said before murmuring something to Vanessa via his mic and earpiece. He drove them in a big circle, taking time as Vanessa did whatever it was back at the office. Finally, he headed back and pulled up into the drive, turning to back in so they could make a quicker exit. "We're good to go. All external cameras are on a loop for the next three minutes."

Clive slid out and opened Rowan's door before she could do it herself. Then he put himself between her and the house while David caught up on her other side.

The front of the house was…fine. There were cameras and the overall security of the neighborhood was excellent. Her home had been landscaped to interrupt sightlines and foil anyone with a rifle and a hate boner for a Hunter or a Scion. This place wasn't nearly as secure. For a Vampire as powerful as Marsc, it seemed lazy. The cost of inattention to such important details could result in someone you don't want about to pound on your front door.

Clive took it all in and shook his head. Clearly disappointed in this Vampire. He'd had his power signature muted in the car, but in the space of a breath, he let it free. The heavy, delicious weight of a Scion rolled from him.

Brilliant. Fierce. Clive Stewart was one of the most powerful beings on the planet and right then, she bet his power was visible from miles away.

"I think the Scion should knock," she told him.

"I think that's a fine idea," he said as they climbed to the shiny black lacquer double front doors.

He knocked twice and then adjusted his cuffs as he waited. The night all around them seemed to hold Clive in its arms. This was his ground and he would occupy it, drowning anyone who dared oppose him with his power.

The human who answered the door started and then bowed low. He swept an arm out, indicating Clive enter. "Scion, it is our honor. Please, come inside."

Rowan followed him with David at her back and the servant who'd answered the door paled. "You aren't alone."

"Why would I be? Please let Mr. Marsc know I'm to be attended to—by him—immediately." Clive didn't bother with any sort of compulsion or glamor because it was unnecessary.

The human looked from side to side. "He's unavailable. What can I do instead?"

Rowan made a sound in her throat. Horror and dismay, if Clive knew his wife. And he did.

She said, icy and disapproving, "You can go to your employer and let him know a *Scion* is standing in his foyer and hasn't yet even been offered a seat or refreshments. Because, as I'm utterly certain you know, *unavailable* isn't an option when a Scion visits. Unless one is looking to be offensive. In which case, I'd wonder why that was."

Rowan turned her attention from the human to a spot just above a china cabinet on a nearby wall.

The human blushed and then went stiff as no doubt, Marsc was using the blood bond to inform him of his unhappiness.

The servant bent very low. "Apologies, Scion. Please, come through to the sitting room. I'll ring for tea and refreshments for you to enjoy while I let Mr. Marsc know you're here. He's been in meetings, that is all I meant. I was clumsy in my explanation."

Clive watched the interplay closely. Rowan usually went out of her way to be patient and kind with any human servants. This time though, she narrowed her gaze at the man until he left quickly.

Rowan didn't bother to sit. She ranged around the room picking things up, turning books out, shaking to see if anything was between the pages.

David examined things closely, but made no move to touch anything. He remained on point should he need to protect Rowan. Clive approved of the rhythm that had developed between Rowan and her valet.

She got a text. Frowned and then smiled before tucking her phone away once more. In a few steps, she'd pressed her mouth to his ear. "He's here. Vanessa tapped into the in-house cameras and there's a suite beneath the main house. Probably where he goes to daytime rest. Possible panic room. But he doesn't appear panicked. He's watching an action movie. She says he's dressed like he sells something for a living."

It was certainly easier than trying to deal with him in a public place surrounded by humans.

He hummed his agreement and breathed her magic in for long moments before she stepped away and slipped back into public mode.

"I'm giving him one more minute to present himself with the appropriate grace. Then I'm going to look for him and he won't like that. I've not only got a warrant, I've got cause to search without it. I can promise anyone watching this video feed they won't like the result of making me find Elmer myself," she said loud enough for anyone watching to have heard.

Clive said, "Darling, please don't be cross with me, but I rather hope they don't believe you. I, for one, love the results of such behavior."

She snorted a laugh. "Fair warning, Scion Stewart. We both know this Vampire is playing games. I'm going to fetch him."

"As you say, sometimes, they must touch the hot stove to learn. Go on, then, burn things to the ground." He stood, waving an arm to indicate she go ahead.

Her heartbeat kicked up and she shot him a—very brief—look that promised they'd both be very sore after they next were able to fuck.

Out in the foyer, Rowan noted the human who'd opened the door. "What's your name?" she demanded.

He looked around the room, but she waited until the inevitable when he had to answer. "George."

Rowan said to him in a quiet voice, "Here's what's going to happen, George. I know you don't have a damned bit of say in whatever Elmer Marsc gets up to. Like you have no say in what I get up to. But you do know what a household is supposed to act like when a Scion comes to visit. And this isn't it."

"Go to *Die Mitte* and ask the front desk for Alice," Clive said. "There are other households who always need more daytime staff. We can help you with that if you separate yourself from him now."

Clive essentially told George to choose the Nation or Marsc. One had a future. A new job. The Nation not angry with him. The other? That way lay uncertainty. Most likely death. Surely pain. Human servants could, and did, defend their Vampire masters all the time. Out of loyalty. Some fear, definitely. But in this case, as

George clearly understood, Clive was the far scarier threat of the two.

"Do you wish to sever your bond with him?" Clive asked.

George's eyes widened and he said quietly, "He said that wasn't possible."

"He lied to you."

Clive hadn't gotten truly angry. Yet. He was getting annoyed though.

"Get my back, David. Which way?" she called out. He had the architectural plans on his screen and consulted.

"Down that hallway to your right," David said as they headed in that direction.

Clive could deal with George, and she'd shut down surveillance so wherever Elmer was, he couldn't access the feed.

Of course Elmer would assume she had no way of getting into his basement lair, much less this control room. Rowan smiled to herself as she punched in the code Vanessa had just texted, and the three red lights above the door went green.

She pushed the door open, sweeping down and to the left while David went right. In the center of the space was a large oak desk surrounded by screens.

That was a lot of screens, even for a seven-thousand-square-foot house.

The Vampire behind the desk stood and showed his hands, palms out. "I do apologize for the delay in attending you," he said.

Most definitely not Elmer, but a scumbag just the same.

"Stephen Baker," Rowan said as she took in the Vampire in front of her. One she'd had a run-in with the first year she'd been in Las Vegas. He'd been one of Jacques's hangers-on. A human at a nightclub in one of the casinos had been harassed by Baker and another Vampire as gross as he was, and Rowan had to educate him—and Jacques—about what one did and didn't do under the Treaty.

"Hunter. What an unexpected surprise."

"Where is he?" Rowan asked flatly.

Her surveillance team would let Rowan know if Elmer moved.

"Shut it down," David said to Vanessa, who'd been connected via phone.

With a few audible keystrokes, her tech queen made David's command a reality.

At her back, Clive entered the room. He took a look, first at all the screens, and then over to Stephen, with a perfectly raised eyebrow. The British arch. And then he poured his Scion magic through the area. It was like he'd sucked away all the air as a hot wave of energy rolled past them and toward the other Vamp.

Rowan was intimately familiar with his power, so she wasn't startled. But she did like the way Stephen jumped back, dropped his gaze, his head to one side, exposing his neck.

"David, do grab all the data cards from these cameras. I want to see everything," Rowan said.

Stephen sputtered, holding his hands out. "You will do no such thing. You are in a private residence."

Rowan strode up to him, right into his personal space, only giving him a breath. "I will do what I want to do. Who's going to stop me, even if I didn't have the right?

You? Golly, I fucking hope you try. I haven't made a Vampire bleed in…hours."

David, ignoring anything but what she'd said, moved and began to collect the data cards. "I'll leave a receipt for everything I remove," he murmured offhandedly.

"You will meet with me now. Not in this room," Clive said.

Stephen was clearly torn as he looked back and forth between the screens and Clive.

Rowan was fairly certain Clive would escalate this little power display to a painful degree if this meathead didn't obey.

He and George left to have this meeting, so she just shrugged her shoulders and got to looking.

Then. Stephen reached out, grabbed her upper arm, and yanked her back. "*I said no.*"

Rowan let him carry her as she began to turn, using the energy he'd already expended as she cocked her fist back and let fly, punching him square in the temple with about half her strength because she used her non-dominant hand.

He folded, crumpling to the ground and at her back, Clive flowed in, hot and full of outrage.

"That's yours." She pointed.

"Who is this Vampire to Elmer, George?" Clive asked and Rowan wanted to kiss him for not asking if she was okay. He knew she was, even if he worried, and he wouldn't weaken her in front of anyone else.

Whatever he'd said to George had turned Elmer's *former* employee into the president of Clive's fan club. He answered immediately. "Mr. Marsc's *head of security*. Stephen Baker."

"Is he in contact with Elmer? Right now? Does Elmer know we're here?" Rowan asked quickly.

"No. Mr. Baker does not bother Mr. Marsc outside an emergency when he's…relaxing before he goes out for the evening. There's another control room downstairs, but Mr. Marsc only uses this one to watch. And he doesn't watch before he goes out."

Aside from the ick crawling through her at what that meant, that a Hunter and a Scion in the front parlor didn't constitute an emergency was further evidence these Vampires were up to something dodgy as fuck.

"Watch?"

"All the rooms, bathrooms, common areas, the yards, pool, pool house, garage, all of it is covered by cameras. He'll watch people he brings back. People who visit. Replays of his own activities. You have fifteen minutes until he'll ring for the car to be brought around so he and his boyfriend can go. There's only one exit and it's through that door there." He pointed. George sounded miserable and there was a pang of pity at the thought of what his day-to-day life must have been like.

"Okay, what's with the italics when you said Stephen's job title?" she asked.

"Baker doesn't act like an employee. They have their own schedule and do…things. But Baker acted like a partner or an equal to Mr. Marsc."

Interesting.

Chapter Seven

A thorough search had begun upstairs. Some of Clive's team had shown up to take Baker into custody and the others had joined Rowan's people systematically going through each room.

"Elmer is on his way up," Vanessa murmured through the earpiece.

Rowan and David moved out of the line of sight, waiting for Elmer to walk out, letting the door close at his back.

The surveillance room was empty but for the three of them. Clive had gone off to handle Nation business and a lot of the equipment had already been removed. Elmer didn't even notice until Rowan threw a pen at the back of his head.

When she'd interviewed Aron, he'd told Rowan Elmer appeared harmless. Warned her to watch closely.

And, as she first caught sight of him when he spun around, she agreed with that. At first glance anyway. She walked closer and that's when she caught sight of the flat gaze of a predator. Such a big red flag that even the most deliberately clueless of humans often had a sense of something very wrong around any being with an affect like that. Blank.

Outwardly, everything about him said he was bland. A vanilla dude who fucked with the lights off and ate a lot of beige food. Just a Vampire out for the night grabbing some potato skins and a drink after his workday doing whatever people did inside an office building.

Those shark's eyes met hers and then skittered off, settling at her right ear, and then he decided to get bold and try to glamor her.

She leaned close, thumb and middle finger enough to get the force for a flick right between his eyes. "Far more powerful Vampires than you have tried—and failed—to glamor me.

"Weird you aren't asking who I am or what I want as I'm standing in your little pervert hole." She examined him closely. Elmer had managed average leaning into attractive. But not too far. He had yellowy-gold hair that he'd artfully let curl just a bit. Green eyes. He was sitting, but she was sure he couldn't have been taller than five ten or so. He appeared soft. Khaki trousers and a button-down shirt with the sleeves rolled up to the elbows. Well made though. Vampires liked a well-made garment. Nice watch, but not a Rolex like she'd found back at his house. Didn't wear them when he went out to find himself snacks, she figured. Good shoes.

Though he'd been Made a Vampire in a time when men wore wigs and breeches, he'd embraced modernity well enough that he wouldn't stand out. Witnesses would forget about him five minutes after they left his company.

But Rowan had been able to spot a monster from before she could speak. Elmer Marsc, through Brigid's eyes, had a dark and cluttered energy. Dirty. This being was a taker. She underlined just how little respect she had for him as She stood back and let Rowan resume control once more.

From the start, when it came to this Vampire, there'd been a *knowing* in her gut. It had led her to this very place. *To this very person.* At the very least, Elmer was a predator who sought out underaged humans to Make. In violation of Vampiric law as well as the Treaty.

There was more. She knew it. The Goddess knew it and now Rowan had to prove it.

"I know who you are and what you do. I've done nothing to merit this sort of attention," Elmer said, and that flare in her belly happened again.

Rowan sent him a censuring glance and cocked her head. "I'm sure that's not true at all or I wouldn't be here."

The harmless act faded, though the flatness of his demeanor remained. Creepy.

"What do you want, Hunter?" he said at last.

Rowan would start out slow and see just what direction Elmer rabbited off to. Vamps like him weren't that hard to goad into saying too much. Their belief in their supremacy was their weak spot. It made them incautious. It meant they underestimated everyone else.

Originally she'd planned to take him through the house, show him his perfect, ordered world was crumbling all around him, but as his first glimpse of real emotion was when he caught sight of the missing equipment, Rowan settled her feet a little wider. Let him stay right there wondering just what else was going on. Confronted with her power over him.

"Let's talk about Aron." It was his interview material that had first sent up a *knowing* within Rowan's belly. Then he'd told her about Elmer's gross little hobby.

The more she found out, the stronger that feeling had become.

Elmer's expression shuttered immediately and the laugh that burst from her lips was all Brigid. The goddess was delighted by that reaction because deep in the pit of her belly, distrust and anger banked, heating up.

Rowan *did* like the way his smug was wiped away by that laugh though she hoped she'd get to use the cane too.

"What about him?" Elmer said, trying to sound tough, but the thread of panic in his words was delicious and she wanted to lean in and take a deep breath. "He left my line seventy-five years ago."

"After you Made him illegally and abused him for several decades."

"It wasn't illegal back then. Anyway, one man's abuse is another man's pleasure. Don't let him convince you he was a victim. He said he wanted to leave. I told him to get on getting the fuck out. There's a hundred more where he came from. He file a complaint?" Elmer's sneer told Rowan what he thought of that. "You going to turn me over to the Nation?"

Rowan made a face, admittedly surprised he seemed to have no idea the Scion was in his fucking mansion with his fingers all over Elmer's illegal bullshit. Rowan could feel his power and she wasn't even a Vampire. "That's between you and the Nation."

He'd simply assume she had and that her answer was what he wanted to hear because otherwise meant a confrontation and he wasn't up to it.

He was more vicious than smart or cunning. That much was clear to her. Viciousness had its uses in the Vampire world. Many of them made their living from it in one way or another. But viciousness without intelligence was a problem. Especially without someone holding the leash.

"What do you want, then?" he asked at last.

"Aron works for Hunter Corp. That makes him one of mine." Let him think all she knew about was Aron. Right at that very moment, the data cards from the house were being examined. She'd done a quick search through the entire house before Elmer had come upstairs, and had located a number of caches. Some appeared to be spell trapped, so Genevieve showed up with Darius and they were now part of the search.

Elmer had no fucking idea how deep his troubles went. He seemed to sense none of it.

"I hear working for you gets a body killed," he said, mean in his voice.

Just when she'd begun to feel a little sorry for what a weak Vampire he was, he had to go and make a reference like that. Before Elmer was conscious of it, Rowan had shifted to his side, and had the tip of one of her blades pressing into the flesh between his ribs.

"And what would you know of such a thing?" she asked, her lips pressed to his ear. The sticky copper of the blood she'd spilled beading down the tip of her knife was a match to the kindling of her rage. Not even two months before, several of her closest friends had been murdered by magic-wielding Vampires as a way to get to Rowan.

It had broken her heart and she'd spent the intervening weeks hunting down and killing every being who'd been involved. The key players—that she knew of—were dead, but the problems remained. And where there were problems, there were aggrieved Vampires waiting to plot about it.

Elmer's intake of breath and gurgle of pain had Brigid delighted.

He said, "I heard. It's all over town. I didn't have anything to do with it, I swear. I would never!"

"You felt pretty comfortable bringing it up. Which makes me really cranky and makes *you* really stupid."

"You're right. I'm sorry. I shouldn't have joked about it," he said in a rush.

"Who Made you?" Rowan asked.

"I don't have to tell you that."

Well, that was an interesting response from a Vampire who was just so eager to abase himself moments before. Rowan pulled her phone out with her free hand and dialed Clive.

Before he could purr her name and get all sexy, Rowan said, "Who is this fucko's Maker?"

"Give me a few minutes," he told her and rang off.

"Well then. While we wait, I should probably let you know just on the other side of this door there's a search of your home being executed by Hunter Corp. Nation stuff too, but the Scion's people can tell you about that." She shrugged, amused by the way his mouth flattened with displeasure.

She stepped away, her back to the door, blocking his only way out. She held her blade in between them, just so he didn't forget it was there.

"This is preposterous!"

"I will give you points for vocabulary, Elmer. Otherwise, honestly, how is it you thought you could just do whatever the fuck, and the Scion would never pay any mind? This one isn't a criminal scumbag like the last one."

"Jacques was the epitome of what a powerful Vampire is."

That made her guffaw. "Yeah? Dead and irrelevant? Is that what you mean?"

Less than two minutes later, Rowan looked at her screen and then up to Elmer. "Well, isn't this interesting. David, did you know Roderick Haigh was this Vampire's Maker?" Haigh was a Vampire she'd personally executed upon finding out he'd been the source for the black-market spells Vampires and a bad-guy faerie had been using to harm innocents.

Clive's tersely worded text told her he was beyond pissed, which was a problem to deal with once they got out of there and Elmer into a cell.

"We're going to go outside and load you into a car. Then we're going to get you somewhere secure so we can have a chat about what you've been up to," she told Elmer. "I can see in your eyes you think you can run. I'll warn you now, that would be a very bad idea. I'm already pissed off. I'll make it hurt if you run." Walking stick or not, she'd be on Elmer's ass before he could gather his next breath.

"I don't have to go anywhere with you," Elmer said, his gaze returning to the blade over and over. The stink of his fear made her eyes water. He was hiding something he desperately didn't want her to know. Which piqued her interest like a motherfucker.

"You're two hundred and seventy-five years old and you *still* don't have the power or ability to take me on. Whereas I have a goddess inside me and the power and authority the Hunter Corp. brings to bear. Your Maker is—sorry, *was*—a very bad Vampire who got himself executed. If you're involved in anything he was, I could serve a warrant on you right here. You'd be nothing but dust afterward," she told him conversationally. "But then I wouldn't be able to have a longer chat with you and I don't want that."

Interrogate first. Then came killing. Logical order.

Rowan said, "David, let's get him out."

David moved to obey, opening the door.

Rowan took Elmer's arm and moved him out.

Patience, one of Clive's top lieutenants, approached with a curled lip in Elmer's direction. She and Rowan weren't pals, but the job she did for Clive kept him alive, so they respected one another.

"Tell him I'm taking this one to *Die Mitte*," she requested.

"I'll get in contact with Alice to clear the way for you," Patience said and headed back into the heart of the house where Clive probably was.

But outside the night seemed weirdly still and she stood on the doorstep a few seconds more to listen carefully.

The hair on the back of her neck prickled, awareness that there were powerful beings in that area. Whoever else was out there wasn't more powerful than she or the Vampire she was frog marching to her vehicle. There were Nation Vampires everywhere on Clive's orders, along with a Dust Devil or two and an incredibly powerful witch.

But she didn't think it was a friendly out there. Paranoid or not, the situation warranted caution, so Rowan shifted so that David had physical control of Elmer. Her valet had been at her side long enough that he adjusted, knowing she was up to something and to be ready in case their prisoner tried to run.

She'd let it play out to see what—or who—Elmer had up his sleeve. It was as she hit the automatic locks that another Vampire raced at her, snapping his jaws as he attempted to rush her off her feet. In an easy movement, Rowan stepped to the side, sticking her foot out before she remembered that was her injured leg and an echo of pain blossomed, but she wrestled it back, not having time for any injury bullshit right then.

His rate of speed combined with his trajectory meant when she tripped him, he flew face-first into her passenger door. That would leave a mark on her brand-new car, damn it. She had to give it to him though. Despite the crunch and spray of blood as his nose had broken, the new Vampire scrambled to his feet and went at her again, trying to rip her open with his nails and teeth. She punched him in his already broken nose and then kneed him in the balls with her good leg, sending him right back to the ground on a gurgled exhalation of air.

"Cease this immediately," Rowan ordered and thought of how Clive had done it, using his voice just so. She pitched her tone slightly differently and the threads of compulsion wrapped around the younger Vamp as she watched. *Ooh!* "Stand up and dust yourself off. And for goddess' sake, Elmer, you're his Maker, find your voice and your spine and tell him to back off or you'll both be true dead."

"Haddon, please," Elmer said. "Stand down."

Haddon had been the name George had given them for Elmer's boyfriend. He'd most likely been the one tasked with bringing the car around.

"They said she'll kill you," Haddon said. *They?* She'd let them think she missed that little slip of the tongue until she was ready to run them over with it.

Rowan saw how young he was. Or had been when

he'd been Made into a Vampire. She sent a glare Elmer's way.

"I'm the Hunter. And I will kill you *both* if I need to. So. Don't make me need to. I'm in the middle of a hunt. Answer my questions. Don't be an asshole and try to bite me. Are you a fucking rabid raccoon or a Vampire?" Still annoyed, her injured leg beginning to throb, she sent a middle finger Haddon's way.

That shut him up.

David put Elmer in the back seat, climbing in next to him. Rowan sent a text to Clive and then jerked her thumb for the younger Vampire to sit up front with her. It took a few minutes to be sure everyone was secure, but Rowan got down to it. She might as well start the questions then, since she had them both subdued and a little scared. Just to take the edge off, so to speak.

"What's your connection to Roderick Haigh other than his being your Maker? You aren't in the Haigh line, I know that. You didn't remain close after he brought you over?" Rowan asked Elmer.

"Why do you care about Haigh?" Elmer challenged. Again.

Rowan sneered at him. "Answer the question. It's the least of your problems right now."

"I was never part of that line. He and I were *particular* friends. His family did not approve."

"I know the Haighs. There are plenty of gay Vampires in their line and no one seems bothered at all. Maybe it was because you and Roderick went out hunting for young people to seduce and change, and they found it as abhorrent as I do." It was a guess based on what she already knew and given the way Elmer's whole body jerked, Rowan figured it was accurate.

Some days being jaded really paid off.

"And you?" she asked Haddon. Haddon? What a ridiculous name. It sounded like one of three last names of an old white guy law firm. "How old were you when Elmer Made you? Don't lie to me. He's a Nation Vampire, which means there are rules."

"I was eighteen. Fully legal."

Sure. And she was eighteen too. Rowan rolled her eyes knowing all she had to do was look up the paperwork for the Change. If Elmer had done it officially anyway. "Did you consent? Did you know what was going to happen?"

"You don't need to answer any of these questions," Elmer told him.

Rowan leaned through to the back seat and punched Elmer's fucking asshole face and then gave one more jab because he deserved it and her leg still hurt.

"Actually, he does. And now so you do. See you like to frequent bars, but you can't get drunk from human alcohol. You know the bars I mean. I imagine you choose classier bars serving blood-added drinks when you're not hunting humans you can manipulate."

"You're grasping at straws."

She'd been doing this too long to miss the slight rise in his voice. The way his words had sped slightly.

To be over two centuries old and still have so little control was a real problem when it came to nearly immortal beings who could make other people into their bonded blood servants or other Vampires.

"See, I don't think I am. I'm going to take a look at anyone who's gone missing from this place and the others you creep around. I bet I'll find a few." The panic wheeling in his gaze told her she'd win that bet.

That electric blip that pinged in her chest a few seconds before vibrated again, stronger this time, echoing through her whole system. She knew without thinking on it too hard that it was Clive approaching and the bond they shared was reacting.

Not even one more question to Elmer and Clive emerged from the main door, his power filling the air.

"If anyone moves from this car or makes any trouble whatsoever, I will shove a blade through your eye. It'll take forever to heal, and as a bonus for me, it'll hurt. And then I'll do it again. Sit your ass in here. David, shoot them in the face if they make you nervous at all. They'll survive and you'll be safer." Rowan opened her door and Star jumped up into the driver's seat. "Uh, hi there. These are the bad guys. Protect David."

Star licked Rowan's nose and then turned her attention back to the Vampires. Rowan closed the door and stepped a few feet away. "Let me get you up to speed."

Clive interrupted. "You were in pain. I felt it through the bond. What happened?"

"I didn't think. Always at the root of a problem." She shrugged. "I'll be all right." No doubt she'd set herself back a little though. Not that she'd admit it outside extreme circumstances.

"You should have called for backup," he said quietly enough she didn't worry he'd be overheard.

"Moving on. Elmer is exactly what I thought he might be. Brigid doesn't like him at all. The pain you sensed came when I tripped his little friend. Emphasis on little because if that Vampire was eighteen when he was Made, I'm the nicest person on earth. And, to top it off, Roderick Haigh is Elmer's Maker. That's a lot in an already eventful day."

"I wish I was shocked Marsc was made by that little gobshite." Clive smoothed a hand down his tie. Anger throbbed from him. Haigh had not only been a traitor on his own, but he'd been the connection to Clive's uncles, who'd betrayed the Stewart family line and could have gotten them all executed by the First. They'd been part of the xenophobic, anti-human movement they called the Blood Front. And the Blood Front had been working with some end-of-days-level bad guys.

It had been a violent, costly mess that had left people they'd both cared about dead. And it wasn't entirely over.

All in all, Clive had every reason to be pissed at the mention of Roderick Haigh, so she relented. A little.

"After spending some time in Marsc's presence, I can believe they were close. Marsc further claims Roderick was his boyfriend. The baby Vamp, the one who tried to bite me like he was a rabid animal, claims he was eighteen when he was brought over. Says it was consensual. But they weren't all that way and I'm doubting Haddon had seen his eighteenth birthday before changing either."

Clive's mouth set into a hard line as he shook his head. "We've discussed this matter. You know full well I will not allow for any Vampire to prey on minors in my territory. Remand these prisoners over to Nation custody so we can deal with it. I vow you will have total access to them for your Hunter purposes."

Only because she knew he'd be satisfied if she let it show, Rowan shoved her impulse to raise her brows at his demands. "*I'm* going to interrogate them both first. This is a direct connection to my hunt. She agrees with me," Rowan said, meaning Brigid. "As I said, I won't get in between you with the illegal Making. Stalking too, most likely. I absolutely agree there's evidence of a feed loop. Lots of young people's lives to ruin. I already have Vanessa working on checking missing persons reports in the general area of these bars. When I mentioned it, he nearly shit his pants. I mean, thank goodness that didn't happen because gross. Not in my new car!"

"Well, let us be grateful you were spared such an event. I think once we give the evidence culled from this house a more thorough examination, we'll get all the information we need. I'll need to find where he nests so we can take care of any possibly traumatized Vampires. I'm not going to play political games with Hunter Corp."

She blew out a breath, allowing herself to soften a little. For him. Because he was capable of a lot of shitty Vampire behavior, but not to harm her or their bond. And because he truly did want to protect those Vampires who were often at the mercies of more powerful masters. Plus, her other prisoners were already at *Die Mitte* so it made logistical sense.

He said very quietly, "Let me help."

How could she resist when he was this way? Well, easily when she wanted to. She was a badass bitch, after all. But she didn't want to. Or need to. "Fine."

Star's bark caught their attention and they turned, Rowan stalking over with a snarled curse. She yanked the door open as David had a gun pulled and pointed square into Elmer's face.

Clive had ceased to be amazed at the amount of trouble Rowan could find herself in at any given moment, but he was impressed by the tableau, nonetheless, as he flowed to stand next to her, not bothering to filter away his true power.

"Do we need to shoot him in the face?" she asked David, calm. Star had her lips pulled back, teeth bared as she growled in the direction of a pitifully young-looking Vampire cringing back against the passenger door.

Both Vampires realized the Scion was standing there, and everything went very still and very quiet. Clive turned his glamor up to ten and it rolled over the area in a warm wave of energy. Rowan had told him it was like a brownie and a hug. Like everything you ever wanted.

He was good with that when it got him everything *he* wanted.

"Well, introductions need to be made," Clive said, satisfied both Vampires in the SUV had taken on glossy gazes and slack mouths as a result of the glamor. "You've been a very bad boy, Elmer."

"You said you weren't going to execute me!" Panic roused Elmer enough to accuse Rowan after she rattled off their names by way of introduction.

"I said *I* was here on Hunter Corp. business. And I am," Rowan told him, disdain dripping from her tone.

Yes, this impacted Rowan's investigation. But. While most of Vampirekind would have ignored making such young humans even fifty years prior, what they knew for sure by that point in their history was if there was something bound to get attention from the authorities that would endanger their secrecy, it was this sort of abuse.

"Shall we move to a more secure and private location?" Clive said, though he made an effort to sound like he asked. His wife was already on edge and feeling territorial, he didn't want to start an argument with her in the open, in front of witnesses. But they needed to get out of the public eye before things devolved any further and eventually neighbors would begin to peek out windows.

"You two." She pointed a knife tip toward the Vampires in the SUV. "Fuck you both if you make him shoot you. And he will. In your femoral artery, which will absolutely ruin my upholstery, so I'll be billing the Nation, and they'll take it out on you. You won't die. Probably. But it'll hurt. Haddon? My dog will rip your nose off and shit it out later, so just for the love of Pete, behave yourselves!" she said and shut the door.

Clive said, "You can question them first. However many times you need to." He underlined that.

There had been times when he'd been placed between the Vampire Nation and his wife. Neither of them had liked it one bit. He had responsibilities and loyalties to the Vampires he ruled and lived with that did not always align with those he had to her. Though she understood those responsibilities—and had some of her own as it pertained to Hunter Corp.—it had exacerbated her distrust of Vampires. They'd spent a lot of time working to avoid such problems in the future. And to always choose one another above anyone or anything else.

Add this ridiculous Vampire lord situation and their threats toward any Vampires working for Hunter Corp. and it paid to be careful to get that balance right.

Clive'd been steadfast at her side throughout this entire situation. As she'd been at his. They had to lean on one another. He trusted that beneath her annoyance, she knew him, and his motivations, while Vampire-centric, were never to cause her harm.

"When this goes left and I have to make someone bleed, you can't complain," she said.

"Darling. I would never."

She snorted.

"I'll take them over myself, but I'll let you arrange with Alice to meet us in the garage so we can transfer these two safely," Rowan told him. "And I still want dinner after this."

"I'll handle it and see you there. I just have a few things to finish before I leave. I'll be less than ten minutes behind you."

"I've done this a few times before," she said, narrow-eyed.

He held his hands up. "You certainly have. Alone even. But you're not alone anymore. Go on. I'll see you shortly." Though he wanted to, he held back his desire to lay a kiss on that curled lip.

Chapter Eight

Once she'd arrived at *Die Mitte* and had parked in the secure access area, Rowan unloaded the Vampires. Alice had been waiting with two guards at her side, and in her very efficient manner, she took the prisoners in with a slight curl of her lip and indicated they head to the elevators.

"The Scion has gone ahead to ready the interview rooms," Alice told Rowan. He must have flown back rather than get a ride from a minion. No traffic jams that way, which was nice as the preparation in the city for an upcoming race had turned the Strip into a parking lot.

Once they all piled into the elevator, Star snorted and got dog snot on Elmer's pants and then looked up over her shoulder to Rowan, doggie smile firmly in place. Goddess, her dog was petty and shady, and it was just the absolute best.

Rowan sent a sunny human smile Star's way.

"It's the point where a Vampire can't even live without a Hunter interfering," Elmer groused.

"Sad day when you can't pick off underaged kids to transition them to near immortality to create an eternal power imbalance with someone who didn't have the emotional maturity to make the choice otherwise.

Is that what you mean?" Alice asked in her best uptight British accent. Rowan wanted to kiss her.

One of the guards snickered as the doors slid open on the secure floor. Interrogation rooms complete with one-way glass lay between the open work area beyond the locked doors just ahead. The enforcement Vampires worked out of offices on that floor as well.

She'd been there so many times over the last weeks it felt like she should have her own office there. Not that she'd bring such a thing up or Clive would do it and honestly the thought of it made her itchy. The cages they'd had built at the Motherhouse were nearly finished, but they were still in the process of being warded, so she didn't want to test their security with prisoners of this level of danger until they were completely finished.

A strange, barbed sensation caught in her belly. She paused, looking around, trying not to hiss at the pain. Once that happened, Clive would be out there, incisors gleaming, ready to fuck shit up. Normally, that would be fine, but Rowan needed him away until she figured out just what was making her guts feel like they were being stabbed with a fork.

Alice looked calm and unruffled. The two guards they'd come up in the elevator with were ones she'd worked with multiple times before. They'd never given her a tingle as far as worrying over their allegiance or behavior and that hadn't changed.

There was a security station they had to be buzzed into and then they waited while their credentials were checked. The same willowy Vampire with ice blue hair and a wardrobe of leather pants and high-necked tunics with side splits that enabled easy movement in a fight was at the desk as she had been two hours before when Rowan had left.

Nothing amiss. Everyone felt fine.

At her side, David had taken note in the change in her body language and shifted his own, hyperaware.

They moved through the first station to the next checkpoint where just beyond lay the holding cells and, to the other side, the interview rooms.

Elmer and Haddon walked in front of Rowan and David. Alice was to Rowan's other side, just in front, while one of the guards from the elevator led the group, handling each step of the process.

That pleased Rowan very much as it had been her recommendation to add this secondary point.

She moved forward as the prisoners were passed through, and that poking fork became barbed wire right as one of the guards who'd been at that door stepped in Rowan's path to halt her movement.

"Who are you and why are you here?" he demanded, putting his hand out to push back against her chest and she stepped aside, ducking contact.

It was a different guard than had been there when she'd left earlier that night. Not one she'd formally met, but she'd seen him around. He certainty knew who she was. And he absolutely knew he had no business attempting to touch her.

Vampire bullshit was always annoying, but Rowan was used to it and mostly she let it roll right off her back. But in that moment, the most important thing was that the goddess really didn't like him. Brigid seemed to burn from the center of Rowan's gut outward, Her distrust of this guard seemed to vibrate through Rowan's bones.

Time seemed to slow as it sometimes did when Brigid

rose to an individual consciousness within Rowan's body and mind. The barbed wire sensation went red hot, and Rowan gave in to the hiss and let the sweat from the pain bead on her temple.

The guard's nostrils flared as he took in the scent of her sweat. A petty bully, the light in his eyes brightened at the thought of her fear. Not that unusual. But the absolute understanding this Vampire was connected to something important to her hunt settled in. Sucked for him, but for her, it was fuel.

Rowan bet he'd watched that video of the ambush and assumed she'd be weak. So, she acted a little cowed, enough that the guard lost his focus, thinking he'd won. He let out a sound of triumph and *pushed* her back into an office chair.

Which washed away all her reasons for not making him bleed. Rowan used the side of her right hand, chopping out and connecting with his throat. Hard enough that he choked, gagged, and staggered back. Then she followed up with the handle of her cane, the hard, heavy metallic wolf's head at the base of the handle making solid contact with the guard's dick.

"You bitch!" he wheezed out. Time seemed to snap back into place, and the terrible pain had eased back to bearable.

In the background, she heard Alice ordering everyone to stand down, felt the slice of power in the words, and other guards, the ones from the elevator, fanned to Rowan's prisoners, each with a hand on a shoulder to make sure no one made sudden moves.

That's when the guy on the door got extra stupid and gave Rowan a defiant, cocky look.

"You got something to say?" she asked him.

"I'm doing my job. I don't just let any riffraff in here." He gave her an exaggerated up and down. At her back, Rowan registered several gasps of offense and Alice's growl as she stepped forward, leaning on her cane until that smirk got a little wider.

Then she swung out with the cane again, working in concert with her fist on the other side. Delivering a double shot angled perfectly to strike the bundle of nerves Vampires had just behind and beneath the jaw. His entire body tensed up and snapped like a rubber band, and he crumpled to the ground like he didn't have bones, leaving him conscious but useless.

"Bet you remember who I am now," she taunted.

There were directions being shouted and Rowan just stared at the guard, letting him see just how much she wanted him to come at her again. Letting every bit of her otherness slip through her gaze.

Clive was moving in their direction at a high rate of speed, Rowan felt his presence larger and larger through their bond, and within a breath, the door at the guard's back opened, revealing Clive and Patience.

Rowan snarled at Clive without taking her gaze from the guard. "This isn't looking good for you, Scion Stewart," she told him, utterly fucking annoyed at being attacked by multiple Vampires in a matter of hours.

David and Star, along with the other two guards that had come with Alice, took Elmer and Haddon toward the interview rooms where they'd be secured until they could be questioned. Rowan had to admit she was looking forward to that part now that she was feeling extra mean.

"The guard was aggressive with Rowan and attempted to bar her entry though I was with her, and I personally let everyone know we'd be in shortly to question our prisoners. In direct opposition to my orders, he put his hand on a Hunter and shoved her." Alice placed her palm over the spot on her own chest, underlining to Clive the guard had seemed to deliberately target the place Rowan had been shot three times and was still healing.

Clive's eyes gleamed with malice.

Alice continued, "It was only then that Ms. Summerwaite responded physically. It's a shameful breach of protocol. He should be grateful she allowed him to live."

Clive looked to the guard. "Yes, he should. Explain yourself," he ordered, using all his Scion power to shove the question into the other Vampire's consciousness.

"I don't give a fuck what his problem is. I have things to do, and if he tries to stop me again, I will skin him and wear him to prom," Rowan said curtly.

There was more than annoyance in her tone. She was upset, and part of him surged forward, needing to address and fix it.

Clive tried to get her attention as she shoved past them all and into the area beyond. He didn't like it that she wouldn't meet his eyes. This wasn't a Rowan and Clive issue. Clive would disagree with her ovcr many things as they pertained to politics, but that was Scion to Hunter. He attempted to use their blood bond to underline that when she shook her head at him, warning him to stop.

It would weaken them both if he followed or called after her, so he put it away to deal with the most pressing issue. This guard and whatever madness drove him to touch Rowan.

Clive looked to the guard but spoke to Alice. "Accompany Rowan wherever she needs to be and see to it she gets what she requires. Patience, with me after the guard is replaced by a *trusted* one."

Alice gave him a conciliatory look as she stepped past, catching up to David. Clive trusted his assistant to handle any potential issues while he questioned this guard.

He followed their prisoner into another interrogation space, glad they'd opted to create a surfeit of cells and rooms. Better to have more than one needed than not enough to meet a problem. It also gave him the perfect excuse to have the prisoners—all of them—at *Die Mitte* and he wasn't mad about that in any way.

"Sit," Clive ordered the guard, pointing. "Answer my questions when I ask. Don't lie to me."

He settled across the table, Patience at his back, guarding the door and serving as another pair of eyes and ears during questioning.

"Now then," Clive said, "you caused a diplomatic incident with a Hunter in my building. On ground I control. I'm waiting for you to explain why it is you acted as if it was ground *you* control instead."

Fear rolled off the guard before he could wrestle it back, and the predator within Clive perked up, homed in on a being who was prey.

Clive leaned close and took a deep breath, taking the remnants of that terror into his lungs, and sat back again, watching.

The guard's swallow was audible. "I stopped her like I would anyone else. I stepped into her path, and she struck first. *She* attacked me. I'm a Vampire guarding Vampire prisoners that she has arrested and will most likely kill. In service to my Scion, it is my duty to be sure every person has permission to enter. She should have waited for permission to pass. She's a *human*."

Rage rolled through Clive, further inciting the predator within. He knew his eyes would have bled to amber as bloodlust began to take root. This guard had derailed the progress Clive had made with Rowan when she'd turned her prisoners over to him to start with.

It was more than that. This other Vampire stunk of deceit. And after the last year spent rooting out leaks and traitors, Clive had zero tolerance for it. He needed to know what was motivating this guard. Or who.

"You must think I'm as witless as my predecessor was," Clive told him, his tone full of sharp edges. The guard's mouth flattened. Insulted. Interesting. "Rowan has other prisoners here. She's been in and out for days regularly. You not only knew she was expected, you went out of your way to escalate a confrontation with a partner of Hunter Corp. Now, why is that?"

"Scion," the guard said, lowering his chin, "I'm sorry if you misunderstood."

At that lack of an answer, Clive sighed, reaching out to grab the guard's throat and squeeze. Vampires could slow down their respiration far beyond anything humans could survive. The guard *could* survive without oxygen, but he'd lose consciousness and Clive had some things to set in motion. And, given the damage Rowan had caused earlier, the crushed larynx Clive had just inflicted would hurt a great deal as it healed.

The guard's eyes rolled up, showing the whites, and Clive dropped him. He had about three minutes until the guard would begin to wake so Clive snapped into action.

He turned to Patience. "I've lost faith in this Vampire. I want a report on him. What's his Genesis? Work history. Bullet points in five minutes, more to follow. Search his domicile, his work area and locker. Pick apart his electronics. He's in breach." Which meant all his access to everything within the Vampire Nation was locked down. His bank accounts, his email, his key-card access to every door and elevator were now inaccessible to anyone but Clive's security team. "I want to know who he's been talking to and what he's been stealing from my organization."

Patience nodded and stepped out of the room to set it all in motion. Clive texted a status request and an update regarding the guard to Alice and by the time he'd finished, his prisoner had begun to surface.

"You lied." Clive sat straighter, letting his displeasure flow over the guard in a swarm of bites and stings. "And then you insulted my leadership and my intelligence by claiming my understanding was at issue. So I'm sitting here wondering just what exactly you're doing."

"It's a setup. She's interviewing rogues to work at Hunter Corp.!" the guard urged. "The Vampire you brought in here is a law-abiding Vampire."

If this guard was connected to that serial sexual predator in the other room, he'd sealed his fate. Clive had no intention of allowing such rot to continue. Vampires like Elmer had to be put down.

"You certainly have a great deal of information as to what the Hunter was doing. Let's take this statement by statement for the sake of clarity, shall we?" Though there was a question mark at the end, it wasn't a request and if this guard wanted to stay alive, he'd follow along and obey.

"Yes, Scion."

"You claim the prisoners we brought in, because *I'm* the one who had them brought here, are law-abiding." Clive cocked his head slightly and let the monster inside him show fully. That monster wanted to roll around in the fear coming off the guard in wave after wave. "How is it you know this?"

"Everyone knows! She thumbs her nose at the Nation with the way she seeks to hire the garbage of our society. She's going to kill one of our own people. Right here. It's an abomination."

Patience had returned to the room and at that response, she hissed. She didn't like Rowan any more than Rowan liked her. But there was a mutual respect between them, and Clive's top lieutenant was as obviously offended by this guard's lies as Clive was.

"You dare speak of the Scion's mate in such a fashion?" Patience demanded as she placed a file folder on the table next to Clive's right hand.

"I'm speaking of a Hunter, not his wife," the guard said.

"And when did you receive this information about an unsanctioned kill? If you pretend not to understand my question again, I will tear off pieces of you until you're feeling clearer on what you need to do," Clive said. "I haven't been able to exercise tonight so you'd be doing me a favor."

"Tonight," the guard squeaked out. "I got a call from a friend who said Elmer was about to be grabbed by the Hunter. Right out of his own home," he said quickly.

Clive just stared at the other Vampire. Waiting for the rest.

"My friend said he heard the Hunter tell Elmer she

was going to kill him right under your nose in the middle of our building. And here she was! Scion, she was here just like the call said she would be," the guard said as if Clive hadn't been there and knew it all for lies.

"Who made the call?"

When the guard looked away, trying to get around a direct answer, Clive had had enough. He flipped open the file and scanned the top sheet. Eduard Garces. Had worked with the office of the Scion of North America for seven years. Started on the secure floor three months before.

He read the Genesis report and narrowed his gaze at Eduard. "Interesting. Jacques was your Maker."

Jacques had been the Scion of North America before Clive. He'd broken so many laws—their own and the Treaty as well—that Rowan had executed him. Frankly, he was fortunate because once the First had been made aware of all the lawlessness that had taken place under Jacques's leadership, what would have happened to him in the dungeons of the Keep would have been far worse than the quick mercy of Rowan's blade.

Jacques had Made dozens of Vampires over the century he'd held North America. Clive had executed a lot of those Vampires when he'd arrived in Las Vegas. Not all. Simply being Made by someone didn't automatically mean that Vampire was the same or shared similar beliefs. It didn't make sense to destroy stock that would be useful, so many were spared and had been an integral part of his transition.

When one was nearly immortal, second chances were important. Clive had once been accorded a second chance by their leader, and there he was, Scion of North America.

Clive read the rest of the information Patience had compiled for him before he stood to remove his suit jacket and hand it off. While he considered just where he'd strike first, Clive rolled up his shirtsleeves to his elbows before he stepped in close enough to deliver a series of jabs to the guard's face and then his gut.

It'd been a while since he'd handled such things on his own when they were in Las Vegas. Clive found it rather refreshing. As he was already annoyed and feeling defensive of his wife, the ability to punch away his feelings seemed just the thing.

"Who provided you with the information about the prisoner?" he asked again.

"I need to protect them. They don't want any trouble," the guard said through the blood in his mouth.

"If they didn't want trouble, why did they spend so much time following someone else to report directly… to a guard working here? This is very confusing." Clive blinked slowly at him.

"The other Vampire knows me. We're friends. That's why. They knew I'd help."

"You're a good citizen, then, are you?"

"I try," the guard said, and the deceit rolled off him.

Instead of ripping his head off and beating his body with his spine, Clive slowly turned up his glamor, taking a bit of power from each of his Vampires to steamroll over the traitor across from him. He'd crush Eduard after he got what he needed.

"How did you know Hunter Corp. was in the process of hiring Vampires?" Clive asked with deceptive calm. He'd deliberately not used Rowan's name. She'd drawn enough fire from Vampires and Clive sure as hell wasn't going to aid that.

But within that calm was a push, an order that guard wasn't strong enough to disobey.

"Everyone knows!" he bust out and Clive broke his arm in three places before the guard had even registered the movement.

"Shall we try again?" Clive asked, this time not so calm. "It seems to me you've got a spy in place. And it seems to me that you've been sharing what happens within my walls with others, as well as getting intel on whatever Hunter Corp. is doing."

The only people who knew were the Scions. Who'd been informed by the First's office. Of course one, or perhaps two, of the Scions had leaked that information to others. Others who currently suffered in the dungeons below their leader's mountainous Keep.

Was this Eduard connected to one of those self-titled Vampire lords? Was there more than one leak?

Never in his years had the Vampiric tendency toward constant political scheming been so utterly exhausting. Nonetheless, it had roused his bloodlust. This was a threat not only to his leadership and the Vampire Nation, but to his wife.

"S-scion, I am as ever on the side of Vampires. I heard it from more than one source."

Who had taught this creature to tell the truth without answering a question from his Scion? Clive didn't like it one bit. There was more to this problem than he could see, which only made him angrier.

Clearly, he needed to turn up the compulsion and add a great deal more painful incentive. "How long have you been spying on us?" Clive asked, leaning in, caressing Eduard with his power before turning it on its edge, using it to slice hard enough the other Vampire cried out in pain.

Eduard's surprise flowed out along with the thin line of blood beading up his throat. Satisfaction rolled through Clive, along with no small pride. A new ability as he aged, and his power continued to grow. Useful. And news of it would get out to others. Sowing fear, reaping power. Both like blood and magic, foundations of the world he lived in.

Clive smiled. A mimicry of what Rowan would term his uptight British man of the manor face. He'd see just what else he might be able to do to punish the Vampire across from him. A project.

"I could make it soft. A seduction. But I find it's far better to make it hurt." Clive's wife was more often the outwardly aggressive one, but his ferocity simply waited for the right moment. By the time he got angry enough to want to cause pain, he was out of patience.

Then he focused his glamor another way, shifting his power slightly so it wasn't just an attempt to control a mind, but to send thousands of tiny sharp metal barbs through Eduard's veins. Still control of mind, but though phantom, the pain would be real.

Eduard's spine bowed as he sweated blood. "Since she murdered Jacques!" the guard burst out.

Nearly four years. Outrage, hot and so big it took him a moment to rein it in, filled him at such betrayal.

"Who do you work for?" Because it was clear this wasn't just some ordinary Vampire with a grudge against the Hunter who slayed his Maker. This was bigger. Damn it all. Conspiracies took up far too much of his time and he was quite finished with them. He tried the barbs again to underline his question.

And it worked, because moments later, Eduard gasped out, "*Sanguis Principatus.*"

Blood supremacy. Clive wanted to groan. Rowan was going to have a field day with this. Why did Vampires have to choose these types of names for their xenophobic little clubs? Hearing the name for this one in particular wasn't a welcome return to the past.

"Who told you Rowan would be coming?"

This time, Eduard answered immediately. "Baker. He texted me that the Hunter had shown up at Elmer's residence. Like I said."

"And how do you know this Baker?" Clive didn't need to let on he'd been there and was the one who'd ordered the prisoners be taken to *Die Mitte*. Not yet.

"He…through *Sanguis Principatus*."

"Elmer too?"

Eduard nodded. "Yes," he added so Clive held back his need to make this Vampire bleed.

"Fill me in on the local chapter," Clive said.

Chapter Nine

"You can't keep me here," Elmer said.

"I could have caught you covered in blood, holding a knife, standing over a dead body covered in stab wounds, with *Elmer Did It* written in the victim's blood, and you'd still act surprised. Oh no, whyever could I be in trouble with the authorities!" Rowan rolled her eyes at him. Alice sat to one side while David was at their back, guarding the door.

"I'm not going to say anything to you," Elmer told Rowan.

"You're very brave for someone who manipulates children," Alice said, and Rowan barely stifled a grin as she leaned back in her chair. Alice was good at her job. She was strong, though people tended to underestimate her because she was so lovely and efficient. But when she needed to be badass, she was stone cold. Such an excellent quality. Especially when it came to her position with Clive. Most importantly, Alice wasn't going to play games and fuck her over.

No denying it'd be less of a mess if the Nation took point on this underage thing. She had enough shit to shovel as it was with witch nonsense and this Vampire lord stuff. Rowan would kill whoever needed killing but had no problem letting someone else draw the fire of the First. The paperwork alone would be a nightmare. And it would do them some good to be on the side of right for a change. They had the money and the staff and she was sick to death of cleaning up Nation messes.

"What is your connection to the guard on this floor?" Alice asked, using her power to push the compulsion to answer straight into Elmer's chest.

He paused as he fought it. Then a smirk. "What guard?"

Alice grabbed a small, silver hammer from a little black bag at her feet. It caught the light as she brought it down on Elmer's hand hard enough that it dented the table beneath where it had been resting. Blood spattered—thankfully away from Rowan—and Elmer howled in pain.

Rowan looked back over her shoulder to David. "Just when you think you can't love her more, she produces a fucking *hammer* and goes to town," she told him.

David fought a smile but lost.

"We're in the same social circle," Elmer gasped out, cradling his ruined hand to his chest.

The hammer flashed as it came down on Elmer's kneecap, creating a sound that had Rowan gagging a little.

"I told you the truth!" he howled, tears in his eyes.

Rowan shook her head. They *always* fucked around and cried when they got called out.

"How do you know the guard working on this floor?" Alice repeated.

Fearing a second shattered kneecap, Elmer finally decided to answer the question he'd been asked and his problem with underaged boys was only a small part of the issue.

"*Sanguis Principatus*," he said.

Of course it was in Latin. They probably used a gothic font like a heavy metal band and wore robes when they met like the self-important pissants they were. Something poked at the back of her brain. Some long-ago mention of this group. The North American capitalist version of Blood Front shit, if she recalled correctly.

David would get Vanessa working on compiling information about this group as soon as they finished up.

Alice sighed and closed her eyes a moment. So disappointed in Elmer. Rowan's crush on her grew by the minute.

Then Alice said, "*Blood Supremacy.*" And heaved a heavy sigh. "I was still in England when they had any real power here in the United States. I'm sure you can guess what this little social club is all about, Rowan." She sat straighter. Neat. Perfect posture. Even the spot of blood on her left shoulder seemed dignified.

At Rowan's amused snort, Alice continued. "Same basic theme. Vampires are the master race. They're at the top of the food chain and humans are cattle and meant to serve. More of an American spin. They liked power and money and wanted free rein to do with humans whatever they wished to obtain it. Witches and shifters and other types aren't as pure as Vampires, but not as base as humans. They'd be suitable employees. Lovers perhaps?"

"It's not against the law to believe any of those things," Elmer said, petulant.

"No. It just lets everyone know you're rather dim. However," Alice held up a finger, "how one sets about making those things a reality may be against our laws. Let's find out. How did Eduard know to expect Rowan?" Alice asked. Rowan figured Eduard was the guard who'd shoved her.

Before he could speak, the shiny arc of the hammer caught Rowan's eye as Alice used her wicked little friend and re-broke the hand that had been healing. "Just to keep you forthcoming. I find it's better for everyone to remain transparent about consequences," she told Elmer.

The confidence Elmer had been wearing had begun to wear thin. "I don't know exactly."

Rowan cocked her head. "I don't think it's true."

Alice didn't ask how Rowan knew. The hammer returned. It hadn't taken nearly as many broken bones to get the answers to the next questions.

"I really don't know for sure!" he shrieked.

"Give me your best guess," Alice invited.

"Stephen would have been on watch. He'd have contacted someone depending on whatever problem arose."

They'd run a loop when they'd first arrived to catch them by surprise, but after that initial three minutes, that video would have begun to run again. Baker would have seen it all but instead of warning Elmer, he'd called *Die Mitte*.

Alice's pupils flared as her elemental nature showed through. Disgusted and outraged by this creature before them.

Scary Alice was Rowan's favorite.

He added quickly, "I like to have someone watching my back. For human cops or Hunters." Like that made things better?

If the Nation didn't handle this piece of shit, Rowan would hunt him down and execute him herself. He couldn't be allowed to continue walking the earth, preying on the weak.

Alice said, "I'll need that same information on any other such *partners* in addition to Baker."

At that point, the fight left him, his spine curved slightly, as if the weight of all his bullshit began to sit on his shoulders.

"Oh and bee tee dubs, Stephen Baker is here in custody too. Just FYI." Rowan gave a slight jerk of her shoulders. "He didn't tell you we'd arrived, which I find *fascinating.* You sat down there in your little pervert bunker watching an action movie while Hunter Corp., the Conclave, and the Vampire Nation rooted through your belongings. I wonder what it could have been that kept him from telling you or Haddon."

There was a pause as Elmer realized a few things. Given the sour expression, they weren't pleasant things. Rowan loved it that he was so dejected and suspicious.

Finally, in a tone that said he didn't even believe what he was saying, Elmer managed, "He probably didn't have the chance, so he made the choice to have Eduard in the loop. Knowing we'd need help. Someone to defend us against this false accusation."

Rowan shook her head at this amateur. "Setting aside the fact that when I came into creeper mansion, none of you would have known what accusations I'd have to level against you, what is it you think a guard here could have done? Other than get himself stuck into an interrogation room with an angry Scion that is."

"He serves as a witness to my mistreatment."

Rowan curled her lip at him. "You certainly have enough cameras watching every angle of each room in your giant house. I'm pretty sure there'll be lots of mistreatment on the SD cards we confiscated. But you're not the abused, Elmer. You're the abuser. I see you. She sees you." Rowan jerked her head toward Alice.

"You violated my home! At the behest of some slut I cast off years ago?"

Until this disgusting pig called Aron a slut when said pig had manipulated a damned kid, Rowan had been moderately calm.

The liquid, quicksilver magic that seemed to fill her veins heralded Brigid's rise to consciousness. She was just fine with Rowan's loss of calm. She'd only made Herself known to reassure Rowan. *You're on the right path.*

"We walked right up to that door and into your secret perv room where we took you into custody after you poked your rodent head out. Then we turned all seven thousand square feet upside down, including the four hidden bedchambers that look a whole lot like holding cells." She shuddered at that. Silk and cashmere on the beds and locks on the outside of the door.

Rowan wanted to speak more with George, the butler, to get more information on that whole situation. Clive would brief her soon enough.

Remembering she'd warned him away from their bond because she was beyond annoyed with Vampires earlier, she let herself open up to it once again. It wasn't about punishing Clive, she just needed to be alone with her thoughts for a little while.

"It's not against the law to have cameras in one's home," he said. "Nor is my sexual preference any of your business."

Rowan curled her lip. "Believe me, I don't care about your sexual preference as it pertains to *legal* adults who *consent* to whatever it is you like to do. But that's not what I'm going to find on those SD cards, and we all know it. Keep on lying. It's not going to do you any favors, but it'll be a gas to watch the Scion strangle you with your intestines. You think Jacques was tough because he was cruel." A theatrical eye roll. "Cruelty is a coward's tool. *I* killed Jacques. As you know. And he wasn't shit. However, I'm married to the new guy, and I can tell you firsthand, he *is* hot shit. So, you'll tell us, or he'll take it from you and leave you a drooling mess. I hope he rips your dick off before the drooling mess part. Either way, I see you, Marsc."

She stood, done with this garbage.

"Don't get comfortable," Alice said as he was on the way out. "The Scion will want to speak to you later."

Rowan loved his expression at that so much she wanted to marry it.

When they were alone, waiting for Haddon, Alice said, "I'm not letting the issue of the *Sanguis Principatus* go. Or of this underage Making. It seemed better to have the Scion handling that. Especially after he speaks with Eduard. I'll assume the Scion will wish for you to be given information about the group and its history, so I'll put that in motion."

"I only have some vague memories, so I'll definitely need to read up."

Haddon was brought in. He'd only been a Vampire four years and while there were parts of him that came off very young mentally and emotionally, he didn't try to evade their questions.

He hadn't been warned by Baker. He'd been waiting in the car he'd brought around for Elmer when he'd caught sight of all the cars in the drive and had hidden, waiting to attack until he'd caught sight of Rowan and David walking his master out of the house.

There was a sort of sad courage about it. More than Elmer or Stephen had shown him.

He said he was only familiar with Stephen. Though he did know Elmer had other older Vampires he had meetings with. Sometimes Haddon would bring friends, young friends, for the other Vampires. Mostly they ignored him and dealt with Elmer exclusively.

He rattled off names and descriptions, not hesitating in the same way his Maker had. His earlier fire when he'd attacked Rowan in the driveway had gone. Maybe while he'd had time to think as they'd questioned Elmer.

Alice motioned for them to go into the hall to speak privately. David nodded that he'd remain in the room so once they were alone in the hall outside—Alice had emptied the space of personnel—she spoke. "The rooms are soundproof so he can't hear us. I need to inform Clive of what we've learned. Are you satisfied with the questioning? Is there anything else we need to ask?"

That sort of thing was one of myriad reasons Rowan not only liked Alice but trusted her word. It made her lose some of her impatience with the process. A process that was often closed to her. But Alice had made sure Rowan's perspective was handled and her questioning of the prisoners hadn't just been about the breaking of Vampire rules.

"There would have been a lot more blood if I'd been doing the interrogation," Rowan murmured. "I'm good. So long as Elmer is incarcerated and punished. And. I will require information regarding this *Sanguis Principatus*, so I appreciate that you've already got that handled."

Alice nodded. "It's my recommendation that Elmer face a tribunal and be sentenced that way. It spreads the responsibility to a group of Vampires instead of the Scion doing this on his own. Haddon? I feel strongly that he should be examined by a physician and a therapist. I know this may not be what you want, given his cooperation with Elmer. But he's…he's a victim, Rowan. He was hurt at an age when he barely had enough sense to get himself through the day. Certainly not a match for a centuries-old predator like Elmer."

Yeah, she was aware of just how little a match a child could be against an ancient Vampire. That was her fucking childhood. And she'd been able to be something more than a plaything because others had given her a chance. She'd dedicated her life to helping others. So, she wouldn't stand in the way of Haddon getting his second chance. "If he can be treated and come out the other side refusing to continue in his Maker's footsteps, that will be enough for me. That and he needs to assist in tracking down other young victims. Otherwise, I will carve a path through you all to get him and see he's punished for what he's done." But Rowan thought Haddon, given the help he so desperately needed, might come out the other side better. And as a source for information on this new cabal.

Alice nodded. "Agreed."

"I will need to deal with all this," Rowan said, thinking of a call she needed to make to Susan and the other partners. "Tell Clive what you and I agreed upon. I expect a full report from all the interrogations. I want to see whatever it is you all find with this guard. I'm sure every part of his life is being examined as we speak. And the guard."

"I'll include transcripts and any video we have from the interrogations, as well as any information we've gleaned from the searches of Eduard's domicile." Alice walked with her toward the doorway where David waited.

Clive came around the corner and they all headed to the parking garage.

"I'll see you for dinner in a bit," he told her.

"I've got calls to make before I can take the time," she explained.

"Make them. I have things to do as well. We'll skip Fleur, but I'll have the food sent home for us. When you leave, let me know and I'll meet you there." For a refusal to change his plans, it was done rather well so she let it go because it was nice to share a meal with him and reconnect that way.

She nodded.

"Are you all right? You're limping slightly," he said as they reached her car.

"I'm a little worse for wear. But I'll sleep, and you gave me blood. I'll be fine. I'll see you in a while."

Chapter Ten

When Rowan finally arrived home it was one in the morning. And yet, she found a pot of tea steeping and a full meal waiting. Having staff really worked out in her favor when it came to a clean house and freshly made food at all hours.

Who was she kidding? Even before she had Elisabeth and Betchamp minding her life full-time, David had been the one to be sure she was fed, and her home was reasonably tidy.

She looked over at him. "So many curveballs tonight. I couldn't have gotten nearly as much done without your assistance."

He blushed a little, looking pleased that she'd noticed. "It's always this way. Nothing or tiny little steps forward and then all the sudden it happens in a rush. One clue leads to the next and so on. It's fortunate you can find the clues. I'm pleased to help you once that happens. Such as when you're appointed to lead up a new workgroup on the *Sanguis Principatus*."

She snarled. "I thought I'd gotten away clean when other people were put in charge of the wolf shifter workgroup."

David chuckled. "That was a very nice turn of events

as you already have plenty on your plate. But it makes sense to leave this *Principatus* issue with you."

It had been unavoidable. She was the Vampire expert, and this was in her territory, after all.

"Not bad for the first middle-of-the-night meeting and work session for all the new staff. Lots of sexy and gory bits to keep everyone interested." There'd been an air of camaraderie Rowan had really liked.

They did dangerous stuff all the time. And they had to keep it secret from most of the world. Having tight relationships at work was crucial to unit cohesion and connection. Trust. The kind of loyalty that had them putting their lives on the line for one another on a regular basis.

She was responsible for them all. For each bright and burning soul who'd pledged to put themselves on the line for what was right. The weight of it could be stifling sometimes. But when they worked together to make something important happen, she was far more impressed and proud than burdened.

Star bounded up with a happy bark to welcome them home. Rowan paused, knelt to be face-to-face, and was pleased when her leg cooperated without pain.

"And how are you tonight? I haven't seen you in a few hours, so I figured you came home to eat and catch a nap after we got Elmer handled."

Star licked her nose as she accepted Rowan's pets and scratches behind her ears.

"I'm sorry to be in so late," Rowan told Elisabeth as they entered the kitchen. She washed her hands while she looked around to see what sort of yummy dinner was in her future.

"You were both working. The Scion had the food

from your canceled dinner at Fleur sent here. It kept," Elisabeth said.

"He's on his way too. I texted him when I left the motherhouse. I'm in for the rest of the night so I'm going to change before I eat. You should go to bed," she told Elisabeth.

"I have worked in a Vampire's household the entirety of my adult life. I'm quite used to being up this late to handle meals."

That and Clive had probably inferred strongly that Rowan needed minding after, especially as she still recovered from the ambush.

"I'll retire once you've both had your meal. Go on and get yourself into comfortable clothes. I'll pour out a cup of tea, so it'll be cool enough to drink by the time you get back."

He came to her because it always seemed that all roads led to Rowan. She entered their sitting room just as he did.

"There she is," he murmured, taking her in. This version of his wife was softer than the one she was outside their home. Here she'd gotten rid of the warrior gear. She'd swapped out stab-proof material and multiple weapons pockets for soft, clingy lounge pants and a long-sleeved T-shirt bearing a graphic of a snarling honey badger holding up one paw giving a middle claw.

She gave him a smile. "The bond is pinging more clearly these days. At least for me. When you get about a mile away in your car, I get that first real burst of feeling. Just a sort of blooming recognition that you're near."

She ducked her head, always shy when it came to expressing tender emotions.

He pulled her into his arms and kissed her until she settled that clawing need she always drew from him. "I believe it's a case of reading it better as well as the bond we share deepening and strengthening."

Satisfied very much indeed, Clive spun her neatly, tucked her hand in the crook of his arm, and led her toward the door. "I'd dance you into your bedchamber right now, but Elisabeth will wait until we eat before she goes to rest."

"I'm home for the night anyway. We'll eat. You can catch me up. I can catch you up and then you can fill all my filthy needs."

Smothering a laugh, he leaned close and breathed her in deep at the nape of her neck and slid the edge of his teeth over the sensitive skin there. Teasing.

He turned as she did, their mouths meeting in a kiss that wasn't slow and gentle. It was a kiss with claws, the gnash of teeth, the slide of tongues, and no small amount of heated need building between them. Need they both knew would be sated at the end of their day together.

"If I don't get you out before your tea gets cold, I will be scolded, so let's get moving," he teased, drawing her to the table where several domed platters sat.

For a few more moments, she was soft for him and then she straightened in her chair, drawing her power back around herself. Clive settled to get comfortable next to her. "Please rest and eat first."

Elisabeth placed a new cup and saucer at Rowan's place. "This is a fresh one. Chamomile with some other bits. I put in some of the blueberry honey you favor. Genevieve's friend Ms. Lorraine sent it over. The tea and the honey."

"For a scary old lady, she's got a very gooey center," Rowan said, unaware of the irony. Though it was only Rowan's soul that was old. She sipped the tea and shrugged. "That's quite nice."

She buttered a slice of bread and hummed happily when she pulled up the cover on the first platter to find roasted potatoes. Rosemary and garlic wafted out as she spooned some onto her plate. Once she'd added chicken piccata and some roasted broccolini, Rowan seemed to take a steadying breath before she took several bites.

They all watched her. David as he filled his own plate. Elisabeth, pleasure written all over her as Rowan so obviously appreciated the meal and her tea. Clive, assuring himself she'd be taking in enough calories to heal. Assuring himself she was okay. Alive. At his side.

"This is exactly what I needed at the end of what has been a totally weird day. You always take care of me so well," Rowan said in between bites.

"Since dinner came from Fleur, there are leftovers for tomorrow. But for after you finish tonight, there's a lemon coconut cake. If you have the room," Elisabeth said with a pleased blush.

"That sounds perfect."

He glared at her when she started speaking. "Please. Just eat for a few minutes. Recharge. Then we can do business."

David gave Clive an approving nod.

Finally, after she'd gone back for seconds, she began to fill him in. "Busy freaking day! Okay, let's see. Procella stuff. As you know, Hugo and Sergio are in holding cells. Antonia is still at the Conclave facility but might be sprung unless I can find something on her. Otherwise, we'll use her as bait."

"You think she's part of whatever it is Sergio and Hugo are up to?" Clive asked.

"I think Antonia and her dad, Alfonso, are cosplaying as modern thinkers who reject Sergio's old-world—all the *isms*—views. But the deeper I dig and see how they all act? It sure fucking looks to me like they're not so different at all. Alfonso is still on the wind. Odd, given that we've got Hugo in custody at this point so I'm assuming he's in on whatever the hell is behind the curtain, along with the rest of that damned family."

"Self-preservation," Clive said. "I wouldn't want you and Konrad Aubert looking for me at the same time. He might be in a closet somewhere rocking and weeping at the horror."

That made her cheer up considerably. "Wouldn't that be awesome? Where is he? Did he manage to get himself on a ship, since he was already down there? Is someone hiding him? I don't think he's back in Vegas. Between me and the Devils, we'd know." She sighed and scrunched her nose a moment. "And the mother on the way back from New Zealand? There is simply no way I believe she's not involved with something sketchy. It's all connected somehow. They can't evade me forever."

David said, "We're doing a deep dive on the cruise company. Vanessa reached out to her compatriot at the Southern California chapterhouse since she's already working on intelligence gathering on the Vampire front. After I'm finished here, I'll make a first pass through the interview and notes from New Zealand."

"Perfect. Coincidences are one thing, but when there are fourteen of them, it's a pattern, not a coincidence. First thing in the morning, I'm going over to the Procellas' mansion to search the servants' wing," Rowan said as she forked up a potato after sliding it through the sauce pooled on the plate. "Gonna do my daytime non-Vampire business while you're all incapable of getting up to mischief. At least in my time zone."

"You'll sleep first, though, correct?" he said. He was prepared to argue if necessary. What he wasn't prepared to do was watch her limp again. Not without clucking at her until she rested and let her system heal itself.

"Yes. Like I said. I'm going to go over that interview. Review my notes on the search already performed at the Procella place, and then I'll go to sleep. But before any of that. Let me get to the Vampire portion of my to-do list. How about we start with this *Sanguis* Whatsits and what Elmer, Stephen Baker, and that fucking guard have to do with it."

"I apologize again for Eduard, the guard who attacked you. That is absolutely my failure. As for *Sanguis Principatus*, let me update you on what I've discovered after a *discussion* with Elmer, Stephen Baker, and Eduard. I have unredacted transcripts of the interrogations as requested so sweetly via Alice, but I'll give you an abridged version with the pertinent bits highlighted as well."

She chuckled at that. "That *might* make me less annoyed at you."

Clive brushed the backs of his fingers down her throat, admiring the way she felt. So vital.

"One does what one can to keep a mate of the quality mine has."

After resting her head against his arm a moment, she got back to her meal.

The sessions were...exhaustive, but he'd gotten some answers. "There's a connection between the three via

Sanguis Principatus. The Vampire who brought them into the group was Jacques. He was Eduard's Maker and, I'm certain you'll be shocked to know, a contemporary of Elmer's. Elmer claims Jacques knew of his little hobby and sent humans who might appeal his way."

"Of course he did. We just got the Blood Front dealt with barely a month ago. Can you all just not scheme for a little while? Just give me six months to deal with all the other stuff I need to. Then you can get back to plotting. I'm one person and you all come up with one thing after the next. I'm tired," she confessed.

"I was thinking rather the same earlier. A getaway would be nice at some point. We really haven't had a break in quite some time."

Rowan surprised him by saying, "After the Joint Tribunal, how about we take a week and go to Venice? I'll call ahead and have the house readied. It'll rain a lot, but we'll be in Venice, and I have rain boots. I think Star would love Italy."

It had been a rather delightful surprise to discover she had a beautifully furnished piazza in Venice, complete with staff. They'd been in the city on the trail of Enyo, a powerful, magic-wielding Vampire who'd nearly killed Rowan. In a satisfying turn of events, it was Rowan who'd ended her.

In Venice Rowan was colorful and full of joy. More open to wandering and spending a few hours just the two of them. It made him feel young to follow as she led them down long and twisty alleys to a cicchetti bar open at night for all the various supernatural citizens of the city unable to amble into one during their more common daylight hours.

There it would be just the two of them. Time to heal

up and have great heaping amounts of sex and limoncello.

"I'd very much like that. We can give some vacation time to Elisabeth, Betchamp, and David as well."

David snorted. "I'll remain at my post so my boss doesn't decide to come back early because she's worried things will fall apart in her absence. I'll claim that week at another time. I promise."

Rowan's snort of laughter relaxed everyone in the vicinity. "It's only because you'll be here that I can even consider vacation."

David ducked his head a moment, clearly pleased by her confidence in him. He stood and ferried his dishes to the machine in the kitchen. "I'm going to finish up a few things, send some emails, and then go to bed. I'll see you in the morning." He gave Rowan a slight bow.

They sent Elisabeth off as well and then settled on the couch in the sitting room to continue their work discussion.

Clive grabbed one of the folded throws and tucked it around her once she rested her leg on a pillow. "Are you warm enough?"

She nodded. "Yes, thank you. Sit and tell me more."

"Elmer attempted to paint himself as an integral member of Jacques's team. I'm not so convinced, but given what he admitted, and what Baker said—he loathes Elmer—it sounds like Jacques used him as muscle."

"Threats from a bland guy like Elmer could actually be terrifying. I doubt he has any moral hesitation about assaulting and terrorizing people to get them to do whatever his master commanded. Lot of that in my life of late."

"That very thing occurred to me, as it happens. Patience is doing deeper background as we speak, but I figured you might like to do it yourself as well. Tell me about your prior run-in with Stephen Baker," he asked. It'd been clear at the time there'd been history, but there hadn't been any opportunity to ask for details until that point.

"Hang on a sec. I want to send some new keywords to David and Vanessa." Rowan tapped on her phone for a minute or two before tucking it away again.

"About a year before I finally executed your predecessor, I got a call from one of my connections, an ER nurse. They'd brought in a woman who'd been found half-naked, raving, the bottoms of her feet torn up from running barefoot. Law enforcement figured it was drugs. But my friend the ER nurse realized the rants were about Vampires. I went over there, got the woman out and into a clinic where she could be treated for what had really happened to her."

Clive blew out a breath.

"Putting together all she'd managed to remember, I ended up on the doorstep of another one of Jacques's inner circle, Tomas Derwin."

Clive snarled at the name. "He was one of the first Vampires I ended when I got to Las Vegas."

"One of your finest qualities. Anyway. Inside Derwin's place were far too many humans in various states of blood intoxication. Stephen Baker was one of the Vampires there and it was his bite pattern on the woman in the ER. Jacques got involved. Intervened to keep me from leaving Baker and his buddies staked out for the sun. Promised he'd keep a tighter rein on his Vampires. Baker paid restitution. I kept an eye on him until I executed Jacques and then had to spend the following year in meetings, testifying and filling out paperwork."

"I'm sorry it's so tedious to kill a Scion," he teased.

She rolled her eyes. "Yeah, Yelena, the human in the ER that night, was all kinds of fucked-up back then. She's a landscaper in Taos now." She smiled briefly.

"Well, that certainly explains why he seems to have such a deep enmity toward you." Clive didn't much care for it. Many Vampires distrusted or disliked her and Hunter Corp. But there was a deeper vein in some Vampires. More than distrust and dislike. Virulent hatred. Aggressive and violent. These Vampires knew Rowan was a force in the universe that could not be swayed from what was right. Their very existence was threatened by her.

Clive would be sure Baker, Elmer, and Eduard never got the opportunity to act on their feelings toward his wife.

"Seems odd he'd be working for Elmer. Like it should be the other way around." She shrugged. "Vampires and their hierarchy. Anyway. Refresh me on *Sanguis Principatus*. I have a bare-bones idea of what they are, but it's been a long time. I put in a request for the librarian at the London motherhouse to create a brief for me so when I wake up, I'll have it."

She was asking him for information but letting him choose how much to share. A few attempts on her life ago, Clive had given up all pretext that he'd ever place anyone or anything above Rowan if he had to choose.

She needed this information. And in the end, whatever she did, it would be to the benefit of the Vampire Nation as a whole because she was a bulldog. She would not quit until the job was done.

"The Blood Front is older than I am. Started by aristocratic Vampire families in the late thirteenth century. *Sanguis Principatus* came along at the beginning of the *twentieth* century. Yesterday to Vampires. I had to do a quick bit of research before I interrogated Elmer to refresh myself. The Vampires who started it were born not Made, but the roots of the organization are far less class rigid than the Blood Front."

"I wish you all would choose to not be rigid about things that weren't plots to subjugate humanity. I mean, that's the aim, right? No group with a name like that is knitting socks for orphans."

He knew she just had to vent, so he continued. "About a hundred years ago there was an incident." He'd already decided to tell her everything, so he did. "A reason I had to do some refreshing was they didn't call themselves *Sanguis Principatus* at first. A group of them interrupted a meeting being held in New York City by high-ranking Vampires who'd been working together to set up power boundaries in the United States."

"What's their angle, then?"

"They wanted what most Vampires want. Power enough to be left alone to do whatever we choose. These upstarts felt that the United States should be ruled, and territories created by an approach as unique as its Vampires. These families—little more than organized criminal empires—wanted a place at the table and territories to control the same way powerful Vampiric families did in other territories. The old guard did not agree."

Rowan said, "In America, power is about money instead of lineage. It took the Nation way longer than it should have to understand that."

Clive nodded. "The First barely paid attention to the

United States until World War Two. It wasn't nuclear capability that got his focus. It was profit. Jacques had many faults. But the reason he was able to steal from the Nation for so long was due to how profitable this territory is."

"That expired gas station sushi wasn't *officially* a creeper like Elmer, but he worked with *Sanguis Principatus.* That's where the connection to Elmer came in. Right? Not over seventeen-year-olds, but money and influence. The Vampire all-purpose high. Okay, so what did *SP* call themselves then and why did they change their name?" Rowan asked, ever perceptive.

"Jacques had been the Scion of North America for a few decades by that point. He set up his court originally in Montreal but moved it to Manhattan the year after that meeting. Back then they called themselves The Brotherhood."

"I mean, less douchey than Latin. But still creepy for myriad reasons. It's always purity, violence, and master race crap."

He'd had that same thought. Even with the words she'd used. Rowan had changed his world in so many ways.

"From what I could track down, it appears they changed their name in the 1960s. Vampires from other territories wanted to join but they didn't like the original title."

"Nothing more American than marketing."

He shrugged. Not disagreeing. Perception was important and the first title scared off potential members who'd bring money and influence. "Everyone loves a Latin name. They've been active—more or less—since 1923 with the same goals. They run drugs for blood feeds. We've got more important problems than petty drug use or distribution. But getting humans involved in this drug trade is a recipe for exposure. And obviously, a violation of the Treaty."

Vampires couldn't really get intoxicated from most substances directly so if they wanted to get drunk or high, they had to achieve it via blood additives. Bloodwine was popular, as was the blood-casked whiskey his father preferred. Those were legal and highly regulated.

Or, humans used one of only a handful of drugs that were effective, and a Vampire fed directly after—a blood feed. Clive had gotten to know Rowan as she investigated a Vampire who'd been using crystal meth via humans he'd been killing. Near immortals and crystal meth did not mix well. Human law enforcement had nearly stumbled into the truth of the existence of Vampires when bodies had begun to drop from the sky.

"I'm wondering if Elmer's little addiction plays into that on some level," Rowan said. "I told him I'd look into missing humans with any connection to his favorite bars earlier and he freaked out. Is he helping connect these Brotherhood dudes with humans to use the drugs for the feeds? When profit is the only motivator, the field of possibilities is infinity big."

Clive pinched the bridge of his nose. "When I woke this evening, the biggest problem was witches we'd already captured. But this sort of trouble is on a totally different level."

"Iceberg trouble. What you see above water is only a small part of the issue."

"They've had spies in my court since the start, Eduard confirmed it. We knew this was a possibility after the way the last Scion was removed."

She laughed, genuinely amused. "Yeah, removed his head from his body."

"Just so, darling. I think profit and power are their motivating factors as you say. From what I know at this point, they don't have a history of xenophobia like the Blood Front has. They've never been of the step on a soap box and yell about some foreign other to blame for all the world's ills. But oversight from a Scion? That gets in the way of power and profit unless the Scion is Jacques."

"And the new guy doesn't care so much about drugs and whatever, but does care about disappearing humans that attract notice. But why haven't they even approached you to see if you'd be willing to look the other way for some cash or whatever? Me probably, right?"

Clive could have been offended that she didn't automatically jump to the conclusion that these Vampires saw his rule as inherently just and knew he'd never overlook wrongdoing. But generally, he didn't care about ninety percent of things as long as they kept their behavior discreet.

"That was my conclusion. It's been nearly four years since I arrived. I've tidied a great deal of mess, and the profits are up. But as we learned recently, there's lawbreaking of all sorts in North America. Consorting with sorcerers and this ridiculous black-market nonsense. These Brotherhood Vampires have continued to quietly make money under my radar. And now because of Elmer and Eduard, I know about them. I expect they'll either come to me to propose a deal even though my wife is a Hunter, or they'll make a move."

"It'll be interesting to see which they choose," Rowan

said. "If it's the latter, I'll kill them all true without a second thought."

He sent her a raised brow.

"What? You don't already know that? I'll burn the world if any of them harms you in any way."

He took her hand, threading their fingers and holding on tight. "I believe that is the most romantic thing you've ever said to me. I'm… I do not jest." Clive paused, searching for words. "I know what your path means. I know what your position at Hunter Corp. means. That you would put me above that moves me beyond explanation."

She smiled, a little shy at the edges.

"And in that vein. The Nation and the Scion are very grateful Hunter Corp. has worked with us so closely on these important matters. Especially leaving these prisoners in our custody. That enables me to make the process public enough that Vampires like the one who tipped you off—instead of the Nation—can see we're not ignoring the crimes against them. And I want these *Sanguis* Vampires to see I *will* punish them if they step a toe over the line. I'm certain news of the arrests have already circulated through the region. We'll see what they do next."

"If they were smart, they'd lay low for a few years. But their greed is going to overcome their wits. Goddess, I'd love to watch you look down your aristocratic Scion nose at them," she said with a grin.

"I'm buoyed by your confidence." Absolute truth. "As for Elmer and his underaged Making; if you'd like to submit a statement, I'll have it added to the evidence. Elmer will not go unpunished for what he did to your new employee or that poor, wounded boy he Made far too young. They're my Vampires, even the rogue ones. It's my duty to protect them and I promise you I will," he said.

"Maybe I believe that, Scion. I'll speak to my new fanged employee to see if he'd like to submit something. Your Vampires should know the personal toll this takes, even if they'll pretend it's just a few here and there, oops no big deal!" Rowan said.

"You said you're in for the rest of the night?" Clive said, and Rowan had to give him credit for how casual he made it sound.

"I have a little more work. Vanessa has been working on a list of properties owned by or somehow connected to the Procellas. I just got a text that it's ready, so I want to look it over. Chances are, I'll put it aside for after I wake, but one never knows what might be found. Otherwise, yes, I'm off the clock until I meet up with Genevieve in the morning to head over to search the Procella mansion."

If Genevieve hadn't been there the last few times there'd been run-ins with witches and magic, Rowan very well could have died. But she left that unsaid as Clive worried about her all the time as it was.

"I endorse plans that include powerful allies," Clive said.

"As the point of bringing in witches and Vampires for special Hunter teams was exactly this type of situation, I'm glad we have the resource when we really need it."

He frowned, probably thinking about her injuries or danger or whatever.

Rowan leaned over and slid the pad of her thumb down the space between his eyebrows. "What have I said about all the frowning you do? You're going to get a wrinkle right here."

"It displeases me that you're the target in some elaborate conspiracy."

She allowed a smile. "You're very grumpy. *I'm* the grumpy one. That's my job. My thing. You do haughty English nobility."

"I have an idea of how I can work through my grumpiness," he murmured, his eyelids dropping to sex-mast.

"You've got me intrigued enough to hear your pitch," she teased.

He laughed and then his mouth was on hers.

It had been days since the last time they'd been together like this as she'd healed from the ambush. And still, he touched her with reined-in greed. Gentle, insistent.

Rowan arched into his arms and he flowed to his feet, bringing her along with him, sweeping her up and into his hold as he took them both into his bedchamber, closing the door at his back.

"I want to fuck you in here so I can smell you on the sheets when I wake each evening," he said as he set her on the mattress.

He was just so good at saying the exact perfectly dirty thing that was also heartwarming. Centuries of getting women into bed had honed him into a killing machine when it came to sex.

"I'm so very lucky sometimes," she told him as he tossed her blouse and bra to the side.

"As you say, you're about to get even luckier."

His hands roved over her skin in long, firm strokes, but when he reached her pants, he paused, gaze flicking to her face.

"Are you well enough for this?"

She managed to sit up so she could take the brace off her leg. "I'm absolutely fine. I'll let you do all the work."

He frowned and that line formed between his eyes, making her snort.

"An orgasm will help my healing. Think of this as physical therapy as well as improving your mood."

His spine lost its tension, and he gave her a smile. "I'm happy to do all the work, as you say."

His clothes fell away quickly to join hers as he slid back beside her, body to body, skin to skin. Everything felt exactly right, and she wrapped her arms around him, breathing him in.

"I love you," she told him. The words were important. That he heard them from her as well as saw them in her behavior was necessary for them both.

"What a joy that is to me. I love you. Beyond measure."

Her soft sigh and the way she seemed to melt into him settled everything within before that fire, low and banked heat, erupted into blinding need.

Forcing himself to be gentle to the body that had been broken just a few days earlier, he kissed over every part of her. Down the smooth column of her throat, across her collarbone and the curve of her shoulders. Each taste a mystery, a homecoming, and a secret only the two of them shared.

He loved the way she held her breath as he kissed down her belly and settled between her thighs, growling her pleasure as he took a long, leisurely lick, circling her clit.

Driving her up, higher and higher until she broke, coming all over his lips.

"Now that the edge has been eased a bit, lie back and enjoy," he said as he settled above her. "I'll let you move your legs wherever they feel best."

"I told you I'm fine," she said, shifting, bringing the liquid heat of her pussy to brush against the line of his cock. "Even better now," she wheezed out as he slid inside her.

He took his time, careful not to rest any of his weight on her. Letting himself remember she was his. This vibrant flame who owned his heart and soul.

There was nothing but the two of them tucked away in the quiet and when he came he stayed pressed deep inside her for some time afterward. Always home when he was with her.

Chapter Eleven

There was nothing Rowan loved more about her job than the ability to absolutely lay waste to the lives of the fucking dicks she had to deal with.

They didn't make any advance contact at the Procella mansion, not even with the guards watching the place. No, they just rolled straight up to the front steps, and when the soles of Rowan's boots hit the pavement, utter certainty seemed echoed out from her middle as the connection she shared with Brigid flared to life so much faster and easier than it ever had. It took Rowan's breath away at the sheer power of it, at the quickness of the transition.

If the sun had been down, Clive would have felt that sonic boom of her energy. As it was, Darius looked over at her and then dropped his gaze. Rowan knew Brigid shone from her eyes at that moment and he gave that respect.

Genevieve stopped just next to the vehicle and spat on the pavement three times and then sang something that sounded like stones grinding and then clicking into place. Rowan wasn't sure how she'd even made that sound, much less sang it.

But even Rowan could tell a spell had dropped over the entire area.

"All magic but ours has been disabled," Genevieve said.

"Cool."

Marco appeared, walking from a shadow Rowan hadn't noticed moments before. He and David exchanged a look that had Rowan raising her internal eyebrows.

They were on the third step to the massive front porch when the doors swung open, Lotte stood there, outrage all over her body, hands fisted at her sides. "What are you doing here? What have you done?"

Genevieve took a slow look at Lotte from the tips of her shined work shoes to her perfect, pale-blond chignon. Rowan secretly admired the suit and wondered if Elisabeth would be interested in something that smart and classy or if it would just get in the way of her work.

"The Conclave and Hunter Corp. had further queries as well as an updated physical inventory to take. We'll need to ask you some questions as part of that." Genevieve turned her attention to Rowan. "I'll let you take the lead on this."

"Delighted." Rowan stepped closer. Lotte was confident in her physical ability, and she thought Rowan was human, so she'd be lazy. Her gaze flicked down to the cane and Rowan snorted. Of course she'd underestimate Rowan.

"You can step aside, or I can move you," Rowan said. "Either works for me." Frankly, she was hoping Lotte gave her a reason. "But if you choose the latter, it won't be gentle."

Rowan caught the shift in Lotte's stance and the way she dropped her right shoulder. She stepped back and to the side quickly as Lotte moved forward. Rowan choked her grasp up higher on her cane, lifted it before Lotte even knew what was happening, and brought it down brutally hard against the back of the witch's leg.

Lotte cried out, stumbling back. She tried to use magic but that fizzled because Genevieve had pulled the plug. Rowan used her free hand to punch Lotte's face in two short jabs as she stepped into the front foyer fully.

The others followed as one of the beefy guards from the day Rowan and Genevieve had come for the first meeting with the Procella family stormed into the room. He raised a weapon, but Rowan spun on her good leg and brought the cane down full force on the arm lifting to aim. The crack of bone made her wince and filled her with victory at the same time.

He screamed, high and shrill, full of pain and the energy of a person about to pass out, which he then did in a heap at Rowan's feet.

"That was very impressive," Genevieve said.

"It's all in the nerves. Know where to strike and boom. Beefy there should up his calcium intake though. Shouldn't have been so easy to break that bone. Ah well." Rowan shrugged. "He'll heal. Eventually. Plus, I practiced that spin while using the cane to hit the target a few times since yesterday." She smiled, showing her teeth at Lotte, who limped over, smeared blood on her lip from where Rowan's punch had landed.

David took all the weapons and then unloaded them all, pocketing the magazines.

"You broke his arm," Lotte said, falling into a heap in a nearby chair. Her outrage had begun to drain away, replaced with a growing realization she was in over her head. Good. The sooner Perfect Suit accepted reality, the easier things would go for everyone.

"Probably in two places given the angle I used. Like I said, he'll heal. At least I didn't shoot him fourteen times." Because it was rude, Rowan snapped her fingers at Lotte. "Stand up. I didn't break *your* leg. I can hit you in exactly the right place to shatter a bone. You understand I'll do it if you push me again. You *know* I will. Understanding is a beautiful thing. Isn't it? So, since we understand one another, we can skip any further attempts to attack me. They'll fail and I will hurt you to gain your compliance. You'll comply in the end, they all do."

Lotte was in good shape. She'd been quick and had moved with strength. She was likely quite formidable with humans and other witches when it came to hand-to-hand. But she was a kitten compared with what Rowan was. She couldn't even dream up the types of things Rowan had done and was willing to do. Even if Lotte didn't realize it, Rowan did. And being the more powerful being came with a bunch of rules about not abusing it. Annoying, but whatever. They'd get Lotte subdued enough to handle the rest of the search and that was what counted.

Rowan looked around. "You can take a seat over there and one of us will speak to you shortly. You're not to move unless there's a fire or whatever, as we conduct the search."

Genevieve said three words and made a hand movement.

"She's secured," Genevieve told Rowan.

"Okay, let's get that one handled." She pointed at the guard, still on the ground but coming to consciousness.

"Then we begin. I'll start in the kitchen. I've been dying to see it after Lotte attempted to corral me in there when I was here last on official business." Rowan sent a sunny smile Lotte's way at the reference to the way she'd been expected to wait in the kitchen while real witch business was conducted elsewhere.

Genevieve came through with them. "Though I'm certain my working would have deactivated all spell traps when I took down everything else, I'll accompany you just in case I'm needed to handle something."

As it was clearly the domain of servants, Rowan wanted to perform the second search of the kitchen herself. There were no new revelations. However, when Rowan opened the fridge, she noted similarities to what was stocked at Sergio's hidey-hole she thought of as his Gloat Palace. They'd searched the upscale ranch house in Spring Valley first thing and had gathered a stunning amount of evidence, including indications that Hugo had most likely been hiding out there before they'd arrested him.

"That's not a label found on shelves of most liquor stores," Genevieve said of the champagne and wine. "Same with the liquor in the butler's pantry. I'm sure there's a bar cart in the main sitting room of each of the bedrooms as well. I imagine we'll find more of the same, connecting to what was stocked at the other house."

"I had a very strong feeling the sidepiece wasn't the one doing all the grocery stocking. Probably Lotte. Bet she knew Hugo was there, too." Rowan curled her lip.

David remained at her side as they moved, quadrant by quadrant, through the first floor. Filming when necessary. Taking notes. Handing her things she didn't even know she needed until they appeared and solved the problem.

Rowan spoke quietly as they ascended to the second floor where all the living quarters were clustered like little apartments. "I guess living with your family would be okay if you had thirteen thousand square feet and they had their own full apartment to be in rather than the living room at all hours, hogging the TV when all your shows are on."

"Do *you* have shows?" David asked, teasing.

"I totally do! That tattoo competition show, for one. Then I can root for the contestant who is just badass and talented and sneer at the one guy who refers to himself in the third person while telling everyone how great he is. It's always the best when whatever bullshit that guy has been doing to others turns around on him so he can act hurt and surprised people would do the same shady shit he has. Honestly, it's a show with plenty of drama, but has great art. If my father-in-law came in every time I was about to watch the elimination tattoo results to talk to me about laxatives or wanted to change the channel to golf, I'd probably not tell the cops where he was if he ran off either, so long as he didn't come back."

"You are as ever, a very complex person," David told her. "I will endeavor to never interrupt while you're watching television."

"You're welcome to watch with me. Bring snacks. Star will share the couch with you if you give her a scratch behind her ears."

"I find it's best to lead with snacks in most every situation."

"Right? Why hasn't everyone figured that out yet?

Clive now just hands me food every time he sees me. As a preventative measure."

David's snort of laughter brought a smile to her face.

Rowan pointed to the left. "We need to cross over to that wing of this floor. That's where all the household staff live." They walked over an open, bright landing that then took a slight turn that led to a series of suite-styled bedrooms. Not as opulent and spacious as the family apartments, but quite lovely, nonetheless.

Rowan looked at her notes. "Let's start with Lotte's room. I bet that galls the hell out of her to be here with the staff instead of with her employer. I also bet the rest of the staff hate her guts. You know she's a cop. Telling on everyone."

"I really do wish they understood how much worse it goes for them when they give you reasons to dislike them. Though it's obviously far more entertaining when they bumble along, and you savage them at every turn."

"I know, David. But villains never learn. I guess that's good for the rest of us always having to deal with them and stop them from villainy and shit. Keeps the lights on and Star in that swanky homemade dog food they spoil her with."

Genevieve came in moments after they had. "I've gone through the rooms in this wing. All clear of spell traps. But that doesn't mean other sorts of traps won't be set. Do be cautious."

"I'm glad you said it," David teased Genevieve.

"I need you to wait in the hall," Rowan told them both.

"I will go speak with Lotte, if you are amenable," Genevieve said.

"Excellent idea. I'll join you in a bit."

Once they'd gone, leaving her alone in Lotte's space, Rowan let herself breathe slowly as she got her head right.

Rowan wasn't a witch. She wasn't a Vampire. Her senses were highly developed just the same. Honed over the years as her connection to Brigid strengthened and she trained as a Hunter.

Intuition was a melding of the physical parts of being an investigator and the metaphysical parts of being... well, Rowan. It had taken a long time for her to accept the magical aspects of herself, as if they could disappear and leave her lacking so she never wanted to be weak. Or that they somehow made her weak.

But it was the opposite, she'd realized. Accepting her gifts as that particular combination of all her various strengths made her better at her job in every way. Her connection to Brigid was a positive. It was supposed to be. She was supposed to lean into it and let it make her stronger.

Learning that—accepting that—had been revolutionary. And a process she was still working through.

Moving to the center of the sitting room, Rowan let her eyes close and reached out for her other senses. Opened herself up to the Goddess inside her.

Pleasure surged through her veins as Brigid rose and settled herself within Rowan. Sharing a consciousness in a way that had begun to feel very natural.

She needed to trust herself more.

That was a Brigid thought.

"Okay, okay," she muttered. Perfect Suit lived in this space. Her energy and magical signature were everywhere.

Interesting. Rowan opened her eyes and then relaxed

her focus, like she was staring at one of those optical illusion posters they sold at the mall. As of just a few days before that, Rowan couldn't really detect a magical signature more than in a cursory way. She'd been able to notice if magic had been used. Could tell when someone was a witch. But what she was looking at just then were little gossamer threads. So similar to the way she perceived a scent trail.

Lotte spent time at the little couch and table near the windows. There was one of those individual-cup coffee maker things and all the pods that went inside were neatly lined up in a little tray holding two mugs and various coffee and tea accessories. A mini fridge sat beneath the table and held food and drinks. Nothing incriminating.

There were bookshelves on one wall but not a lot of Lotte's energy was there. Rowan followed those little threads into the bedroom and knew immediately that this was where Lotte spent most of her time when she wasn't working.

She might be a stuck-up bitch, but Lotte had good taste. The furnishings were elegant and clearly well-made with luxury materials and finishes. There was a vanity nearest French doors leading to a small balcony, and on the other side of the room, set in an alcove, was a beautiful desk. The gleaming cherrywood was smudged at the drawer pulls with those threads.

"This is a very cool new gift," she murmured to the Goddess.

Somewhere in her head, Rowan heard a laugh as warmth flowed through her.

She knelt and looked under the bed, noting the room had hardwoods but the bed sat on an area rug.

"David!" she called, straightening.

He came in quickly. "What do you need?"

"I want to move the bed and the rug it's on. There's something under it."

"Let me call Marco. He's just at the end of the hall. You might reinjure yourself."

She considered arguing but Marco appeared in the doorway. "Did you need my assistance?" he asked… David.

Oh for fuck's sake.

Fine. It'd give them a little flirting time and Clive wouldn't hear she was moving furniture.

"There's something under the bed. I need it and the rug moved," she said.

Genevieve seated herself across from Lotte, taking her time settling, letting the other woman get more and more nervous and uncertain.

Darius had retreated a few feet away, near the doorway to the grand foyer. Close enough to intervene should she need it. Or should he want to. He did pretty much whatever he wanted anyway. Who or what could stop him?

"Who is Sergio's paramour? The one who lives out at the Lakes?" she asked at last.

Surprise registered on Lotte's features briefly before she schooled herself. "If I knew, I wouldn't tell you."

"Okay. You'll be held in Conclave custody until a tribunal decides your fate."

"My fate? For what? I have broken no laws! I have rights." She tried to shoot to her feet, but Genevieve had secured her in place.

"Lower your voice or I'll do it for you." Genevieve

raised a lazy hand, the bracelets clacking and jingling with the motion. "You are withholding information regarding a current investigation. You've been given multiple opportunities to cooperate and have chosen otherwise. I have no idea why you all act like humans are beneath notice but you try to cling to their laws when you're in trouble. Human law isn't applicable here. It never has been. Mainly that's been about our protection from them. But sometimes, we end up in situations where we're the threats. And then the Conclave has to step in and handle it before your hubris gets the rest of us unwanted attention. Like contracting wolf shifters to murder a Hunter in the middle of the day. On camera in one of the busiest intersections in the world."

Lotte sneered. "And look at her now. A pathetic human upstairs right now pawing through the belongings of her betters. She's nothing to the Procella organization."

Rowan seemed fine with people underestimating her, but Genevieve was not. "She's free to do her very important and powerful job while you're held to a chair being interrogated, and your employers are all under arrest. I'm entirely clear about who is who's better. As will you be when she finds whatever it is you're hiding." Genevieve gave Lotte a once-over full of disdain.

If there was something to find, Rowan would find it. She had a way. And now she had some built-up spite to apply to the problem, which fueled Rowan like nothing else.

"None of this has anything to do with Mr. Procella's private life." Lotte nervously twisted her fingers.

"Tell me or I'll make a call and have a transport sent over to take you to be held until trial."

Lotte's spine curved slightly as she finally understood her fate.

"Mr. Procella was married for nearly a century. He was devastated when his beloved wife died. In the thirty years since she passed, he has had a long-term relationship with two women. He kept them away from this home, which he built for his wife and their children."

Genevieve figured that might explain the fact that in all the photographs and video they'd located featuring the Procellas out and about at various society and work-related events there wasn't a single instance of another woman. She wondered just what the current girlfriend had to say about that.

"What happened to the first one?"

"They grew apart." Lotte's brief answer was loaded with judgment.

"Name." Genevieve looked Lotte over again. "I can use magical means to get the answer. This isn't even a particularly deep secret, so it'll be easy enough to take. But it won't be pleasant."

A deep secret was more difficult to uproot. A working to reveal it was most effectively performed with precision of intent. Genevieve didn't know enough about Hugo and Sergio and whatever they were up to, so it was difficult to even know the questions to ask. But with Lotte and what she needed? Easy. And she wouldn't even be sad if it hurt given all the pain the Procellas had brought. The sooner they had more information from those around Sergio and Hugo, the sooner Genevieve could uncover answers.

"Why do you need to know?" Lotte asked.

"You know why we're here. You know why Hugo ran off and that he was hiding out at the house in Spring

Valley. You know why Sergio and Antonia are in custody and you know why Bess Procella is being detained. You *don't* need to know the exact reasons I'm asking. That's, how do you say? Oh, above your pay level.

"If they haven't done anything wrong, I'll find that. Speaking to people will give me answers. If they have? I'll find out anyway. It'll be messier and more painful, and it'll take a little longer maybe. But make no mistake, I will get answers. You can tell me, or I can make you tell me. This is where we are. Your option is to answer the questions I ask or be arrested."

Marco came in holding a tea tray he laid out next to Genevieve's seat. He poured her a cup of perfectly doctored milky black tea. The way she preferred it. Very sweet.

She nodded her appreciation, and he retreated after an inclination of his chin, showing her respect.

"That tea set is priceless," Lotte said, her tone going up in pitch as Genevieve sipped. "Once owned by a tsar. A gift to Mr. Procella Senior from a business associate. It was in a *locked* cabinet. That's not a set we use daily. It's for kings and notables."

"Ms. Aubert is as close as you will ever get to royalty," Darius said, filling Genevieve's belly with butterflies.

"Back to Sergio's first mistress and her name." Genevieve turned the delicate cup in the saucer slightly and then set them down. It *was* a beautiful set and while she had no concerns for what Lotte felt, she wasn't going to destroy something that couldn't be replaced.

Pausing, she bent to pull a pipe from her handbag. The bowl was loaded, and the sticky, sweet scent of marijuana filled the space as she took a hit—bigger than was actually necessary—and blew it out, delighting in the horrified look on Lotte's face.

There were times when all the various disciplines and teachers in Genevieve's life and magical study were voices in her head. All telling her what would be best. What was a problem. They weren't negative voices. They never said cruel things to or about her. But they could be overwhelming to the point of being debilitating. She'd discovered several centuries before that marijuana seemed to help and left her clearer than alcohol and other types of things she'd used before and after.

Her connection to the Dust Devils and their Trick had helped immensely with her facets, as Darius called them. They still clamored for attention, but it wasn't overwhelming as often.

They really didn't like Lotte, that much was clear to Genevieve. Which was understandable because she didn't like Lotte either.

"Hugo and Sergio will most likely be sentenced at a tribunal. You won't see them in your lifetime. Antonia? That remains to be seen. Alfonso is running from our inquiries. We'll find him eventually. And when we do, we'll also find who's been giving him inside information to help him. The way *Hugo* was also fed information." Genevieve paused to look over at Lotte, delighted as the truth hit her and she realized they knew she'd been helping Procella father and son. Then she decided to toss out, "Oh, I suppose you might be wondering why Hugo hasn't gotten in contact with you over the last day and a half or so. Well, as it happens, he was captured after he attacked me and the Hunter with negative magic. *Again.*" She sent a faux smile laced with

Chapter Twelve

Rowan strolled into the room right as Lotte was speaking. She placed the box she'd carried down from upstairs on the low table between the couches and chairs. David had another box he placed next to that one.

"I caught the tail end of that conversation as I entered. *Found nothing* is such an interesting way to put it." Rowan held up a cell phone, loving the expression on Perfect Suit's face. "Surprise, it's nothing! I'm obviously much smarter than you, but kudos to you for not warding the little cache space built into the floor beneath your bed. That's why no one found it." Well, that and the way they had only given a cursory glance at the staff quarters but whatever, that was a Conclave problem. Rowan had enough of her own to go borrowing theirs.

"Because the magic of the wards would have indicated something was there when a scan was done," Genevieve said. "That is very clever indeed. So how did you find it, Rowan?"

She wasn't going to give away this newly risen talent for seeing magical imprints. She could trust Genevieve of course, but there were several witches from the Conclave who'd come at Genevieve's summons, as sympathy. "I see from your expression that you didn't. Ah. Well, you do now in any case."

"You people have done enough and found nothing. This is persecution, plain and simple," Lotte said, her cheeks going pink. Her panic and fear stunk up the air. Genevieve felt that if one were to involve themselves in conspiracies of the type Lotte had, one might have a stronger disposition.

well as the guard whose arm she'd broken, tied up and miserable in a chair on the other side of the hallway.

But it wasn't the only thing that had led her to that hiding place. The rest had been intuition and detective work. Stuff she did all the time.

"Criminals are never as clever as they think they are. All the bedrooms in the staff wing are staged in the same basic way. A large area rug the bed sits on while the rest of the room has wood flooring. I had a hunch they didn't look beneath the rugs because the beds were heavy and probably hard to move."

Genevieve's left eyebrow rose slowly. It had been lazy not to move the beds. They'd made a quick calculation and bet against something being probable. They were dealing with assholes who took out a hit on a cranky Hunter, and some stalking of another witch. Rowan figured the witches Konrad had sent were well trained enough that if the search had been urgent, they'd have been more careful.

But if they had worked for her, she'd make them all go get more training at the very least and it appeared Genevieve agreed.

"Imagine my surprise when David and Marco began to shift the bed and discovered a latch on the footboard that unlocked. The whole thing, rug and all, was on little casters, so they just had to tug to move it all at once. Easily. The cache was pretty large and was chock-full of things Lotte didn't want us to find. Then we looked in the other staff and guest bedroom suites. About half had such a system but none of the rest had anything inside, nor did they have the setup Lotte did with the casters to move the bed easily. David has gone back up to search the family bedrooms." Marco had volunteered to help so Rowan knew he'd be safe while she handled other things.

"My." Genevieve set her cup down a little harder than necessary as she swiveled to take Lotte in better. "As you heard when you came in, Lotte was just telling me she had nothing to say."

"The phone had a bunch of calls made to the same number over the last few days. Several to and from the landline at Sergio's Gloat Palace. A lot to Hugo's number before and after the attack, though the after went unanswered." Rowan shook her head. "So sneaky. I admire that, actually. Anyway, since we had the unknown number with all the calls, we were able to locate the signal and find the phone, along with Alfonso Procella, in one of the presidential villas at an oceanside resort in Laguna Beach. He'd been there since Lotte told him we were looking for Hugo, five days ago. Konrad is involved and sent someone to the scene."

Genevieve hummed. "Well. Lotte is very industrious. It's really too bad they'll all be incarcerated. Maybe we can find ways to turn these criminal tendencies into virtues. I do believe you will have some things to say at this point."

"What would you incarcerate Alfonso for? You said yourself Hugo was in custody. You were searching for him to ask about Hugo's whereabouts. Now you know. What crime is there?" Lotte asked.

Genevieve's smile turned into something darker, sharper. Rowan had seen that a time or two and it had never ended well for whoever she was looking at. "Alfonso is in a great deal of trouble and an overwhelming amount of it isn't even related to Hugo. The irony is, we wouldn't have noticed any of this if *you* hadn't been so rude to Rowan and Hugo hadn't acted like a predator."

Rowan chuckled. "Right? Hard to be thirsty for attention and a successful criminal at the same time. One will get the other caught. For beings who like to think they're better than humans, you sure act like them a lot."

Lotte's face darkened as she registered the insult.

Goddess, Rowan *loved* offending assholes.

Amused, she dug around in one of the boxes from upstairs. "There are some memory sticks and," Rowan's words were cut short when a concussive explosion rolled from the northern-facing part of the house toward them. The hair on her arms rose as she hit the floor, bounding up to her knees again to grab Genevieve and pull them both under the table, yanking all the protective magics she could imagine around herself, feeling the *snick-snick-snick* of that power weaving around her. Over that, the cool metallic shell of Genevieve's magic seemed to bubble around their bodies.

Then the heat came, a molten hot flash that sucked all the air from the room, like a fucking freight train of fire barreling through. She tried to hold back the panic over how David was faring. The Devils would likely be all right. Marco was with him. Marco would keep him safe. He had to be safe. She could not stand losing anyone else.

Be calm.

Brigid's words soothed as they sounded inside her head, a steady stream of warmth coursed through her veins, full of comfort and strength. Those moments allowed Rowan to gather her wits and get herself under control. There would be a point coming when the explosion itself would die, and she'd need to be up and in action.

The fire ate everything in its path as it roared through, high-pitched and relentless until it finally died off.

The protections around Genevieve and Rowan fell away.

The stench of burned things rose—people, furniture, plastic—and Rowan's breakfast lurched in her gut a moment.

Thoughts of David got her moving again, as she reached to push the table aside. Before she could though, Darius was there, lifting it, and then Genevieve before he handed Rowan her cane and took her weight a little as she got to her feet.

A circle of space around the table had been totally untouched, including the boxes of evidence she'd found under Lotte's bed.

"I've got to see if David is okay," she said, trying not to panic as she took stock of her physical state. Nothing new appeared to be broken.

Then she caught sight of what was left of Perfect Suit and the guard whose arm she'd broken and winced. Not even enough for DNA identification.

Darius put a hand on her arm briefly. "He and Marco are fine. We need to leave now before the authorities arrive. There is nothing incriminating left. We'll take the boxes with us."

Rowan had been ready to rush upstairs anyway, but David hurried up, clearly as concerned for her as she'd been for him. "I'll drive. Are you hurt?" he asked as she willed away her tears of relief.

"No. I'm fine. I think a combo of Genevieve, Dust Devil, and Goddess magic protected me and our evidence." No use talking about that twinge in her upper arm and the low throb of general discomfort. She was alive. They'd come through that fire when everyone and everything else had been turned to ash.

Gratitude was in order. When the adrenaline wore off, she'd most likely be hurting a lot worse.

"Good," David told her as he hustled out with her and the others after the boxes of evidence she'd had with her were loaded into the back of her SUV.

The once obscenely large mansion still smoked, and though the main walls still stood in most places, the roof was gone. The windows had been blown out. Whatever that spell was, the way it hit hard and fast and had burned *everything* in a matter of seconds was quite concerning. Rowan would address that with Genevieve once they had gotten clear of the place and couldn't be overheard.

Whatever Devil magic it was, her vehicle, along with the one the Conclave had sent over, had all survived and they got the hell out of there.

"What the fuck was that?" Rowan demanded as they sped away. She typed rapid-fire notes to Vanessa to handle all the emergency services overwatch.

"That was a series of spells set in a pattern, triggering the next in a cascade until the energy is powerful enough to set off a mage firebomb. Only a Genetic witch can make it." Genevieve said all that while she too was typing away on her phone.

"I need to go back to examine the scene. Did a witch have to be there to fire the spell off? Is it a multiple-witch deal like with the black market sorcerers? You said only Genetic witches can do it but is it a one powerful witch deal, or a five witches with a powerful spell deal?"

"There are times you ask questions when I am more impressed by you than anyone else I've met in hundreds of years," Genevieve said.

Pleased, Rowan tried to play it off with a shrug. "Truth is, I don't know as much about the world of magical practitioners as I should. Working on it, though."

"That will displease a great many, I'll say up front," Genevieve said. "But add I think it's a necessary wake-up call. Reckless behavior will get us exposed. We need to get ourselves under control. You can be the monster in the closet."

Rowan snorted.

"I sensed three different magical imprints on the magic. I will need to return after the authorities leave to take another, closer look. It's very complicated, *big* magic. A great deal of energy would need to be managed and directed without blowing back against the user. Whoever it was has a great deal of control. A spell with mage fire could have taken out not just the Procella mansion, but the houses to either side and across the street as well. But it didn't leap any further than the outer walls of the house. These are not merely Genetic witches with a lot of Talent. Once I can be in the spot they were when they launched the magic, then I can gather more identifying information."

"Okay. So my next question is, if they're so powerful, will that make things easier? Like you have a list of the biggest powers in the Conclave?" Witches were hyper-private. Instincts to survive honed over a long history full of being hunted, persecuted, and murdered. They were driven to hide. Rowan knew she wasn't going to have full access to lists or anything of that type. She just needed as much information as possible to figure out a solution.

"I have a general idea. It's not an exceptionally large pool of candidates, I can say that. But in the hundreds. It's a start. I'll have Samaya break it down into something manageable." Samaya was Genevieve's David, and Ms. Lorraine's daughter.

"I don't think it should get out that Sergio, Antonia, and Alfonso were not at home when the spell went off," Rowan said. "That ignorance might be very useful. Plus if these witches think they killed everyone but Hugo—the story about him is already out so we can't change that—they'll ease back a little. That gives me time to home in on them. They'll make mistakes trying to cover up. Then we'll grab them. Hopefully before any more spell bombs go off."

Genevieve blew out a frustrated breath. "This is the third time in less than a week that witches have nearly killed you. Your Vampire isn't going to let me come to your house for play dates if this keeps up."

Rowan snickered, so tired. "Meh. You're not that unique. People try to kill me regularly. We're all alive and the evidence we found was saved. Did the attackers know we were there? Was it about us? Was it about the property and destroying whatever could lead back to them? Ugh! I hate not knowing things. It makes me very cranky."

And when Clive rose for the evening, he'd wake to the news of an explosion. She'd need to finish up with her interview of Antonia. Then she'd tie up as much as she could and be waiting when he opened his eyes.

Rowan tried to ignore the growing throb in her chest

and leg. "David, please alert London as to what's gone down. Darius, can you please take us to the motherhouse? I want to drop off this evidence to get them started on the electronics before we head over to speak to Antonia."

Back at work, Genevieve followed Rowan into her office and closed the door at her back. "You're in pain. Let me help."

Rowan's shoulder and chest on the side where she'd been shot so many times had healed. Mostly. But it had happened only days before and super blood and a goddess inside her aside, her body was still knitting itself together again. Which was why it had started to ache.

Genevieve's healing magic was a flavor Brigid seemed to enjoy and then amplify with her own power, all aimed at alleviating Rowan's pain.

At the end, as her friend stood back, the waves of discomfort had eased, and she could think more clearly. And she didn't feel as guilty or nervous about how Clive would react.

"I'm going to check in with Konrad regarding Alfonso and Bess. I'll meet you afterward. Darius and I will watch you interview Antonia from the other room, so don't start without us."

Now she didn't have to push the topic of Genevieve not being in the interview. Antonia showed off for her and Rowan didn't want her to have that. Plus, that whole family was in on what Hugo had done to Genevieve. Fuck them all.

"Gotcha. I've got this stuff and we're heading out shortly. I'll see you there."

Star trotted at Rowan's side as they made their way through the main floor. Rowan needed to pause here and there, sign things, give her opinion and the like. Naturally everyone wanted to dote on the dog, and Rowan didn't blame them. Star was looking very fluffy, and she loved being fawned over.

"Is this your way of forcing interaction between me and my employees?" she asked Star quietly.

Star snorted and sat on her rump and staring up at Rowan, clearly in the mood to communicate something.

"Okay, then. I'm only here briefly to pick this up." She held the file folder with the material she needed for her chat with Antonia. "Are you coming with me to magic headquarters when I question Antonia?"

Nothing.

"I'm not going back to talk to Hugo or his pepaw until later today at the earliest. I've found out some juicy stuff today and I want to punch them in the face with it at the right time."

Still nothing.

"You'll just show up wherever and whenever you please?"

That got a yip, and Rowan said, "All right, then. I just wanted to make sure you understood you were invited."

To which Star snorted as if to say of course I am.

David approached and tossed Star another treat.

"I just gave her three snacks," Rowan said without rancor.

David scratched behind one of Star's ears for a moment. "And now she's had four. Busy day ahead, she'll need the calories. And so will you. Don't forget that."

"Yeah, yeah. Genevieve and I are having a meal after I'm finished chatting with Antonia. Then I'll have to figure out what will happen next depending on how close we are to sunset. I'll need to go home to deal with Vampire stuff when the sun goes down."

Understanding shone in his eyes. "Ah. Yes, I imagine so. I have a call with London in just a few minutes to update Susan and the others."

"I am so fucking glad you handle all this stuff. I trust your ability to inform them on that front." He was the head of US operations for Hunter Corp. and he knew how to give a report.

Clearly pleased, he continued, "I've got some calls and a meeting with Vihan and Vanessa about the data we need extracted from all the things we brought from the Procella mansion and the Gloat Palace. All of which should be over by the time you're ready for me. I'll meet you wherever and we'll hit the next steps of whatever plan. Do we need to pull someone to be your driver until I can attend you?"

Goddess, he was so efficient and pretty much unflappable. Whatever would she do without him?

"Past Rowan was so smart to hire you," she told him.

Her valet gave her a look. "I had to beg you to stay when I showed up at your door. And then you were ordered to keep me or lose your job."

"The journey is its own reward, David. We're here now, aren't we? And if I was opposed you most assuredly would not be. Obviously."

He chuckled with a shake of his head. "Obviously."

She'd panicked at the prospect of a far softer and younger David, and the orders that she train him and let him serve her as her valet. Her life was dangerous. People in her orbit got hurt. Killed.

Susan, her former trainer, and mentor, had forced the decision on her, knowing Rowan would not walk away from being a Hunter. It had been right and good, and he was seriously amazing at his job and in her life.

Rowan worried about him. Their world seemed to flood with violence on a far-too-frequent basis. She made powerful enemies regularly. He wasn't even ten years younger than she was, but he was in so many ways like her son. With all the complicated pride and fear wrapped tight around the other. But in the end, it meant she had to let him fly and trust his wings and her ability to step in if necessary to protect him.

"Yes, I have a driver," she said tucking the file under her arm. "I'm on the way out now."

"Wait a moment," he told her, leaving and returning within five minutes with a cup of coffee in a travel mug and a still-warm ham and cheese croissant. "Now then. I'll walk you to your car."

"Marco is waiting. Let's bring him some coffee too."

David made a neat circle and returned with another mug and croissant. "I don't know what he takes in it, so I included little creamer and sweetener packets. I'll carry it, as I said. That way you can hold on to the railing with one hand and your cane with the other. Don't give me that expression. Your leg is still healing, and you just survived an explosion. Again. Why would you endanger yourself unduly over something so silly?" He also snatched the file and tucked it under his arm.

"Babyface David didn't talk back," she said as they headed out.

He laughed again. "In the years I've spent around you and those in your life, if I hadn't gotten tough, I'd have been sent packing. One does need to be ready for anything and to stand up for it when one serves Rowan Summerwaite."

"Didn't I just give you a raise recently?" she teased.

"You did. And I was awarded a valorous service bonus as well. My investment portfolio is looking pretty good these days." He moved ahead of her to open the door to the parking lot where Marco waited, lounging against the side of her new vehicle.

Since Darius was with Genevieve and David had work, Marco volunteered, and Rowan had accepted his very generous offer. He was a tank, and she wasn't a fool. Plus, it helped that she could tell Clive she had a guard with her the whole day while David could get things done at the motherhouse.

There was a coffee and baked goods handoff between David and Marco. And more flirting.

"The backup today is very helpful," she said as they headed to their destination.

Marco had short, very thick dark hair, soulful and slightly terrifying hazel eyes that sometimes went ice blue at the outer edges. Olive skin. That day he wore black pants and a long-sleeved black shirt. More stylish than some of the other devils without being ridiculous. Probably didn't *need* weapons but he had them in a few of those pockets, Rowan had no doubt.

He wasn't much taller than she was. But he was immense when it came to energy.

Even when he had it tucked away such as when they were out in public, it was impossible not to sense the energy surging all around him. Probably kept most of the tourists walking on by. But given the arresting looks and all that energy, Rowan had zero doubt it also drew a few of the thrill seekers closer.

"This vehicle is very nice. Handles well. We did an excellent job."

The devils ran a number of side businesses and one of them was installing privacy windows that also had sound dampening and anti-magic bells and whistles. There was a long waitlist she only had to get shot fourteen times to get to the head of.

"Clive and Darius made it happen so quickly. I like it too."

"For a Vampire, he is tolerable," Marco said of Clive.

She wanted to laugh but she didn't know him well enough to predict he wouldn't be offended.

"He really is," was what she settled on. "The previous guy though? Total shitbag."

Marco grunted. "We weren't expecting you. You rolled into the city, took that asshole's measure, and when you had enough on him, you'd lopped his head off. That's when we decided to let you live."

All that was delivered in such a deadpan manner she wasn't entirely sure it was in jest. "Well, that's good," she managed without sounding terrified. "Please drive past the Tempest."

She hadn't been at that intersection where she'd been ambushed since the day it happened. Before that, she'd had several prophetic dreams and knowings, and some of them had led her to that spot. In front of the casino resort owned—in part—by the Procellas. There were many symbols that had been swimming around in her subconscious. She was still working through them all. But a recurring one had been storms at sea. Tempests.

Thanks to the Devil at the wheel, they'd discovered one of the meanings of the name Procella was *storm*. Far too many coincidences to be anything but connected. The Procellas were at the center of whatever the fuck was happening. She just had to figure out the connections.

"I'm only seeing glimpses of what's going on. I just need to look at it from different angles until I see it clearly," she explained even though he hadn't asked.

"Fair."

She wasn't sure what she expected, but there wasn't any great lightning-bolt moment as they drove past the scene. The glass had been cleaned up. No weird energy remained that she could detect.

"Would you like me to approach this intersection again?" he asked.

"This was useful. I'm good for now." She'd wanted to see if there was something she'd missed. Some new bit of information but none was there that she could sense. Satisfied for the time being, she looked through the file and her notes, added some new ones given what they'd learned that afternoon and got herself into an interview headspace.

Chapter Thirteen

As they got caught up in the usual Las Vegas traffic madness, Rowan's phone buzzed with an incoming call.

Nadir. One of her father's Five. His own personal special ops squad universally feared and respected in the world of Vampires. She was the Voice. The only one of them who ever spoke aloud in public. Theo's official spokesperson. Sort of like the Pope and God to Catholics.

Rowan's relationship with not only Vampires, but these very powerful Vampires who'd been a part of her upbringing—for all the good and ill that came with it—was a work in progress. Love was complicated.

That afternoon, Rowan figured she had enough goodwill built up with the Nation right at that moment, so she picked up.

"Well, hello."

"It's good to hear your voice so I can reassure your father. We just got news of a magic bomb in your city at the home of a witch," Nadir said.

Aw, fuck. Damned Nation spies. Now they knew before Clive knew and that would be a whole thing. He'd be pouty and there'd be dominance displays until he felt more even again.

"You can pass along to him that my healing is going well. They removed the cast and I have a brace instead. Cane instead of crutches. My physician says I'm freakishly quick to recover." She wanted to avoid talk of the explosion altogether and emphasize how well she was getting. If Theo learned she was involved in yet another attempt on her life there'd be no stopping him from poking his nose into the situation.

She had enough to manage without an ancient being with more power than sanity showing up in full paternal protection mode.

Rowan chose evasion. "I'm currently miles away from that explosion."

"He will be relieved," Nadir said of Theo.

While the Vampire was feeling grateful, Rowan said, "So hey, tell me about *Sanguis Principatus*."

Nadir hissed. "I haven't spoken to Clive about this yet."

"That's between you and the Scion who is still at daytime rest. This is the Hunter asking the Voice. This group is here in my city. They're up to something and I need to figure it out. It'll only hurt the Nation if it gets worse. You know that."

"Jacques, that fool, was one of them. At that time, it was economic. A union of like-minded Vampires with a lot of money and power who enabled one another to make more money and thereby earn more power."

"How would you compare them to the Blood Front?"

"I would say the Blood Front is the great uncle, yes? Older. In the world of Vampires, until now at least, more powerful. More populated by old families. The *Sanguis Principatus* are younger. New world. Same basic focus on the supremacy of Vampires. But…being American means they're less evangelical about that supremacy and more interested in living lives motivated by profit."

Rowan thought that sounded worse. People got up to all sorts of dire bullshit over a few dollars.

"What's the news on the dinguses in your pain basement?" Rowan asked instead.

Two weeks prior, a group referring to themselves as Vampire Lords—complete with silly capitalization—had shown up on letterhead from the Vampire Nation. Hunter Corp. had made changes after a series of bloody betrayals had nearly destroyed them from the ground up. One of those changes was to create special teams that would include a Vampire or a witch to go out into the field with a Hunter.

Rowan knew the other parties would be pissy that she was hiring them. Fortunately, the Conclave was fine after a few tweaks. But the Vampire Nation sent a snippy little missive ignoring the declaration of these new teams and instead trying to time waste and involve her in endless negotiations, so nothing ever happened.

Rowan had ignored that letter and had gone about her business because she was never seeking permission anyway. She didn't need it. Vampires were attention-seeking narcissists, so she'd expected theater.

Vampires being extra was one thing, but they'd crossed a line with a second letter, declaring any Vampire employees of Hunter Corp. would be executed on sight. And they'd done so very publicly. On Nation letterhead. Which had driven Theo to send out one of his Five, Andros, the one they called Silent Death. And now these shitlords were imprisoned in the dungeons beneath the Keep. At the mercy of whatever Theo decided to do to them.

What really bothered Rowan was how the attack from these Vampires had come at her out of the blue. She didn't trust that. Very little Vampires did was random. They consistently had long game plans. It was their vibe. All plans, all the time.

Nadir coughed out a laugh. "The guests below have been marinating, as Andros puts it. Tomorrow, maybe the day after, we will begin to converse with them."

Converse. Ha!

"I'll be interested to hear what your conversation merits from them as to their motivations."

"You are not alone in that."

"You're the one who let them into the process," Rowan said, frustrated.

The entire situation with the Vampire lords escalated to the point it did because Nation leadership allowed them in. Otherwise they could have threatened all day and night and it wouldn't have made a difference because no one took them seriously. But their names showed up on Nation letter head on official correspondence and that would not have happened without Nadir's permission.

Nadir was quiet for some time. "When we are face-to-face and sharing gossip, we will discuss this."

She wasn't going to say anything over the phone or in writing. Which meant it would be the truth.

"All right."

Rowan knew it had been political. And that regardless of how it came about, it had happened. But now, she had some power because the Vampire Nation's fuckups had ended with a giant mess that had caused harm to Rowan. Even if Theo had done it to get her attention—which was what Rowan believed—he hadn't done it to hurt her. And that hurt occurred meant he'd be eager to punish people to make up for it. And thereby avoid his own culpability. That was his vibe, too.

The world Vampires inhabited wasn't soft and sweet. It could land you in a torture suite in Theo's dungeon. It got you *conversations* told in blood and bone. It used to be something she wanted to change.

By that point, she left it up to them. They invited this bullshit, so that's what they got.

"I do hope we can find the time for a drink or a meal during the Joint Tribunal where we can catch up, Nadir to Rowan."

The Joint Tribunal they'd had to push out several weeks from the original date after Rowan had been ambushed the first time would be held in Prague. A meeting of the various parties to the Treaty, Hunter Corp., the Vampire Nation, and the Conclave of Witches met in different configurations once every quarter or so. Rowan had been made the liaison a few years back and every damned time someone had tried to kill her.

"I hope so too. We can sneak off and gossip." Sure, it was sarcastic, but it was true as well. She found herself building a real friendship with the ancient Vampire she'd grown up around. As an adult, Rowan could understand a lot more context for why Nadir acted the way she did.

Still, she had shit to do now that she had some answers.

"I will tell him you're well and will contact him sometime this week. If you don't, he'll come looking for you," Nadir said of Theo.

"Yes, all right. I'm recovered enough that I can try a video chat. I'll coordinate with staff about it, so he's got everything he needs set up in advance." Otherwise, if he got frustrated he might take it out on everyone in the vicinity.

"Good."

"I would like access to Nation files on *Sanguis Principatus* to aid in my investigation." She gave a quick and loose update on Elmer and that fuckheaded guard.

"*Jacques.* I am gratified you killed him true, but he remains a mess I must clean up. I can give you access to *some* of our information."

"That will aid my work," Rowan said, skirting around saying thank you outright.

They ended the call and Rowan moved on to the next item on her to-do list.

Soon enough they had turned onto the road where Konrad Aubert had set up shop there in town. And Rowan had no idea until that week.

She needed to get herself together and keep her eye on the ball.

Like she'd said it aloud, Marco replied, "Lots of magic and supernatural shit going on in Las Vegas," as he pulled into the parking structure next to their destination.

He had that right. A lot more than she'd assumed before the last few weeks. Shady magic shit *she* had to deal with. It would be really nice if people just kept their untidy business to relatively harmless stuff. Then she could ignore it.

But *nooooo*, they had to be taking out hits and attacking in broad daylight in front of cameras and dozens of tourists.

The introduction of wolf shifters into this whole situation only made it messier than it had already been. They'd been one of those out of sight out of mind deals.

Rowan knew they existed, but generally they stayed out of her line of sight. She'd had so much bullshit to handle coming from the Vampires she'd been focused elsewhere.

Marco gave her one last sigh that said he totally got how big a pain in her ass it all was, but that was the world they lived in, and they headed into the building.

"You know, I don't get you," Rowan said to Antonia Procella several minutes later.

"I don't know what you mean."

"I think you do, actually. But let's pretend you don't. Your family is in a lot of trouble."

The dark-haired witch across from Rowan widened her eyes and managed a sheen of emotion. The big-eyed thing was designed to tug at the heartstrings. But Rowan wasn't a fool. Under that mask, Antonia was the type of person who poisoned her husband slowly all while pretending to be respectable.

None of it mattered to Rowan anyway. Not respectability. Not rich people doing rich people shit. That's why she was sitting across from Antonia instead of Genevieve. Antonia couldn't use those familiar and easy weapons against Rowan.

"I book different acts to appear in our properties and on our ships. I don't know anything about whatever Hugo is up to. But if Hugo is involved, I fear it's because of my grandfather." Her voice—and Rowan really admired this—was modulated perfectly. A babyish octave but pitched to evoke a need to soothe and take care of rather than annoy. *Oh look at me, I'm too pretty and helpless to be a threat.*

At Rowan's side, Konrad remained on high alert. It

would take more than a cunning bitch wearing a helpless mask to fool either of them.

Rowan told her conversationally, "This sort of subtle play of agendas takes too long and you're not worth my energy or time."

"I'm sure if I could just speak with Genevieve, we might clear this up," Antonia tried as she looked around Rowan and Konrad as if Gen was going to pop out and say boo.

Instead of addressing that, Rowan said, "I've spoken with the Shanks. The shifter crime family that does your wetwork. Wetwork is such a strange term, isn't it? Gross. But what they do is gross, so I suppose it's apt."

Antonia's body froze up a moment, panic in her eyes before she got herself under control once more. The deepest, darkest, most feral part of Rowan perked up.

"Wetwork?"

Rowan took a few moments to look Antonia over. "I'm sure that's probably not what it says on the check memo line, though it doesn't say kill Rowan Summerwaite either. But you paid a wolf shifter pack with bespelled paper to kill me in public. And as you can see right now, that didn't work out. Patrick Shank wasn't that thrilled either. About me surviving certainly, but mainly, he knows he wasn't even *paid* for the way he'd just betrayed his pack. I bet you can only imagine how eager the remaining shifters you hired were to speak to us and answer our questions."

Antonia shook her head, obviously anxious. "I don't know what you're talking about. I didn't have anything to do with this."

"See, that's bullshit. Oh, you bat your eyes and pretend you're just the innocent one in the family. But I've spent my entire life around scumbags and liars of all sorts. I know one when I see one."

Antonia's intake of air nearly made Rowan giggle. Instead, Brigid surged and showed herself to the witch across the table. It was the Goddess who said, "You think you can evade me. You won't. Not forever." Satisfied with her point, She dropped away and Rowan asserted herself again smoothly, tipping her head toward Konrad. "The whole Conclave is looking at you. Your family is involved in some serious fuckery. *You are out of your league.* Whoever you've made this fool's bargain with won't protect you forever. You've made them angry with this public foolishness. Whatever you're doing can't be something you want noticed. And yet here the Procellas are taking out hits and showing their ass to the point you're all in the custody of the OG warlock here and me, the fucking bitch you've tried to kill multiple times. You're going to talk. We only have to play the numbers. One of you will spill. You know what a stupid, reckless dick your brother is. Your grandfather is a greedy, bloviating, self-important ass. Your dad, well, he's got a serial sexual predator as a son he and the rest of the family has enabled. And a liar for a daughter, so now that we've found him and brought your mother—she's a piece of work, eh—back to the US, one of you, chances are more than one, will tell us either by a brag or by mistake. You are all so predictable. And you're all incarcerated." She shrugged her good shoulder.

"*I didn't know where they were.*" Antonia's voice rose. She was losing her control. "I never even thought about that house my grandfather keeps. My mother has been in the middle of the ocean for months. My father was just taking a little break at the spa because of the stress."

Rowan chuckled. "You do realize you just admitted you knew where your father was, right? Anyway, back to my point. These people you're working with will know that one way or another we'll find our way back to them. Who knows what people like that would do to you when their shady business gets threatened? That's a rhetorical question. The answer is they blow up houses."

Antonia jerked back, unsure if Rowan was being serious or hyperbolic. "I don't know about any of this," she repeated, the tremble in her voice real this time.

Rowan just stared at her and then sighed. "I should write a textbook with people like you as examples." She might, actually. Hunters needed new, updated training materials all the time. Why not do a lesson of some sort?

"Let me go home. I have nothing to do with any of this, whatever you think. I book lounge singers and magicians to work on cruises. You say you have Hugo and my father, so why am I in custody?" She grasped at control. Rowan had to admire the way she hadn't given up entirely.

"As Ms. Summerwaite says, you're in way over your head," Konrad said in smooth tones. "You can't go home. It's a crime scene. Maybe you think you could go stay at your grandfather's three-bedroom place where Hugo hid. The search has already been conducted so you're clear to stay there."

The blush climbing up Antonia's neck was all Rowan needed to confirm the witch had known where Hugo was the whole time.

"Fortunately, before your house exploded, we were able to recover *so much* information from a cache underneath Lotte's bed and it's given us new insight on your situation. More by the moment, I imagine."

Rowan stood, done with this woman.

"Wait!" Antonia called out.

"Go on, then," Rowan allowed, but kept standing.

"Did the house really get bombed?"

"I hope for your staff's sake, there was some sort of burial benefits in their salaries. And that your mansion was insured, because all you've got left there are the outer walls and lots of ash. They don't know—*yet*—that you all weren't at home. But eventually they will. And when they do, they'll start searching for you to finish the job. Like I said, at least one of you will tell us what we need to know and the rest of you can fuck off. I don't have any desire to protect you from the logical outcome of your actions."

"I have a right to an attorney."

"I'm done with this useless twit," Rowan told Konrad and left the room before she gave in to her desire and hit Antonia with her cane.

Ignoring her protests, Konrad ordered the guards to take Antonia away and then he and Rowan went to the other room to speak to Genevieve and the others.

Chapter Fourteen

Die Mitte was a different animal during daylight hours. Humans who served as daytime help ran things while the Vampires were at rest. They were the most loyal of all staff to be trusted in such a way.

She'd been attacked—more than once—at *Die Mitte* by Vampires. Never a single time by a human.

That afternoon John Liu, Clive's human head of security, was at the front desk and when he saw her, he stood at attention.

"Stand down, John. I'm here to see the wolf shifters, please."

"I heard what happened with that asshole Eduard," John said, sneering as he said the Vampire's name. "We had to watch the footage. More than once, you know, so we could be up to date on what was going on here. That chop to his neck was beautiful."

Rowan chuckled. She hoped tales of just how soft Eduard had been had already spread like wildfire.

"I don't want to talk to him just yet. But if you have anything to share regarding Jacques and Elmer or these *Sanguis* jackwagons, I'd appreciate the information."

"I do have the report of the search that was done at Eduard's apartment and through his work computer.

Patience sent it to me with instructions to get it your way when you came to see the prisoners."

It was…not altogether awful that Patience had done something helpful. On purpose. Though certainly Clive would have ordered all relevant information be turned over to her, they didn't have to make it easy.

And… Rowan and Patience had a complicated history. Mainly it was that Patience wanted to bone Clive and instead, Clive had gone and hitched his wagon—and his bone—to Rowan. Nearly four years in though, the two had come to an understanding. Patience didn't have to like Rowan's place in Clive's life. But she respected it. Rowan had earned that respect by being the sort of partner he was to her. She'd give her life for Clive and had not only protected him, but Vampires, over and over. In return, Rowan had come to grudgingly respect the courage and honor Patience had shown. She'd fucked up a time or two and Rowan had been the one to call her out. But she'd taken the critique to heart and had adjusted her training and the way the security teams within Clive's domain were run.

This information was a peace offering.

She took the packet from him. Humans, she could thank. So she did.

He nodded. "I'm always at your service, Ms. Summerwaite. As for your questions? I wasn't up here while Jacques was Scion. I worked downstairs with the human guests mostly. My predecessor in this job had a different set of priorities and was very close to Jacques."

"I know." She'd killed that human right before she'd killed Jacques. He'd come at her, shooting. Rowan didn't much like having to kill human servants. But it had been her or him and she'd made sure it had been him.

That was all unsaid, but given John's expression, he knew that.

"Good riddance to them both," John said. "Even in those days I saw Elmer get into the elevators up to the private floors more than once. He was a sort of body man for Jacques. He's not a good Vampire. He likes hurting weaker beings. He used to visit the house, I'm told."

Jacques's ridiculous house had been an over-the-top nightmare. The things he'd done there were even worse than the terrible decor. The humans she'd been able to free that day were still fucked-up despite years of treatment.

"I'm real pissed at myself for not knowing Eduard was a spy. I knew Jacques had Made him. I knew he was part of that circle. But that's Vampires for you. When the new Scion came, some stayed. And thrived. But many of the inner circle of the prior one left this territory."

Rowan wanted to laugh. Those Vampires who'd been in Jacques's closest service had scattered like roaches. Not only because Rowan had killed their boss, but because Jacques's sins against the Vampire Nation had been made known to the First. A few of them were still alive. She'd lay odds Recht, one of Theo's Five, knew the location of every one of the remaining cronies who'd suffer a few centuries at the very least of being suspected and surveilled by the First.

Rowan blew out a breath. "Just because a Vampire is Made doesn't mean they automatically believe all the same things their Maker does. And a Scion being replaced is a rarity to be sure, but the Vampires who hold large territories in the Scions change up regularly. This is what they do. And sometimes, well, no, all the time, there are political spats high-ranking Nation Vampires have to deal with in their regions. Even former friends can become enemies. Again, this is what they do."

John nodded. "Understood. But I'll be twice as suspicious next time."

"Good. That's how it goes. Were you friends with Eduard?"

John tried valiantly not to sneer so Rowan accepted that answer.

"This *Sanguis Principatus* business? Now and again, it would pop up. In a whisper like they're something to be awed over. Also in derisive tones, if you catch my meaning."

Vampires did love power and position. Not as much as they loved gatekeeping so no one they thought was unworthy got much of those things.

"But I'm in the employ of the Scion. I run the daytime security operations of this building. I'm not a person who gets included in any sort of Vampire supremacist organization activities or gossip. I do, however, get sought out by those who have been told or invited and found whatever they were told to be so dangerous or repugnant they felt the Scion needed to hear it."

Rowan did like the idea of Vampires feeling protective of their Scion.

"If you remember anything else, or can think of someone who'd be willing to talk with me about it, let me know."

"Got it. So, I saw on social media there'd been an explosion at a house and when they said the address, I realized it was the Procella mansion," he told her.

She went with frank. "I was trying to figure out how to tell you without making a political mess because none of the Vampires in this territory will know this for another three hours. The First knows. I've spoken with the Voice."

John's brows rose quickly.

"It's fine. He's been assured I'm unhurt." Unhurt adjacent because her hip ached like a motherfucker. Still, if Theo got into a place where he decided he had to come to Las Vegas to see to her safety himself, the potential for things to get dire very quickly was high.

It would be hard to enough to deal with Clive when he awoke for the evening.

"And Mr. David?" In his gaze, Rowan saw he worried she might lose another person she was close to.

"Fortunately, everyone on our team is all accounted for and unharmed. There's no way for Hugo or Sergio to know this yet. I want to be the one to tell them. Which means if Felix shows up or anyone from outside—other than Ms. Aubert or her father—attempts contact, they need to remain sequestered. I'll tell them when they need to know, but that's not now." There'd be a time when it would get her somewhere.

"I'll make a note in the logbook here and when Patience comes on at eight, I'll tell her myself. Will you inform the Conclave guards, or shall I?"

"Konrad has been in contact with them so that's handled. I'm just going to pop in on Sergio and Hugo. Just to poke at them both. And then I want to chat with some wolves."

Twenty minutes later, she walked out. Rowan hadn't bothered with an interview room for either Procella. She wanted the sameness to drag on them. Wanted them to sit in the reality that they had no power whatsoever in the situation. It was working. Sergio's argumentativeness had softened past sullen and into hopeless. Soon enough he'd break down. Then she'd pounce.

"I'll come back tonight," she told John.

At the doorway to the interview room Patrick Shank waited in, something caught Rowan's eye, a flash of light. She went to her haunches to examine it closer.

"What is it?" John asked.

"It's," she picked it up with a pair of tweezers from her tool pack, "a dick. A metallic phallus. Ha!" She stood and John leaned closer with a laugh.

"I know what that is. One of our people is getting married and is having bachelor party. It's penis confetti. They were put in the envelopes for all the invitations. I spilled some when I opened it too."

"When did these invitations show up?"

"Today. About two hours ago when he got to work. Shift change. You know."

Rowan nodded.

"You want to see the feed for the time between when he got to this floor and now? It shouldn't take too long."

Clive had made an excellent choice in this human. Efficient. He anticipated what she'd need and provided it. All while controlling what data was shared with an outsider. Even an outsider married to their Scion.

At his station, she sat at his side as John scanned the surveillance in that time frame and then sat back. "Here. The human male in the center of this group of three walking down this hallway? That's Matthew. The guy who's getting married."

They watched as the two others with Matthew opened their envelopes and one of them spilled tiny glittery wieners they all tried to pick up.

"Looks to me like how it got there was innocent enough," she said. She wanted to soothe John's worry.

But it was absolutely *no* coincidence that she found it right outside the interview room where Patrick waited.

Over the last weeks she'd been having prophetic dreams and waking fugue states. Various symbols echoed through them that had led to the Procellas over and over. Storms at sea. High waves. Waves battering shorelines. Empty spaces like malls and schools. And confetti. She'd gone back and forth on the meaning and symbolism of confetti, but those sparkly little dicks had been a metaphysical arrow pointing at the wolves.

Just to be totally certain, she had a brief chat with Matthew and a few others. Everything they said backed up what she thought had happened. She made a mental note to have a present sent to the wedding.

And then she went to talk to Patrick Shank.

He didn't complain he'd been kept waiting. Rowan was fairly certain he'd been in jail or prison at some point because he seemed very at ease with the truncated freedom of incarceration. So she commented on it.

"Doing time is doing time." He shrugged, answering her question with a nonanswer that worked just the same.

"I imagine doing time here instead of county is preferable. Especially when you don't have to pretend you're not a being that can shift into an animal form."

He shrugged again.

"I just stopped by to see if you were feeling chatty about the Procellas. They're here too, by the way."

His blank mask faded, replaced by...satisfaction. Well. She couldn't blame him really. They'd fucked him and his crew over, and he'd fucked his own family over because of it.

"What do you want to know?"

"Has the Shank family worked for the Procellas before?"

"Yes. For years now. My dad used to do jobs for him before we were born. Mainly body work. Rough someone up. Burn their shit to the ground. Extortion. That sort of deal. The grandson? The one who wanted to move the hit on you up?"

"Hugo."

Patrick nodded. "Yeah, that little fucker. He hired us to find some women a time or two. One had run to London. The other to Manhattan. Both had high security protection."

Rowan sat, seething. It hadn't been enough that Hugo had tormented those women, he'd continued to do so after they'd reached an agreement with the family that he would stop.

"Did the family have to pay for that? I mean, I'm certain you're aware the Procellas were ordered to cough up a lot of money to pay those women off because of Hugo."

Patrick laughed and Rowan was glad. It meant she didn't have to feel bad for whatever was coming this shifter's way when she was finished with him. She curled her lip.

"We informed the old man about it before we made a move. We didn't do anything without his say-so. He told us not to supply the exact locations to Hugo, but that we could give him surveillance photographs of the women."

Each new thing she learned about Hugo made her

hate him more. Keeping him off the streets would make a lot of people safer.

"What else have you done for them?"

"I'm not doing this for free," Patrick countered.

That made her laugh so hard tears came to her eyes before she managed to say, "I'm not paying you shit. You don't have the power to make demands like that. We both know I don't need you to handle this. There are other shifters in these cells." She wiped her eyes and sobered a bit. "Your information will help bury the witches who fucked you over, paid you in magic paper, and exposed your failings to your father and uncle, who, I'm given to understand, are the ones who control everything within the Shank pack. Maybe they'll even let you come home again if you do this right."

They totally wouldn't, but she didn't care.

An hour later, her head hurt so severely she texted David, asking him to come to *Die Mitte* to drive her home. She'd hit her limit, and it wasn't such a surprise. She'd been gravely injured less than a week before. All the goddesses, Scion blood, and excellent medical care in the world wasn't going to heal her instantly. It was happening but at an accelerated rate. That was why it seemed like all she did was eat and sleep.

"*Deesse*," he murmured as he caught sight of her. "Are you certain we shouldn't be taking you to see Dr. Jenkins? Or upstairs to the Scion's apartments? You can rest there until you're ready to move elsewhere."

"I'm fine. Dr. Jenkins told me headaches might happen as I heal. If I'm not better when I wake up from a nap, I'll call her. I promise."

She pretended not to see the look David and John

shared. She held that pretense in place even as her vision had begun to gray at the edges. It wasn't just a headache. That heavy blanket of unconsciousness that frequently came with her prophecy dreams had begun to descend.

Rowan needed to get home. Be safe. Before the dream settled in.

"I just want to rest," she told David. "Then I'll tell you about this afternoon with Patrick Shank."

He drove quickly home and once there, Elisabeth clucked and Betchamp stepped to Rowan's other side and helped David get her to her bed, complete with pulling her boots off and placing a lightweight blanket over her body.

The last thing she remembered was the familiar thump on the mattress followed by the warm weight of Star, who'd jumped on the bed and laid herself over Rowan's legs.

Chapter Fifteen

When Clive woke, he reached for their bond. Instantly and automatically. Pleased, he found her nearby. Healthy.

He pulled on casual clothing and headed to her. Wanting to establish that sort of contact as well. Needing to see for himself she was whole.

He found her in the sitting room, having a whispered—annoyed on her part—conversation with David.

"Good evening. Look at my beautiful wife all in one piece. I confess my delight." He risked getting close enough for a quick kiss and then straightened, pulling back. "Less delightful though not less usual, tell me why you smell of death."

"Okay. So maybe sit down first because it's been a whole ass day, let me tell you."

He frowned but settled, pleased to see the teapot waiting there.

"You know we were going to do another search of the Procella mansion today because I had a feeling Lotte would slip up."

David gave her a stern glare and then pointedly looked toward the teapot and two cups of tea. She rolled her eyes, but leaned forward to hand Clive one and then took one for herself before sitting back against the pillows.

She was lovely and vibrant there next to him, which allowed him to relax enough to take her hand, kissing her knuckles over the ring she wore that marked her as his.

"I was right."

"Obviously," he said.

"Right? Anyway, we found a cache. Had a few of her burner phones in it. One she'd been using to contact Alfonso, Antonia, and Hugo. We got that info to Konrad immediately and he got to work locating Alfonso, that dick."

David said, "Vanessa's already running through the thumb drives and data cards we found. Naturally she created a filter like it was easy. It's working now that we've broken through the firewalls."

"Excellent." Rowan turned back to Clive. "Then there was an…explosion I suppose is the best way to describe it. As you can see, I'm totally fine," she said in a rush and sent ice-cold dread through him.

Clive took a bracing breath and reminded himself that yes, indeed, she was totally fine. He placed a hand on her thigh, needing the contact. "Go on."

She explained Genevieve's theory regarding the type of working it took to set off the type of magical explosion of fire that had destroyed the interior of the mansion. She then quickly added that a combo of goddess, witch, and Dust Devil magics had kept them—and their evidence—safe. "The death part you smell even though I showered? That was Lotte. And a few Procella guards who'd been there. I broke someone's arm, but I guess that's moot now that he's dead and all."

She sat back with a satisfied smile, and he couldn't have loved her more.

"You'll be less pleased to hear the news had hit the Keep by the time I'd gotten back to my office. Blame the spies planted around the city who ran off to tattle to Theo immediately."

His spies should have waited to report to him or one of his Vampires once the sun had gone down. They either disregarded his instructions, or they were Nation spies put in place by the First to watch Rowan and Clive's business at the same time. He had spies in the courts of other Scions and in other major cities so it wasn't as if he could be outraged.

"All this before sunset? My, you are a busy bee when I'm at rest." He allowed himself a quick brush of his fingertips along her throat.

Her attempt at annoyance was half-hearted at best. "I get into trouble sometimes. Usually because someone else is being a bag of concrete." She paused. "Though I suppose when you add water it becomes useful. So maybe more like unsalted, ice-cold fast-food fries at the bottom of the bag."

He gave her a look and she snickered.

Clive looked over to David, who watched her, but not in a way that said he was overly worried. "How did he take the news of the explosion?" The First was already close to jumping on a plane and showing up to see for himself that Rowan was well.

A Vampire so ancient was best kept at home. Or in areas that were sparsely populated. They lost their hold on the present sometimes and got caught up in the past. It left them prone to striking out. The First of their kind had been on very thin ice for long months. His emotional state and worry over Rowan had led to a great deal of bloodshed. Clive didn't need the complication of the First in his territory and he truly didn't want Rowan under any more stress, which her father would bring.

"I had Nadir tell him I'm fine. I have to do a video call with him now. Something else to make the Procellas pay for. Oh! But in exchange, she's allowed for some access to Nation data on these *Sanguis* fuckos."

Nadir most likely assumed Rowan would steal it if it wasn't offered. And the fact was, Rowan and Hunter Corp. were doing them a favor by investigating *SP*. Especially as they'd just been exposed in his territory.

"And? I'm certain there's more."

She shot him a dark look. "There's so much more. Let me take this chronologically. So, we did a search out in Spring Valley. Then we headed to the mansion and that was exploded. Then I went to the motherhouse, changed clothes, and headed to *Die Mitte* to have a quick check-in with Hugo and Sergio." Rowan laughed at that. "I'm letting them stew some more. On my way out of Sergio's chat, I let him know I'd been to his house in the burbs. Then I asked him if he was seeing a doctor because I'd found blue pills and had been told Genetic witches don't usually suffer with ED issues. His eyes bulged out and he started denying it. I said maybe Hugo had left them there since he'd been hiding out. And then of course I realized that was probably true. Genevieve said it was possible the magics Hugo had used habitually to try to victimize women could kill his boner. Then I swanned into Hugo's cell and asked him if his dick was able to get hard again since they'd removed all those magics from him. He started yelling and burst into tears. It was, quite honestly, amazing.

So I left him and his soft pecker behind and headed on down the hall to have a chat with Patrick Shank. Before I opened the door, I stepped on something slippery between my boot and the tile. Confetti."

"Just on the ground on a secure floor of the court of the North American Scion of the Vampire Nation?" He said it with so much hauteur she knew he'd been as surprised by that as she'd been.

She explained she'd found the source and that she felt it was innocent enough. "Then I went into the cell to have a talk with Patrick and he's feeling friendlier today. Said they'd been doing work with the Procellas, including Antonia and Alfonso, for two decades and before that, a different shifter pack did their dirty work. Up until recently most of it was about roughing people up, not killing. They've popped the odd enemy here and there for Sergio, but until me, they'd never been asked to take risks like that."

"This is why Vampires rarely hire them. Loose lips."

Rowan rolled her eyes at him. "Whatever. You have your own hit squads, I guess. But anyway. He's understandably angry and embarrassed because his actions have impacted the pack. I've put in a few calls to the leader of the Shank family. I want to talk to them about all this."

"I imagine they've all gone ignored."

"Yep. If I wasn't recovering, I'd hop on a plane and show up on their doorstep."

"Ah. But you *are* recovering."

She growled. "I started feeling achy and sick to my stomach in the middle of my interview. My head started hurting so bad I called David to bring me home so I could nap."

Now it was Clive who growled, leaning in closer to her.

"I'm much better now. I slept for an hour and a half. And I had dreams."

"*Dreams* or dreams?"

"The prophecy ones. Mainly the same symbolism as before. But there was something new. A bird and a sprig of greenery. I had to do a quick image search because I wasn't sure if it was a nightingale or a sparrow. It was a sparrow. I think the plant was holly, but I can't say for certain. I don't know what's up yet. It's not connected to something in a way that's obvious to me yet. But I'm trying to trust that I will when it's time."

"This debilitated you? In the middle of your workday? I do not much care for that," Clive said.

Rowan understood his fear. Accepted it. She worried for the people she loved—including him—too. But she wanted to make him understand she saw all this as a positive.

"The thing is, I knew one was coming on. And I had the time to get David over to *Die Mitte* and drive me home safely. Which he did. Then Star protected me. I'm good. Learning how to deal with this new aspect of my gifts is a big step. I could have gone to your private apartment at *Die Mitte* too if I'd needed that. The point is, I had options, and it *didn't* hit until I was safe. Each time one of these things happens, a dream or a knowing, I learn from it. This is a good thing. I promise."

He adjusted cuffs he didn't even have and yet, he made it work. She sent him the *knock it off there are people around* expression, and he ignored it because he was contrary like that.

"I don't like it. It puts you at risk. And yet I know it's

as much a part of you as eating cookies while in bed. I admire it. Not the cookies-in-bed part. But the rest. It makes you stronger. Better. It's rather attractive, as you well know."

She sent him a look under her lashes and David cleared his throat. "Let's all have dinner, then. Before you head back to the office instead of working from here."

She pointed at David. "You are such a snitch."

"I'm not tattling," David said, spine rigid. "I'm merely doing my job. You've been working since nine this morning and it's already nine in the evening. Twelve-hour workdays are tough even when you aren't convalescing from an ambush and a mage firebomb."

"She can work here," Clive said to David. Like they were planning a playdate for a baby.

"*She* is right the hell here and getting cranky enough to start slapping the shit out of assholes who talk around her."

"Will you please have dinner with me before you head out again?" Clive allowed and though she wanted to kick him in the taint, she also knew he was trying to sound like he was asking.

"It might be nice to remember it's not just you, alone, against the world all in your head. We are here to help. We care for you, and it hurts us too when you don't put yourself first in these types of situations," David said.

All these friends and found family meant she had to take their feelings into account, and she was used to doing whatever needed to be done. Things were easier before. But. A lot lonelier.

"I appreciate being cared for and looked after. I'm told we're having fish stew with fresh bread," she said.

Rowan wasn't going to stop being who she was simply because people she cared about wanted her to. It wasn't who she was. And both the men currently staring at her needed to understand that. She could meet them part-way sometimes. And she did by agreeing to eat dinner at the table with David across from her and Clive at her left. Which she knew he did to let her eat more freely with her dominant hand. And it was her sword hand. A fact he always respected.

"This really hits the spot. Knowing I can come home to something soul nourishing is invaluable," Rowan told Elisabeth.

Elisabeth gave a deep, clearly pleased bow, blushing. "I'm so very pleased to hear that. Betchamp and I know how hard you three work, so any time we're able to lighten that load, even with a good meal, is what we aim for."

"You clearly do. Our household is very well kept, as are its occupants," Rowan told her.

At her side, Clive practically throbbed with pride. As his wife she had a responsibility to everyone under his protection. She was a hard-ass to most everyone. But never to those who served her. And rarely ever to those who served at all.

One of myriad reasons he adored her. The unexpected kindness she showed had ceased to surprise him, but it always made him happy. And when she showed it to those in their household? It stoked some fire in the heart of the man whose mate did the things to make their lives better and stronger. Primal.

Conversation rose and fell as Clive surreptitiously monitored her food intake. If she felt like he was doing too much, she'd push back. Sometimes out of habit. Their little interplay was always delightful. But he had no desire to poke at her for amusement just then.

He needed to connect with his people. And if one of them didn't report this explosion immediately, he'd be quite vexed.

The house phone rang, and Elisabeth moved to answer before she returned. "Alice is here," she told them.

Of course Alice would be there to deliver the news personally. He'd lay odds she wanted to assure herself Rowan was in one piece as well.

"She's not one for blood wine, but I'm absolutely certain a cup of tea would be appreciated," Rowan said quietly to Elisabeth, who nodded and bustled off to procure another cup and saucer.

Clive wanted to cosset and pet his wife. He was so very delighted with her right at that moment. Thinking of Clive's people as her own. The way Rowan avoided direct eye contact even though their bond thrummed with attraction and desire said she knew exactly what was on his mind. As that petting would definitely be skin to skin.

He stood, pausing to bend and brush a kiss against Rowan's temple on his way.

Alice Lovecraft had been his assistant for a century. She was efficient. She saw complexity in ways most others didn't. She was powerful and clever and had included Rowan in the people she protected. Which Clive approved of mightily. And, he'd learned more than once, Alice was a champion at hand-to-hand combat.

He'd asked her to come to the United States with him, to serve him as assistant to the Scion. He'd been honest. He knew she could have had her pick of other assignments, even leading her own line if she chose to. But she'd been part of the Stewart line the entirety of her life, as had her parents and two other siblings. The position serving him was a huge honor and she took it as such.

He hadn't regretted bringing her along. Not a single time.

As she entered the house, her arms full, Clive and Betchamp moved to take some of her burden.

"The files are yours, Clive," she said. "The green bags are for Elisabeth. My housekeeper has a very large garden. She doesn't know I'm not human, so she constantly leaves me food. I figured it'd get used here more than at my place."

Betchamp bowed slightly. "She will indeed be most grateful," he said and then left Clive and Alice alone in the front part of the house.

"I assume you already know about the explosion?" she asked quickly. "I knew you wouldn't be at the office yet, so I wanted to come here to speak in person."

Clive nodded, appreciating her discretion. "She went back to work right after, I'm told." A fact he did not like, but certainly wasn't going to argue with Rowan over. That there'd been another prophecy dream, well, he *did* like that. Because these gifts from her goddess made her stronger.

Stronger meant her chances of winning rose.

"She's already been in contact with Nadir, so the First knows she's well. There will be a video call at some point so that he can see for himself."

Alice let out a breath. "Good. I'm sure that will be useful for both Rowan and her father."

They walked back to the kitchen where dinner had

been set up in the eating nook. Alice gave Rowan a discreet look, but it was done quickly.

Another quality that made Alice invaluable was her rapport with Rowan. A genuine sense of friendship and fraternity had developed between them. It was one more set of eyes watching Rowan's back. And, without a doubt, when the mate of the Scion showed kindness and care toward any of those within the territory, the news traveled. She'd already made fans of many of his staff, especially the notoriously temperamental ones like his chef. It was a good reminder to him that being a leader meant many things, including seeing to the emotional well-being of those they led.

Soon enough tea had been poured and another bowl of soup had been ladled up for Rowan, so Clive took his seat at her side once again.

"Just so you both know, I've been tasked to lead a workgroup on *Sanguis Principatus*," Rowan said.

Vanessa had already procured a list of the Vampires—the ones still living—who'd been part of Jacques's circle. They hadn't needed to steal anything as Hunter Corp. had been watching them anyway because of that connection. There were a few left in Las Vegas. She'd look at them. Eventually, she'd find the links she needed.

As for what would result? It wasn't against the Treaty to hate humans. If *SP* was indeed active again, all they could really do was watch. When they stepped over the line like Elmer had, they'd be punished.

Rowan would happily use Elmer and Eduard as object lessons about those lines and what her response was when they were crossed. In the end, her best hope was to strangle them of opportunities to do anything truly harmful.

"They're going to hate Elmer and Eduard for calling attention to them." She laughed pretty hard at that. As long as Elmer wasn't able to harm humans anymore, it would at least be a victory.

Clive looked over to Alice. "I assume there's an update in here on the searches that have been done on Eduard?"

She nodded.

"Please go on. You may be frank," he said to Alice, giving her permission to tell Rowan Vampire business.

"Patience has already been hard at work on taking every Vampire who'd ever said more than two words to Eduard into custody for questioning. Searches of Eduard's electronics, his workspace, and the condo he lived in have yielded quite a bit of data, which was worked on during daylight. We have Elmer's address. Not what he put on his official registration paperwork. But his nest. I only got this information on my way over here. Haddon told us. No one has entered. It's being monitored. I thought you might want to handle that yourself," Alice said.

An hour later, they stood in the front hall of Elmer Marsc's nest. The place a Vampire lived and rested during the day with others of their line or family. Their official homes were quite often a ruse because no one wanted anyone to have the information regarding where they were most vulnerable.

The condo was in a newer building near the Strip. It contained daylight locks on all bedroom doors. Three of the bedrooms had been used within the last week, Clive said after doing his Vampire scent thing. Haddon and Elmer shared the master suite. The bedrooms to either side were connected Jack-and-Jill style through bathrooms.

"I guess Elmer liked keeping his Made very close to his bed." Not exactly unusual. Vampires had looser perspectives on sex and the size of their relationships than most humans did.

"That room held a Vampire. Barely made. Less than five years I'd say. And that one? A human. I know what Stephen Baker smells of, he has not been here in this place for months, given the very faint scent. Not in the bedrooms. In the kitchen."

Maybe one he was using to feed on? Someone he was preparing to Make to join his line? A one-night stand? Did Stephen come over to grab one of the humans he helped Elmer round up to take them back to his place?

"We can ask Haddon about some of this. And Eduard, I'd say," Alice told them. "I rewatched his interrogation with you, Clive, and it seemed to me Eduard would gleefully murder a human for the cause, but he does *not* like Making underaged humans. His morals might be terrible, but on this, he seems to be firmly repulsed by that aspect of Elmer's behavior."

Clive cocked his head a moment. "I do recall him claiming not to know about any of that. He said he knew Elmer from *SP* but had nothing to do with any sort of Making young humans."

"Jacques, who he seems to worship, routinely kidnapped and drained young female humans. How's that any different?" Rowan demanded.

"Putting it plain," Alice said, "it's one thing to use humans up and throw out the carcasses and quite another to bestow a Making on them. These types of Vampires tend to see humans as resources but not good enough to be Vampires. Elmer's behavior is predatory in ways that serve his own twisted desires."

"Okay. Okay. I can totally see that distinction. Gross as it is," Rowan said.

They headed toward a home office where a file of photos Rowan never wanted to think about again brought on a wave of exhaustion.

On the way back to *Die Mitte*, Rowan said, "You're going to be far more effective at discussing this with Elmer and Eduard. And I don't want to scare Haddon any further, so I'll let you do that too."

Clive gave her a suspicious look. Alice and David were in the back seat, both with phones pressed to their ears, ordering other people around for Rowan's benefit.

He asked quietly, "Why are you being so easy?"

"I can go in and fuck them all up enough to finally spill but frankly, I don't want to beat anyone else up tonight. I'm tired. I have a meeting with Genevieve at ten in the morning and since it's just us two, I can admit I need the rest."

He turned the car toward home when the next ability to reverse their direction came. "Let me take you home."

Across the city, Genevieve and Darius stood on top of a little hillock near the remains of the Procella mansion. "This was where they set the spell in motion," she said.

The police and bomb squad had cleared off, but the end of a bit of yellow caution tape flapped in the breeze. From their vantage point they could see the collapsed roof. With her othersight, Genevieve could detect the magics that had ignited the first of the cascade of spells that led to the mage bomb.

"I see three different magical signatures," Darius said quietly.

"Yes, as do I. Some of it seems familiar but I can't say off the top of my head who it could be. That I can rectify with a quick pass through some of our logs. However, I know who it isn't. So those names can be removed from the list of witches powerful enough for a working of this magnitude and complication."

"This is why there are no high points that can see into our village. If they lived a lifestyle that got this sort of response, they most definitely should have worked far harder on their security."

The Dust Devils were organized into a group they called a Trick. And when they settled in a place, they tended to build or buy up/rent places in the same area and create a large space between themselves and the outside world. Those little communities were called villages.

Genevieve lived smack dab in the middle of one and she could absolutely attest to feeling totally safe there.

"They've lived here for years without any reports of problems like this. We checked law enforcement records. State, county, and city. Nothing. Nothing at the Conclave other than the financial crimes and stalking. What on earth did the Procellas do to draw *this* type of attention?" Genevieve shook her head.

"Come on, then," Darius told her twenty minutes later, after they'd viewed the property from a few other vantage points. "Let's go home. I have some scented bath salts I can't wait to smell on your skin."

Chapter Sixteen

Genevieve turned in her bed and rolled toward Darius. With her eyes still closed, she put her head on his chest as he wrapped an arm around her to hold her in place. The delightful warmth of it seemed to blanket her.

"Are we waking up?" he asked, sleep in his voice.

"We should." She hadn't opened her eyes yet, but the noises from the house began to make themselves known. Lorraine was out there making breakfast.

He made a sound that could have been *a yes let's wake up* or a *huh, let's wait for Lorraine to yell our names* before squeezing her to him. "I think we might find a way to spend some time before we begin our day."

She finally opened her eyes and looked up into his face. By the old gods, he was so beautiful. That amber ring around his pupils seemed to burn with the same intensity he gave off.

He easily brought her body upward so he could kiss her awake.

Genevieve had lived a very long time, and this man made her forget everything before. Made her forget what it was to awake to an empty bed. Which was its own sort of magic.

His taste was made for her. The weight of him as he

rolled them over and settled between her thighs seemed not perfect, but absolutely right. Part of the immensity of how he made her feel terrified her. But not enough to overcome her pleasure at his presence and all the delights he'd brought to her life.

There was no sound other than soft sighs, the slide of skin on skin, and the occasional groan or growl because when Darius worked his way inside her body, she writhed, shifting her knees up, taking him deeper.

Those long minutes with him, skin to skin, open hearts, had a way of trickling into her darkest parts and soothing. Erasing wariness and grief. Making new memories.

She'd known love before. But her connection to this being was a recipe. They'd created something she'd never known to expect, much less desire.

He was her partner. Her protector too. But not in a way that lessened her power. No, the exact opposite. He respected and admired her strength and that was delightful and also foundational to what they had.

He kissed a lazy trail down her neck, changing his angle enough to brush the tips of his fingers over her clit in time with his thrusts, driving her out of her mind with need as he built her climax and shoved her hard into it.

Her ears were still roaring when he pressed deep and came as well.

"I really must confess sleepovers at your house are far more fun than sleeping alone in mine." He smiled before kissing her and sending her wits flying the way he always did.

There was something to be said for over four thousand years of experience at sex. He learned her each time he touched her. Used what he found to drive her to new heights the next time they found themselves alone together.

In the kitchen, Lorraine called out that it was time to awaken and take a meal.

"You know she doesn't do this when you aren't here, don't you?" she told him as she rolled from bed to get dressed.

"She doesn't?" He came up behind her, burying his face in her hair and breathing deep. "Why?"

"She likes you and wants to see you before you shimmer away." She made a motion with her hand and then laughed as he spun her in his embrace. "She's going to come knock on the door very loudly in about two minutes," Genevieve warned him.

"I'd face her wrath for just one more kiss," he murmured in the French of her youth, before delivering a sweet brush of her lips with his.

She was still wearing a silly smile when she entered the kitchen right as Madame had been turning toward the hall where her bedroom lay.

"Good morning. He'll be out shortly," Genevieve told her. Lorraine wasn't a house manager or an assistant. She ran Genevieve's life in a way that kept her safe and heading in the direction she needed to go. She was part mother figure, part vice president of Genevieve's life. Her daughter, Samaya, ran Genevieve's office at the Conclave. Bastien, her son, was a green witch of some talent. He worked for the Conclave and ran their very comprehensive gardens for every type of spellwork imaginable. He'd also created the strain of weed she preferred.

Lorraine's mother and her grandfather before that had worked for the Auberts. There was a lovely symmetry in continuing that, though Genevieve thought she'd most certainly gotten the better end of the deal with the family, considering all they brought to her life.

Still, Lorraine was an opinionated witch with a very healthy sense of self-respect, and it didn't matter so much that Genevieve was technically her boss. To Madame, Genevieve was her charge and she needed to let Lorraine do her job.

Everyone seemed happiest that way. The house they lived in had bedroom suites to either side of a large living space, so each witch had their privacy. And there was an extra bedroom on Lorraine's end where Bas or Samaya would stay over.

The Devils who lived in the houses surrounding theirs had taken to them both. Genevieve they'd given their reverence but also a sort of sweet affection. Madame was feared. They yearned for her attention, which she seemed to know how to give in whatever way it would be received best. It was part of her magic, Genevieve believed.

"Samaya hand couriered some files for you. She just ran to the car to grab something. Sit."

Fresh juice and pastries already waited at the table but soon enough there was coffee and a spinach omelet.

Smiling, Darius followed the trail of her magic. She threw it off like leaves on the breeze and there were times it was a struggle to free himself from the fascination she filled him with. He didn't try very hard anyway.

Samaya was speaking to Genevieve at the table, and Madame gave him an imperious cheek he bent to kiss before she shooed him to sit and eat.

"We've locked down all information regarding the

Procellas. Just in general, controlling what information gets out when we don't know who to trust or even who is working with who is a smart move. Though the explosion isn't a secret by now to the magical world, we've been able to continue to keep it from all the Procellas except Antonia. Alfonso is in custody now at the Conclave Senate building. He claims he was worried for his son and had gone out looking for him. Says he didn't want to lead anyone back to Hugo if he did reach out to his father for help."

Genevieve's sound of disapproval, along with that shrug of hers, told Darius she didn't believe that for a moment.

"I have a meeting with Rowan in an hour. I'll update her. You can work from an office at the motherhouse today if you like," she told Samaya before turning back to Darius. "I've got things to tell her."

"There are links to three very prominent Conclave families on the phones we took from the Procella mansion. And on the phones we took from them when we took them into custody originally. Multiple incoming and outgoing calls over the last year and a half or so. Samaya was able to pull the phone records for the business numbers of these families and there are calls to those numbers too," Genevieve told Rowan.

"What do these other families do?"

Samaya answered, looking at the page before her. "The Clares run rail freight across the lower part of the country and a little into Mexico. The Sansburys run a variety of businesses. A few travel brokerages nationwide. There's a car service with various locations served. Formal events. Airport trips for businesspeople. There's one in wine country that takes people from their hotels or rentals to a bunch of wineries. The Salazars own several resorts in North America from beach all-inclusives to a few mountain lodges. Some have gambling, but only about a quarter."

Rowan said, "Are they sketchy? Whatever, don't look concerned, I don't care about ninety-five percent of whatever illegal fuckery they get up to. But are they salt of the earth never would do a bad thing types or are they on the Procella side of the spectrum?"

Genevieve thought a moment before saying, "All three of them other than the Procellas are old European lines. There are aristocratic titles held by some of them to this day. Entitled. Even during the various crusades and trials. They hid in plain sight then. Remaining in Europe while the fervor ravaged here. Their money is generations old. The Procellas are a younger line, yes? They've always been here in North America. They're a different type of witch."

"Crass? Is that the word? Though I will say despite Lotte being dead and all, the suits she wore to work were pretty fantastic for a guy with as little taste as Sergio."

"That comes from Bess, I believe," Genevieve said. "Samaya brought all the items taken from Bess in Auckland, so you can go through them if you like."

"Where do these Clares and Sansburys and Salazars live, then?" Rowan asked this instead of demanding to know why Genevieve was being so accommodating.

"Two of the three live in Southern California," Genevieve admitted. "The Salazars live in Miami."

"They all need to be questioned about this business. Obviously."

"Agreed. I planned to handle that myself. Zara is

on the way to Florida now, to deal with the Salazars. I assume you might want a Hunter to meet her there?"

"I'll get in contact with someone in Miami right away. Get them Zara's number so they can connect." David left the room for a few minutes to handle it.

"You cannot come along," Genevieve said. "You're still recovering."

"I have a physician to dispense medical advice," Rowan shot back.

"Would you *like* to accompany me to this meeting with the Clares and the Sansburys?" Genevieve asked, frustration in her tone.

It was on the tip of her tongue to say yes. Because the point was, she was part of this investigation. But looking at Genevieve, Rowan felt slightly bad about making her friend feel as if she wasn't being trusted.

Then she remembered something Carl had said. Carl, her own personal sage. Only hers always showed up out of the blue and nearly always at the wheel of some sort of public conveyance. He loved taxicabs but one time he'd picked her up in a water taxi. He always had whatever advice hidden in what were usually stories about animals or the land. He was kookoopants and she loved him even though he never gave her plainspoken, clear advice or warnings.

He'd told her that at some point it would be on the tip of her tongue to give an answer, but she'd argue with herself. He'd urged her to go with her original answer. Rowan wasn't sure if this was that situation or even if that situation had already passed. Which was part of her generalized impatience with sages and the way they went about their business. But in the end,

Rowan decided that since she'd thought it, it was the right moment.

"I would very much appreciate the opportunity to go with you to this meeting today."

"I must take a plane to get there in time," Genevieve said, wary.

"It's Los Angeles. I can get us a private plane to Burbank, and we can be there in an hour once we take off."

Genevieve's left eyebrow rose as she waited.

Rowan growled. "Fine. I'll be sure Clive knows." She didn't say she'd already checked in with Dr. Jenkins to see if it would be safe to fly to Seattle—should the need arise—and was given the green light for any trip under three hours. To Southern California it was even quicker.

Genevieve lost her wariness. "We'll go after dark because you have to wait until after sunset to tell him anyway. I'll prepare for both of you because he's not going to allow you to do this without him. For now, I've work to do so I'll leave you to yours."

Rowan wanted to stomp her foot or break something from frustration because her friend was right. Clive was most assuredly not going to wave goodbye and tell her to text when she got there.

"He has his own job to do," she muttered as she pulled her phone out and sent a note to David to deal with getting a jet and a pilot for them all to fly into Burbank that evening. She was a grown-up with a goddess inside her! She didn't need permission.

But at sunset, after a very busy day, Rowan finally called Clive to deal with it.

"Hello, darling Hunter," he purred, and it sent a wave of pleasure racing over her skin. She barely withheld a giggle in response.

So, she snickered. "Stop that. Genevieve is heading to Southern California to interview a few witches."

Before she could say anything else, he interrupted. "No. She can give you an update when she returns."

"I was not actually *asking* for your input. I was keeping you updated on my activities. I stopped to see Dr. Jenkins this morning on my way in. I did ask her about air travel." He didn't need to know she wanted to see if a flight to Seattle to go bug some wolves was possible. "She okayed anything under three hours. Burbank is just over an hour. The people we're going to speak to live within twenty minutes' drive from there. I'll be back far before sunrise."

"In that case, I'll meet you at the airfield. Don't argue, I know you're going to use a Nation jet and you need my pilot. I'm coming along. I can get work done while you're off interviewing people. I'll bring food."

Then he disconnected, leaving her gaping, and pretending not to be impressed by the way he'd just invited himself along.

Darius was at the wheel because like Clive, he'd simply bullied his way onto the plane. Clive and Darius both seemed to be in accord, and undoubtedly having a Dust Devil along with them would only make them all safer.

So, Genevieve had taken it all with grace. But between the airport and their first stop, she'd put on her armor and mask. When she stepped from the vehicle, she would be Genevieve Aubert, Senator of the Conclave of Witches. A power so massive, so old and deep, none could oppose her and remain standing.

"I'm just going to say it outright, is this your ex's house or his parents' or what?" Rowan said.

That made Genevieve laugh and loosened the tension in her chest. "Tristan—the fool I divorced a very long time ago—he's not particularly Talented. Especially given his line and age. His parents still live in England. Thank the stars. We are to meet with Joseph Sansbury, the uncle. He's the designated emissary in the United States and to the Conclave. He *is* powerful."

Rowan thought for a moment. "He's the second son, right?"

Genevieve nodded.

"They're either murderously ambitious or lazy to a fault. I rarely meet any other type in our universe," Rowan mumbled.

Clive choked out a laugh.

"He's the former," Genevieve confirmed.

"Won't this be fun?" Rowan said. And meant.

There was a gate around the tony neighborhood, but as they approached, it swung open, admitting them.

"I imagine we handled this in advance?" Rowan asked.

"Why give notice someone's about to knock on the door?" Darius asked with a flick of his wrist that indicated Devil magic had opened the way.

"Truth. Being surprised is a first strike. I'll take your lead," Rowan said as the energy and power around her began to rise but was quickly extinguished when Genevieve's friend tucked her true strength away.

They pulled right up to the front door, but Clive said, "Wait."

Everyone did, watching the Scion as his eyelids went half-mast and his nostrils flared. After a few breaths, he shook his head. "You know what to do if you need backup," he told Rowan, who nodded that she did.

"Vanessa just texted to say she's taken over the security system so no alarms will go to the authorities," David said. "I've got the feed on my phone should we need to examine it."

Darius had already informed Genevieve he was coming with her for all her interviews that night, so he got their door, and she pretended not to see the way Clive took Rowan's hand and kissed her knuckles gently.

"There's no one here," Darius said as they approached the front door. "No humans. No witches. They have animals, but none of them are here either."

"There are wards. Hold a moment."

Genevieve called up her magic as she viewed the warding spells laced over the home and yard. They were quality work and appeared to be Conclave provided. Genevieve knew most of the witches who created wards via a multitude of services scattered across the world.

She sang an unweaving. A song older than any of the magics that held the wards closed. The words rose on the breeze and found the hinge points, weakening them until they broke. At that, Genevieve was able to call another sort of spell, this one via the movements of her hands as she threw the broken wards off, leaving the main house unwarded.

Three claps, three stomps, and three exhaled words and all magic but theirs had been nullified.

"Someone is coming," Darius said as headlights hit the curve of the drive to the front door.

"It's Joseph." Genevieve knew his magic because he'd tried it on her when she'd left Tristan a century before. She'd humiliated him that day, besting him easily.

He'd made noise about opposing the divorce but while the Sansburys were a very old and influential line, hers was altogether another thing. Aubert would suffocate everything in its way should he have tried.

"I don't like that tone," Darius said quietly as he moved to stand to her side and slightly ahead. "He will be disappointed if he hopes to harm you."

"He knows from experience that would be impossible. Still, don't kill him if you can help it," Genevieve urged.

"Unless I have no other choice, I will let you handle this business. But I will confess to you hearing that tone in your voice, knowing this witch put it there, makes me very angry."

And what could she say to that? She barely resisted the sigh of pleasure at the way he'd appointed himself her protector. Genevieve knew she couldn't let him push too far or he'd take over. But that didn't stop the warmth in her belly. The satisfaction that he wanted her safe.

Just to her left, Rowan shook her head as she glanced toward the vehicle where Clive sat. Telling him to stay put.

Joseph Sansbury sprung from the back seat of the Bentley that had come to a stop. "You there! What are you doing?"

"He's one of *them*?" Rowan asked Genevieve, making her want to laugh. "A thousand percent indignation he can't have his way in all things? Tips five percent. Hasn't paid a bonus to staff ever. Since he's old, he thinks he's the Earl of Whatever? I'm really good with those types."

"You!" Joseph snapped his fingers in their direction but then as he got closer, he recognized Genevieve and pulled up short.

"Me," Genevieve agreed. "Let us go inside and have a chat."

He was shaken but managed to attempt to reassert control. "I'm rather busy at the moment. I can make time for you in the morning."

"I'm certain it wasn't a request. I am here as a representative of the Conclave, and I have questions for you."

"You go too far. Being Konrad's daughter won't protect you," Joseph said.

"From what exactly? Do tell, Joseph. What do I need to be protected from?" Genevieve asked. A hundred years ago she'd been strong, and her father had supported her immediately when she decided to end her disastrous marriage to Tristan. But the witch she was right then was light-years stronger. Was more powerful and since her ascension to being the priestess to a Trick of Dust Devils and close friends with the Hunter mated to a Scion, was more well connected.

She had *nothing* to be afraid of when it came to the witch in front of her.

And she let that show. Wanted him to understand she knew it too.

"I think a better question might be, who will protect *you*, witch?" Darius murmured and the sound was a slow-rising fog. Full of potential. Full of warning.

Joseph stepped back at that voice. Still agitated, but there was fear lacing his tone when he said to Genevieve, "You could have given me some advance notice you were coming."

"I could have." Genevieve simply stared at him. This exchange, despite their history, was strange. A visit by someone of her status should have him stumbling over himself.

"We can talk out here. I'm good with that. How about you?" Rowan sent Joseph a sunny smile. "Before you demand to know who I am and I'm expected to pretend like you don't know or somehow that I am your inferior yadda yadda, I'm Rowan Summerwaite. A Hunter. My office did contact yours. When did you get back from Bali, by the way? That's where you were visiting, right?"

"Er, yes. I'm sure my secretary has your request waiting for my return. As you can see, no one is here. We've all been—"

"In Bali. Right. So. Let's chat now. Lead the way, Joey."

Amused, Genevieve stayed quiet while Joseph made his grudging way to the front door, but it wasn't until they stood in the soaring front foyer that he seemed to realize there was no warding left. He tried to draw power for a working but there was nothing.

He made a few more attempts and finally gave up, his shoulders slumping slightly. Even at that very moment he was trying to work his way around what she'd done. Thinking he could just figure out what she'd done, he could counter it.

What she'd done was create nothing. A null space all around him and every other magical being except the ones she came in with. A bottomless pit with unclimbable walls. A yawning nothing between him and the power he tried to draw.

She'd studied for a few years with a witch who hunted demons and other infernal summoned creatures. It had been terrifying work, especially at first. But it had taught her a skill very few possessed. Taught her to access types of magic no longer known or practiced.

In many ways the manner in which she'd been *educated* had come at a terrible price. She and Rowan shared that history. But that education made her a force. A force few could ever hope to overcome.

She let that show in her eyes when Joseph opened his mouth to speak. Then Genevieve said, "I'm not the same witch I was a century ago and I beat you then too. Do not think you can best me."

Joseph drew a breath and stood a little taller. "Follow me through to my office. We can meet there. Briefly."

He spun and scurried off. Genevieve looked over to Darius and then to Rowan and David, before they headed toward him.

Rowan didn't like this prick one bit. She especially didn't like the way he tried to look down his nose at Genevieve even though he was as helpless as a kitten without claws up against her.

She was really going to like finding more of Joseph's weak spots and manipulating them.

The house was one of those places that had been built within the last decade after whatever had been there before had been torn down, but it did have some beautiful elements. The carpentry was fantastic and the art—some excellent reproductions—was overwhelmingly inoffensive and done by the rich-people artists of the moment. But here and there in a nook were elegant and very expensive statues. Rowan recognized the artist's work from the larger statues gracing the waiting area and bar of Fleur, the award-winning restaurant in Vegas the Vampire Nation owned and ran. All the subjects were female and managed to be classical and modern all at once.

The stuff on the walls had been bought. But the statues…they felt collected. Most likely not the same two people, which made her wonder about Joseph's spouse or whoever it was that had sought them out versus the aggressive inoffensiveness of everything else.

Rowan waited until Joseph had entered his office, and then David moved up to give her a little cover while she snapped several photos before turning on the recorder she had in the middle button on her shirt. Approval coursed through the bond she shared with Clive. Of course he was happy to spy on others and keep an eye on her at the same time.

The office was…bland. The furniture was well made, and the rugs were similarly expensive. But again, there was nothing personal there. It felt like a furniture showroom, or as if it had been staged to sell it to another family looking to spend their money on being as vehemently mediocre in taste as the former owners.

Aspirational mediocrity. For fuck's sake. This state of beige life was more offensive to her than when people decorated with terrible swap meet art they loved. Sure, those little sayings were clichéd, but frankly, she'd rather live, laugh, love than look at middle-distance landscapes done in muted colors that left you feeling… nothing.

Joseph wanted to blend, Rowan realized. Not socially invisible, because he was an entitled, powerful witch who most likely gave orders and rarely took them. She tucked the thought away. He had something to hide, and he acted like it.

She figured she may as well get started destabilizing Joe's life so she could find out what he was so busily trying to distract everyone's attention from.

Status was a thing witches—and powerful people in general—got all wet over. So Rowan gave a slow glance around the office before she said, "Are you getting ready to move? Who did your staging?"

David looked at the opposite end of the room, suddenly fascinated by the bookshelves full of everything but books. Fucking chock a block with shiny metal pseudo lungs for bookends that sat to either side of other shit like the weirdly menacing ceramic horses. Rowan bet those were expensive. Nightmare fuel wasn't cheap. But those would make a delightful sound on the hardwood at their feet, she bet. And she'd seen the same ones here and there on shelves in offices like that one. Dear in cost, but not in stock.

"Moving? Why would you think so?" Joseph asked, affronted.

In familiar territory, Rowan settled in to play with his head. She gestured around his office. "Well. It looks…generic. Like it's been staged so, I mean I just… assumed." There was no need to say more. He'd fill it in a dozen ways over the next however many days.

Genevieve looked down at her hands for a moment until she'd wrestled her smile away.

"What is your relationship to the Procellas?" Genevieve said, going from zero to light speed, kicking old Joseph in the butthole while he was still puzzling over Rowan's insults.

Joseph wasn't a newbie though. He reacted, his color blanching. But it was quick as he wrested it back and pretended not to be alarmed. The predator part of Rowan perked up.

He steepled his fingers in front of his lips. Classic liar's tell, for fuck's sake. "*Relationship* seems an overstatement. We're both Genetic witches and of course we do see one another at Conclave social events and the like. We both run businesses that do occasionally line up with one another to make some sort of deal. Why?"

"When was the last time you made *some sort* of deal with them?" Genevieve asked.

"I really must know why you're here without warning in the dead of night asking questions about things that are simply none of your business. As I said, being Konrad's daughter won't save you," Joseph told Genevieve with a sneer.

A hot wave of disapproval rolled from Darius and over the other witch. He jerked back slightly and finally seemed to register who was standing in his office.

"Go on, then," Genevieve invited. "Call whoever you need to come and…apprehend me for doing the Conclave's work?" She waved a hand.

"You don't know your place," he said, mean in his tone. "You never have."

Before Rowan could slap his fucking face, Genevieve began to laugh. As she did, magics swirled all around them until she snapped her fingers and it fell away like misty rain. That was a very cool spell and it had left Joseph shaken.

"My place is on the Conclave Senate. My place is leading an investigative team. A team already approved and sanctioned by the Conclave leadership. You reach above yourself, Joseph. See what it gets you if you try that again. Answer the question because I am beginning to wonder why you're working so hard to avoid discussing what I assume are legal business dealings with another prominent Conclave family."

"These are privileged business details," Joseph said weakly.

Rowan strolled over and grabbed a nightmare horse

and looked it over carefully. A reproduction even. She threw it to the floor with force, loving the dull splat and then the pieces shooting away from where she stood. Over the years she'd developed a throw that usually spared her any cuts from flying debris.

Joseph stood, hands balled at his side like angry Arthur, and David turned to face the witch. The nulled witch.

"You will calm yourself immediately," David said, his tone and his stance full of menace.

Rowan stared at Joseph, keeping her expression bland. "What will you do? No one is coming to help you. You're fucked."

"She's on three right now," Genevieve said. "Sit down or I'll let her escalate."

"Oooh, that's fancy and scary. I like it," Rowan said before she turned her attention to Joseph again. "The staging company has insurance to cover accidental loss probably. Though, they might get mad about the rest of the art on the walls I'm about to destroy. I bet you had to pay a deposit for that, and it most assuredly won't be accidental."

He looked confused and she couldn't have found it more delightful. What a fucking pencil.

"Why do you…what's happening?"

Rowan said, feigning—badly—patience, "This can all be over if you just answer the questions. When you don't, I'm going to get a little destructive. It's a good thing no one lives here, and all this is rented. Imagine what I'll do to the contents of the other rooms."

David coughed again.

Rowan snapped her fingers because he'd get offended. "I can see you're working up some sort of *well see here* in your chest. Don't waste your breath or my time. *Answer* the fucking questions you're asked."

"As I said, I may have bumped into Sergio or Alfonso from time to time at various widely attended social events." Joseph looked at Rowan and curled his lip. "For Genetic witches only."

"Oh no, I'm not invited to Thurston Howell the Third's white people party. I'm super sad about that. I'm sure I'll miss so many fascinating discussions about tweed and all the people you're so much better than."

Genevieve soldiered on after a slight wobble of her lips. "So it's been years since you've done business with the Procellas and the only time you've seen them was at *widely attended social events*. How long ago was that?"

"If you'd just tell me what you wanted to know, I could give you the information."

"Do not get testy here, Joey Snickerdoodle." She flashed a grin at David, pleased with her improvisation. "She's telling you exactly what she needs to know when she asks you the questions you're working overtime to pretend to misunderstand."

Genevieve said, "When did you speak with any Procella last? A decade ago? Ten minutes ago? Six months ago? Surely you can recall. Otherwise, if I'm not specific you won't know what you can lie about."

Red stained his cheeks as he registered Genevieve's insult. "I honestly can't say."

To that Rowan stalked over to a painting on a nearby wall, snatched it down, and then, using her uninjured leg, she kicked through it. Next one, she'd use the cane to see how that worked.

Better than therapy.

"You destroyed my painting! That cost fifteen grand."

"I told you. Just contact your staging company to file a claim. Though I do suppose they might not cover you being a dumbass and me having to wreck everything between you and the answer to our questions."

"*I'm not moving!* Why do you keep saying that?"

"This place looks like a furniture showroom. Or the rental office of an apartment complex. I never thought anyone would strive for that level of bland on purpose. Wooow. I mean, go you I guess?" Rowan said, pleased AF to see the vein on his temple start to throb.

"You can just look on your phone for goddess' sake, man!" David exclaimed. "In your outgoing or incoming calls. Surely you can do that."

Because we can hung in the air, unspoken.

He paled. "Yes. Yes. His granddaughter is seeing one of my cousins. That's right."

Genevieve said, "So. You've spoken to Sergio because Antonia is dating one of your cousins. And when was the last time?"

"I can't recall."

"And the last time you had contact with Sergio was due to this dating relationship? No business dealings?"

"As I said, we've done business in the past. I can't remember when it was."

"Have you ever been to the Procella home?" Genevieve asked, deceptively quiet.

"I may have. I don't know for certain."

"They live in Las Vegas. Their house blew up yesterday, as you well know. As the whole fucking world knows. Have you been there and don't lie." Rowan underlined that by tossing a small vase at his head.

Sadly, he moved and it broke when it hit the wall at his back instead.

"What are you doing? Stop this instantly."

"No." Genevieve spoke this time. "I don't think we will. Answer the question or I'll let her leave this room."

"How can I be expected to remember every place I've visited?"

Rowan strolled out and when Joseph started after her, Darius grabbed him by the back of his neck like a fucking puppy and then dragged him into the hall where Rowan headed straight for the reproduction vintage lamps that still would have set them back at least ten thousand bucks each.

She knew this fact because not too long ago she wanted something for her bedchamber at home and had looked into the exact type she wanted based on an art nouveau original.

Her cane was a very handy tool, and it gave her extra reach so when she swept through the shades, sending glass everywhere, she was far enough back to be safe.

"I need to work on my upper-body strength," she said. "Recently I was ambushed by shifters. Hired by the Procellas to kill me. In public. I'm sure you saw it on the news. Don't pretend like you didn't because I'm already embarrassed for you enough as it is."

Joseph blinked swiftly, taking in the swath of destruction she'd already created. "The Procellas caused that scene in the middle of the daytime? On a city street in front of cameras? That's…it's outlandish."

"It is rather shocking, no?" Genevieve said. "A violation of our most sacrosanct laws. A danger to everyone."

"It's asinine."

"It's like you've never met the Procellas. And yet we know you have even if you've spent the last forty minutes pretending not to understand the questions about them. So, my thing is we have important business to be about. If you want to waste more time, waste it with someone else," Rowan told him.

Genevieve sucked in a deep breath and said with extreme patience, "Frankly, were it me in your place, I'd be doing all I could to disassociate myself with them. And that starts by telling us what your relationship with the Procellas is."

"Just business! I'd certainly not associate my family's reputation on such recklessness. Making a profit with someone does not mean one shares their feelings or methodologies. I have nothing else to add."

By the time they left, Joseph had been wrecked and in tears. He'd admitted, sort of, that his company and the Procellas had done business regularly, but insisted he had no regular contact with them. Such a stupid lie. So easily verified.

Genevieve had put some sort of tagging magic on him, so she'd know if he tried to leave the area.

"Let's go visit Gerard Clare. I think we've both hit our second wind," Genevieve said once they'd gotten back into the car.

Chapter Seventeen

Gerard Clare's Mediterranean-styled villa sat in the Hollywood Hills. Unsurprisingly, his home was also in a gated enclave. The gates proved to be no more problem than the ones at Joseph's place.

At the second set of very high, wrought iron gates with spikes at the top, Rowan muttered, "Even I don't have this much security." Maybe they needed it for the same reasons she did. She should try to be nicer.

Ha.

When they pulled up, unlike over at the Sansbury place, lights blazed from inside the home.

The door opened before they'd reached the third step, revealing what Rowan silently considered a stereotypical butler in a stereotypical butler's suit. Though this one didn't look more than thirty.

"Please tell whoever is at home that Genevieve Aubert is here."

Genevieve had been snickering at something or other in the car just five minutes prior, but this version was cool, beautiful, and very much in charge.

The butler started at the name before he bowed low and stepped back from the doorway. "Please, be welcome," he said with a sweep of an arm.

Now *that* was how a household should welcome a VIP guest.

Darius went first. Rowan could pretend to be offended, but mainly she was just fine. One, he could protect Genevieve better that way. Two, he was far more powerful than Rowan. And three, she was absolutely all right with letting him take any sort of hit that might come. It'd bounce off that giant chest anyway.

Heh. Very giant. Like a big, broody, sexy tree.

She got that thought right out of her head before Clive picked up on it and decided to be possessive.

"I'm Giles. Please make use of the sitting room while I seek out Mr. Clare. Would you care for some tea or coffee? A cocktail?"

If he was startled by the appearance of four supernatural strangers on the doorstep at ten p.m. he didn't show it. It was certainly a far more understandable reaction to Genevieve's presence than it had been over at chez Sansbury.

Genevieve asked for tea and Giles was off to butler it up, leaving them alone.

"Surveillance has been fed to Vanessa and Pru at the LA chapterhouse, but disabled internally," David said quietly as he walked past. Pru ran the Southern California Hunters and should they need assistance, there was a team nearby ready.

Konrad hadn't liked the idea of Hunter Corp. having such inside views of Conclave business, but to his credit, he'd sucked it up. Rowan was absolutely going to use everything she discovered to keep the magical community from violating the Treaty, yes. But they needed her help, and she was going to do it anyway, so working together had been the best option.

Rowan already felt guilty that she'd left so much of this witch stuff alone while she dealt with the Vampires. They'd gotten a toe hold in her city, and she'd barely noticed because she'd been drowning in murderous bloodsuckers.

She nodded that she'd heard and stood to wander the room. Unlike the Sansbury place, this home was clearly lived in. There were books on the shelves. Though most were of the coffee table variety there were also some biographies and the odd bit of fiction here and there.

Lots of photos. Mainly of the same couple either alone or together with this or that celebrity or important person.

"This is an unexpected surprise."

Rowan turned to watch a man—the same from the photos in the room—enter and head straight for Genevieve.

"We are honored to have you here," he told Genevieve with a bow.

David had shifted so he was slightly behind Rowan, to her left. Out of the way should she need to draw a weapon or fight in close quarters.

Darius narrowed his eyes as he took in the bow over Genevieve's hand. She'd held it out to shake but Clare had taken it, turned it and kissed her knuckles instead.

Genevieve did not cede ground though. She held in place as she took her hand back.

"We have some questions for you, Gerard," Genevieve told him.

He looked around Genevieve to Rowan and David. "I'm Gerard Clare. You're Rowan Summerwaite, correct?"

Rowan nodded but did not put a hand out to shake.

"This is David. He manages Hunter Corp. United States." He didn't need to know David's last name.

"Welcome."

He turned to Darius.

"This is Darius," Genevieve said.

"Astonishing. I've never seen one of you up close before. Aren't you out of your territory? I suppose you just do whatever you please."

Rowan barely muffled her gasp. They were welcomed and Darius was…whatever Gerard was doing.

Darius stared at the witch, unspeaking. Genevieve's tone had gone from cool to icy when she said, "As I said, my associates and I have questions for you. That doesn't include passive-aggressive commentary to a guest."

He blushed slightly. "Apologies. I was fascinated and forgot my manners. My office is just through here."

Giles showed up nearly immediately with a tea tray, remaining until he'd poured out with a request that they let him know should there be anything they needed.

"Least *he* knows how to act," Rowan said with a tip of her chin toward Giles before she took the chair next to Genevieve.

Clare looked like he was going to say something so Rowan waited. She fucking hoped he did because after his behavior, he needed to learn a few things.

He must have understood her eagerness because he dropped his gaze and she sat back, settling her right hand on the top of her cane just in case she needed it to knock the shit out of him.

"What do you need to speak to me about?" he asked Genevieve.

"The Procellas. And your connection to them."

Gerard's swallow was audible and Brigid's attention,

the hunter's heart within Rowan, perked. Focused on the man across from her. *Prey.*

"We run in the same circles socially," he said. Outwardly he was calm, but Rowan caught the racing pulse-beat at his neck. "And we do business from time to time."

Pretty much the same line Joseph Sansbury had given them. Rowan made a mental note to avoid any circles that included scumbags like the Procellas and these guys and then wanted to laugh when she realized they were the majority of the dinguses she had to deal with regularly.

"What type of business?" Genevieve, too, was outwardly calm. However, she leaned forward slightly because she was on the scent.

"Freight. They have cruise and ship connections. My company moves freight overland via rail. There are situations when we need the space in the cargo holds of ships. Sergio or Alfonso are the brokers between us." Gerard's lips compressed at that last. Ha! He hadn't meant to say it in that way. *Us?*

Genevieve asked, "What is your opinion of them?"

"I deal with them mainly," a new voice said.

They turned toward the woman who'd just entered the room. She looked to be in her early forties, but Rowan knew from the background she'd been given that Fiona Clare was over two hundred years old.

She extended a hand to stay their movement. On the third finger of that hand, she sported a ring with three large diamonds that caught the light and sent it dancing. "Please. No need to stand. I'm Fiona Clare. I run the business with Gerard."

Her husband brought a chair to sit next to his and then sat once his wife had.

"I should apologize for eavesdropping," Fiona said

without actually doing so. "Important Conclave guests at a late hour? My curiosity got the better of me." She shrugged.

Fiona had shoulder-length, brownish-red hair. Her makeup was flawless. Highlighting her large green eyes and the curve of her bottom lip. In her ears—just one piercing in each—she wore diamond studs. Rowan wasn't a jewelry expert, but her husband gave her a lot of it. She figured the earrings were two carats each. Clothes were the affluent version of at-home wear. Charcoal gray trousers with a house-shoe-type loafer deal, and a green cashmere sweater.

Genevieve looked over to Rowan briefly and then she said to the newcomer, "What is your opinion of the Procellas?"

Where Gerard had blanched slightly, Fiona just got… harder. Her mouth flattened and she smoothed her palms over her thighs as she fought for control.

Fiona didn't like the Procellas at all. Whether it was one or the whole family, Rowan wasn't sure.

It was her thirst for attention or maybe her need to control Gerard that brought her into the office. Whatever the cause, it was quite clear who was truly in charge. And they knew that now. Honestly, villains could be so egotistical. It's what got them in trouble time and again. Rowan was grateful they were consistent at least.

"Business wise, or personal?" Fiona asked.

"As you pointed out, you run the business. Let's hear that. To start," Genevieve added.

While Fiona attempted to talk shit about the Procellas cloaked in business speak, Rowan paid attention to Gerard. He'd calmed at the appearance of his wife, but he was nervous still.

Fiona shrugged. "We are aware of the charges pending against Hugo. We are also aware there have been other women he's stalked. No big surprise. It's why I preferred to deal with Antonia as much as possible. But Sergio played favorites."

"And Hugo was his favorite," Rowan said, letting Fiona set up the story she was trying to sell them. Rowan bet Fiona was aces at manipulating people to get what she wanted.

Rowan wasn't most people though. The woman across from them didn't like any of the Procellas any more than her husband had. Gerard? He'd gotten angry and then shoved it away when they'd brought up the Procellas. Fiona *loathed* them in a way that told Rowan the connection between the two families and their businesses were far closer than they wanted to portray. Which meant they were most assuredly more important.

Fiona swallowed hard, like she was parting with the words but only after a struggle with herself. She poured on the regret as she latched herself to Rowan's gaze. "Yes. Sergio would do or say anything to cast doubt on why his grandson was in trouble. He'd attempt any wild story to excuse it."

Damn. Fiona really should have been an actor instead of a CEO.

Whatever the case, Rowan's curiosity was well and truly piqued about just what sort of wild story she or Gerard thought the Procellas had told about...them.

"Mainly Sergio is an entitled old gasbag with a shitty, indulged predator as a grandson," Rowan said. "His stories are pretty boring. But some of them are... interesting. Without context, they could be pretty explosive."

That bloviating assface hadn't said shit about the Clares. But his phone records did. And there was certainly no harm in letting Fiona believe he'd been telling on them.

"I suppose that's a moot point now anyway," Fiona said.

"What is?" Genevieve asked.

Fiona said, "The news about the explosion at the Procella home has been fairly nonstop all day. Obviously I hesitate to say anything else negative about Sergio given his tragic death. Hugo was suspiciously out of the way of violence I hear."

"Do you think Hugo had something to do with that explosion?" Genevieve asked, sounding so very surprised by such an accusation.

Fiona wasn't the only actress in the room.

"I couldn't possibly say. It would be a terrible thing to associate someone with. Though you've met Hugo, so." Fiona shrugged. "I'm sure it's just a coincidence that he's left in charge after the entirety of his family perished."

Shew! Fiona was really working this angle. Did Hugo give someone she knew, or even herself, the stalker treatment?

Rowan wasn't going to say anything. This was Genevieve's situation to handle. Eventually it would get out, but that control of information had already netted them some good information.

"Bess Procella is alive." Genevieve let that hang for a bit.

"Oh! Yes, the cruise," Gerard said.

Interesting that they knew about the round-the-world trip Hugo's mom had been on.

Fiona gave a shake of the head. "No one would put

her in charge of anything." She looked to Rowan. "She's not the brightest. I suppose her people will step up and be there for her during this time."

Rowan had found Bess self-centered and not very maternal, but she hadn't come across as silly or stupid. On the contrary, she had a calculated manner a great deal like Fiona's. Moreover, the deeper they'd dug into Procella business matters, the bigger Bess's role had become. If these people did the sort of routine deals with the Procellas they claimed to, it seemed rather impossible for them not to know she was the exact opposite of *not that bright*.

"She's on her way back to the United States now."

Bess was already there, but Genevieve had her reasons.

Fiona said, "I'm pleased she's alive and well. Though certainly it can't be good news to return home to. I suppose there is no home now."

Rowan watched a very small smile form and then ghost away from Gerard's mouth.

"Have you also hired the Shank family to do work for your company?" Genevieve asked.

"We've certainly employed shifters to do some side work for us. Many witches do, of course. They're frightfully efficient when it comes to getting local humans to get out of the way of progress." Gerard spread his hands out a moment in a *what else can you do* gesture.

"And what about say, more hands-on behavior?" Genevieve followed up.

Gerard sat up straighter, attempting to affect offense. "Now see here, we do not pay to have others harmed. There are times when shifters go too far. But that's their nature, you see. One must take a stern hand to be sure one is clear."

Rowan couldn't stop the guffaw. "The Shank crew tried to kill me in broad daylight in front of cameras and witnesses. Is that the kind of *too far* you mean?"

Fiona's eyes widened this time as Gerard paled. "We'd heard you were attacked. As you are looking fairly whole, I assumed the news had been exaggerated. Are you saying one of the Procellas hired the Shank family to harm you? In public? Whatever for? What could they possibly gain from that?" Thing was, Fiona sounded *emotionally* invested. Frustrated. Truly wondering why. Interesting.

And for fuck's sake. Pretending they hadn't watched the footage of the ambush on her was such a stupid lie to tell. That attack had been everywhere online and on news outlets across the country. And it had involved members of the supernatural community, which would have created an intense curiosity in their circles. They'd all want to see. Hell, Rowan had watched the video multiple times too, wanting to be sure there was no evidence she was anything but a very resourceful and lucky woman who defended herself until help came.

She played along though, describing her wounds, and then tapped her cane on the floor three times. She wasn't entirely sure why she'd started that, but doing things in threes had become second nature.

"If the extent of your injuries is to be believed, how is it you're standing?" Gerard nearly scoffed.

Genevieve interrupted, "You dare accuse a guest I've brought with me of deception? Are you addled? She is standing because she's a Vessel to a goddess and mated to a Scion. Do you realize the sheer level of power she possesses to be as recovered as she is right now? If not, you are every inch the fool she's got to believe you are."

Aw. Rowan didn't say anything or even make any outward indication of her feelings, but it was rather nice to be defended that way.

But Genevieve wasn't done. "Did you know Sergio and Hugo had contracted with the Shanks to do this deed? Do not lie to me."

Fiona gave a frustrated growl. "Why on Earth would we have known? We've done business with the Procellas, as we've said, but that doesn't mean they'd take us into their confidence for whatever it was they were thinking to do. I suppose in some way it's a shame they're all dead—except Bess and Hugo—given what they've done."

"Hey, before Genevieve says anything else, let me ask you something. Earlier when you were talking about your dealings with the Procellas to use their cargo space, you said they were the connection between *us*. If the Procellas were a middleman, so to speak, who's the other party?"

Sweat broke out on Fiona's forehead. Huh.

"I misspoke. I meant when they might be contracted on a ship versus it being their ship."

Rowan cocked her head. "Did you though? Because what it sounded like was Sergio or Alfonso or whatever hooked you up with another party to move some cargo."

Like perhaps the Procellas were a needed ingredient so they had to deal with them to get connected with some other party. Which would explain why anyone would tolerate them longer than five minutes.

But now they scrambled to protect this other party, which told Rowan that was who she needed to identify.

Neither answered. They most likely knew if they lied it would make things worse so they avoided speaking at all. Rowan had been in their place a time or two, but never because she was a murderous asshole.

"Oh, and one last thing," Genevieve said. "The Procellas—all of them—are alive. They were not in the mansion when the mage firebomb hit it."

"Mage fire?" Fiona said. She was going for shocked to hear it, but missed that by a mile.

"Can't hire out to wolf shifters for that. No, this was an all-witch-type situation. Interesting, right?" Rowan said with a fake smile.

"I'm certain that can't be. Perhaps it was one of those sorcerers. You said some might have escaped," Gerard said of the conspiracy between those in the magical community and some shithead Vampires. Many had suffered. Many still did. Rowan thought back to two weeks before and the little house in Long Beach they'd looked at where three young people, two of them witches, had lived before they'd disappeared.

"Borrowed or stolen magic can't make mage fire. A Genetic witch makes mage fire. You know that as well as I do," Genevieve said.

"How do you know? There are human accelerants that can do that type of damage."

How was it they believed Genevieve wouldn't have gone to get magical signatures from the scene? Signatures that led them right here to these witches.

Genevieve chuckled and the menace in the sound sent goose bumps racing over Rowan's arms. "First be glad the human authorities are as clueless as you assume I am. I was at the scene. So was Rowan. I guess we forgot to mention that part. It's a good thing we all possess a great deal of protective magics of our own. I cannot imagine how the Dust Devils would have responded should I have died. Why, whoever was behind it may as well have walked into a volcano because they'd have been hunted down and executed."

"We will still do that," Darius said in a rumble. Within that rumble were sharp edges and heavy stones. "Our priestess was in that home. And more than one other who was under our protection."

"So you see," Genevieve said, "it's important we get answers so we can meet this threat. Because that's assuredly what this is." As she spoke, the energy in the air seemed to build. "Once again it is our own who are responsible for this sort of deranged violence. We, who pledge to always be shelter to one another against the outside world, are proving to be our own worst enemy. We are Conclave. We have existed for thousands of years, and we will continue to do so. We will find out what is happening, and it will be dealt with. Should you decide to remember anything useful regarding your business with the Procellas, contact my office immediately."

They got up as one and headed out to the front entry.

"I know you are withholding information," Genevieve said. "You are playing a very dangerous game. One I've played for centuries longer than you have. Come to your senses before it's too late. Don't leave the city."

They left while the Clares still made excuses.

"I managed to get into their home Wi-Fi network and Vanessa piggybacked into their system. She's making a clone as we speak," David said. "I'll get everything shared with the Conclave as well once we begin to get data."

Chapter Eighteen

Rowan awoke at roughly nine the next morning feeling better than she had since she'd been ambushed.

She'd flown down to Southern California, ruffled a lot of feathers, found some important connections, and had come home where her delightful husband had talked her into taking some of his blood. Naturally that'd led to some intense sexytimes where she had to do little more than lie back and let her man do his thing to all her parts.

It didn't suck, that was for certain, having someone care that way for her. Even when he was bossy and nosy.

She told Star, "I'm going for a walk. If you want to join me, now's your chance."

Star hopped up and did a little tippy-tap dance on her way to the door.

Rowan wasn't a huge fan of running. Or exercise in general. But she needed to do it. To regain the strength she'd lost after the ambush, and to keep sharp. One never knew when a mage firebomb would be set off, so it paid to be at a state of readiness.

It kept her alive.

Used to be, she exercised like she ate and slept. Purely to survive. Now she had reasons to take the time to enjoy a good meal with people she enjoyed and trusted. She slept in a bed her Vampire husband had bought her as a gift. Lived in a house he gave her.

Such a different—and better—life than she'd had before.

Today she opted for a brisk walk at a park a few miles from the house. The mountains stood tall and imposing all around her as the two of them began. They gave off magical energy the Devils and witches in the area seemed to gobble up. The sky above was that impossible blue of autumn.

There were a million things she needed to do, but mainly she was doing them all. The issue was nothing seemed a direct path. In the past two years, each time she'd thought herself at the end of a conspiracy of some sort, there'd be something worse behind the next door. Another layer of complication. She and her friends had been across the globe multiple times, getting the shit kicked out of them, fighting back the chaos eventually to fight another day.

So many next days.

There'd been the Blood Front. Which had flowed into the sorcerers who'd been working with a faery who'd been banished to this world from his. Witches had joined in and now there were werewolves?

Good goddess what a fucking mess.

"They could all live excellent lives without any of this murderous behavior," Rowan told Star. She'd left the leg brace behind, and they'd started walking slow and steady. Why not bounce some ideas off Star while she was at it? "These Blood Front Vamps. The ones still alive. They could be Vampires in this world. They're already moneyed and entitled! But noooo, they have to start new clubs every ten minutes. Human-hating clubs.

They could have bocce ball clubs, or book clubs. Instead they have *Sanguis Principatus*—because of course it has to be in Latin. Though honestly the Brotherhood sounds racist as fuck, so I get the rebrand. And these fucko witches are up to some shady shit. For what? They could just be fabulously rich and paranormally powerful. That's a pretty fucking nice life. One *I'd* get if they'd just stop being assholes."

Star barked her agreement.

"So right now, I've got these *Sanguis* Vamps. *And*, the Vampire lord dinguses in Theo's dungeon. Doubt that's connected. But they're both Vampire related. Add the witches. And because of the witches, murder shifters. What a fuckin' motley band of scumbags. I'd very much like to have most of this in hand before we have to leave for the Joint Tribunal."

The gentle incline on the path gave way to something more challenging. Rowan kept herself aware of the strain on her healing muscles, but so far, she'd remained limber and strong.

"I do like to think your being here with me means we'll all survive. So you know, silver linings and all that."

Rowan threw the stick Star brought her, content to watch as the dog retrieved it, brought it back to her so she could toss it again and run after it. Over and over for the next forty five minutes or so until they got back to the car.

"If it's ever a choice between me and him," Rowan said quietly to Star, meaning Clive, "make it him."

Star snorted, getting dog snot all over Rowan's forearm.

"What was that for? Ew!" She used the sleeve of the light zip-up jacket she'd brought along to wipe it off.

Star growled, not something she'd ever done to Rowan. Others, yes.

"Lady, ma'am, would you like to explain just what it is you're doing?" Rowan asked her.

Star snorted again and then turned in a neat little circle and gave Rowan her behind. The silent treatment.

"I still want you to save him if it comes to a situation when it's him or me," Rowan said as they drove back toward home.

Then Star farted the grossest, most horrifying wet dog food stench. Rowan had to roll the windows down, laughing at how petty her dog was.

Star jumped from the car when they got back home, trotting to the door and waiting for Rowan at the base of the steps leading to the main entry from the garage.

"I'm leaving the windows down because that was so awful," she said.

Star yapped and ran inside, tail wagging, smile on her face.

After a shower and some breakfast, she and David headed to the motherhouse where Rowan was about to have a call with Theo.

He looked healthy. Rested. Part of that nervousness that always rose before she could see with her own senses just what state he was in relaxed. His gaze was clear.

But he was pissed. She could see the lines next to his mouth as he gave her a long look via their video connection. That day—night where he was—he lounged in a wine-colored chair that complemented the navy sweater and gray trousers. His silver, waist-length hair had been caught away from his face.

Intense. Angry. But sane. She could handle that.

"Petal, I do not much care for yet more news of your involvement with a violent event."

Not like she much cared for it either.

"I am well," she said. Rowan found with him it was best to lead with a reminder that she was alive and fine. That way he couldn't derail. "I'm out of a cast now. I have a brace and a cane. You'll be pleased to know the cane makes an excellent weapon. I broke several very expensive pieces of art with it just last night."

He laughed then with a clap of his hands. "Tell me about it! Who did you do this to? Not my Scion, Petal?"

"No, no. Our home is filled with lovely things I would never be so careless with." She told him a very edited version of the situation the evening before at the Sansbury house.

"And you believe these witches are responsible for this spell that could have killed you?" The menace in his tone sent chills racing over her skin.

"A witch helped keep me safe, *vater*." She reminded them both who he was. The last thing Rowan wanted was Theo deciding to go starting a war with the Conclave over this. "The majority of witches are no more responsible for what a few of their number did than all Vampires are responsible for the things the Blood Front and this *Sanguis* thingy do."

"And what of the witches who tried to have you killed?"

"Oh, they're totally responsible. And they will pay. I'll see to it myself."

He examined her features carefully for long moments and then nodded. Accepting her assurance.

"If you need anything you will seek it from my Scion

or my Voice. If I am sleeping, you will contact the daytime staff. I will not hear no to this," he said finally.

"As you wish. If you are feeling magnanimous," she began carefully, "some information from the First regarding *Sanguis Principatus* would be quite useful."

He wanted to play a game. She saw that in his smile.

It amused him to make her win the information. Normally, Rowan would go through it, giving him what he demanded. But she was *tired.* It shouldn't be some sort of complicated dance every time she needed information to keep herself alive!

There was no use complaining. What would that change? This was their world and though his methods had been—and remained—unacceptable, there was no denying they'd hardened her enough to survive.

Love was…complicated.

"And why should I assist the Hunter Corporation?"

Because your Vampires have spent the last several years trying to kill me at every turn. You claim to be concerned for my well-being but you allow these murderers access to the process.

She settled on, "Because you are the First. These creatures are ultimately your responsibility."

"My Voice his informed me it is in our best interests to share information with you regarding these fools," he admitted. He'd wanted her to dance to entertain him even though he'd already given permission?

In anyone else, Rowan would have delivered a response so blistering her victim would ache for weeks to come.

But Theo was not anyone else and Rowan knew that.

She inclined her chin slightly in appreciation.

"They are a different sort of threat than the Blood

ront, but it is the same direction. There are times, Petal, when it is best to let boys break their toys, grumble, and plot because it lets them release their negative emotions. Mostly they never get past the talking stage. These *Sanguis* Vampires like coin."

"And blood?"

His lips curved into a smile that was more frightening than amusing. "Blood is coin in our world, Rowan. You know this better than most. They have, for the most part, remained out of our notice. Small transgressions are not worth my energy. Them trying to harm you? Well, *that* is worth notice."

She thought so too. But as with everything else, it was the why.

Then he said, "Planning for Yule and New Year has begun in earnest," reminding her of the deal she'd made just a few months prior. She'd done it to save Clive's life. Clive's family line, who'd always been loyal to the Nation with the exception of two who'd been *handled* by her spouse and father-in-law. She'd had to go to her foster father and do some bargaining, giving him what he wanted most, her presence at his Keep as his daughter.

She'd be paraded around. She'd have to wear ridiculous clothing and jewels and it would be horrible. However, Clive and House Stewart would continue to rise in stature. That mattered to her most.

Plus, though he sweetly pretended not to, being the son-in-law of the most powerful being in the Vampire world and having ten days of parties celebrating them both thrilled him and his family. They should fear it. Theo noticing you wasn't a good thing always. It was best, she'd realized early on, when he forgot about you.

But if she could protect them all, she would. And

though she'd hesitate before admitting it out loud to anyone but Clive, Rowan loved Theo.

So. They'd attend fetes and dinners. They'd light candles and go ice-skating on the pond at the Keep. She'd be transported to a place where the modern world wasn't absent as much as the past dominated.

Electricity and running—hot—water, yes, thank goodness. But there were also times when it felt like she'd walked into the pages of a historical novel set in myriad times from before the current era to modern-day touches.

The man still liked a horse-drawn carriage, but instead of heated bricks, his modern conveyance had interior heating.

"I will have cook, who is doing most of the planning, connect with your young valet. He holds the keys to your kingdom, I've discovered."

Cook had a name. Dina. She was lovely and undoubtedly had three-quarters of the staff already at work on whatever ridiculous display Theo had in mind.

"David controls something far more important than my kingdom, he is the keeper of my schedule. He does a fine job."

"He has grown into it from what I have been told and have observed. The first meeting he wanted to run screaming from the room." Theo chuckled.

"*But he didn't.* He was barely twenty-three years old when he was confronted by the first Vampire to exist and he stood his ground. For me. He is my protected." She wanted to reiterate that. It wasn't so much that she thought Theo was going to hunt David down to execute him. But he got jealous from time to time. He lost… sight of himself and his responsibilities sometimes and in those moments he was more dangerous than anything she'd ever been confronted by.

If such a time popped up, she wanted, somewhere in the back of his mind at the very least, him to know there were lines that if he crossed, things between them would be broken forever.

"He must be very brave to serve at your side. I expected nothing less. How is my Scion?"

Wary, Rowan chose an answer he wouldn't consider rude while she tried to figure out what he wanted.

"He is a very fine husband. He buys me more sparkles and baubles than I could possibly use. And weapons. I can and do use those regularly."

Not a lie.

She hadn't expected marriage at all. Much less to a Vampire. An ancient. A fucking Scion, for goddess' sake! But as she'd come to figure out in the years since they'd met, love didn't work on any schedule but its own.

She hadn't planned to love Clive Stewart. But she did. Each day he gave her more reasons. The infuriatingly attentive Vampire knew what she needed before she did sometimes. It was alarming even as it thrilled her to be in his attention.

"His territory appears to be lawless."

Rowan drew a careful breath. There was no way she'd let Theo go down any road that ended with him believing Clive wasn't doing his job.

"Like Europe? Like Asia, Russia, and Africa like these lords of yours? In your own Keep I was nearly murdered during a Joint Tribunal. *Twice.* What I can see, being a person uniquely qualified to see such things, is that Clive Stewart, Scion of North America, in the handful of years he's been here after Jacques drove this land and her people into the ground, has addressed the rot he's found. He was given a task most would fail within the first week. And here he is years later, bringing the Nation a steady flow of profit. He may be a Vampire, but he is an excellent husband and an even more excellent Scion."

He was quiet as he looked at her intently. She allowed it, giving him only what she wanted him to see. Clive wasn't just important to her, he was everything. She would screw up her courage and push back against her father if it meant Clive was protected.

"All right. Did Nadir tell you we were letting our guests get used to their new surroundings before we had a conversation with them?"

Theo's *we* was the royal type.

"She mentioned Andros letting them stew a little. I can't imagine it's very pleasant below. However, I'd very much like to know just what it is they're up to."

"Power, I'd suppose. But Andros is a conscientious worker and tells me discussions will begin tonight."

"I've looked at these Vampires and their holdings. Given who they are, they've reached the pinnacle of their station. Offending me does nothing for them. What do they gain by entering the process and derailing it the way they have? What is their goal? It's not as if I am unaware of what Vampires get up to. Even the greediest and stupid have some sort of end goal. So. What is it? It can't be to mess with the Hunter. Big deal. They all do. And as you know, I will still hire who I need to. If these lords can't imagine why, that's your problem and I'd be concerned about Vampires in any way beholden to your prisoners."

"I am certain they will imagine why once they have been spoken with."

The light in Theo's eyes was a dangerous one. Full of violence and retribution. Rowan was simply glad none of it was aimed at her. Or Clive. If she had to throw these douchelords at Theo to keep his attention off those Rowan loved, so be it.

Truth was, Rowan had empathy. And sympathy. But she didn't waste it on those who didn't deserve it. These lords made their own mess, and she would not intervene to help them out of it. They lived in a very hard world.

For thousands of years Theo had operated under the type of control unimaginable to nearly every being on the planet. There were times he was lost to the past. Times when the years of his life had blurred the present, confused him, left him scared and angry and he reacted—usually murderously.

"I only wanted to play a game with you," he confessed at last.

This glimpse of his…contrition was terrifyingly arresting. Tears stung the back of her eyes and she let Brigid soothe that anxiety so she could get herself back on track.

She couldn't allow this sort of thing, or he'd try it again. Rowan had enough trouble to manage as it was. "By letting these Vampires dress up as lords."

"I knew you would see how ridiculous they were. I wanted you to laugh. But they threatened you. They took our game, and they ruined it."

So fucking glad she was across the world instead of chained in a cell beneath his feet, Rowan breathed through the stinging nettles of his upset. An ocean between them, along with half of two continents, and she could still feel it.

Rowan hoped it was a remnant of the blood bond she'd had with him as a child. Because if he was powerful enough to manifest physical responses at such a distance, Theo was gaining in strength.

When he spoke again, it was in the old dialect. Their original Vampiric language. "My Voice advised me not to allow these lords into the process. She did see my humor, but she had concerns they might step out of the box they'd been placed in."

This language helped her maintain control. English was her emotional language. This one she only spoke rarely and in ceremonial situations. That formality gave her some space between the words and her feelings.

"The problem with fools is they act foolish."

He wanted to play more than he wanted to think. Sometimes he was more like a toddler than an ancient predator.

"I have made mistakes, Petal. So many they plague my waking moments. When you allowed me to be in your life again, I made a vow to myself that I would not be careless with you as I had been. These lords... I was careless."

"You were."

Surprise registered on his features a moment and then he sent her a cheeky grin. "There's the little Hunter all my Vampires quake in fear of."

He really was spoiled. That was the absolutely nicest thing she could have said other than nothing at all.

"They wouldn't have to if they'd stop acting up and threatening Hunters. I will be most interested in what their motivations were because frankly, what could they be that they would risk exactly the outcome they're experiencing?"

"Can I trust my Scions?"

Oh shit.

"In what capacity do you wish my answer?" she asked with a calm she did not feel.

"Tell me as a Hunter."

She took a deep breath. "You can trust Clive. And as annoying as he is, Warren is loyal. I saw it myself when we worked together. Paola's territory is full of old powers, and she does not make waves. She does not grasp for things outside her reach. I have seen her loyalty to you and the Nation on multiple occasions."

Though she'd just touched on the Scions of North and South America and Europe, the other two Scions she wasn't entirely sure of. Nor did she want to start some bloodbath because her dad got pissed and acted before thinking.

"And the other two?" When he wasn't on the verge of violence, he was very sharp.

"To be absolutely clear, *I have no evidence* that the other two are not loyal to you. My concerns as a Hunter are that they allowed the powerful ancients in their territories access to your internal political process and when it went off the rails, they did not react as quickly as I'd have preferred. That does not mean they have done anything wrong," she repeated. "Both have served you for centuries. Were I in your place, I would give weight to that."

"And how would you deal with them sending these Vampires my way to start with?"

Frustrated, she only barely withheld a snarl. "*You* allowed them into the process, *vater*. You. And yes, you saw immediately they were shallow and silly, and I'd laugh. But they inserted themselves into a process and proceeded to offend you. *That* is the issue here. I would want to know if Tahar and Takahiro simply opened the way between their people and their leader—which is a normal thing—or if they sent Vampires to you to cause a problem. One is understandable. It's how things work in your world. Scions are the conduit between their Vampires and the First. They don't have to like the Vampire they send your way. Or even agree with them. Conversely, being deliberately provocative? Well, that's reckless. I'd want to know why."

She hoped that was enough to keep Theo wanting to talk to Tahar and Takahiro instead of executing them. She wanted answers too. And, she didn't actually loathe either Scion. Killing a Scion would be hugely destabilizing in an already chaotic time.

Star wandered in; clearly Rowan had been forgiven whatever sins the dog had been annoyed by. She gave a sharp, pleased bark at the screen, placing her front paws on Rowan's unhurt thigh to look at Theo better.

He caught sight of Star and an altogether different smile showed up. A younger Theo. Pleased with a dog.

Rowan tucked it away. Knowing at some point she'd be mad or sad about his bullshittery and the memory of that expression would get her through the moment.

He spoke to Star in an old language. Long dead. Rowan could only pick up a few words here and there. Theo praised her and then…told Star to watch and protect. Maybe defend?

Whatever it was, Star seemed to understand. She yipped and then licked Rowan's nose in a sneak attack that had her laughing.

They spoke a little longer before she was able to break the call and face the rest of her day. In the light.

Chapter Nineteen

When they arrived at the Motherhouse, the parking lot was full of familiar motorcycles and on those motorcycles *usually* sat Dust Devils. None of whom seemed to be around.

"They're here to help Bastien with some sort of installation of plants in the lobby," David said.

Bastien was a green witch, and Lorraine's son. "Oh. Makes sense. It did seem like a lot of them just for Genevieve." She indicated the bike bearing intricate metalwork. "Marco's on-site."

David blushed and fought a smile.

"Yeah?" she asked him before they went inside. "I thought there was something in the way he was around you."

Plus, Marco had saved David's life at the Procella mansion. It was really fucking sexy to have someone save your life when you were into them on a sexytimes-way level. She and Clive had experienced some of the hottest sex they'd ever had right after one had saved the other's life.

"Things went nowhere with whatsherface? The archivist?" He'd been flirting hard-core with the witch who headed up the Conclave archives. He'd described her with terms like brilliant and witty. Busy, busy man. Rowan liked that he was paying attention to other parts of his life besides work. He deserved romance.

Then a wave of uncertainty hit. Should she add something to indicate she wasn't judging? Goddess. She didn't know how to be the sort of friend you chatted about romance with, but more than that, she was so… proud he'd want to share with her.

David caught her hesitation and reached out, touching her arm. Just a brief brush of his hand. Enough to say he understood the unspoken and things were fine.

"She and I have a date for drinks next week. She's coming to Las Vegas for work of some sort. Marco is… well, unexpected. But I find I rather like him."

"You're young, you have a great job, you're gorgeous and intelligent, and you always know exactly which bagel from the dozen I'm going to want first. Although that's not really relevant to you and your very exciting romantic life. Go, you," she told him.

"It *is* very exciting, I must admit." His expression was so adorable she wanted to pinch his damned cheeks. Instead, she let him open the door for her as they entered the lobby.

They had originally considered leasing space on the first floor to various businesses but had decided to use that space as an atrium with plants and water features that would pump the place full of not only cleaner air, but soothing sounds and green magic. It would be a spot they could find peace in. Even if only for minutes.

There were three Devils with Bastien, helping with bags of soil and setting up all the machinery for the various components of the overall space.

"You can certainly feel the magic here," David said. "And yet, it still feels like our place."

Rowan had been fervently hoping that would be the case. It had been her idea to bring in witches and Vampires to create a few special Hunter teams. She'd been the one to ruffle the feathers of the Vampire Nation as well as the Conclave. Not every idea worked out. Most didn't. But it was gratifying to see the results of her choices. Of the risks she'd taken to open their doors wider.

Malin waved them over to the reception desk, handing David a stack of things before they went up to the secure floors that made up the heart of the Hunter Corporation's Motherhouse in North America.

There was a guard stationed at the elevator and then beyond him two different types of biometric scans. If the person attempting entry by that point was an imposter, an alarm would go off, locking that security point with the person inside until they could be identified or removed.

Beyond that were the stairwells and the elevators to the floors holding their workspaces, some dormitory-styled bedrooms, a kitchen and lounge, a library, archive, and the most secure space in the building, the weapons locker.

"This feels like an action movie sometimes," David said as they passed through the main doors to the floor where Rowan and David's offices were. Just a few weeks before they'd just been getting it furnished. And now it hummed with activity. All sorts of various trainings appeared to be in progress. Young fresh faces and no small number of wary gazes made up the group.

"You chose well," David told her in an undertone as they headed into her office.

It was a good mix. One needed the other. It was so easy to forget there was a reason they did what they did. And all that excitement could get you killed if you didn't think twice. She hoped the combo would create a sense of family.

Hunter Corp. had to face and deal with all manner of threats to humanity. It was more than a place you showed up to every day to punch a timecard. As such, Rowan had learned over her time as a Hunter just what support was so desperately needed in the field.

She wanted them to have an unshakeable certainty they had many fellow Hunters who would always have their back. They need not face those monsters in the dark alone.

Once, Rowan had imagined she could do it herself. She'd been wrong. And beat to shit all the time. At least now when she got beat to shit, there were many who showed up to help her heal. It still made her nervous sometimes. She liked to feel like she was a solitary individual. A loner who needed no one. And for years and years it had felt close to true.

She looked up from the stack of mail he'd put on her desk to him.

It hadn't been true. Now that she'd accepted these people who'd shown up for her time and again, she'd accepted it had been loneliness that had driven her to that point. Now her life was full of creatures who chose her. It was a gift.

One she wanted the others working for Hunter Corp. to have as well.

"First let me procure you some coffee," David said, "and then we can go over everything that's come in."

She didn't argue with that.

Especially when she had to sift through reports on the various searches they'd done in the prior days.

"I recognize some of these Vampires in the photos we took from Elmer's house. A few of Jacques." She held it up toward David. "Purple velvet low-rise bell-bottomed trousers with a matching vest. He even had those wide sideburns." It made her want to comb through photos of Clive to see what he looked like in the seventies. Her mother-in-law would have some, Rowan bet.

There were some photos that had Aron in them. Taken in the thirties through when he left Elmer's line. "Goddess he was young." She touched the earliest image. "Elmer is such a fucking creep."

"It seems so," David said.

"I'll show these to Clive, get him to identify the others," she said, setting the stack aside to look over the list of what they'd pulled from the thumb drives and data cards they'd taken from the Procella mansion and the Gloat Palace.

David rose. "I've got a number of meetings ahead of me. Vanessa is available if you want to speak with her regarding any of this."

"Great. I'll probably pop over to see her just to say thanks and to see if there are any updates on the list Vihan was building with her."

Vihan had arrived in Vegas two weeks prior and had already become integral to their little ragtag crew of Hunters. It was good that David had his own valet. The job of taking Hunter Corp. into the future was a big one with many moving parts.

"I have that information," David said, pausing at the doorway.

Rowan waved a hand at him. "Go do your whatever it was you need to do. I can walk my ass over there."

And when she tapped on the open doorjamb of the tech playground, Vanessa turned her head and when she saw it was Rowan her smile, goddess, it was pleased.

She should have done this more, Rowan realized.

"Hi there. Do you have a moment? I wanted to talk about the list of missing from the various cities we'd identified two weeks ago."

"I do. Come in."

Vanessa pointed at a rolling stool that Rowan deposited herself on and glided over to the desk full of monitors the purple-haired woman sat at.

"Okay, so." Vanessa made a few mouse clicks and typed some stuff. The data that had been on the screens disappeared and new information popped up. "Originally, we realized the concentration of cities. Seattle, Portland, Southern California, New York City and Nashville. Highest numbers per capita of disappeared is Southern California followed by Seattle."

Rowan leaned in, looking at name after name. Address after address.

Then she paused. "Wait." Rowan pointed. "Scroll back a few screens."

Vanessa did as asked, pausing each page to let Rowan read through, and then found it. An address on Holly Drive.

"Holly," she murmured.

"What does that mean?" Vanessa asked.

Rowan briefly explained the various prophetic dreams and knowings she'd been having. Including the most recent that had featured greenery she now realized was holly.

"That's the address you and Genevieve went to. In Long Beach," Vanessa said.

Well, fuck.

Rowan pulled out her phone and looked up the time for sunset. "I need this data with filters for some words. Is that possible?"

Vanessa rolled her eyes and then pushed her berry-red eyeglasses up her nose. "What words?"

Rowan thought for a moment. "Holly, sparrow, bird, storm, ocean, ships. Too generic?"

"I think we can do it. It's a wide net, but how many of these addresses could have any of those terms? It should be relatively easy once we have a filtered batch of data to cull what isn't useful. Then we have a small enough sample that it might give us a direction."

"Great. That will be a big help. Even if we can't figure out who it is from the results, we'll know who it likely isn't. That's an answer too."

Vanessa turned to Rowan. "You've brought me to the field more than once and it teaches me new things each time. No one before you has given me that trust. And I know this might sound weird—I don't want to make you sad—but it feels very much like Carey has been here too, keeping an eye on me."

It was hard. Letting them out into the field meant they'd be exposed to danger. The kind of danger that had caught up to Carey and murdered him.

Carey had been hers. One of the first friends she'd made within Hunter Corp. He'd been killed for that loyalty. In all the rest of her days, when she looked for him, he would not be there. He would not come back. There would never be another moment in his company and that was still a hard realization.

It hurt. Grief wasn't new to Rowan's life. Her parents, both long dead, were simply the beginning of the losses she'd come to endure over and over. She hated it. No matter how many times she told herself grief was the price one paid for love, it still yawned in her belly. So big and dark it was one of the few things that truly scared her.

Because there were others whose loss she could not imagine surviving. David. So human and fragile compared with those creatures out to harm. The son of her heart.

Clive. The unexpected other half of her. The one being in all the universe who saw her so clearly and… celebrated all the things others had sought to punish her for. He celebrated her strength. Her darkness and her sharp edges. Was proud of them. To be seen by him so well and loved because of it was a miracle she wasn't sure she'd ever understand.

But she'd accept it nonetheless because by that point, she simply never wanted a life without her vexing Vampire. And because being understood and known was a beautiful gift she'd never felt worthy of, but she'd never give up.

"Can you do a more thorough search of that address? I know we've been looking at the people who went missing, but more details, if possible, would be good. On their jobs. Friends. There's a connection. The more information I have, the easier it will be to figure it out."

"I have every confidence you will. These missing people are fortunate that it is you who seeks them," Vanessa said quietly.

Rowan told herself it didn't matter that Vanessa had such false confidence. People died around her for goddess' sake!

But that was a lie. It mattered. Their confidence in her, even when she fucked up right and left, was a gift, and she was too weak not to take the solace that trust offered.

"I've gotten the new filters applied. Give me some time."

"I have every confidence you too will prevail," Rowan said, echoing Vanessa.

She stood, taking the folder Vanessa had prepared.

"I'll keep you apprised," Vanessa said as Rowan got to the doorway.

"Appreciate it."

Darius felt the pulse of magic as it echoed toward where he stood in Genevieve's office, looking out over the mountains just beyond.

The sun was tumbling from the sky. Darkness was already rising. The city changed so much in this moment, as day slid away, and the night took her place like a queen.

Gone were the hikers and other adventurers. They'd headed back to hotels and condos to shower and reemerge dressed for fine dining. For dancing and flirting. For gambling of all types. So many risks being taken.

He breathed in deep. The flavor of the magic, of the life energy that was essential to his and the rest of the Trick's existence, had changed as well. Anticipation spiced it now. Longing. They'd start to flow from their rooms and into the night to play and sin and provide a feast with their emotions.

Darius had been thinking that the fading light changed her too. His brilliant witch whose power was a beacon in the darkness. In the night her magic was velvet and sensual. Her light was still a beacon but there were shafts of reds, golds, blues, and bronze in her. As if her power were reflected through stained glass.

And then the pulse heading toward them.

Darius spun to her, their gazes locking. She stood and held out a hand. “No. Let it come. It’s mine.”

He eased that shield back and he knew she’d been telling the truth as that magic flowed through him and he tasted her on every single nerve ending.

His attention locked on her, she tipped her head back with a sigh as the spell swirled around her and then seemed to settle over her skin before sinking inside.

He’d never been more aroused.

She glowed with energy. With the power she was born to. And…the power they’d brought her when she’d become their priestess.

He saw it in her. In those shafts of light. Devil magic had twined with her own. It coursed through her, utterly part of Genevieve. It was a punch. That realization that such an important part of what he was lived in her.

Satisfaction followed. He’d marked her. Deeply and irrevocably. He might have felt guilty over it. If she was someone else perhaps. But she wasn’t naive or innocent. She knew what he was and she’d accepted every part with open arms and a curious, eager mind.

Nothing else would have shattered the walls he’d erected around himself for millennia.

He was in love with Genevieve Aubert.

As he thought it, her eyes opened, her attention seeking him until she found him in a breath. “I set a warning spell at that house in Long Beach. With the missing witches. Someone is there.”

“Let’s go tell Rowan,” he said.

Chapter Twenty

Clive woke and automatically he reached for their bond. Assuring himself Rowan was alive and well.

There she was, practically shining with her power. Not just alive, but thriving. Despite all the attacks, all the setbacks.

He showered and changed into a suit, but before he'd even made it to the living room, Rowan called.

"Hello, Hunter," he replied as he answered.

"Evening, Scion. Want to take another trip to the Southland tonight?"

"What's going on?"

She told him about the street address of the house in Long Beach she and Genevieve had been at just two weeks prior and that she felt it was connected to her dream.

And then she said, "Genevieve set some sort of trap spell at the house. So that if anyone entered, it would be triggered. And it just was, about five minutes ago."

Relief that she'd waited until he could be given the choice to accompany her or not rushed through him. Leaving him pleased and stupidly in love with his wife.

"I'll have the Nation jet readied and meet you on the tarmac. Give me fifteen minutes."

"Thank you," she told him softly.

As if he'd be anywhere else?

He called Alice as he headed toward the kitchen, giving her instructions on what he needed done. On his way to meet them, Clive paused to feed. If Rowan asked, he'd be able to assure her he'd taken care of himself.

They'd both discovered it was important to trust the other was doing all they could to not only live but thrive in that life. His prickly wife did not like it one bit when she thought he wasn't feeding regularly or resting well. And Clive found her interest in his well-being the most intensely pleasurable thing in his existence.

He'd never imagined having a soft place within the fortress she'd build around herself. Instead, she'd given him a key.

The plane was being readied as his car approached. Alice waited at the base of the steps.

"She's inside already. There's a dossier at your seat you will want to look at as well. Ah." Alice raised a hand, waving at the car approaching with Patience at the wheel. "Dinner for everyone. I'll handle that part. Go on inside. I'll accompany you to provide overwatch."

Alice said it in a tone that brooked zero argument, so Clive nodded his thanks and headed to his wife.

That evening she wore slim-fitting black pants with several pockets and weapons loops, and a long-sleeved shirt. Her hair was pulled back into a fighting queue, leaving the lines of her face exposed to his hungry gaze.

"Dressed for a fight I see," he told her in a murmur as he settled at her side and then leaned to brush a kiss against her temple.

That she not only allowed it, but leaned into his touch,

was victory. He'd try not to crow about it. Out loud in any case.

She caught his satisfied smirk and sent him a raised brow. "And you're not wearing a suit. Slightly disappointing. You're so very handsome in them. Still, a treat as your own tactical gear fits you like a second skin."

"I too, am dressed for a fight." Once she'd called, he'd swapped out his business attire for an outfit similar to hers. "Tonight, I won't be staying in the car."

She opened her mouth to argue but he wasn't going to make it easy for her. He interrupted.

"I have a dossier here." He flipped open the top tab of the envelope and peeked inside. "Ooh. Photographs and secret Nation intelligence. I'm willing to share for a price."

"Like me saving Vampire butts?"

He chuckled, nodding to Alice as she climbed up the steps and into the plane.

"Prepare for takeoff, Scion," Alice said before finding her seat.

Clive told Rowan, "You're in a Nation jet for that. No, darling Hunter, my price is my presence at your side." He could protect her better that way, and he had a very strong feeling it might be necessary. Even if it wasn't, being prepared for the possibility pleased him far more than the alternative. "Think of all the deliciously secret things I might see."

Her annoyance faded with a snicker. "Fine. Did you eat?"

"As a matter of fact, I did. And, as a delightful bonus of my presence, dinner for you all has been brought as well. My chef sends his affection. I ought to behead him for the crush he has on you," he grumbled, but mainly to rile her up.

"But then who would make me miso butterfish?"

"That is my quandary."

"That, and his crush is unrequited. I've got my own sweetheart, and he doesn't share," she told him in a voice only he would hear.

"Gimme," she said after she finished her dinner and the attendant whisked away their dishes.

He handed the file over. "I haven't even looked yet."

"I also have a call log from the various phones and data cards we found at the Procella mansion. Vanessa shoved them at me as we left the office," Rowan said as she opened up a file of her own. "Another set of eyes is a good thing." She handed over a few pages each. David began to highlight and identify the numbers as they made their way toward their destination.

About twenty minutes later, the picture was beginning to form.

Rowan scanned the page that held the key David had made before she took one last look. She didn't want to say anything until she had.

"Lots of calls back and forth to Fiona's work and private number. About half that with Gerald. She did say she was the main contact so that tracks to a point. Loads with various Sansburys. Joseph, Rosemary, and Tristan. The Salazars are counted here, but in lesser numbers than the others. We don't have all the data culled yet, so there might be more to be found. Or he called them on a different phone. Or they only used carrier pigeon. Whatever. People are sneaky as fuck when they are up to crime." She looked over to Genevieve. "We know who Tristan is. Who is Rosemary?"

"Rose is Tristan's sister. She's…if you think Bess is cold, Rose makes her look like Mother Goose. Tristan took the Senate seat and Rosemary worked with their father running their businesses in Europe. This data says she lives here in the United States and is working with her uncle."

"What are their European businesses?"

"I looked it all up recently," Genevieve said. "Wanted to be sure as it's been a hundred years since I've been part of their family. They run housecleaning services all across Europe as well as a chain of self-service laundry shops."

Rowan sat back in her chair and thought a while.

What she had for certain was a sense that this was all tied together. It bore out through each bit of evidence they found. What she didn't know was exactly what was up. It had to be bad, or they wouldn't be willing to blow one another up over it.

"Well, we know they're connected. All these calls and their own words confirm it. We know it was their magic on that bomb at the Procellas'. So whatever it was they were up to, it was worth killing over. And killing is a pain in the ass. Once you do it you have so much hiding to deal with. Body disposal. Crime scene cleanup. Avoiding the authorities. It's a whole thing. That's why they hired the wolves, right?"

Genevieve blew out a breath. "Point taken. I agree. They don't know I've identified their signatures from the scene of the mage firebomb. But they do know I'm aware it was magical and not some sort of chemical used by humans."

"Excellent." They'd start to panic. Even longtime criminals who were good at hiding their behavior tended to make mistakes when they panicked.

There were two armored SUVs waiting for them when they landed and behind that, a line of motorcycles.

Rowan looked over to Genevieve, who appeared to be as surprised as Rowan was.

Darius had been on the plane with them and there was no way they could have driven from Vegas to Burbank in the time it took to fly there. And yet, six Devils sat on big throaty motorcycles, waiting patiently.

"Well, then. This is a surprise." Rowan said nothing further. They'd traveled in a Nation jet. One of the SUVs was driven by Pru and the other had Genevieve's second-in-command, Zara, at the wheel. It was already a multi-organization operation so why not add some chaos demigods to the mix?

Darius stalked over and had a chat with Marco before returning to them. "They'll follow and watch. Nothing will sneak up on us." He opened the rear door of one of the SUVs. "My lady."

Genevieve started to speak but closed her mouth and said over her shoulder to Rowan, "See you at the house. Don't go in without me. I mean it. I've set trap spells."

"Okay. See you in a bit."

David climbed in the front with Pru and Alice sat in the back with Rowan and Clive.

"We looked through a stack of photographs earlier today. Stuff we took from Elmer. There were some from the 1970s that had me rolling. Please tell me there are some of you in a velvet suit and platform shoes."

His look of horror made her day.

"I'm afraid I'll have to disappoint you."

"Only as it regards platform shoes and a velvet suit," Alice said. "I can confirm he did wear wide bell bottoms and had sideburns."

Rowan guffawed. "Pictures?"

"Most likely. I'll have a peek for you," Alice said, and Clive groaned.

"There's a painting in my in-laws' home of Clive with his father. 1740. He's wearing the most incredible brocade vest. And hose and shoes with a heel."

"I do not miss wearing hose. Or tricorn hats," Clive muttered.

"You have really nice legs though. However, I prefer the one in my bedchamber."

Clive's mother had sent it to Rowan as a gift. In it, Clive is wearing buckskin breeches and top boots. A white linen shirt with a perfectly folded cravat under a navy blue cutaway tailcoat completed the look. He looked like the prince he was. Sexy. Saucy. Supremely convinced of his worth.

"I bet you he sullied ladies all across the ton back in those days," Rowan teased but he shrugged with a smile. "No lie, I'd have let him back me into a darkened garden or take all the dances on my dance card," Rowan said and while it was a tease, it was also true. Even if he probably wouldn't have looked twice at Rowan at that point in his life.

"Darling, I'd have snatched you right up. Every waltz and quadrille. You were made for candlelight."

She was glad it was dark so no one could see her blush.

"Though I will tell you how many layers of clothing women had to wear back then. So many buttons and skirts and underthings. Rather makes a quick assignation difficult."

"Not impossible though."

His chuckle was a caress. "Never impossible when one has the determination."

He took her hand and squeezed it before bringing it to his mouth for a kiss. She would have let him ruin her in a carriage or whatever the fuck it was that happened back then.

Still, thank goodness for modernity when it came to access for those quick assignations her rakish spouse liked because he knew how to get himself inside her right quick.

"On the way back, there's a stack of photos I want you to look at," she said as they got off the freeway and took surface streets to get to the house. "I recognize some of the Vampires, but others, you'll know more than I would."

"All right." Clive nodded.

"If you wish to speak to Alfonso or Bess Procella while we're here in the area, your home here has been readied. You can stay until sunset tomorrow, if necessary," Alice said.

How spoiled was she that she hadn't even remembered they had a house in Southern California to stay in when they were both doing work-related stuff in the area?

She teased him, "I hear some people buy flowers, but you buy houses."

"You need houses more than flowers."

"You also buy me flowers," she muttered. He'd sent her dozens of red and pink peonies because they were her favorite.

"Someone needs to spoil you," he said in her ear. "Don't deny me my pleasures."

"Who denies you anything, Scion?" she teased.

"Only one very stubborn Vessel. Everyone else falls in line."

"You'd be so bored if I was that way."

"True."

"Well. As for staying tonight? I guess we'll play it by ear to see where we are after we check out this place and whatever tripped the alarm spell thing."

They rolled into the neighborhood where the missing witches' house was, and Rowan felt the weight of magic in the air.

"We're here," Pru announced as she parked behind the other SUV. "We've had a watch set up since you called to alert us the spell had been triggered. No one—not us anyway—has entered or left since we arrived."

"Perfect." Rowan texted Genevieve, who replied she'd go first, pull down the spells, and then Rowan should follow.

"I'll accompany you," Clive said. "David and Alice will provide excellent overwatch."

Rowan gave him a narrow-eyed glance, but it was a good use of resources, so she spoke quietly to David, waited for Genevieve's signal. And when it came, she and Clive slid from the car and headed across the quiet street.

"It doesn't look terribly different than it did when we were here two weeks ago." Rowan took in the yard and the exterior of the home beyond. The lawn had been mowed recently, but David had said there was a service for that paid for by the landlord, so it wasn't evidence of anyone being there for any other reason.

Chapter Twenty-One

Rowan headed toward the pile of trash at the side of the house. People threw out all sorts of incriminating stuff, so she'd give it a quick riffle to see what was there.

But when she was just a few feet away, she saw movement. Fucking raccoons.

Clive growled low in his throat, which meant he saw it too.

"Better not give me rabies," she muttered and then froze as a sound came from that pile, and it wasn't a raccoon or a rat. A whimper of pain.

"Shit. Someone is down!" Rowan called out as she hustled over to what wasn't garbage at all.

It was a woman. A woman who'd been severely beaten.

Rowan wasn't even sure where to touch that wouldn't cause more hurt, her heart squeezing with pity as she went to her knees next to the woman. "I'm here," Rowan murmured. "I'm going to help you. Please don't be afraid." She opened herself to Brigid, who rose instantly, healing and soothing magic flowing from Rowan into the injured woman.

Genevieve approached at a run and slid to a stop, kneeling. "Ah, there you are," she said quietly. "Rowan, this is Dorothy Decker. One of the witches who went missing."

David arrived with a first aid kit. "Shall I call for an ambulance?" he asked.

"Let me see to her immediate injuries," Genevieve said, distracted as she ran her palms over Dorothy's body. No. Not on the body, just above it. Rowan now saw the flickers of magic that rolled in waves from her friend. That magic surrounded Dorothy like a blanket and then it drew taut with a snap. As Rowan watched, something dark and heavy lifted from her.

Dorothy moaned and gasped, her back bowing, and then she went lax again, her eyes drifting closed.

"I've put her under. Hopefully that will help the pain."

"She's been fed upon repeatedly," Clive said, kneeling at Rowan's side. He brushed Dorothy's hair away from her throat, exposing bites that hadn't healed.

Cold fury slammed into her. This wasn't simply a blood exchange. This had been torture. She'd been left with open wounds that had continued to bleed intermittently because Vampires had anti-clotting agents they released as they fed. It eased the blood flow, making the feed quicker as well. Normally, the Vampire would then lick over the bite as their saliva contained healing components to close the tears in the skin.

"They did this on purpose. To prolong her suffering." Which meant a particular kind of Vampire. One who liked to feed on fear as well as blood. Or they tried to use pain to get her to do something she didn't want to. As a witch, she'd have some basic protections against glamor, but powerful Vampires manipulated and glamored their food in different ways all the time.

"It appears so." Clive's voice was tightly controlled but Rowan heard the echo of her anger in him. "I can have a team take her to one of our medical facilities. She will get treatment. No further harm will come to her."

While she appreciated the offer—and believed her husband cared for this injured human—that was the last thing Dorothy needed. Vampires had been the ones who'd done this to her to start with.

Rowan said to him, "I am grateful for the offer of assistance. Given the wounds and how she most likely received them, I'm going to caution her away from Vampires. At least until we get her stabilized and she's conscious enough to make her own choices. In her place, I imagine just seeing a Vampire would be a blow after whatever she's endured."

He nodded. "Understood. The Nation stands by to assist however it can. You know the Scion is very much opposed to such behavior and is doing all he can to deal with it."

That for all the years before he'd come along such a thing hadn't been true was something she knew Clive was committed to handling. *Was* handling. But it was what Vampires did. And had done for generations. It took time and energy to undo that.

He bent close to Dorothy and breathed in deep. Running all those scents and patterns any Vampires would have left behind through his big Scion brain.

Genevieve tipped her chin in appreciation of his offer. Relieved Rowan had said no so she didn't have to. "I've just asked Konrad to send a medical team. They should arrive shortly. She is stable. Once she's settled and conscious again, we'll be able to speak to her."

"Okay. Good."

David settled a blanket he'd retrieved from one of

the vehicles over Dorothy. "I'll stay here with her. Go see if the others are inside."

"Good idea," Rowan said as she stood.

Pru had joined David. Keeping a watch over Dorothy. "Go. Nothing will happen to her."

Genevieve looked back toward the young woman who'd been so misused. Her guts twisted a moment and then she shoved it deep. Far away. She needed to work. She'd feel sorrow and rage afterward.

The back door had been broken open and it was clear someone had been there.

"David said the cameras he put up all went out at the same time as your spell was triggered," Rowan said.

The interior had been tossed. Furniture had been tipped over or shoved sideways.

"They were looking for her," Rowan murmured as she moved through the house. "See? Big stuff has been moved but to check behind or beneath. The drawers haven't been turned out, but the cabinets have been opened."

"She came here but was it before or after they had?" Genevieve asked.

"When we first arrived, I thought she was a bag of trash that had been left. If Dorothy was smart enough to get away from wherever she was, if she was smart enough to get here, she was smart enough to hide because she saw her captors, or knew they'd come soon. It's only been two hours since the spell alerted you," Rowan said.

"Do you think they're watching?"

Rowan turned in a circle, taking in all the details. "I don't know. I would be. They were smart enough to disable the cameras inside."

"Not smart enough to avoid setting off a trap spell," Genevieve said. "Not smart enough to look around the yard. They turned over a desk, but they didn't look in the side yard where she was?"

"A few scenarios occur to me. They were obviously in a hurry. Which means she got loose. They had her and she escaped. But she's in a state. Looks like she's been fed on for a while. Some of the bites I saw looked a week old. She couldn't have run very far without collapsing. Someone might have helped her and then run themselves to take their attention off her. When we can talk with her, she'll be able to give us some answers."

Genevieve said, "One hopes."

"This is important. Integral to what is going on. That's why I dreamed it and that's why we're here. Without food or water, she'd have perished within twenty-four hours. I was meant to be right here right now. Which means she's got something to relate to me. I'll know it when I hear it."

Genevieve nodded again. She agreed with those points. Prophetic dreams and fugue states like Rowan had been experiencing were extraordinary. And rare. These gifts were powerful tools.

"Medicals are here," David said from the doorway.

"I want to go with her. See that she gets seen to and settled," Genevieve told Rowan. "Come along. She'll be in the same building we're holding Alfonso and Bess Procella. I imagine you might want to chat with them."

In the car, Clive put an arm around her and pulled her to his side. Her nerves were jangled, he knew.

And then very quietly he said, "She's been fed on by three Vampires. She's an adept."

Adepts were humans or witches with a certain type

of genetic makeup that rendered their blood perfect for Vampires. They had only identified the protein compound in the blood of certain humans and witches that made them adepts two years before that.

Even before they had a name for the protein, they had a name for those who were the most sought-after blood donors. They were the ones who were kept long term. The most spoiled and protected.

From what they understood, it was a protein compound that reacted to the physiology of Vampires in a way that unlocked nearly every last bit of nutrients and power from their blood.

"Theo always claimed adept blood tasted better. But I've heard others deny that."

"Some Vampires, like some humans, have no discernment." To Clive, the difference was marked. Rowan's blood was like the finest champagne. Light and full of energy. Like a secret on his tongue. Her taste at once unforgettable and yet it wisped away after a breath.

"You're an adept," he said, his lips against her ear as he drew her into his lungs a moment. "You taste better than anything I've ever experienced."

She let a little shiver roll through her. Then she remembered herself and her surroundings and turned to send him a look. Which only made him madder for her.

He kissed her then. Just a brush of his mouth against hers. Reassurance for them both, he realized. "I've found adept blood does have a unique taste though it's difficult to explain it. There's a quality to it you notice when you're drinking from someone who isn't."

Alice said, "It's the difference between low-sodium tomato juice and the regular V8. There's a fullness, perhaps that protein, that spices it up somehow."

Rowan nodded. "Okay. I get that. Was she taken because she was an adept? Or was she kept because she was one? Is there a list you have? Within the Nation I mean?"

Clive shook his head as he considered how much to tell her. "Of all humans and witches who are adepts? That's a great deal of information of a sort that makes it difficult to collect."

Rowan rolled her eyes at him. "So yes." She held up a hand to forestall his argument. "But not a dedicated one. Not yet. It's like you met me yesterday if you thought I'd miss that evasion."

Naturally. But it kept her on her toes instead of thinking about that sad woman they'd found nearly drained of her life.

"Not a specific database. However, those who are in service who are known to be adepts have it noted in their files," Alice said.

Better Alice to reveal such things than Clive. It made things easier when he was asked if he'd told Rowan something.

"I wonder if the other two roommates are adepts?" Rowan asked. "Are they in your system? Perhaps a family member is in service or has been at some point?"

"We wouldn't have had cause to have run their names through our system. Until now." Alice held up her phone. "Let me get that started," she said after Clive nodded his head once to give permission.

David leaned in to give Alice the names and other details as Clive sighed.

"You had your own messes to clean up," Rowan murmured to him.

It had been a Conclave issue and after the Blood

Front nonsense, as she'd said, he had his focus on other things than missing witches and humans.

"I made a mistake in thinking that the end of one particular chapter was the end of this very long tale."

Vampires had a focus on the long game. The big picture that took time and slow, patient energy to create.

"We don't even know there's a connection."

"Rowan." Clive kissed her knuckles and then kept her hand in his. "We found an adept who'd been misused. A witch who'd gone missing."

"Well, for fuck's sake. I didn't see any connection either, and not because I'm stupid. It's because those witches had gone missing to fuel spells for an exiled Fae and stolen death magic wielded by a bananapants ancient Vampire. Both are true dead. And in the interim, there's been a hundred different things going on what with ambush murder attempts and mage firebombs. The witches have a problem and that's where we've been looking."

"Well, there's certainly a link now," David said. "Dorothy and her roommate Jaylin are both witches. And now we've found one who's obviously been at the mercy of Vampires who appear to have none. Now that we know, we're looking."

They passed through an industrial area and on the edge of that, as it began to turn into residential here and there, the SUV Genevieve was in pulled into an alley behind a squat four-story stucco building that looked to have been constructed in the early seventies.

The loading dock door slid up and they helped bring Dorothy inside. Then one of them pointed to the next entrance where a gate slid open to a small parking lot.

"They're taking her to the clinic here. They'll notify

me when she's stabilized. I've filled them in on how we found her and what we suspect happened to her." Genevieve swept through a door Darius held open. In the background somewhere Rowan heard the roar of motorcycles and knew the Devils were out there on patrol.

They went through a security checkpoint where everyone received specialized badges indicating their access level.

If anyone had anything to say about a group that included a Hunter, some Vampires including a Scion, and two Dust Devils, having Genevieve and Konrad opening the way for them seemed to address their concerns.

Rowan liked that because even though it would be fun for the moment to get into it with someone, they had bigger problems to focus on.

"They'll bring Bess in first," Genevieve said as she led them all into a conference room with a few computer stations set up and a worktable in the center. "It's going to take a few minutes so if you want to work in here while we wait you can."

Rowan sat. "David, find out what we can about Rose Sansbury. And check on those other numbers we highlighted that might be his whatever we call it. Girlfriend. Mistress. I want some names so I can work them into this discussion I'm about to have with Bess."

Rowan flipped through the various packets and files she had before she brought out a stack of photos. "These are stills captured from the video we gathered while at the Sansbury and Clare homes. There's a connection between them and the Procellas. Joseph, Fiona, and Gerard all three admitted that they did business. The Procellas haven't said anything about them. Nor do they know their home was blown up by their business associates. That will be a fun reveal. I want to drop things on them both until I make someone bleed answers."

"Ever a poet."

Rowan snorted at Clive's whispered comment.

Rowan spread out five at a time as Genevieve identified the witches in them and David took notes.

"Here are the ones we took from the Procella mansion on the first search."

Lots of Sergio with Hugo and a petite brunette Rowan recognized from the video of the interview they'd done with Bess Procella.

"Ah, here's one at some swankfest." Rowan pulled one out of a bunch of witches in formalwear, champagne flutes in hand, jewels dripping off the women. "Fiona and Gerard are in this."

"The couple to Hugo's left are the Salazars. Camila and Jorge. That's Rose Sansbury in between Joseph and Sergio." Genevieve pointed to a pretty blonde whose smile didn't reach her eyes.

They looked through more photos and then Rowan pulled out a few envelopes that had been tucked in the bottom of a box of files. It was one thing to put a photo on a wall. Or in an album. Photos that had been tucked away—kept but not acknowledged with a frame—could be very good bits of information.

Turns out, the smile didn't reach Bess Procella's eyes either, Rowan realized as they sat across from her. Rowan didn't bother with one, fake or otherwise.

"Why am I here? I have been taken from my cruise and brought back here like a criminal. Held against my will. This is outrageous."

Rowan sighed heavily. "You're all so fucking tedious. You know why you're here. You know your son was a stalker. You know your father-in-law and son hired a hit squad and you know your family is deeply involved in things so illegal the Conclave is paying attention."

"I have no idea what you mean."

Rowan had been up against people like Bess scores of times. They always thought they were better than everyone else and that was their weakness.

"Whatever it might be, Bess," Genevieve said, so cold and remote it sliced through the air, "it was enough to respond to with a mage firebomb that destroyed your home and killed six of your employees. A mage firebomb with a trigger spell so complicated it took *three* Genetic witches on-site to ignite."

Bess had emotion in her eyes then. Rage and then terror.

Rowan watched her fight herself. Neither emotion was going to do her a favor, so Rowan let Bess be her own worst enemy.

Genevieve said, "I looked Fiona Clare in the eyes when we talked about the bomb and how you didn't die. I watched her guilt and then I saw her put it away. But that doesn't matter because I have her magical signature. And Gerald's. And, in a twist, Rose Sansbury. I was thinking it was Joseph. I was married to Tristan so I'm familiar with the way the Sansbury magic looks. But I was assuming. It was Rose there with at least one of the Salazars and the others to create the spell that blew your home to bits."

"What are you saying?" Bess, wide-eyed, stared as if she willed them to deny it.

"I'm saying your business partners, the Clares, Salazars, and Sansburys, got fed up with the Procella family after a series of disastrous and reckless actions including a murder attempt in full camera view in front of two dozen tourists. Sergio and Hugo have gotten high on all that entitlement and privilege, and they've gotten you all tarred with that brush."

Rowan loved the way the truth seemed to wash over her and stripped away her defiance.

A text showed up on Rowan's phone. From Genevieve. It said, "*I just realized the splinter of magic from Dorothy's house belongs to Rose S.*"

Well, now. Two weeks before when they'd come looking for Dorothy and her roommates, they'd found a suspiciously clean-of-magic space, except for one tiny fleck that had been missed.

And it was another connection to the Sansburys.

Bess said, her voice starting to fray with emotion, "My home has been destroyed? How have I not heard?"

Rowan slid several photographs of the burned-out shell of the Procella mansion across the table. "I guess you should be glad you were all in custody at the time or you'd be dead too. But they know you're alive now, so I'm going to guess they're working on that. Whatever are you up to, Bess?"

"Just cargo. That's it."

"What sort of cargo has the people moving it using hidden rooms and under bed rigs? Oh, I should mention I found the ones at your house before it was blown up. So much data on those phones and cards. Fortunately the bombers don't know about the ranch home where Sergio kept all his incriminating evidence, or that love nest he has out in the Lakes that he keeps for...what's her name again?"

Rowan pretended to look for it just to draw it out longer and mess with Bess's head. "Teresa Davis. We're looking for her now, but it appears she left her three-million-dollar town house, and hasn't been back for several days. No sign of the Mercedes Sergio gave her." They'd only just learned that right before they started the interview and it hit Bess hard.

"This can't be happening," Bess murmured with more emotion than she'd shown up to that point. "Teresa. Are you saying she's involved?"

"What's her story anyway?" Rowan asked instead.

"She used to work for Fiona. She was with Hugo first. Then when Sergio's first mistress, Greta, was put out to pasture with a big fat payoff and a warning to never come back, Teresa found her way into his bed within weeks. She's been with him for the past several years. He's been talking about marrying her, but he's never even had her at the mansion, so I'm not convinced. Alfonso and Hugo are opposed for obvious reasons."

"Which are?"

"She's a...secretary! What does she know about anything but fucking the men in the family?"

"Including Alfonso?"

Darius asked that, surprising Rowan enough she had to steel herself to keep still and not gape at him.

"No! Not for lack of trying."

"She's the one who brought you all together for this...business venture that's just cargo?"

"We'd done some business together over the years. When we ran ships across the Atlantic to bring people here from European ports and into the modern age. But."

Bess seemed to realize she'd been sharing and shut her mouth.

"So in between trying to nail Alfonso and then dumping Hugo, her second choice, for Sergio, who wants to marry her, making her your…mother-in-law, Teresa is just in your words, *a secretary.* So you're all responsible for whatever you're up to."

Bess sat forward, spurred on by the specter of having to bear responsibility for something she'd done wrong. "No! She and Fiona started a side business with Rose and that's when she convinced Hugo and Sergio to buy in."

"Buy in to what?" Genevieve asked.

She started to speak but then couldn't. Over and over again. She tried to write but the page remained blank.

Finally Rowan said, "Are you under a geas?" A geas was a spell that prevented someone from discussing something out loud. It could be a person or a topic. Or an event. They were old magic. Very strong and only broken by the death of whoever laid it, or upon their release of the magic. Theo had been bound by one for centuries. Rowan had killed the Vampire witch who'd put it on him, freeing him.

Clearly pissed off, Bess nodded.

Alfonso was similarly bound. Which left them with an understanding there was some shady business going on but not exactly what.

"We need to find Rose Sansbury."

"As it is already midnight, I'm going to suggest we stay here overnight. The house is only about twenty minutes by car and Clive can reach it in about half that time should he fly instead," Alice said quietly as they went back to the conference room they'd been in previously.

Chapter Twenty-Two

Rowan paced a little as she ran through what they knew. "So, current girlfriend used to work for Fiona. Fiona, who is also distantly related to Bess. Let's figure out if old Terry is really a secretary, or if that was just Bess's jealousy talking. Via Fiona, Teresa meets Rose. And at some point, Hugo sees Teresa and they start a thing. Goddess, I hope it was consensual. Even if Teresa is a scumbag, no one deserves what he tried to do to you and the other women he stalked."

Genevieve made one of those French sounds. A grunt, but less vulgar. An acknowledgment she'd heard and also agreed.

Rowan said, "I should have an answer quickly with Rose's address. She's got to be either here or in Las Vegas. Her magic was at the house on Holly and at the Procella mansion. She could still live in England with the other Sansburys. But I doubt it. Speaking of doubt, are we sure which Clare and Salazar were the ones doing the spell?"

"Until we talked with Fiona, I would have said Gerard. He's the public face of their family. But she's the power. I don't think she'd have allowed him to do it and mess things up."

Rowan agreed with Genevieve on that.

"Her magic has hints of blueberry in it," Darius rumbled. "His was raspberry. The part of the trigger the Clares wielded was hers. Her spell and her power."

"Well, that's very helpful," Genevieve said. "I don't know which Salazar. I've only met them a few times over the years so I'm afraid I'm not much help on that. However, Samaya was running a search to see which one of them flew out of Miami to come help perform the working. That'll be our answer. And then we can get that to Zara so she can use it when she arrives in Miami."

Samaya came in just five minutes later. "I've got Rose's address. And it was Javier who flew out to Las Vegas. He hasn't gone back yet. His return isn't for three more days. I called their business line asking for him. They said he was on the West Coast for business. I got the hotel information. Konrad is sending a team to apprehend him now."

Rowan looked up Rose's address. "She's in Manhattan Beach. That's about twenty-five minutes or so from here. Holy fuck, her rent is eighteen thousand dollars a month. Damn. I guess whatever nefarious criming she's up to pays well. Let's go say hello."

When Genevieve got out of the car and the salt from the nearby ocean met her senses, her power seemed to double and redouble. Salt in the desert along veins, salt in the ocean—she'd found out only recently that she was a salt witch, able to use ambient salt in the atmosphere as fuel for her workings.

As salt repelled a lot of magic, it was the sort of hidden weapon that elevated her magical power to levels she'd not even contemplated before.

"For over two hundred grand a year in rent, you think there'd be a doorman," Rowan grumbled.

"There's decent security," Clive said as he took the eight-unit building in. "Three floors, she's in the middle. North side on the corner. I see external cameras on the front on both corners of the building and over the front entry."

"A moment," David said, and they all paused. Three minutes later he said, "Vanessa has taken over the surveillance system here. On our approach she'll buzz us in and get us access to Rose's floor."

"Overwatch in place," Pru said over Rowan's earpiece. "Let's go ruin Rose's day."

Genevieve took the lead because there was simply no way she was allowing Rowan to get attacked by a witch again. Not on her watch. Naturally, Darius took the lead in front of her. The entire evening had been bizarre. Each new revelation worse than the last. And now she was about to come face-to-face with her ex-sister-in-law, who was up to something bad enough they blew up a house and everyone in it to keep it secret.

"There's no one at home but in that apartment on this floor," Clive said, and they all stepped to the side so she could ring the bell.

No one responded so Genevieve knocked.

Rowan stepped up. "I got this." She pressed her finger on the doorbell button, and after noting it was a long tone, she pressed again and kept the pressure as the bell continued to sound on the other side of the closed door.

"I've got all night, Rose. Answer the door because you aren't going back to sleep until you do."

In the background, Clive snickered, and Genevieve allowed a smile.

Then she began to alternate three kicks, three pounds and continued to ring the bell.

"Normally, I'd climb up onto her balcony and kick my way in but that's a little out of my physical limits just now. Genevieve, are there any spells on this door?"

Genevieve used her othersight and noted the apartment was far better warded than any of the Procellas' properties had been.

"Hold."

The warding used salt as a way to frustrate a witch trying to unravel the protections. But Genevieve's magic gobbled all that salt working up and it simply amplified her own. Within six minutes, she'd managed to clear away every layer of complex warding until the door was safe.

"Clive? Kick this door in," Rowan said while looking right into the doorbell camera. "Back up, Rose, this big heavy door is about to demolish whatever's behind it. Hope it's not art. Or people."

Rowan was so delightfully devious.

As Rowan had figured, the sound of bolts sliding free and locks being flipped came, and the big door slowly opened to reveal the same woman from the photographs. Only in person, her eyes weren't flat and emotionless, they were brimming with malice.

Rowan walked inside, bumping Rose's shoulder on the way. "Hope we didn't wake you up."

"Get out of my house!"

Ugh, a screecher. "Eat shit." Recorder on, Rowan gave a slow turn to take the front entry in. She didn't want to go farther until Genevieve had assured them there were no spelltraps because Rowan was sick and tired of getting the crap beat out of her by witches and their sneaky spellcasting.

"She's with me," Genevieve said as she closed the door at her back and stepped fully into the foyer. "It's very rude to keep a guest waiting."

"It's nearly one in the morning. I was sleeping. You can't just harass me like this. There are rules."

Rowan turned and sneered in Rose's direction. For someone who'd been sleeping she had a full face of makeup, and her hair was still in place. She'd been awake and trying to duck their visit.

"The greatest irony in the world is how people who break rules right and left without a fucking thought or care as to how that might affect others are always the first to claim rules when they get caught out in their bullshit." Rowan raised one shoulder. "So, yes let's have a discussion about rules."

Genevieve made a sound as she went through a series of hand and wrist movements. Her bracelets clacked and jingled, and her eyes stared at something far off in the distance. Then she stomped and yanked on the air and Rowan felt the warding all around them fall to the ground like rain and then it was gone.

"That was really impressive," she said to Genevieve, who looked very pleased with herself.

"I made it myself," Genevieve teased back. "Now, Rosemary, shall we move to your office or a sitting room?"

"No, you may not. You need to leave, or I'll call the police."

Rowan and Genevieve froze at those words and then anger came.

"Oh, you will?" Rowan asked. "You'll call the human police?"

"If you think I won't, you're wrong."

"I think all I needed to know was that you were willing to involve humans in a supernatural matter, which is a violation of the Treaty. I'm Rowan Summerwaite and in a cruel twist of fate for you, it's my job to be sure it's not violated."

Genevieve said, "Exposing us to humans is a violation. You're going to be taken into custody now. Then we'll see you in about two hours to have a chat."

Because main Conclave operations were in Southern California, there'd already been a team waiting to take her in and Samaya showed them to the apartment.

"You can't do this."

"You all say that." Rowan shrugged. "I'm here. Free to come and go. You're under arrest and I'm about to riffle through all your things. Understand this. You aren't in charge. I am. See you in a bit, Rose. Can't wait to get to know you better."

They searched the two-bedroom apartment from top to bottom. Warding indicated multiple hiding spots rich in all sorts of things. Phones. Data cards and storage. In the last was jewelry and watches.

On the way back, they talked through what they had.

Rowan said, "On the surface, there are many things about this situation that aren't unusual. Lots of warding? She's a single woman living alone. Same with the secure building. Rich people love to have hidey-holes to keep their treasures near to look at and also not get stolen from the top of the dresser. A hundred grand seems like an excessive amount of cash to have on hand, but I bet it isn't to a certain level of businessperson." At her side, Clive made a sound that said they probably had that much cash in a safe at her house and she chose to pretend not to hear it. "Eight phones though? All hidden. All used regularly. There is a system with the calls. You can see that with each one. Steps in a process of some type."

"Some of them are to the various parties in this little conspiracy," Genevieve said. "I recognize Sergio's number, as well as one of those belonging to the Clares. We know they do business together. But this seems an unusual process."

"It does. Maybe it's a legit business thing and she keeps it all separate for tax purposes or whatever. Why hide the phones though? Corporate espionage? She's worried someone will steal something proprietary?" Rowan didn't think so. But it was always useful to figure out what sort of excuses someone might give in advance to be prepared to refute or clarify.

"Go back to the house whenever you need to," she told Clive quietly once they arrived.

"Sun won't be up for three and a half hours. I'll stay until the last moment and hope to drive home with you. If not, you'll have Darius, Genevieve, and David with you on the ride back since they're all staying with us. I know they'll be safe with you."

He deliberately chose to say it that way. Instead of them protecting her, which was far more likely.

Satisfied he'd take care of himself, they went inside.

"You're going to regret this," Rosemary said as she and Genevieve entered the room a few hours later.

"One of us will, certainly," Genevieve said as they sat.

"You didn't have a warrant. You can't just arrest me like this. I need a lawyer."

"Dorothy Decker."

Genevieve lobbed the name of the witch they'd found, brutalized. The witch whose home they'd found a bit of Rosemary's magic in.

Rose froze for a moment and then shook it off. "Should I know that name?"

Rowan took a leap. "You should. It was on several of the lists kept on more than one of those data cards you had hidden."

They hadn't had a chance to open those before they arrived. David and Samaya and one of the tech people from the Conclave were on that just a few doors down and Rowan was fairly sure she'd just told the truth.

"Surely you saw there were many lists with many names. How could I possibly remember them all? If you told me what this was about, I might have the context to remember."

Rowan wanted to give her a slow clap. Because the way she'd just responded only verified Rowan's suspicions.

"Tell me about your business dealings with Fiona Clare," Genevieve said.

Ooh, keeping Rose on the ropes. She and Genevieve would tag team to keep her off-balance and unable to spin lies and excuses.

Relieved, thinking she could handle that question, Rose said, "We're in the same industry but different aspects of it."

"Let's assume it would be far more helpful if you could give us concrete examples," Rowan said.

"For instance," Rosemary said, "the Sansburys run tours in wine country in Northern California. Limos and party busses, that sort of thing. We pick them up at their hotel or a central point in downtown and a driver takes them to multiple tastings. We partnered with the Clares, who were bringing cruise passengers through southern California. They now have a scenic leg of their trip after the cruise, or before, to take our tours and stay in some of the hotels owned by another witch family."

"The Salazars," Genevieve said.

"Y-yes."

Rowan jumped in. "And the Procellas? Oh, let me guess, they're the part of this deal with the cruise. Those people offload Procella-run or -controlled cruises, get on a Clare train to Napa where they ride your party limo things, and stay in Salazar hotels. Is that right?"

Rose's back got stiff with insult. "Many magical families work with one another. It's how we keep our businesses thriving when we are so very curtailed in our ability to use our gifts to earn a living. It's a very lucrative deal and we've expanded it to Seattle in the summer and fall as well."

Rowan curled her lip. "You mean when you can't use your magic to manipulate others into doing whatever you want. Yeah, tough world. I'm sure you cry yourself to sleep every night in your eighteen-thousand-dollar-a-month apartment."

"You can't just talk to me that way. You aren't even a witch."

Rowan responded like Rose was a pet, or a toddler. "I'm Rowan. We met at your place. Do you remember that?" Then she hardened. "As I said to you earlier, I can and will talk to you any way I want because I'm in charge and you are not. Now. Let's get back to the point, shall we?"

"It's not illegal to work with other witches. It's not illegal to make a profit from that work."

"It is illegal to use a spell trigger to set off a mage firebomb that killed nine witches and humans," Genevieve said.

"You're making things up because you're mad at my family."

Genevieve laughed, delight in the sound. Rowan found that scary as fuck and clearly Rose did too, because the other witch's eyes widened and then she tried to scoot her chair back and found she'd been chained in place magically as well as physically.

"Notice you didn't deny it, though," Rowan said.

"It's a preposterous claim."

Genevieve chuckled at that.

"The way I see it, Rosemary, you're involved in some very dangerous activities with some very dangerous people. Witches, to be specific. But see, you're doing these things in my territory and all of it is just a big giant *violation of the Treaty*. That and you're involved with the people who paid to have me killed. So I'm a little extra cranky about that. My car cost a ridiculous amount of money to replace. Normally, I'd just think it was the cost of doing business in my line of work. Except you live in an apartment that costs eighteen grand a month. For whatever reason, that really, really pisses me off. Bystanders could have been injured. Human bystanders. The attack was on camera so I had to hold back so it wasn't clear I was anything more than a very strong human. That resulted in several more gunshots I could have avoided."

"And then you blew up a house we were all inside at

the time," Genevieve added. "Just a great deal of violence over some wine country limo tours."

"I had nothing to do with that business on the strip. As for this claim that I was part of a working to blow up a house? Preposterous."

Rowan sat back a little in her chair. "I was raised by Vampires. So, I've spent every moment of my life having to parcel out who was telling the truth and who was using true things to avoid answering a question they didn't want to lie about. Most people don't notice. Which is how people like you get away with it for so long." Rowan used two fingers to point at her eyes and then toward Rosemary. "I see you, Rosemary. And I see what you're doing. You aren't fooling anyone."

"You have no proof."

Rowan's laugh was mean.

"But we do, Rose." Genevieve shook her head. "Even our youngest are taught their workings leave evidence. Marks and impressions that are theirs uniquely. Like a fingerprint."

"That's just stories they tell kids."

"That's what witches who *don't* have that gift like to say. But I do. Have that gift, I mean. When I stood up on that little rise you three used, I saw your magic there. Like I saw Fiona's and Javier's. If we hadn't been there at the time of the explosion, I might have missed it. But I knew the direction the magic came from and that was the clue I needed to find the spot you launched the spells from."

"That's a lie," Rose said.

Rowan waved a hand and rolled her eyes. "Here's the deal, sister. You can help us and give the tribunal a reason to show leniency with your sentence. Or you can keep up this charade and be sentenced anyway. Before you begin to counter like this is a negotiation, don't. Those are your options, and this is not up for debate."

"You have no standing here. You're not a witch."

"I am Rowan Summerwaite." She stood and leaned down on her arms as she got right into Rose's face. "I am Hunter Corp.'s sword arm on this *entire continent*. What are you? A half-talented witch who is fucked. Your actions, documented with all sorts of concrete proof, are a violation of the Treaty the Conclave is a signatory to. Which means *you* are beholden to it as well. To me, if we want to be poetic. And I do because I'm the only one of the two of us with standing. I am absolutely within my rights to execute you this exact moment. And to be super honest and transparent with you, I'd love to do it because you are a danger to everyone around you."

Rose's bravado faded, replaced by pallor and wide eyes.

"Yes, look shocked because that means you're closer to true comprehension here. It means you understand me when I tell you I could kill you, go out for pancakes after, and then sleep a solid eight hours, content in the knowledge you could no longer blow up buildings with the gifts you could have used to win at life instead. So, fuck you, Rosemary, and your simpering bullshittery. I see you for what you are. I know you for what you are."

David sent her a text that said Dorothy had regained consciousness and wanted to speak to them.

Genevieve must have gotten the same text because she said, "Last chance to be useful, Rose. We're going to head out to speak with some witnesses who'll gladly fill in the blanks you refuse to."

"What does that mean? She just threatened to kill me. You're a witch too. You're supposed to protect me!"

"My job, the job of all witches, is to protect our weakest and stand shoulder to shoulder against threats. You're the threat this time. As for what Rowan told you just now? The truth."

Rose clamped her mouth closed and after a shrug, Rowan turned and said to the witch who'd just opened the door to the hallway, "Please take her back to her cell."

Chapter Twenty-Three

"She's not going to say a word." Genevieve used a keypad to get them through to another part of the floor. "She knows we have her on the explosion and that we know there's *something* going on between these families. But she thinks she can wait, and we'll give up."

"If you set her free, I'm going to hunt her down and end her myself. Don't test me. I beheaded a fucking Scion, that bitch in there is nothing by comparison."

Genevieve's laughter relaxed the witch whose back went stiff as she overheard Rowan's words. Rowan's serious, totally honest words.

"She won't walk free for the next century, maybe two. That bomb I can absolutely track back to her. She's responsible for the deaths of all those witches and humans and she did it in a public way. However, I can't deny the pleasure I will feel when she finally figures out she's done for, and nothing and no one can help her."

"I like this side of you," Rowan told her.

"I'm exhausted by these machinations. If we didn't need to know more from them, I'd simply send them all away immediately, stripped of their magic for eternity. Now, let's go see this poor girl that woman brutalized."

"I still think her magic needs to be stripped away for eternity. She's used it to harm others more than once."

Genevieve was leaning toward the same perspective. "We're not going to set her free to let her hurt anyone else. Of that you can be certain." She'd make the recommendation to Konrad, and he'd take it into consideration along with whatever Hunter Corp. and the Dust Devils had to say.

Standing just outside the double doors leading to the small medical clinic, Rowan was hit by a wave of… certainty. This was where she needed to be. Answers were coming.

A soft yip had them turning to catch sight of Star trotting toward them. Since the last time Rowan had seen her dog was in Las Vegas several hours before it was a bit of a surprise, but frankly, Star was far more often a help than a hindrance.

And Rowan didn't want to fail. Not the woman on the other side of the door or her missing friends.

Star went to her back legs and braced her front paws almost delicately around any possible sore spots on Rowan's chest. Then she touched her cool nose to Rowan's and gave her a quick kiss before going back to all fours.

It was hard to be sad when your dog touched noses with you. Rowan gave Star a scratch behind her ears before she took a deep breath and got her head back in the game.

"Dorothy is the key," she murmured to Genevieve. "My dreams keep sending me here. And with all the bites, there's obviously a connection to the Vampires." Clive was already on the hunt for whichever fanged fuckheads were responsible. Rowan would be delighted to help in that endeavor once they were able to speak with the injured witch.

Genevieve said, "Your foresight brought you here. So this is where we need to be."

Rowan wasn't sure why, but that assurance settled something within. She didn't have to be believed by everyone, that came with the territory. But it was…nice to have support in her corner.

The doctors in the room cautioned them Dorothy was still groggy and recovering from some of the treatments she'd gone through. They said nothing about a dog, even when Star put her chin next to Dorothy's arm and gave her those pretty eyes.

Pity squeezed in Rowan's chest at the sight of the witch in the hospital bed. The bites had been treated, the worst of them had been covered by bandages. But there were so many of them, at least half of her body was covered, especially the most-used feeding spots like the throat and arms.

Why had Vampires mistreated her so badly? Yes, Rowan was familiar with the ways asshole Vamps harmed those they were supposed to protect, but for the most part, they didn't hurt those who gave their blood to their household. It was threaded into their culture. This looked like an overreaction, but Vampires rarely did anything without a reason, usually four or five of them. So what exactly were they up to?

Tears welled in Dorothy's eyes as Genevieve brought two stools to her bedside. "I thought I was going to die." A sob stole her words and Rowan had to lock down all her emotions before she ended up crying too.

Star sighed softly and shifted herself to lay her head

against Dorothy's arm. The witch paused a moment before a smile crept over her mouth and she ran her fingertips across Star's fur.

"Hello there," she said, and Star gave an adorable little snuffle snort.

"You lived, Dorothy," Genevieve said. "The universe needs you, and your attackers underestimated you. Living is your victory, yes?"

Dorothy swallowed hard and blinked back tears.

Rowan began, filling her tone with a flood of comfort and empathy, which Brigid fed her in a steady stream. "We know you're hurting and confused, and we don't want to rush you into talking. We need to know what happened so we can better try to find your friends."

She'd reached not for violence and menace, but comfort. Compassion. That too, felt like it was exactly how it was supposed to be. Knowledge, *knowing* slammed through her as all the parts of herself that had been running at top speed in what felt like totally different directions threaded together.

Like lightning, liquid power—*magic*—rushed through her veins, leaving harmony in its wake. In all her life she'd been waiting for this moment and hadn't even known it consciously.

Genevieve turned her attention to Rowan, her eyes widening as she drew a breath to speak.

Rowan lifted a hand. "I am well," she told her friend. And also to everyone watching in the control room so Clive understood he didn't need to react.

"Your voice," Dorothy said.

"I am a Vessel to Brigid. Her magic is heavy in the room, but it's good magic. Like Star is good magic."

Rowan then realized that much like Brigid being a

triple goddess, Rowan, Star, and Brigid were of three in a similar way.

The warmth returned in Rowan's chest. Pleasure, she realized. Brigid was pleased with this new accord between them, like a high-speed-train connection.

Amazing.

"I want to help," Dorothy said.

"Thank you," Rowan said. "First, know there are multiple teams out as we speak looking for Jaylin and Kerry. My valet is taking notes right this very moment and he'll get any details to them. Take your time. If you need a break, just say so."

"Two months ago, Jay came home from work and said he'd won some contest he entered at the chain restaurant near his job. The prize was a four-day cruise to Cabo, and he called to ask if three of us could go instead of two and they agreed as long as we all shared a stateroom. We were excited, you know? Anyway, there was a party with the winners, a dinner sail that set out from San Pedro. Afterward, when we got back home, Kerry, our other roommate, said she wasn't going on the cruise."

Dorothy took a break to sip some water and catch her breath. They'd given her some medication and also had used various spells to keep her calm and comfortable, so the pain was more emotional than physical. Far harder to manage.

Dorothy was strong, though. And after a brief pause, she continued with the story. "Some creep harassed her the whole night long and we were on a boat so she couldn't escape him. I knew the guy she was talking about. He was a witch. There were several witches there, along with a few humans and a Vampire. She didn't want to repeat it over days of the Mexico cruise, and we didn't blame her. In fact, Jay and I decided not to go either because the whole night had felt like theater. Like there was some other thing happening that they didn't want us to see.

"He told the cruise people, and they started offering all sorts of assurances. Then as we kept saying no, they got mad. They insisted the guy Kerry was talking about wasn't even going to be on the cruise so there was no reason not to go. But by that point, we all had a bad taste in our mouth over it and their reaction, so we thanked them again but refused and hung up. They called multiple times afterward, but none of us answered.

"And then two days later they came to the house. I had just gotten out of the shower but everyone else was still sleeping. The bathroom door opened up and before I could fight, they hit me with a knockout spell. By the time we regained consciousness, they'd moved us. We only saw three rooms of the place we were at first. The bathroom, a bunk room where they kept us, and..."

Dorothy lifted a hand to her mouth, covering it as her lips quivered.

Rowan knew from experience that some things were hard to speak of, especially right after they happened. Genevieve, too, understood that pain.

They needed her to tell them what she knew. But she needed to understand they would not force her to part with whatever it was. It was hers to tell however she could manage.

So Rowan and Genevieve waited until Dorothy got herself together and resumed. "They drugged us and then put us in the other room. Where the Vampires came. At first, they were nice. They fed us and talked to us. Made sure we had showers and all that. Then one of them bit me and took blood. *I didn't want to be fed on.* I said so over and over. They didn't care. They said it was time for us to come live with them. They took Kerry. I don't know where. She was gone for a few days and then the Vampire—he was different from the other two—who took her did something wrong. I don't know what, but it made all the other Vampires nervous. They argued and then even physically fought." She shivered. "Jay and I were drugged into unconsciousness again and when we came to, we'd been placed in a different house. No Vampires. It was witches. Two of them. For several days they acted like they were helping. They treated some of Jay's injuries. He'd been caught up in the brawl between the Vampires," Dorothy explained.

"You said the Vampire who took Kerry was different. What did you mean?" Rowan asked her.

"It was his accent. His inflections and pauses were unlike anyone I've heard before. But it did remind me of a teacher at the Conclave building, Tinto Gaddon. Not the same accent, but the quality of it. He was *old*, I think, Kerry's Vampire."

Genevieve nodded. "Tinto is at least a thousand. It might be that the accent is from a language and culture that's changed or even been lost over time."

Okay so most likely an ancient, or a Vampire who lived in a part of the world Dorothy hadn't encountered. The audacity certainly screamed old age. Those Vampires liked what they liked, and they'd liked it long enough to not want it any other way. If they saw a human or a witch they wanted as a blood servant, they'd certainly believe they were entitled to take whoever they pleased.

The picture she was beginning to see clearly was not a pleasant one.

"Thank you. Please, go on," Rowan urged, and Star nudged her side gently. Just a *hey I'm here*.

"Then *she* came. Another witch. She said time was up. Jay and I were about to be bonded into Vampiric households and it was an honor. That if we just cooperated, we'd grow to like it and once we'd earned our Vampire's trust, we'd have more freedom. It paid more than our current jobs. We'd have nice things and live in a mansion. We asked over and over where Kerry had gone but no one would say. I stopped cooperating. I tried to run but they caught me, and the Vampires came back."

Fear sweated from her pores as her voice went a little breathless.

Clive's rage churned through his bond with Rowan. Most Vampires, big assholes or not, wouldn't do such things. But some did. Rowan could kill thousands of Vampires true dead but there'd still be of this sort of thing unless the Nation dropped on them like a house every time one poked a head out.

"It was the same two as from the other place. Jay, they did something to him. He was leaning toward accepting this new plan. But it made me mad instead. They couldn't just take me where I didn't want to go! The feedings began again and this time, they left their bites open to make me *compliant*. That's when Jay started to change his mind. Maybe it was the shock of seeing what had been done? I don't know. I just wanted revenge, so I knew I had to hold on for the right opportunity and Jay was back on my side. It was stupid luck, but one of the witches who always scurried off when the Vampires came left her stuff behind. Her keycard had been tucked between the pages of her book. Then we had to wait until midday when the witches ate their lunch, before the shift change when the one whose key-card I took came back and would discover her card gone.

"We waited until the right moment and Jay and I ran. Well, he ran. I stumbled, but he helped me. The house they were keeping us was only a few miles from our place. It felt like years getting there. We didn't want to call the police because the one witch who came to tell us about the Vampires said they had connections with the cops, and no one would help us. We wanted to get home. An old teacher of mine knows someone in leadership at the Conclave. We just had to get her number from the house so she could help us."

She told them about how once they'd neared their neighborhood, a car full of witches had begun to cruise through, trying to find them, which slowed them down further, so they took refuge in the backyard of a neighbor's house. How Jay had left her there to jump into their own yard and get into the house through the back door.

And then how she'd crawled to the street, trying to escape as Jay had led them away, yelling as he did. He'd created a diversion to keep her safe. She made it as far as the bags of trash and passed out. That's where they'd found her less than two hours later.

Rowan said, "Can you describe the witch from the dinner cruise? The one who harassed your friend?"

As she did, Genevieve scrolled through her phone and then turned a photo around for the other woman to see.

"Yes! That's him."

"His name is Hugo Procella. And he's got a history of

stalking women. He's in custody and he won't be hurting anyone again," Genevieve said. "He stalked me too. Your friend was right about her instincts."

Dorothy described the Vampires and Rowan took notes, dread creeping into her gut as she began to see all the connections.

"Can we show you some photographs?" Genevieve asked. "Once we identify these witches, we'll be able to find them quicker."

"And Vampires, if it's not too much."

"Will you stop them from hurting anyone else?" Dorothy asked Rowan.

"When I find the Vampires who did this to you, they won't be able to harm anyone again."

Rowan was entirely unsurprised to find David waiting with the file box of photos they'd taken from Elmer's house. "I took the liberty of selecting the ones I thought you might want to show Dorothy."

As she sifted through the various photos, setting aside shots including Vampires Rowan was fairly sure were involved, Konrad told her, "The Vampires, your local Hunters, and my teams have been fed all the identifying information we received from your interview so far."

"Alice is coordinating a team of Vampires on scent trails leading from the house on Holly. They're reporting back with the others in real time," Clive said.

"Excellent." She took the file David handed her and opened it. "There are a lot of creeps in these. I'm fairly certain one of the Vampires she described was Stephen Baker." Rowan paused as she slid the contents of a manila envelope onto the table. "Well, what do you know? Here's one of Stephen from the sixties. That's Aron."

She pointed to the Vampire on his left. She put that one on her stack and added one of Elmer in a crowd shot.

Konrad made a sound that had Rowan's attention landing on him. "What is it?"

He shook his head. "It's nothing. Just remembered back in the day, Fiona did variety." He took a photo from Genevieve's folder and pointed.

Nineteen twenty-two, according to the writing on the back. A black-and-white crowd shot taken on a stage with striped curtains at their back. At one side of the group was an older gentleman with what looked to be a dog act with a collie and a poodle. There were a few dudes in suits, a man playing the mother role, still in his wig and dress. Some musicians, a child, and smack dab in the middle was a sultry-eyed Fiona Clare in a dark-toned gown.

"I bet that face sold a hell of a lot of tickets," Rowan said. "What was her act? Dancing? Magician's assistant? Nah, she's no one's assistant."

Konrad chuckled. "You're very good at reading people. I saw her perform a time or two. She's got a beautiful voice. They called her the Sparrow."

"Well, now." Rowan blew out a breath and plopped her butt back into a chair. She didn't want to give away all her secrets, but the prophecy dreams were known by the people in that room, so she quickly explained to Konrad about the holly leading them to the house in Long Beach and the sparrow in her most recent experience.

"From the moment Fiona entered the room when Genevieve and I were at their home, I had a visceral response to her. Don't mistake me, she's deadly and intelligent. I respect what a badass she is. On the surface. But

I had a deep distrust of everything she said. I obviously knew she and her husband were involved somehow, but while he's certainly a participant, she's in charge. The symbolism in my dream just underlined it. I want to go speak to her again after we're done with Dorothy."

"I have a strong feeling we'll have a lot more of an idea of what's going on by the time we're done here," Genevieve told her. "Are you ready to see what else we're about to find out?"

Over the next few minutes, Dorothy had identified Rose as one of the witches she saw on the dinner cruise and also at the second location they'd been taken. Sergio had come to the first location. Dorothy recognized Antonia from the dinner cruise, along with Gerard Clare.

Rowan knew Antonia had been way more involved than she'd claimed.

Rowan showed a picture of Baker and Dorothy backed up, alarmed. "That's the one who bit me. The one whose household I was supposed to be bonded into."

Rowan drew out the next, the crowd shot of Elmer and his pervo friends, and turned it to Dorothy. "Him." Elmer. "Him." Another Vampire not well known to Rowan, but Clive would know. Then, "What's *she* doing there?"

That sound…a sound of discovery and certainty, drew Rowan's attention. "Which?" she asked, using her control to not rush Dorothy.

Dorothy pointed to a redhead off to the side, standing not with the Vampires posing, but with a smaller group. "That's the witch who showed up to tell us we were going to be sent to Vampire households. She's the one who ordered me punished."

Genevieve took the photo. "I don't know her. But that's easily remedied. Just outside the door are several people, including my father, who know just about everyone. Failing that, we have the ability to do an image search. We're going to find these people and make sure they can never hurt anyone else."

A few minutes later, they let the doctor—also a witch—take over and put Dorothy into a healing sleep.

Chapter Twenty-Four

Clive knew she was taking things hard. Like he knew she'd never allow him to bring it up in mixed company. He didn't want to weaken her further, so he and David, after a look, had teamed up and had food delivered, along with plenty of tea in to-go containers.

Not that she'd have an appetite after hearing that poor girl tell her story. But she'd need the calories and something to do other than rage and grieve. Though she'd do both.

"Vampire update. Patience has been in contact with Seth back at *Die Mitte*. We've already got Baker and Elmer in custody. You know we located his nest and those Vampires and some humans he'd been feeding on long term are either in a cell or they're in a locked medical facility being evaluated. I'll go meet Alice in the field while you and Genevieve go to the Clares'."

Her surprise edged through their bond. She'd expected him to horn in on her trip and normally he would without hesitation. But there were multiple situations going on at once and with dawn on the way, he was focused on giving her what she needed while also taking care of the mess Vampires had busily been making.

"Depending on what happens, I may join you or I might go home for daytime rest."

"I'll speak to them all when we get back to Las Vegas. Hunter Corp. needs to be satisfied they're being treated appropriately. And by that I mean if one or more needs killing, it had best be handled. I'm not concerned you're going to hurt any innocents." She waved a lazy hand.

Was it any wonder he was mad for her?

"I'm pleased to hear it."

"Do you know who this woman is?" Genevieve asked Konrad as she handed over one of the photos Dorothy had seen.

Clive leaned in to take a look as well. "I recognize many of the Vampires here." Jacques, the former Scion, Elmer, Baker, and… "Rowan, this Vampire here bears a striking resemblance to Mardoc."

She froze and then cursed. "Mardoc? The one who was part of this Vampire lord thing? You're shitting me."

Everyone moved to peer at the group shot.

"This photo, along with a few others, had been tucked into a manila envelope. It was at the bottom of a file cabinet drawer. Not hidden as much as forgotten," David said. "There's no date on it. Ignoring the Vampires who never stick to current trends, this witch is wearing Chanel. Early nineties. She's got great taste. The others," he paused a moment, looking closely, "I'd say no earlier than '90 and no later than '95 or '96."

"So handy with your fashion info," Rowan said. "So who's the redhead?"

"Samaya, can you run this through an image search in the Conclave archive? I want to say I know who she is, but we'll need more information than I have to verify. I believe this is a witch in the Clare line somewhere.

Not in a powerful position. Or so I thought. I can't recall her name."

Samaya and David bent their heads over a screen as they got to work.

"Her name is Teresa," Samaya called out. "She's been married a few times and changed her name each time."

"Current isn't Davis by any chance?" Rowan asked, using the name of Sergio's mistress.

Genevieve looked to them, eyes wide a moment.

Samaya nodded. "Yep, that's her."

"At a party with a bunch of Vampires. The absolute worst Vampires," Rowan said.

"Vampires also connected to the Procellas and the Sansburys," Clive added.

"The link with the Salazars will be there too. And," Rowan stabbed a fingertip in the direction of the single named Vampire lord, "now this creep who is handily in a torture dungeon with the most deadly skilled inquisitor and hunter of all Vampirekind. People don't actually forget about Andros, they just want to pretend him away because if he comes for you, it's over. I'll send his office a text about this, along with a copy of the photograph. What about the other lords in custody? I didn't really recognize any of their names and I did run them all through the Hunter Corp. database but nothing overly alarming came up. Which could easily mean they're good at being horrible by staying under the radar."

"I hadn't considered them any part of this situation, which was only barely developing when they inserted themselves into the process the way they did." Clive couldn't even be angry at himself on that one. This twist came entirely out of the blue. "But I'll get my people on it to figure out what their connection might be to this situation."

David came back into the room and handled that on Rowan's behalf, but Clive could see his wife chafing at giving him even more work instead of doing it herself. As if she hadn't nearly died less than a week before. As if he'd ever forget that.

He flicked his gaze to her cane and sent her a raised brow. Mainly to needle her because he needed to keep her on her toes, and she liked being agitated. But also, to remind her he wasn't going to let her guilt herself sick over giving David work instead of trying to do the job of eight people at once herself.

"Sunrise is on the way," she said.

"I've got ninety-three minutes. Tell me before I head out, what are you thinking at this point?"

She huffed a breath, and he suppressed a smirk.

"Assuming all the basic disclaimers about how we don't know everything yet. I think the Vampires and witches are working together to locate, woo, and, if necessary, traffic potential blood servants into Vampiric households. I bet part of it is even aboveboard and consensual. There are plenty of humans and witches alike who *choose* to work for Vampires in one form or another. Every part of this conspiracy isn't going to be as nefarious as what they did to Dorothy and her friends. Maybe it even started out as purely aboveboard. But it happened once, and then again. Each time it got easier. They can tell themselves it's really a good deal for the blood servants or whatever, since Vamps pay handsomely in many cases. But they know what it is. They only ask for permission until someone says no. Then they take what they want just like they'd planned all along."

Clive knew her chill demeanor was a lie. She was on a Hunt, and it was clear to him that she was correct in her suspicions regarding the witches and Vampires.

"I think there's a lot more we don't know. But the pieces are all here. We just need to take it step by step to put it all together," Rowan said. "To think I believed the Blood Front were the biggest bad we'd faced and here comes this *Sanguis* bullshittery. There's no way I believe they're not part of this mess. Elmer, Baker, *and* your little guard Eduard were in these photos. Eddie might not be the same kind of pervert Elmer and Baker are, but he's definitely involved." She rubbed her hands together. "Can't wait to chat with him. I'll wait to see what Andros gets out of Mardoc and then use that to bury him alive."

"Won't that be fun?" Clive sent a smirk only she could see as his back was to everyone else.

"It will be if I do it right. Now. I have some witches to go harass and you're going to be Scion and hunt scumbags. I'll see you after sunset if we don't connect first."

Genevieve and the others left the room, getting ready to head out in different directions.

"I should go with you," she said. "What if there are still Vampires or witches there?"

"Alice will protect me," he said, deadpan.

That made her laugh as she stood and leaned into his embrace for a few moments. "If you can't make it before sunrise, just text me or I'll worry."

"I'll text you if we find anything, or if I have to take my rest away from home. I will be careful and so will you. I love you." He kissed her forehead quickly, before she could duck away, and led her from the room.

Darius waited at the front doors leading to the parking lot. He tipped his chin in their direction. "We've located the second location Dorothy and her friends were held in and my Trick nearly has the first location locked down."

Rowan put aside her thoughts of Fiona Clare as they changed plans and headed over to a four-bedroom single-story house on Twentieth, less than two miles from the house on Holly. The neighborhood was a mix of apartment buildings and single-family homes with an elementary school nearby. Quiet enough but with plenty of people coming and going.

On the way over, she texted Andros to inform him of the possible connection with Mardoc. She left all the Vampire Nation stuff to Clive, but suggested to Andros there might also be ties to the others in the dungeon. Whether or not a Scion knew or was involved? Well, that was going to be something she had to stay out of for the time being.

If Tahar or Takahiro were part of this, Rowan was perfectly fine letting the Nation handle all the necessary executions. And it would be execution because there was no way Theo was going to let it slide that they did all this so publicly, using his process to mess with Rowan on top of it.

It would save her a lot of time and effort to let them do it, and the responsibility would stay where it belonged. Delegation. Everyone was always telling her to delegate and this time, she planned to listen.

As long as she agreed with whatever their discipline was.

Genevieve and Darius went first to deal with what turned out to be multiple spelltraps. Deadly ones.

"I expect these witches to be punished for that," Rowan said. "Anyone could walk in here and get injured or worse. This is more very public wrongdoing and I'm not here for it."

"The wipe here is markedly similar to what they did at Dorothy's house. Quickly done, so it's not complete." Genevieve shook her arms and wrists, jingling and clacking, and on an exhale she said something, and a warm mist of magic seemed to fall all around them.

A team of witches and some of Pru's Hunters rolled through to gather evidence once it was safe. Whatever Genevieve had done, suddenly all the smudges and sparkles where magical workings had been performed seemed to bloom into life.

No one had been left behind, but the imprint of several witches was clear, and Genevieve made a call.

"We've found the original location," Clive murmured to her. "Stephen Baker's scent trail led us."

"Well, isn't that a delightful irony? Since he's in custody, he's less of a threat."

She itched to find Dorothy's missing friends. Jaylin was a maybe, but with the specter of Mardoc or another very old Vampire having taken Kerry, Rowan knew their window for finding her alive was getting smaller with every moment that passed.

"They've arrived and are locking it down."

Konrad had gone with them and after they did a check of the house, the group joined everyone else at a mixed-use commercial building in San Pedro.

"Super close to multiple cruise terminals," Rowan said as they pulled to a stop around the corner.

Darius opened the door. "First thing. Some of Genevieve's team located Jaylin. He managed to make his way to the house again and called the Conclave. They've taken him to the clinic where Dorothy is."

Rowan breathed out all the anxiety she'd been swimming in as she'd worried over him. "Good to hear."

He nodded once. "There are life signs inside. Three."

Clive had melted from the car, disappearing off somewhere. Rowan figured it was to check in with his team.

Darius looked her over carefully and then nodded once, apparently judging her capable of whatever might lie ahead.

The sun was coming, so she—and Star, who'd turned up to trot along at Rowan's side—made for the post the others had created in the neighboring building, in the back room of a clothing store.

"What have we got?" she asked once she got there.

"One Vampire on the third floor," Patience informed them. "Two witches on the second in a room fronting the street."

"On watch?" Rowan would handle the breach of the building differently if they were.

"They've been stationary. One appears to be in a bed and the other is sitting."

"There's a television. The one sitting is facing it," Konrad said as he approached from outside. "I sent a team over to the Clares' home to be sure no one leaves."

Once they finished planning how they'd enter the building and handle the apprehension of all those inside, Rowan caught Clive to the side. "Sun is coming. Go home. I'll see you after sunset. I won't go back to Las Vegas without you unless it's absolutely unavoidable."

He took her features in carefully and apparently was satisfied by that promise, because he gave a nod. "Have a guard with you at all times. No driving. Don't kill any of the guards outside our house here. I adore you and expect you to be careful and not get any more injured than you are."

"You must think because there are lots of people around you can be bossy without getting socked in the taint," she whispered in his ear.

"You always bring the party wherever you go. But as I value my wife, I'll repeat my request that you be careful." He risked a squeeze of her hand. "Once you're inside safely and the three there are secured, my Vampires and I will leave to take to our rest."

"I love you, Scion."

He gave her a sexy smirk. "What a lucky Vampire I am."

Chapter Twenty-Five

Rowan knew without a doubt this place had been used multiple times over at least a few years. There was a great deal of energy fairly throbbing from the walls. Plenty of powerful Vampires had been there.

There was a main room the team skirted, as they'd discovered it had cameras installed. Furnished comfortably. All the windows to the outside had light tight coverings. Big kitchen. Swanky formal dining room but also a smaller space in the eat-in kitchen.

Rowan wanted to talk to the Vampire before he lost consciousness when the sun rose, so they headed to that room while Genevieve and Konrad were handling the witches on the floor just below.

She breached the door quietly—but not quietly enough a Vampire wouldn't hear. The Vamp took the bait, rushing at her, and Rowan hopped to the side to avoid his attack. Easily and with a great deal of force, she brought her cane up, striking him as hard as she could in the throat, resulting in a pretty gross *thwack* of crushed muscles and tendons.

Brown eyes widened and then watered as he gagged, bending, bracing his hands on his thighs. Rowan used that momentum, kicking out the side of his right knee.

He screamed, high-pitched and full of pain, as he crumpled to the floor with a thud.

"Do not," Rowan warned as he presented her with a mouth full of sharp teeth and his hands bent into claws. "My name is Rowan Summerwaite and you're under arrest. I have a warrant issued from Hunter Corp. and the Vampire Nation. I have the freedom to serve it as an order for execution. If you fuck around, I will cleave you in half."

At her back, Marco chuckled. She hadn't realized he'd come in. Instead of being pissed she'd missed it, she chose to be grateful for the backup.

"What are you arresting me for? You can't just come in here like this. You broke my knee!"

"My goddess, I wish you fucking scumbags would come up with some new material. If I had a dollar for every time someone I was serving a warrant on told me I couldn't just do this or that thing I totally can, and absolutely will do, I'd be able to retire and not have to deal with the dregs of society like you and your criminal buddies." She flipped him off. "Your knee will heal, just like your windpipe did. I'm arresting you for multiple violations of the Treaty. Kidnapping, assault, attempted murder, and you'd best hope I don't find out any of the people you took died, because I'll hang that around your neck too. You've done all these things so recklessly you've threatened to expose our existence to humans. Oh! The Vampire Nation has a bunch of its own charges too. That's if you're alive after I'm done with you. David, light this fucking room so I can get a photo of our prisoner."

Marco hit the lights and David nodded his thanks

before taking pictures and sending them to all interested parties.

"What's your name?" Rowan asked.

He sneered—because of course he did—so she grabbed the arm restraints from the backpack she'd brought along, jammed a booted foot into the small of his back, and cuffed him. He tried to fight but she was by far the stronger. Plus, his knee popped out of the socket twice, and she got pissed and gave him her cane to the back of his head. Soon enough he sagged, defeated.

The cuffs were something Hunter Corp. Research and Development rolled out recently. When fully cinched and secured, movement was painful. Escape—in Vampires like this one with middling power levels—was next to impossible with a Hunter within arm's reach.

"There's a wallet on the top of that dresser." Rowan tipped her chin and David grabbed it, tossing it her way. Inside was five hundred dollars in cash, parking garage stubs—handy to track movement—a punch card for a coffee chain and a burrito stand, as well as a California driver's license.

When some states began to have evening hours at their licensing bureaus, Vampires could manage to be law-abiding citizens and get their licenses. The Nation encouraged such things. It kept that mask on between the supernatural world and the human one. For whatever reason, it was harder to believe someone was a Vampire if they had an official state identity card.

"Brandon Forman." She called the name out to David, who nodded and tapped his screen at a high rate of speed.

"Alice is sending light tight transfer," David said, anticipating her next sentence.

"Whether it's a body or a still-living Vampire will be up to Brandon."

The Vampire's eyes wheeled with panic. "We didn't have anything to do with those two running off. The witches are the ones in charge. It's their fuckup. I'm just a go-between."

"You're not a born Vampire. Given the hair I'd say you were Made in the early 1980s. Certainly you're old enough to understand what is going on here. There is no putting the blame on the witches. They're dealing with their own troubles just now. This is what you have done, Brandon." She shrugged.

She sent him a glare that promised blood if he said a thing.

Satisfied with his compliance when he shut his mouth, Rowan continued. "Here's where we are. Like I said, I have the paperwork—and certainly the will—to kill you true and be fucking done with you. Goddess knows the world will be safer without you prowling around hurting people. However, I prefer not to have to ruin these pants because I like them a lot and frankly, I'm tired. Killing Vampires takes a lot of energy and there'll be more paperwork I have to fill out. So. Here's what you're going to do to save your life. Answer my questions. Honestly. Starting with the big one. Where did Mardoc go after he left with the human woman?"

Less than an hour later, they'd handed Brandon off to Alice's Vampires when they showed up in a windowless serial killer van to take him away. Alice also informed Rowan she'd sent all the information Brandon had given about Mardoc's possible movements with Kerry to Andros.

Then they'd headed over to the Conclave headquarters in Pasadena to have a little chat with Teresa and the other witch who'd been at the place in San Pedro with Brandon.

Genevieve paused at the first set of double doors. "This is a null facility. I do not think it will impact your connection to your goddess, but I always find it uncomfortable, so I wanted to warn you up front."

Warmth bloomed through Rowan's veins. Brigid didn't seem worried.

"Explain. Please," Rowan added. She wasn't opposed to any of this, she just wanted to know exactly what was happening. "It comes back when we leave, though, yes?"

"All prisoners are stripped of their magic before they're sent here. We are under no such liability. However, beyond this set of doors, *no one's* magic works. A null cage has been created. The simplest way to explain is a bubble exists between the walls of this building and the outside. No magic can pass through. For witches who are interviewing or otherwise not under arrest, their magic returns once they leave."

It made sense in that way that really didn't make sense if you examined it too closely. Which, Rowan felt, most magic seemed to be.

"What about the geas? Can we bring the witches who have one here so they can be free of it?"

"A geas is far more complicated than nullifying a spell or magical talent. It's old magic. Oath magic. One of the few things we can't simply wipe away. If we can't get whoever set the geas on the other witches to undo it themselves, it can be unraveled, but it takes a lot of time and multiple practitioners. We're already starting. But it'll be at least six months, perhaps eight or ten, until we can erase it from just one of them. Then it starts over for the next. Messy, time-consuming business."

Genevieve sounded tired and totally pissed off. Rowan could identify.

"So we need to break whoever created them on first. Save a bunch of work on your part and hopefully find our victims quicker."

There was a joint Vampire/Hunter team assembling in Nigeria to move on Mardoc's compound in neighboring Chad. Brandon confessed that all the adepts Mardoc had *acquired* were sent there. Since Mardoc was at the Keep, Rowan had to hope someone was taking care of Kerry's needs. If there were other survivors there, help would be given to them as well.

She'd hear back within the next hours, so she tried to put it out of her mind.

"Let's question Teresa first."

Genevieve had never met Teresa Davis, but she was relatively unchanged from all the photographs they'd seen of her over the years. Shoulder-length coppery hair. Fair complexion. Green eyes that landed immediately on Rowan and narrowed.

Genevieve wanted to laugh at that. If Teresa only knew what she was about to go through with Rowan, she'd change all the calculations she was furiously crafting in her head. But, as Rowan herself liked to say, sometimes they needed to touch the stove to know it was hot.

"I demand to speak with an attorney," Teresa said.

Rowan looked over to Genevieve, shaking her head. "I thought you all would be smarter, as a whole, than

Vampires. How wrong I was. Present company excluded, of course."

"Hello? I asked a question." Teresa snapped her fingers.

In a blur of movement, Rowan slammed her fist into Teresa's face. "Don't be rude. You didn't ask a question. You made a demand no one is going to comply with. If you don't want another shot to the teeth, you'll stop this nonsense immediately."

Teresa's eyes widened and her skin paled with shock.

"There we are," Genevieve said smoothly. "You understand your place in this little play. No attorney. You played human games, but you're a Genetic witch. The Conclave is in charge. You and your friends have engaged in a conspiracy to stalk, kidnap, and traffic in adepts. Selling them for a minimum of a hundred thousand dollars a head. In addition to forced imprisonment, assault, attempted murder, and murder. We have evidence from multiple sources. There are a dozen of you in cells with the Conclave, as well as Vampires who are in the dungeons below the Keep where the First resides. Hunter Corp. has shifters, witches, and Vampires in its custody. Imagine, if you will, how many of them are angry and scared and oh so eager to be the first to take the offer to answer our questions truthfully. And then imagine not being one of those who are helpful. It's entirely up to you which one you are."

Rowan snorted. "Terry, everyone in this room knows what you are. Let's hear it."

"My name is Teresa," she said.

Rowan waved it away. "Whatever. Are you going to chat, get a chance to brag as well as make sure we understand just who did what? Or, are you going to try to be snooty about your name to a person who does not give one tiny fuck in a high wind about your opinion of whatever you're called?"

"When did you start this business?" Genevieve asked.

Fiona Clare hadn't been prepared for Rowan—actually Darius, but on her request—kicking her fucking door in at nine twenty-two in the morning so it was icing on the cake as she came rushing down a beautiful curved staircase, rage on her features.

"Get out of my house!"

"Hi, Fiona! We're here to arrest you and your husband." Rowan waved her cane and opted to strike a rather beautiful vase sitting on an antique table. The sound of the porcelain shattering shut Fee right up.

"You really should speak to a therapist about the pleasure you take in breaking things," Genevieve teased.

"I don't need my destructive tendencies fixed. They're a prerequisite tool for my job."

In the background, Fiona had made it to the entry and gotten over her shock enough to start screeching again.

"Shut your mouth," Genevieve snapped and the magic in the command formed as Fiona's lips met. "Don't bother trying to undo the spell. It's beyond your skill level and your magic has been nullified."

"You can try to punch me if you like," Rowan suggested.

Genevieve fought a smile. "Let's stop goading our prisoner."

Gerard burst out of a side door with Konrad at his back. Rowan waved at him.

Two other witches from Konrad's team stepped into the entry.

"David, please go with a few of Konrad's people. Search every last inch of this place," Rowan said.

Marco turned up. "I'll accompany them all. Help disable any traps."

Since it had been Marco's magic that had protected David at the Procella mansion, Rowan was absolutely all right with that.

"What is happening?" Gerard demanded.

"Teresa says hello," Rowan said. "She's a survivor, that one." Once she'd realized they meant it, and she could take a deal and roll or she'd be the one the rest testified over, she'd started talking.

Naturally, she shifted the blame, made herself a bit player, and they'd let her believe they didn't know any different.

Teresa also divulged everyone but the Clares had a geas on them as it concerned their little enterprise. And that it was Fiona who'd done the spell. Which meant she'd have to be the one to lift it.

First, it meant Rowan was free to get info from Hugo and Sergio as it pertained to the attempts on her life because that wasn't part of the geas. They were going down. But she wanted them to confess their bullshit with this little adept ring of theirs too. Or at the very least, be free to deny it even as they were convicted.

"My cousin Teresa?" Fiona asked, yanking her attention back.

"Why'd you unseal her lips?" Rowan rolled her eyes at Genevieve.

"I asked a question." Fiona tried to be imperious, but Rowan lived with a Vampire, so it was a pathetic attempt by comparison.

"You're under arrest by order of the Conclave," Konrad said.

"For what?"

Rowan rattled off the charges and added, "All that, plus using coercive magic in the commission of those crimes. There are some other charges that will follow. You moved Vampires, witches, and humans across state and international lines. You used your magic to blow up a house in a neighborhood full of humans during broad daylight. You used your familial connections to break into Conclave records to locate many of the adepts you were selling to the Vampires. It's all very serious." Rowan used her uninjured leg to kick a shard of expensive vase in Fiona's direction. "Those are violations of the Treaty."

"What Rowan means for you to understand is those same charges are leveled by the Conclave as well. Your property is forfeit. Your businesses are forfeit. Everything you own, everything the Clares own as a familial line is now ours. I personally identified your magical signatures at multiple crime scenes. Not only the mage firebomb, but both locations you held adepts before they were bonded into Vampiric households. That has been verified by *four* other Senators."

Once they'd located the places, Konrad had brought multiple Senators into the process and, in doing so, created an airtight case.

"Don't start with your outrage," Rowan warned, pointing her cane at the couple. "You knew this was coming."

They didn't listen, naturally. Fiona yapped about having no real proof, so Rowan walked over and punched her right in the kidney. Softer target than the face shot she'd landed on Terry. She didn't need to break a finger.

"Second Clare I've punched since sunrise." She looked over to Gerard. "Want to make that three?" He stared at her, shocked. "You don't have to say anything," she said over her shoulder as she walked away. "We know everything from multiple other sources. Whoever talks first gets the best deals. I'll see you later today."

Konrad did something to shut them up as both Clares were loaded into a transport.

They searched the house but a few hours in, still hadn't found much. She stood, hands on her hips, in the formal living room on the first floor.

"It could be they're too smart to have any real evidence against themselves here," Konrad murmured. "We'll keep looking. They're not perfect and I'm very patient."

"I'm not patient at all. I need to walk a little. I'm missing something. There are answers here. *I know it.* This whole time it was that I was missing key parts of the picture. That's all this is. I just have to look at things from an angle I hadn't considered yet. I just don't know what that is yet."

"I agree and I will do the same in the opposite direction," Genevieve said.

"And then you will go home and sleep for several hours," David said quietly. "You've been awake for over a day."

She wanted to snarl at him. But he was right. She needed to rest and if Clive found out she hadn't, he'd never let it go, and he'd be right, so she'd have to apologize, and he'd be smug.

So Rowan nodded at him and wandered from the room, letting herself zone out and follow whatever pattern her subconscious chose.

Another hour passed as she considered color patterns, types of doors and drawer pulls. Whether light landed on something or was in shadow.

Nothing.

"This is some bullshit," she muttered, turning to leave the guest room she'd been standing in. Then as she reached out to run a palm down the switch plate and turn the lights off, the corner of a painting caught her eye.

Rowan looked behind it. Nothing. Sighing, she rehung it and took in the subject. A playground spinny toy thing. She got out her phone and after a few attempts, she learned it was called a merry-go-round. She turned back to it. It wasn't a joyful thing. The colors rendered the tableau bleak. No kids were on it or near it. The whole blacktop was empty of people.

Like in her dream. Empty places.

She called out Genevieve's name.

Chapter Twenty-Six

Rowan wouldn't admit it out loud, but the four solid hours of heavy sleep had been exactly what she'd needed. After a quick shower, she followed the smell of food and found Elisabeth and Betchamp in the kitchen.

"Come and sit at the table. The Scion was clever enough to have the house stocked so when we arrived, we were able to get a meal prepared for you. Betchamp conferred with David, and we brought some clothes and necessaries for you."

"Ah, I was wondering about all my toiletries being here, along with a change of clothes and pajamas." She'd just figured Clive made it happen. "Thank you for doing that."

Genevieve came in just a few minutes later and plopped down at the table. "Konrad called and said Jaylin is awake and happy to speak to us later today."

David put his phone down and said, "They searched Mardoc's compound and the surrounding area. Empty. No staff. No adepts. No one. Adaeze and her team are tracking and will keep us apprised as they do." Adaeze was the Hunter in charge of that part of Africa. She was sharp and mean as hell, so Rowan had every confidence things would get done right.

"Let me call the Keep. I need Andros to know this."

She excused herself, taking her plate to the adjoining room.

Andros answered on the fourth ring.

"Like I said in my text, I've got a positive identification that it was Mardoc who contracted with witches to identify, track, kidnap, and coerce a human named Kerry. My team searched his compound to find it empty. She's still missing. Where is she, Andros?"

In one- or two-word questions, he satisfied himself of the accuracy of her information and then said, "I began our conversation just after sunset. He has continued to claim ignorance. I am disappointed in this Vampire."

"Are these other lords in the dungeon part of this trafficking scheme? Is that why they decided to insert themselves into Nation protocol with Hunter Corp.? Why I can't imagine because all it did was piss me off enough to pay attention to them."

"There were six lords total. Two were stripped of their holdings, all their staff, had their Made severed from their bonds of affiliation. They are not in custody as they were forthcoming immediately. They do still suffer, and they will not repeat their past mistakes with you."

Damn. To sever affiliation was to cast the Vampire at the head of a line adrift. Without their holdings or staff, they'd have to start over. And do so under the intense scrutiny of the Vampire Nation. All for swinging their dicks around.

"As for the rest, there are four guests below. Two have been very cooperative. Like the ones I just told you about, I believe them to be ego-blinded fools who thought to gain power in our world by challenging

Hunter Corp. when they perceived it to be weakest. Their allegiance belongs to the First and they squandered it on a being like Mardoc."

Rowan couldn't stop her snort.

"They now understand what weak is. And isn't. They will remain here as well as suffer the same fate as their brethren above. For a time."

"How *much* of a time?"

"However long your father wills it. He is very angry. Nadir is very angry. I am annoyed by having to hunt down riffraff who should know better."

"Pays to keep sharp these days," Rowan said.

He grunted. "The third Vampire of the four is Vincent Armas. He believes he can evade the truth. That he can talk his way out of a cell. Or he did before he had some time to reflect. I will speak to him again and let him know your father has been asking to speak with them directly. This will most likely loosen their tongues."

Yikes. Better them than her.

"And the Scions who assisted these Vampires by bringing them to the First and allowing this Vampire lord nonsense? What of them?" Rowan asked.

"That is Nation business."

"Respectfully, that's bullshit. It was Nation business until they threatened to kill my staff on sight. It was until one of them came to my continent and contracted to kidnap an adept. His fourth, I should add. Where are the others, Andros? This is bigger than them lying to Theo. They horned into a process that has led to multiple incidents of public exposure of our world."

"The death threat situation has been handled. Are you demanding the *witches* do things?"

"I sure as fuck am!"

"Language," he said, and it made her want to laugh.

"I demand they do things all day long. *This is my job.* I am administering the Treaty. Witches are in violation and so are Vampires. In fact, they're working together to pull all sorts of shady shit that will absolutely get them caught. But they're so blinded by money they're high on fantasy. If one or both of the Scions who forwarded these lords to Theo did it because that's what you do when ancients in your territory ask, or because they don't like me and wanted to make waves, that's one thing." Childish Vampiric posturing, but that was who they all were. "However. If one or both Scions are connected to whatever Mardoc has done? The Nation must answer."

"What does your husband say?"

"Do not condescend to me. This is a Vampire Nation issue. I am speaking to one of his Five. I am not running Hunter Corp. protocol by *any* Scion, even if I'm married to him. I'm bringing it to you because *it is your job.*"

He was silent for so long she thought he might have disconnected. Until his laughter sounded over the line. "Your claws are still sharp. Good. It'll keep you alive. Recht and I have investigated the Scions involved quite exhaustively. They both came to me freely, as it happens. Neither wants war, or to be removed from positions both have held for a considerable length of time. Neither is overly concerned with how much trouble it caused you or Hunter Corp. either, but they both grasp the gravity of their very poor choices. I am satisfied they are not involved with this trafficking ring."

"Hunter Corp. needs to be assured both Scions will examine the Vampires under their rule in their territory.

If there are any adepts who've been bought through these witches or any such scheme, those Vampires must be investigated, and the adepts examined. We are not prepared to let this continue and all the Scions need to clean up their territory."

"I will speak with the others about this and possible wording and get back to you. Will that satisfy?" he asked.

"For the time being, yes. What is the connection with the *Sanguis Principatus*? I know there is one. I found out just a few hours ago that Mardoc is one of them. I have photographs of him with Jacques and others from this little group. I know they're members and I want to know if this is their new business plan, or if these assholes are traffickers who *also* belong to this stupid club. And before you tell me it's not illegal to belong to such a club, I don't care. I do not care about their little fantasies of world domination and their bigoted bullshit. They're as ridiculous and worthless as humans who do the same. We both know what's the legal issue here. Elmer and those like him seem to pluck up humans and anyone else they decide they want like they're shoes. That's not going to continue on my ground. And if that attitude extends to adepts? You better find them first because I will wipe them off the earth."

He blew out a breath. "I will apply some pressure on that subject."

"Okay. Andros, help me find this human. She doesn't deserve whatever horrible thing they've done to her."

"I will do all I can. I'll update you." He hung up and she took her things back into the kitchen.

"When we get back to Las Vegas I want to head directly to *Die Mitte*. I want to talk with the Procellas and with Elmer and Stephen too. Now that we've got the link between the witch families, we bring the hammer down on Sergio. Hugo is a fool. But grandpa isn't. He's been suffering and wallowing in his circumstances over the last few days. It'll be time. And we'll use Teresa to strike the blow. If we can't get Fiona to undo the geas, we can still get information from him. The bonus will be that I'll get to rattle him some more." Rowan thanked Elisabeth for warming up her cup of coffee.

"I'm looking forward to seeing his face when we let him know all we've discovered," David said.

"Who is this Mardoc, then?" Genevieve asked.

Most of the planning for the raid had been done while Rowan and Genevieve had been tasked with a dozen other things, so she hadn't really had much opportunity to explain.

"Mardoc is a six-hundred-year-old Vampire. He's one of those self-proclaimed lords who caused all that mess with the Vampire hires at Hunter Corp. Powerful enough for what he is, but no big showy past history. He's got a compound in N'Djamena," Rowan explained of the largest city in Chad. "There's a Hunter Corp. chapterhouse in Kano, Nigeria, and as you know, they did a joint raid to see if Kerry was at this compound. I'm told normally he's got about two dozen humans and Vampires living there, but it was totally empty today. Adaeze, the Hunter in charge, says it looks like maybe a week or so since anyone had been there. Probably scattered when Andros started hunting Mardoc. Hunters are tracking, along with some Vampires, trying to locate the staff or Kerry. Andros is going to question Mardoc about Kerry as well."

Rowan skirted around some of the more complicated

Nation issues. That was Vampire business. She didn't want to give away more than necessary. And she'd do the same if it was witches she was discussing with Vampires. Everyone was just trying to do the best they could while serving their goals.

"Let's finish eating and head back out to make all sorts of people uncomfortable," Genevieve said.

Rowan sent Fiona a smirk as she sat across from her an hour later. "So, we searched your house from top to bottom. We found some incriminating stuff."

Fiona pursed her lips like she had a secret and Rowan openly rolled her eyes. Honestly, liars were so stupid.

"But not a lot of it. Certainly not enough given the sort of shit you've been getting up to with the Sansburys and the Salazars. And sadly, I'm around criminals so often, I knew there'd be more but where was it?" She tapped her chin, pretending to be perplexed and then pulled the keycard they'd found in the painting in the guest room, and put it on the table between them.

Fiona's face fell and Rowan laughed.

"Right? I knew the moment they pulled the obfuscation spell free, and the keycard fell out. *This* was what I'd been looking for."

"It was a good spell," Genevieve allowed. "You placed it in such a way that it wouldn't have been found in most searches. Even if the painting had been pulled off the wall, as it had been, nothing would have been discovered if Rowan hadn't noted the small scratch at the corner of the frame."

A tiny, magical hinge had opened, and then Genevieve had been able to see the spell hiding something.

"Then, of course, we had to find what the keycard

opened. Which might have taken us another hour, but I realized there were other paintings around that had similar themes." Empty places. Just like her dreams. "A deserted Times Square in the garage seemed strange. You'd have been smarter to use something totally unconnected, but I imagine you like feeling cleverer than other people. That hidden room under your garage floor was quite a treasure trove!"

"It's a nice thing witches are such excellent record-keepers," Genevieve told her. "Now we have ever so much more concrete information connecting you all to one another. After this, we're headed to speak to Tristan and Joseph. Joseph is already about to jump out of his skin at the hint of being connected to you. Started confessing on the drive over—what he could, anyway, as he too was operating under a geas you put on him. I'm quite certain he'll have many more things to say once we're finished with you. He seems very dedicated to finding ways around the prohibitions in the spell."

"The point is, we don't need you," Rowan told Fiona. "You can decide to clam up and pretend it'll help you. But *Teresa* has plenty of information she's been sharing. She's quite the braggart. Naturally, everything is *your* fault. And since you're not a very nice person, the others will roll, and boot you over a cliff without a second thought."

"She's a stupid skank who only has her power because she opens her legs."

The *real* Fiona glared at them. Disgusted by her lackeys and their inability to keep themselves under control.

Rowan wrinkled her nose. "Ew. What's your excuse then, Fee? Hmm? You were right there with her this whole time. Slut shaming your cousin who was your fucking *procurer* is a bold move."

Fiona pointed at Rowan, her anger fully engaged. *Good.* Angry people made mistakes. "Talk to Rose! *She's* the problem. I'm not going to jail for her."

Rowan guffawed at that. "*You're* the one who put the geas on her. Release it and I'll talk to her all day long."

Genevieve added, "Don't make the mistake in assuming if you don't remove the geas, we won't come for you. *We already have you.* And the entire Procella family. Which, if you recall, aren't all under magical gag orders when it comes to a good chunk of this conspiracy you're involved in."

In other words, just because Sergio couldn't directly talk about their little *workgroup* didn't mean they wouldn't get all sorts of useful information from him by coming at him sideways.

"And, of course, you know that being under a geas means they'll all be treated with more leniency in sentencing because they're unable to defend themselves against any accusations." Genevieve hummed, pleased. "Unlike you."

Fiona's mouth was tight from holding back all the vitriol she bit back. Rowan wanted to rub her hands together with glee.

"You're wasting time and resources you should spend on witches in need instead of harassing successful business owners." Fiona attempted to look down her nose at them.

"Go on and tell us about this successful business, then," Rowan invited. "How can we understand your side of things if you won't explain?"

"There's nothing illegal about connecting adepts with Vampires who wish to engage their services."

That tired line.

"Sure. I'm certain you won't have any trouble producing the names of the Vampires you sold adepts to. So that we can verify ourselves they're all in place of their own free will. Seems like consent has been a tricky issue for you in this business venture," Rowan said.

"I'm bound by a nondisclosure agreement."

Rowan laughed long and hard at that. "No, you aren't. Even if you did such a ridiculous thing, it doesn't matter. You can't NDA your way around this. *NDA.*" She laughed some more. "You're not some starlet going to a celebrity sex and drug party up in the hills. You're stalking and trafficking in humans and other witches to sell off to Vampires to use up like a carton of milk."

"They're treated like royalty!"

"I've got two witches recovering from being your idea of *royalty* and another still missing." Their physical wounds were healed, but the emotional and mental damage would take a great deal of time and effort to process. That spurred Rowan on. "Both have identified *you* as being at the scene of multiple events. I should add this lest you get ideas, that Vampire who bought Kerry? He's in Vampire Nation custody. In a cell in a dungeon kept by the First. *Nothing* you could even dream up would be half as bad as the reality he's facing. I spoke to his inquisitor a few hours ago. He texted me twice to let me know they were getting somewhere. Mardoc is not going to protect you. He can't even protect himself. And when he's offered a chance to get a reprieve from his interrogations, we'll know more about *you.* You're fucked. So, you can make it worse by refusing to tell us what the hell you've done. Or you can at least raise the standard of the type of fucked you are by answering our questions."

"For over thirty years everything was legal," Fiona all but snarled. "I said all along we didn't need the ones who weren't interested. There are plenty of adepts over the years who jumped at the opportunity. More than enough profit for everyone. Our stop-loss rate was very low. Those adepts who didn't wish to be bound to a Vampire rarely even made it to the stage where the Vampires met them and began to…we called it courting because they would get to know each other. Vampires are very charming.

"But Teresa got greedy. She and Rose decided even that loss of a few adepts a year was too much. Teresa ran to the others to tattle. Convinced them we lost too much money each time we allowed anyone to leave because we had to start the process over with new recruits."

Recruits. Stop loss. Rowan shoved her disgust deep, trying to keep a blank expression to encourage Fiona to keep talking.

"By that point, Teresa had moved on from Hugo to Sergio. And she convinced the others to let the Procellas join the group. Her big selling point was that Sergio had Hugo on a leash and Hugo had a talent with coercive magics. Worse, she arranged a premium! The Vampires she was dealing with directly were willing to pay more when it wasn't willing and extra measures like magic and other types of discipline had to be employed."

The casual way this witch spoke about the depraved things they were doing to adepts brought a rage so hot it scalded. It was more than just Brigid being upset; it was a union between them. Each new thing she learned was worse than the last. These witches and Vampires needed to be ended.

It was like a cork had been popped as Fiona continued this torrent of bitter truth.

"Joseph is weak, and Rose is, well, she's a sociopath. She only did it for the entertainment. Like pulling wings off flies. The Sansburys don't even need the money. The Salazars live a quiet but very expensive life. The new bonus and premium system seemed to put paid to any qualms they may have had. Gerard and I were outvoted. What could we do by that point? At least there were people on the inside who tried to ensure the adepts were willing by the end of the trial period."

Rowan showed her teeth a moment as she leaned over the table slightly. "So when they weren't willing and you ordered a witch to be bitten repeatedly and not have her wounds healed? This is the discipline you mean? Why not use Hugo to change her mind? Why torture her?"

"Cases with reticent recruits are very rare. The female witch needed discipline because she had a natural resistance to Hugo's coercion magics. The other one with her, the male, he was swayed and most likely we could have turned the woman around too. But we didn't have time and then she escaped. Gerard and I didn't have any choice. Were we supposed to call the Conclave to turn them in? Walk away from a business I was instrumental in starting and running for over three decades when it hit a bump or two?"

"But you, the face and power within the Conclave as it pertains to the Clare line, were…helpless against a witch you described as a secretary? This is rather confusing." Genevieve cocked her head.

Fiona flinched, but to her credit, she soldiered on. "It

didn't start out that way. A hundred years ago Teresa worked for *me* doing administrative tasks. I still had a stage career, but the Clares have always run a business empire, so she worked on that side of things. Teresa isn't very bright, but she's vicious, petty, and greedy. She used everything she could to gain power and influence all while she ingratiated herself into the family business. Like a tick.

"Then in the seventies, she met and attached herself to Rose. And the two of them liked Vampires. A lot." Fiona curled her lip a moment. "They partied in Las Vegas with the Vampires there."

Bingo. That's how they hooked up with Jacques and the other Vampires and discovered the world of adepts. And the Clares discovered *Sanguis Principatus*. Damn all these long-game feints Vampires were so fond of.

Fiona kept going. "That connection to the Vampire Nation and the Scion was quite profitable for us. We arranged parties and events with er...*paid* entertainment who were all adepts. That's how it all started. And it only allowed Teresa to dig her claws in deeper to the family and the group until she worked out what each member of the group wanted or needed and manipulated until *she* got whatever *she* wanted."

Genevieve huffed an annoyed breath. "Then you decided to come to the Conclave for permission to use more coercive magic on humans? You didn't think this could get our attention when you were already breaking our most sacrosanct laws? What sort of madness is this?"

"Those fucking Procellas!" Fiona threw her hands up, rage on her face. "Truth is, none of us even knew about that petition to the Conclave until right *after* they'd done it, and it was too late. Sergio and Teresa figured since Hugo had the gift, they could use it on their various properties to fleece humans more efficiently. She said she wanted to diversify her arm of the business. She sold it as a way to also keep an eye out for anyone they might recruit for a Vampire client. We've had a great deal of success in attracting adepts through our various entertainment-based events so that's what she claimed when we called her out." Fiona sighed deeply. "All that greed made Teresa even more stupid because Hugo is not only a pig, it was that petition that ended everything!"

Genevieve shrugged. "Well, it was the petition that made me look twice at what *you were all doing*."

Rowan added, "That and trying to have me killed in the middle of the day on one of the busiest and most surveilled streets in the country."

"Of course their vulgarity ended up with *werewolf assassins* on the Las Vegas Strip. And of course it's my bimbo cousin who's put us in this position. We are legitimate business owners. We made a mistake, but it was to rely on family. Surely you can see that."

"Who's the connection with the Vampires? Not back in the day when you ran adept hookers for their parties, but now," Rowan asked instead of replying to Fiona's bullshit.

"Teresa used to sleep with some friend of the Scion. Not the one you're married to," she said to Rowan, "the one before him. She was always at their parties. Eduard something or other."

The guard who'd attacked Rowan at *Die Mitte* and a known member of *Sanguis Principatus*.

Fuck. All sorts of things began to shift and began to make sense.

"He and Mardoc, the creepy old Vampire, were friends from way back." She looked at Rowan with a smirk. "Then Mardoc got himself in big trouble for threatening to kill Hunters. The other Vampires in their group lost their minds as they should have, because this sort of thing should be private! He and Hugo, absolute creeps. We had to send the two recruits we had left to another location because of the brawl the Vampires started and then disappeared after everything began to crumble around us. The male, Jaylin, had been engaged by a Vampire recommended to us via Mardoc. He was supposed to have gone with the human Mardoc took, but Mardoc ran off with the human and left Jaylin behind. I don't know where Stephen is. He's the one who engaged the services of the female witch, but he's ghosting us. And Eduard hasn't returned my calls either."

"That's because Stephen and Eduard are in custody of the Vampire Nation." Rowan stared at Fiona. "But back to your story. You're saying Teresa met up with Eduard and hung out with all those Vampires who were buddies with Jacques and then you hatched this trafficking ring?"

"It's not trafficking! For over thirty years we simply brought parties with the same interests together. A lucrative introduction service. Teresa is the one who changed things five years ago. I can't be responsible for that. It was her idea."

They could call it whatever the fuck they wanted, but it didn't change reality.

"Where did Mardoc take Kerry? If you help us find her, you might escape with your life," Genevieve said.

Fiona paled. "Life?"

"Have you been paying attention at all? Is the situation not dire enough for you?" Rowan snapped.

"If you do not cooperate—and that includes removing the geas you've placed on the others, as well as giving us the location of our missing—you will be executed for your part in this conspiracy. It's up to you."

Chapter Twenty-Seven

Clive took his wife in as she stalked down a hallway toward an interview room. She'd only found out minutes before, as they were flying back home to Las Vegas, that the missing human woman, Kerry, had been found. And it hadn't been good news.

He knew Rowan was taking it personally. Full of guilt that she was unable to figure out this twisty, fucked-up conspiracy in time to save Kerry's life.

The set of Genevieve's mouth said she felt the same guilt as Rowan, and as much as Clive would shove someone in the way to take a hit that was not Rowan's, it wasn't Genevieve's either.

The witches had a lot to account for. As did the Vampires.

Christ. The absolute shambolic shit show these *Sanguis Principatus* Vampires had created; the layers of discipline Clive had to administer as well as the scorched-earth way he would have to react to this would be a massive undertaking.

He had other things he'd prefer to deal with, which only made him angrier.

"Send Elmer next," Rowan said to one of the Vampire guards. "I don't need him for this part. Eduard first."

The former guard physically recoiled when Rowan entered the room and she narrowed her gaze at him, the predator inside going sharp and still. Goddess she was magnificent.

"*Sanguis Principatus* has been involved in a scheme with a bunch of witches to stalk, kidnap, and enslave adepts. You were so very high and mighty when you were questioned at first. Remember that? Oh woe, the Hunter found out my pervert best friend Elmer has been sniffing around teenagers. That might endanger my deal with Stephen Baker for all those sweet adepts, so I'll pretend I'm morally outraged. You're fucking pathetic."

Starting strong.

Clive simply sat back and let his wife do what she did best. Whatever was left of Eduard when she was finished with him, Clive would crush under his boot.

Eduard jerked back with the end of each sentence, his mouth dropping open for a moment at the end.

"You see," Rowan continued without waiting for a reply, "many Vampires like to think they're smarter than everyone else because they're older. Or because they have superpowers. It's your weakest spot and goddess love you all, you just keep doing it. Over and over and over. I come in, things are hinky as fuck and I run you all to ground. And I do, because you're stupid and think self-control is for other people. So here I am, Ed. Looking at a stupid motherfucker—yet again—who thought with his ego instead of his brain."

"I don't know what you're talking about," Eduard managed.

"Teresa says hi. She also said you were terrible in bed and never made her come unless you took her blood.

I'm not surprised at all to hear you're too lazy to find a clit and give it some attention."

Eduard's color rose and Rowan chuckled.

"I'm talking to Stephen after this. And Elmer. So you know the deal. First one to talk gets a better deal from Hunter Corp."

Certainly not from the Nation. But she'd said it that way to keep Eduard's mind off that fact.

"These crimes are judged by a panel. A panel we've already charged with examining all the evidence we've collected," Clive said. "Being cooperative is imperative to your very existence."

"Shall I tell you how I think it went down?" Rowan asked with deceptive calm. Clive felt the surge of her emotions, knew she would never lose control, but also understood she wanted to. "That night when I arrested Elmer, Stephen called to let you know I was about to arrest Elmer. And you both knew Elmer was a liability to your little trafficking ring because he's a scumbag with zero concern about how whatever he did would bring you into the spotlight eventually, so you let him get caught and figured you'd handle him when he arrived here to be thrown into a cell." Rowan waved a hand. "Anyhoodle, your little stunt by putting hands on me was you panicking, but also a signal to let Elmer know you saw him. You wanted him to think you were protecting him, but he also knew it was a warning to shut up since he was in a cell here and at your mercy. You saw that footage of the ambush and that I was using a cane and you assumed I was weak. You could have made your point and backed off, but you underestimated me, and I knocked you the fuck out. Taintweasel."

Rowan tipped her head back and laughed. Brigid rose

then and seemed to fill the room up as an amber halo of power radiated around Rowan's body. The air was thick with magic. Rowan's unique magic as a Vessel.

Eduard blinked fast and swallowed audibly.

Clive watched Rowan level her gaze on Eduard, freezing him there in terror for long moments.

Finally, he said to Clive, "For thirty-one years, *Sanguis Principatus* provided a service to our members. An introduction to the sweetest feeds possible. No Nation laws were broken, nor was the Treaty violated. Jacques was a real Scion who served his Vampires."

"He's not going to respond," Rowan interrupted. "You and I are talking about your little club and all the years *after* the first thirty-one when oodles of laws, Nation, Treaty, and the Conclave, were being broken. Focus."

Eduard licked his lips. "I wasn't part of that. I have blood servants. Adepts who willingly serve me. I don't need to force anyone. You can't pin that on me."

"Look, let's not do this. You're trying to quibble here; claim you didn't use magic and violence to break an unwilling adept, so you're not like the others who did. But if it's not a deal breaker to you, you're exactly the same. There were underage adepts. Your little introductions for Elmer."

A guess, Clive knew. But when the words landed, Eduard's change of expression said it was an accurate one. His wife's intuition remained undefeated.

"Not in the years since Scion Stewart took over."

Before that, the territory was lawless when it came to such rules and the Nation had been on the other side of the ocean, and as long as the profits rolled in and appearances were kept, they'd been left alone.

"He was fine for a few years, but he wanted more,

and we didn't want the possible problems, so we said no. Offered him adepts who were still young, but legal adults. He started hunting again to get his own. We have nothing to do with that. You can't hold us responsible for it." Eduard tried to fold his arms over his chest, but his wrists were shackled.

Rowan made a low sound in her throat. A growling snarl as she processed that information about Elmer.

"We know you're the one who has been feeding Mardoc and his ridiculous lords information about Scion Stewart's territory and my activities," Rowan said, standing. "Armas, one of his little friends and the Vampire who was expecting delivery of Jaylin Prince, confessed."

Mardoc had bragged about his deal with *Sanguis Principatus* and the various other services they provided members. Armas had only been an official member for a few months when Mardoc had convinced him and the others that Rowan and Hunter Corp. were weak, and it was time to cause them trouble and keep them hobbled and ineffective.

"Don't judge them too harshly," Clive said. "They've been guests of the First in his dungeons. Andros has been attending them all."

"Theo came to visit Mardoc. That loosened his tongue, I'm told." Rowan snorted.

Clive suppressed a shudder. At one time in what felt like another life, he'd had been subject to the First's displeasure and discipline.

"Tell us everything or I'm walking out of here. No more games. I'm done with you," Rowan said, her hand on the doorknob.

"Fine!"

Rowan knocked on the door and David came in, seating himself, reading for notes. Alice was doing the same.

"Start at the beginning. You and Teresa."

An hour and a half later, an insulated mug of coffee at her left hand, Rowan and Clive sat across from Stephen Baker. They'd moved Elmer's interrogation again, knowing they'd get more information from Baker to pile on Elmer's head.

"So, chief of security for Elmer Marsc. Wooow." Rowan drew out the last word, grating on him. "I'm sure your parents are super proud."

Her chuckle was genuine, so she went with it.

Stephen opened his mouth, and she slapped her palm down on the tabletop. "No. It's not your turn to talk. I'll tell you before you start squawking, yes, we have every right to hold you. Yes, you absolutely understand why you're here and no, we're not letting you go. So, to continue. I hear you and Elmer share a love of questionably young humans. What a thing to have people know about you. I mean, I guess if you're Elmer's lackey you don't have any shame left."

Stephen's face twisted in anger. If he was human, he'd be red-faced and panting. Goddess, she wished she could goad him into a heart attack. Sometimes things weren't fair. Ah well, the least she could do was reduce him to tears.

Before she sent him off to prison.

"Everyone works for someone," Stephen said. "Last I checked having a job wasn't against the law."

She clucked a little. Disappointed. "Really? I'm cringing just imagining taking the fall for a pervert like Elmer. Dude, he's just so fucking stupid and led by his dick, which isn't that unusual for those who have dicks, even when they're Vampires. I guess that's something you knew was a possibility when you linked up with him in this scheme of his."

"I don't need to manipulate boys who are barely over eighteen. Whatever his...predilections, they've been over eighteen, even if only by minutes, when he Made them. For the last four years."

"He means after I separated Jacques's head from his body and you took over as Scion and started making them obey the laws," she said to Clive, who fought a smile for a moment. "You're the one who follows Elmer around cleaning up his messes, licking his boots. He laughed about that."

She was such a liar. Elmer hadn't said anything like that. But Rowan could read Stephen like a book. And Stevie didn't like Elmer and the idea that Elmer would mock him would uncork Steve's truth.

"*Sanguis* pays me. *We* mocked Elmer and his ridiculous life. The man is a degenerate, and he can face the sun for all I care."

"He's a massive asshole, for sure. But you *served* him for how long?"

"Seven years."

"Like a fanboy? Just sniffing after Elmer, trying to steal his shine?" That might be laying it on a little thick, but she went with it.

Stephen's curled lip cheered her. "Elmer was a direct connection to Jacques and then Eduard. Jacques used him for heavy jobs. So he had a lot of dirt on the old Scion. Enough to keep him alive. Plus, Elmer's money, power, and connections have been of great use to *Sanguis Principatus*. And we built a nice little file on Elmer for when he outlived his usefulness. He can choke on his laughter."

"Oh, you mean on one of the multiple data cards you had tucked in the safe at your nest?" Clive asked. "My staff has busily been unlocking and decrypting the information and compiling it. I'm pleased to know we'll have more evidence against Marsc."

"You entered my nest?" Oh, that tone wasn't going to please her Scion.

Which he proved when he spoke, voice icy and full of power. "I am the Scion of this entire continent. You provide overwatch to a Vampire who lurks at sports bars to prey on impressionable humans. *We are not the same.* I go where I please. And it pleased me to have your nest searched from top to bottom. Like it pleased me to remove every last one of your staff and blood servants and get them the support and help they need."

"Everything is unraveling, Stephen." Rowan shrugged. "If Mardoc hadn't played his little game and threatened Hunters I never would have looked twice at him. If the Procellas hadn't gotten greedy and petitioned the Conclave to be allowed more power to coerce humans, the witches wouldn't have taken note of their adept trafficking business. If you hadn't abused Dorothy because she didn't want you, she might not have run straight into my investigation. I knew there were some dark things going on, but I never would have put it all together if you all hadn't let money and power go to your heads and got reckless. Entitlement makes people so lazy. Or maybe it's lazy people are entitled. I don't know. But what I *do* know is if I was involved in the process of kidnapping and selling adepts, I'd keep my shit locked down because it turns out that's not legal. Even if it's via a luxury concierge service. Especially one that has begun to resemble human organized crime, complete with public assassination attempts on enemies."

He froze for a brief moment. Not so brief she missed it. *I've got you, motherfucker.*

"Fiona Clare is looking for you." She smiled at him. "She thought you'd ghosted her after you went and damaged the whole-ass witch you attempted to buy like she was a new car. Dorothy. She's amazing. Strong. Courageous. *She remembers everything.* Some witches, it turns out, have varying levels of immunity to coercion magic. You tortured her to break her, and that, Steve, makes me dislike you intensely."

He opened his mouth to speak before thinking better of it and closing it again.

"Look at you. Learning like a big boy. I have a dozen other witnesses, all now free of the geas Fiona Clare had put on them, chatting like their lives depended on it. And they do. The First and Andros have had Mardoc and his ridiculous little lords in a dungeon and they've all seen the wisdom in telling the truth. You're fucked. So if you want to help yourself, dispense with all the excuses and lies and tell the truth."

Clive said, "This is your opportunity to help us understand your perspective. Because, as Rowan said, we have a dozen other perspectives, and as you might imagine, their portrayal of you isn't the most flattering."

"I can see from your expression that you're considering continuing to deny the truth. So I'm going to stand up and leave this room if you don't start telling us what we want to know. Then I'll go next door where your buddy Elmer is waiting. I'm sure he has loads of helpful things to share."

"In the decades *Sanguis Principatus* has worked with the witches to procure adepts, less than a handful has needed *convincing*," he finally said. "A handful! Less than a dozen who are all settled now serving their Vampires as they were meant to! In the end they all want it. Dorothy and modern women like her don't know what they want at first. So we help them be what they're born to."

"Gonna be honest here, I'm having trouble finding something to say. Give me a moment."

Rowan breathed carefully through her anger. All these machinations were about control and loss of control so the last thing she needed to do was emulate that.

But oh how she wanted to hurt these Vampires and witches who'd just decided a whole group of people didn't deserve even the most basic rights of bodily autonomy because adepts have blood that tastes better.

"It has been Elmer from the start. He's the problem! He was never satisfied. Caused issues to the point where the workgroup refused to let him use their services. He started hunting on his own again. Getting high off blood feeds with nineteen-year-old humans like an embarrassment. Calling attention to himself in ways that would have harmed the rest of us. So I stayed to keep him in line. Then Mardoc and that stupid fucking stunt he pulled put so much heat on us we couldn't handle Elmer in the way we'd planned for the last year. Too much attention someone might have noticed him missing. Elmer and Mardoc both are to blame for this mess. *Sanguis Principatus* and her members have done nothing wrong."

"Except for that whole kidnapping, false imprisonment, assault, and murder stuff, yeah."

Chapter Twenty-Eight

Clive placed a hand at her elbow to stay her.

They'd interviewed multiple Vampires and witches and a werewolf or two over hours and hours and had been able to piece together the big picture of what exactly had happened.

She turned, her features softening in question.

"It's two in the morning. Might I tempt you into going home, eating a meal with me, and decompressing from everything we've learned over the last three days?"

Her brows drew together as she frowned. "I have to write up everything. I need to conference call with London and the other chapterhouses. I should check in with the clinic. Genevieve went over there to inform them in person when we got the news about Kerry."

He took her hand and tugged her close. They were alone so she allowed it. Which only made him want her to rest more. "You can do all that from home. David and Vihan are already working on writing everything up. You can add your perspective when they're finished. Rowan, you're knackered. Physically and emotionally. You've flown back and forth to Southern California multiple times in the last few days. You've kicked doors down and broken ever so much rich people shit, as you so charmingly put it. Even a Vessel needs some downtime." Especially when one was still recovering from multiple attempts on one's life.

She gave him a raised brow and then she snorted. "I'm too tired to argue."

It wasn't until they'd safely arrived home and had settled at the table with a meal—Elisabeth had it all ready when they arrived—that Rowan said, "My Goddess. All the twists and turns over the last few weeks. Like a fuckin' ride at one of those carnivals they set up in abandoned mall parking lots. Screws all over the ground. Smells like gasoline, puke, kettle corn, and the blue stuff they squirt on snow cones."

Having never experienced such a horror—gladly—he still got the basic idea.

"For decades they had their little business. Sketchy at times, but from those adepts we've been able to speak to, consensual. The witches are making bank. The Vampires are able to get their sweet adepts via a process that makes them feel even more important. They even add their side businesses in with day trips to woo the adepts and all that shit."

Greed and self-importance wrecked the best of things.

"Teresa flitted around, doing her thing, making deals, tucking away her cash, collecting rich lovers to get those connections and to further the life she wanted to live. Also, whatever, plenty of people do stuff like that and for years she's able to do what she wanted. But Hugo, oh he's got this *gift* that means we can just keep all the adepts we pull into our net! The rest, literally all the rest just went along with it! I don't care what they say now they've been caught. If a bad bitch like Fiona doesn't want to do something, it's not going to be Teresa who makes her. They all knew and they all at the very least tolerated it."

"I rather wanted to throttle the fourth one of them who claimed it was only a handful of witches and humans who'd been bespelled or harmed to achieve compliance."

"They're going to stick to that forever. Until they believe it. How else do you face the world if you don't downplay your monstrousness?"

They'd been able to identify seven adepts, four humans and three witches, who'd been abused by Hugo's magic. Two of their Vampires had physically dealt with Hugo when he'd started sniffing around after their adepts he'd used his magic on. Clive had to pull Patience off to the side after that had been revealed when she flew across the room, nails out, toward Hugo when he confessed that bit.

"I do appreciate your leaving the Vampires involved with the purchase of these adepts who'd been tampered with by Hugo to the Nation," he told Rowan.

"I trust you to handle it. And if the Nation doesn't, those Vampires are known to me, and they *will* be held responsible one way or another." She shrugged one shoulder. "The Conclave is dealing with the witches from this workgroup, so it seemed best to let Vampires do the same. They're already in your custody and Theo's custody as it is. Why make more work for myself if I don't have to?"

"But you'll watch us?" he teased.

"I'll watch you and the witches too because this happened right under our noses and we didn't know until a few weeks ago when we went to that house on Holly where Dorothy, Jaylin, and Kerry lived and had gone missing. And when we're in Prague for the Joint Tribunal, you can bet I'll expect a full accounting from the Nation regarding this issue. And, while I'm willing to accept Takahiro's and Tahar's word that their involvement was only as a Scion passing on concerns of their Vampires to their leader, understand Hunter Corp. is already paying far more attention to them than we have before. If even a whisper of wrongdoing reaches me, there will be a problem."

Clive grimaced. "These lords are radioactive. Any involvement or perception of involvement with them will be sure to gain your father's attention. In the worst way. If I believed either of those Scions knew in advance of this outcome or this adept scheme, I'd kill them both myself."

"Aw, romantic! Scions stepping out of their lane will always gain Theo's attention. Well, Nadir or Recht's first, and then his. It's not like either Scion is new to this, so they're welcome to whatever this stirs up. As for these pathetic lords? The two who'd been freed will most likely remain so. But the others in the dungeon? Most of them will probably be freed after a decade. Armas knew more and fooled Andros, so that's going to hurt. He'll be there as long as Mardoc now." She shook her head. "If he's released before at least a century, I'd be surprised."

"My territory has registered a strong recommendation that Mardoc be executed." Clive wanted to kill Mardoc himself for all his part in not only the suffering he'd caused the kidnapped adepts, but the ruthless attacks on Rowan.

Vampires were bloodthirsty. They battled and bloodied one another all the time. Sometimes they went too far, and one might die. Regrettable, but not frowned upon, usually. But they were also rare. Old ones like Mardoc rarer still. But officially sanctioning true death was only for the most acute violations of their laws. In most other circumstances, Clive would support imprisonment, as would the other Scions.

But his wife wasn't just anyone, and she'd had enough violence from the Vampire Nation. Mardoc's crimes had put the Nation in danger of being exposed, and he'd created major political problems with the witches and humans.

"That's one of the sweetest things you've ever done for me."

He took her hand, kissing it.

"He's too old to be this reckless. It's a danger to us all. As for my internal leak problem, every single employee at *Die Mitte*, as well as all Scion-funded and -controlled positions in Las Vegas, are undergoing upgraded training and security screens. It helps that Eduard and Stephen kept such good records pointing us in the right direction. Every contact that we discover will be rounded up and dealt with."

"This won't be the end of *Sanguis Principatus*," Rowan said as she dipped her bread in balsamic and olive oil.

"No. But this cell here in the West was controlled by Vampires most of whom are in my custody. That will leave them off-balance for a while. It's too much to hope they'll go away entirely. And for those who weren't part of this kidnapping scheme with the witches, they're staying on the right side of Nation law. They'll lick their wounds and, in the meantime, I'll be working to destabilize them across the territory."

"Good idea. Get yourself someone like Andros and Recht combined. A spy who can get into their leadership and rip them apart." Rowan hummed her approval of that idea. "What's the situation with Elmer, then?"

"He's being transferred to Recht's custody in a few days," Clive told her. "He'll serve his sentence in Munich."

Theo kept a Nation prison just outside the city. High security. Light tight. And not Clive's problem.

"Brrr." Rowan shivered. "The Conclave is transferring many of the witches to their various null facilities. Then I sincerely hope they do some major deep cleaning. I think they will, at least given what I know from Genevieve and Konrad. If Hugo and his grandpa weren't so greedy, how many more would have been taken before they were found out? These are unprecedented times and the risks we all face grow every day. They have to pay attention."

"I think it's fate," Clive said, surprising them both. He gave a slight rise of his right shoulder, slightly embarrassed.

She took him seriously immediately. Turning her gaze to him. "How so?"

"There are times when a situation hits a sort of mass. Roiling, building to something far worse. Over my life there have been instances when coincidences began to build up to the point they could no longer be ignored. First the Procellas put in their request, but it sat on someone's desk because Genevieve's time had been taken up on the sorcerer crisis. Even as it began to work its way through the system to get to her, Mardoc had begun his campaign to the Scions to be added to the official Nation response to Hunter Corp. in the wake of your announcement of hiring Vampires. That took time as well. That both inciting events finally surfaced within such a relatively brief time between them, in such disparate ways, says to me this was meant for you. Which I find myself hating because of how beaten up you are every time you take on an enemy. But your record of overcoming your enemies is undefeated, so I hold that confidence in your ability. And now I know I have this rot in my territory, and it needs to be burned out."

"You can't hold yourself responsible for what Jacques germinated for a century before he was terminated. Ha. *Terminated.* See what I did there?"

"I can hold myself responsible as Scion for what happens in my territory. I thought I was brutal when I came into the position, but I clearly showed too much mercy. A fact I will spend the next year correcting."

"You know how sexy I find it when you're very tough. But. I want to say mercy is never a mistake." She reached over to cup his cheek a moment. "I'm not arguing with the fact you have a mess to clean up. I'll happily watch you do it and lend a fist whenever you need it. I don't doubt your ability. Vampires are notoriously troublesome. You're going to have to create a process to be more thorough in each major quadrant of North America. If Patience wouldn't be offended, I'm happy to talk about some of the ways Hunter Corp. is attempting to clean our own house worldwide."

Just when he thought it would be impossible to adore her more, she proved him wrong. Over and over.

"I mean, don't get it twisted, offending Patience is

like my morning coffee or whatever. But not generally about this sort of thing. It's a big job and despite her boner for you, she's made a lot of improvements in the years since you came to Las Vegas. She can learn. That's important. Don't tell her I said that. I don't want her thinking I like her."

No danger of that.

"I appreciate the offer. I will bring it up. Naturally and not rehearsed," he added because his wife was about to tell him that.

"Okay. Good."

Star wandered in, her nails tapping on the floor. After a quick look to see what Rowan had to eat, she headed to her water dish and slurped it with gusto enough to have Rowan snort with amusement.

"Hi there," Rowan said and then tossed a piece of strawberry Star caught neatly. "She's going to come to the Joint Tribunal with us. I just said that without even conscious thought." She turned to Clive, eyes a little wide.

"Then that's what will be. Darling, these dreams and knowings have manifested themselves on you and they've led you to the truth over and over. If Star needs to be in Prague with us, by all means, we'll pack her best toys and dog bed and put it on the plane. Elisabeth and Betchamp are coming along so she'll have plenty of people to feed her, scratch her ears, and accompany her on walks."

"I don't always know how to process it. I'm more comfortable with punching my way to a solution to my problems. This sagey, woo-woo stuff is…it's part of me I'm working on. I accept it as a gift. But I'm going to need to sharpen those skills like all my other gifts. It's a trip to dream of confetti and find actual confetti outside a werewolf's cell. Those abandoned human places? The paintings, but also I think it was about the kidnappings. Storms and tempests, we got the Procellas and their casino right in front of where I was ambushed. Then Holly Drive and Fiona's stupid fucking vaudeville nickname. I wonder if it's like this for Carl."

"If so, let us hope you do not take on his sense of fashion or love of taxidermy."

"Roger that. Rather than have to travel back to Southern California to interview Rose, that nutbag, since she's free of the geas, Konrad is moving her here, along with Bess and Alfonso. But since we have all we need for the moment, I'll let them stew awhile."

"What about Teresa?"

"She's a shark. Rose is a robot whose only pleasure seems to come from hurting people for amusement. Fiona is a boss bitch and all that, but she's so greedy and entitled she's gotten herself in over her head. And she knows it's her own fault. If she wasn't such a goon, I'd like her. Gerard, the husband, he's all booming voice and backslaps, but he's mean underneath it. Joseph, gods, what a dingus. Money. Power. Education. Talent. And he's just useless unless he's being directed. Rose holds the reins there. Still, he's too dangerous to be free. I hate this for Genevieve, but her ex-husband Tristan is tangentially involved. Someone else has taken over that part of the investigation. The Salazars? They're tight. Work as a unit. It would be nice if they weren't working to kidnap people and sell them to Vampires.

"The rest of these witches got high on money and control and since they already think they're better than not only humans, but non-Genetic witches, the road to get them to a place where it's acceptable to use adepts like goods instead of people wasn't very long. They're devoid of empathy. I'm sure some Conclave psychologist will be writing papers on this for years."

They got up to put away their dishes, but Elisabeth materialized with a tray filled with two large slices of coconut lemon cake, a pot of tea, and all the various accoutrements.

"I'll take this to your sitting room and then come back to deal with the dishes," Elisabeth called out as she walked past.

After thanking Elisabeth, and being left alone, Rowan moved to the love seat and fit herself against his side, allowing him to wrap an arm around her shoulders. The ease of her choice had been a hard-won battle. He hoped he never forgot what a gift she was.

"So, Teresa. She absolutely does not see anything she's done as wrong. There was a market for adepts. She filled it. Described it as *job creation*. Positively crowed about how her business brought together multiple parties of witches to make money off Vampires. The witches and humans she stalked are nothing to her but columns on a balance sheet. Rose is honestly, she's the closest to true sociopathy I've seen in a witch. But Teresa saw that and weaponized it. To make money off. To build her own power from. She bragged about being self-made. When we told her Kerry hadn't lived, she said it wasn't her fault that Mardoc couldn't treat his stock better. *Stock*." She shook her head. "I wanted to punch her, but she's…there's nothing redeemable about her. Nothing. Even if I punched her, I'd have a sore hand and she'd still be irredeemable. By the way, she knew about the mage firebomb at the Procella mansion before it happened and said nothing. She didn't know none of the family were home at the time."

She sighed and sadness trickled through their bond.

"What a remarkable group of assholes, darling. I'm sorry you had to deal with them. Especially the ones who tried to have you killed."

"Oh, and that's a whole new thing on my to-do list. I've got to suss out this shifter situation. I can't have these superpowered tree-trunk-sized people forming hit squads at the behest of witches. I don't give a fuck what the witches have to say about that. That's a Treaty no-go."

"Prague first. The shifters in my cells will hold until after we return from the Joint Tribunal. Then we can go to Seattle. I haven't been there in a few years. I want to swap out some of my Las Vegas people for some of theirs. Bring them back to *Die Mitte* and train them properly before we send them to their territory once more. Alice is creating an itinerary for visits across the United States, Canada, and Mexico. You can combine Hunter Corp. business if you like and accompany me."

"Okay. I think I can do that. I have my own inspections to do. You cannot buy me a house in every territory we visit," she warned.

"I do believe you said it best, I do what I want, Hunter."

That made her laugh and lean her head on his shoulder. "I love you, Scion. Thank you for everything. The last months especially, I don't know what I would have done without you. But I didn't have to. That's…well, I didn't have that before."

Her blush always delighted him.

"Let's save this cake until after you rut upon me."

"I do love a good rut. I promise to be gentle as you're still healing." He wanted her every moment of every day. But not more than he needed her to be healthy.

"You do know where everything is. It's a fine quality."

"Of course I do. They're all my favorite places." He stood, pulling her into his arms and carrying her into his bedchamber, kicking the door closed.

* * * * *

Acknowledgments

I started this series well over a decade ago, after a trip to Las Vegas with friends. I had this idea while waiting for my flight home that started with *What if Vampires were real and that show on the Strip was a cover?*

Eight books later and I've loved every glimpse into Rowan, Clive, David, Genevieve and Darius's world and I hope you all have too.

Over the years, I've had so much help with beta reading, editing, cover art, etc. This wasn't done alone so thank you to everyone who had a hand in Goddess with a Blade, honestly I couldn't have done it without you all.